A TROUBLED COURSE

DAVID DONACHIE

McBooks
Press

Essex, Connecticut

McBooks Press

An imprint of Globe Pequot, the trade division of The Rowman & Littlefield Publishing Group, Inc.
4501 Forbes Blvd., Ste. 200
Lanham, MD 20706
www.rowman.com

Distributed by NATIONAL BOOK NETWORK

Copyright © 2023 by David Donachie

British Library Cataloguing in Publication Information available

Library of Congress Cataloging-in-Publication Data

Names: Donachie, David, 1944– author.
Title: A troubled course / David Donachie.
Description: Essex, Connecticut : McBooks Press, [2023] | Series: A John Pearce Adventure | Summary: "John Pearce discovers that Madrid plans to desert the British-led coalition and join the enemy. In company with Lord Langholm, he has taken a Spanish treasure ship. But a violent Atlantic westerly forces them into a deep bay overlooked by Spaniards, who have created a trap with cannon on the heights aimed at the narrow entrance. Pearce must find a way to get Lord Langholm's frigate and the damaged Santa Leocadia through the same bottleneck. Will he succeed, or will John Pearce, HMS Hazard, and the Pelicans pay the ultimate price of failure?"—Provided by publisher.
Identifiers: LCCN 2022014206 (print) | LCCN 2022014207 (ebook) | ISBN 9781493068883 (hardcover : alk. paper) | ISBN 9781493070664 (electronic)
Classification: LCC PR6053.O483 T76 2023 (print) | LCC PR6053.O483 (ebook) | DDC 823/.914—dc23
LC record available at https://lccn.loc.gov/2022014206
LC ebook record available at https://lccn.loc.gov/2022014207

To David and Margaret Rose
and in memory of
their lovely librarian daughter
Caroline

CHAPTER ONE

John Pearce was sure everything would have gone as planned if the weather had not changed so drastically. Such an occurrence could hardly be a surprise given the position they occupied on the Atlantic shore of the Iberian Peninsula. It was an area subject to huge rollers at the best of times, as well as being at the mercy of sudden changes in the conditions. Severe storms could come in from the Caribbean or the Southern Ocean, creating the kind of monstrous and crashing waves which had, over millennia, shaped the rocky shoreline and, no doubt, the character of the people.

It was only later he reflected on this, reasoning that folk who lived by and depended on such an unpredictable sea, and too often died from the way it behaved, had a natural resilience not gifted to everyone. Yet, even if the increase in the strength of the wind was noticeable, creating the need to watch out for the unexpected movement of plates and goblets at the dining table, there was no expectation of danger. Neither he nor his fellow commanding officer, Captain Lord Langholm, felt the need to react to the changing circumstances.

The need they might be obliged to do so was flagged up by both the sailing masters, of Lord Langholm's vessel HMS *Lively* and Mr Williams of HMS *Hazard*, who were alarmed not just by the increasing wind but also by the cloud formations visible on the horizon. The news was imparted in a whispered exchange by his man to Langholm, he being the senior, and this happened as the officers of both vessels were near to completing, in all respects bar one, what had been a capital dinner.

The circumstances surrounding the recent taking of the Spanish frigate, the *Santa Leocadia*, less than twenty-four hours earlier, welcome as the result had been, provided a raw memory for John Pearce and his two lieutenants, Hallowell and Worricker. This applied as well to the acting-lieutenant he had mustered under the name of Macklin. The braying self-congratulation of the *Lively*'s officers meant that bitter recollections had to be kept hidden, nothing less than the relative merits of who had done what to affect the said capture.

The bulk of the action and the danger therein had been borne by the crew of HMS *Hazard*. It was they who had engaged the Spaniard in an exchange of gunfire, which had prevented it from making its escape. Then Langholm and his much larger complement (Johnnies come lately) claimed the glory and the prize at practically no cost to them in terms of either the effort or casualties sustained.

It was telling that the surgeon of *Lively* was present and busy getting drunk. His opposite number, Mr Cullen, was still aboard *Hazard*, dealing with the casualties the action had engendered in a fiercely contested and opposed boarding. Naval good manners might demand that such a variation in recent experience could not be openly referred to, but it would have been a blind man who failed to notice the peaked expressions from the *Lively*'s guests, when their hosts loudly praised their own gallantry.

Offsetting such justifiable pique was the nature of what the *Santa Leocadia* had been carrying, and indeed the reason why she, an ostensibly allied vessel, had been intercepted. In her holds she was transporting an extremely high-value cargo of South American silver, needed by the Spanish government to facilitate a policy of betrayal. If she was accepted as a prize, it could make a great deal of money for all attending the dinner.

It was impossible not to compare the rewards with that which had been awarded to the frigate *Active*, in company with the sloop

Favourite, in the year '62. They had taken the Spanish vessel *Hermione* only to find, in her holds, bags of gold dollars and ingots of silver. This and the ship cannon and head money together led to the largest payout of prize money in the history of King George's Navy.

In the case of both captains, who were entitled to a three-eighth share of the proceeds of the recent capture, it would render them seriously rich, though Langholm would be obliged to pass on one-eighth to his commanding admiral. John Pearce, sailing under Admiralty orders, had no such requirement. Their inferior officers and midshipman, also well rewarded, could go from impecunious lieutenants to sought-after fellows in the article of matrimony, while the crew, from warrants down to the meanest waister, could look forward to sums that would match years of pay.

Both captains knew it would be necessary to manage expectations, there being a process in such matters, which could take years to reach a conclusion. Prize courts could be fickle and pernickety, while there were any number of people dipping their beaks into the trough along the way: assessors, lawyers and, not least, the agents acting on their behalf, who would extract a high commission. It was also the case for the common seaman; they were signed up for the duration and no amount of prize money would alter this.

'Gentlemen,' Langholm said as he got to his feet, something which attested to both his youthful appearance, allied to his lack of inches, 'The King.'

A toast which was mandatory also served as an indication that the gathering was nearly at an end. So, once the monarch had been acknowledged and praised, the conversation flagged and the well-wined guests slowly made moves to disperse, no doubt still discussing how they would spend their windfall. It required no obvious signal from Langholm to John Pearce that he should hold back, with the latter being naturally curious as to what had been whispered in his colleague's ear.

'I am bound to say,' was the reply, when told, 'I have a limited amount of faith in Mr Williams.'

In imparting this, John Pearce saw no need to elaborate, to say the master of HMS *Hazard*, on one previous occasion, had come up seriously short in his weather predictions. Langholm's response was to insist that the opinion he held on his man, McAllister, was the polar opposite: he trusted him absolutely. He then invited Pearce to look at the barometer, pointing out the mercury had fallen considerably.

'So, I suggest we take a look at Mr McAllister's troubling sky ourselves.'

The words were accompanied by a wry smile. This implied, Pearce thought, it would be more for appearance than any desire to question those held to be expert or the mercury reading just taken. Coming on deck, the change in the weather was many times more obvious than it had been when seated in the great cabin, where the only evidence had been an increase in the rocking motion. The warm wind, previously steady, was now much stronger and gusting, tugging at both their coats and the anchor cables, at its peak requiring a hand hold on to their hats.

The sun, previously bright in a clear sky, now had a watery quality, it being partly obscured by haze. But it was what lay far out to sea which presaged a severe deterioration, high banks of cloud, in which the darker tumult of activity was obvious even at a distance. Also, outside the cove in which they were anchored, the increasingly disturbed sea state was palpable, while the run of the waves and their increasing height raised questions as to the safety of their present anchorage.

The outer part of Pontevedra Bay was protected from an easterly gale by the Island of Ons, but it was dangerously open to anything approaching from the southwest, the quarter from which the menace threatened. It was natural for Pearce to cast an eye over their capture, which lay alongside *Lively*, and take in once more the damage inflicted on the Spanish frigate by *Hazard*'s cannon. He then had good cause to wonder if the repairs so far undertaken, work which was continuing as he watched, would be sufficient to stand, out in open water, the kind of blow which appeared to be in the offing.

The massive damage to the stern of the *Santa Leocadia* was easy to hide by the use of planks and stretched-over canvas, visually reassuring, but hardly sturdy enough to cope with a heavy following sea. More importantly, the wounded masts, both main and mizzen, would be a worry. It had been the intention, following an inspection by bosuns and carpenters, to use battens and frapping to make them more secure. But again, would this hold through what might be a proper tempest?

'An opinion, Mr Pearce?'

It was, in a sense, a reprise of an earlier exchange, which referred to the notion of HMS *Lively* escorting the Spanish frigate back to England. Pearce had posited it would be risky for such a damaged vessel to spend too much time at sea, a danger made worse by the waters through which they would be required to sail. Apart from the risk of interdiction by a vessel of the French fleet, based in Brest, the waters off the Brittany were among the most treacherous in creation. Safer, he maintained, to take the shorter route to Gibraltar.

For Pearce, this posed a conundrum outside what the damaged vessel would and would not withstand. Having established, without doubt, that Spain intended to desert the coalition fighting Revolutionary France and to instead ally with Paris against Britannia, his duty and orders were clear. He was to proceed immediately to Corsica to advise Sir John Jervis, the admiral in command of the Mediterranean Fleet, of the peril he now faced from such a naval combination. He had the ships necessary to contain France and Spain piecemeal, but it was seriously questionable if he had the force required to face them both.

Quite apart from the inadvisability of Langholm weighing for Pompey with a serious storm brewing, added to the other dangers to be faced, Pearce was looking at a vessel full of the said Peruvian silver, the value of which he could only guess. He was loath to part company and leave what would follow in the hands of the man he was standing next to, being far from prepared to repose so much trust. Also, there was more the possibility of substantial wealth to be gained once the cargo was landed in England.

A degree of glory and public approbation would ensue as well, which might be to advantage in his personal relations. Although Pearce might insist that such a thing as fame and glory held no attraction for him, there had to be a residual desire to share in any which was going. Quite apart from his private life, it would serve as a poke in the eye to those numerous officers who hated his very name. This ill will arose not only for the way he had risen from midshipman to his present rank of lieutenant, but also the employment and good fortune he'd enjoyed since.

'Would it be sensible to take an already damaged vessel to sea, carrying the cargo at present in her holds, regardless of the proposed destination, when we know, the weather is set to deteriorate?'

'With which I can only agree,' Langholm drawled.

Pearce was wondering what thoughts were going through his mind, behind a bland expression, for another possibility must have occurred to Langholm, namely, to transfer the silver to *Lively*. The option of Pearce using his own ship was impossible. *Hazard* was too small, not that the frigate was gifted with an excess of space. With such a cargo taking up what little existed, it would be a severely overcrowded ship, one which would be required to plough its way to whatever end point was agreed upon.

And there was another problem. Silver in such quantity was heavy, so would affect the sailing qualities of any vessel which had it aboard, dangerous should a recapture be attempted. This would lead to a fight, or flight, if the opposition was too strong. Indeed, both men had failed to realise, in the recent action, how this very problem must have impacted on the decision making of their Spanish opponent.

'I think my cabin, Mr Pearce,' was a very non-committal response, from a man who could draw as many conclusions as the person addressed.

They entered a space clear of the extra leaves in the dining table, with a bulkhead thrown up to turn the foremost section into a place of work. Langholm, after another quick look at the barometer, followed by a frown, whipped off his hat, took his chair and invited Pearce to follow suit. This was done silently, which continued as the man began to tap fingers on his desk, clearly deep in thought.

'Would I be permitted to enquire as to your thinking?' Pearce asked finally.

'If the mercury is telling the true situation, we are in for the kind of blow to make any notion of putting to sea inadvisable even for our own ships.'

'I would counsel such, if asked.'

Was there a note of resentment in the response? A full post captain, Langholm seriously outranked Pearce and, in normal circumstances, would have been in a position to issue orders. But with HMS *Hazard* sailing under an Admiralty pennant, Langholm's seniority did not apply. John Pearce could ignore admirals if he so chose, but it seemed wise for him to be emollient.

'And I would most assuredly have asked, sir.'

'It is paramount we preserve both our own vessels as much as the *Santa Leocadia*?'

It seemed an odd point and obvious, to which there was only one answer, and it was in the affirmative. At which point Langholm called out, 'His master should be asked to attend.' The fellow who obliged, the one who'd whispered in his captain's ear at dinner, was not long in coming. He was a bulky fellow with wild grey hair topping a face so ruddy, it evidenced the extent of the weather to which it had been exposed.

'Mr McAllister, have you had a chance to survey the holding ground?'

'Put a couple of my mates to it right off, soon as we anchored.'

'And?'

'It's not where I'd want to be a'laying in a south-westerly gale. Seabed is soft sand and, under pressure, we could drag our anchors.'

'Which is what you reckon we're going to have to contend with?'

'Looks that way, sir, and Mr Williams concurs.'

The languid Langholm eyes took in Pearce's then, obviously an invitation to comment, and one which was declined. Opinions vouchsafed to a fellow ship's commander were not to be shared with others of a lesser rank.

'And your solution?'

There was a moment where John Pearce felt a tad uncomfortable. It was as if the question posed was one to which Langholm already knew the answer. The whisper at dinner had not been either one sided or overly short in duration. Yet he had such a laconic manner it could easily be that he had misread it.

'You know what the risks are as well as I gentlemen,' McAllister replied, his look taking in both officers. 'This is no bay in which to be cast loose, what with the rocks not far off in the southern part of the roads, just awaiting to rip out a keel. Best off inside the bar protecting Pontevedra Bay, there not being any weather known to man to cause us bother there.'

Pearce required no deeper explanation. He had been made aware of those very dangers just alluded to before he engaged the *Santa Leocadia*, information which had dictated much of his subsequent actions. The actual bay was a deep bight surrounded by high hills, but to access it required any vessel entering the inner section to dogleg through the said bar, by way of a narrow channel. Relatively safe at high tide, the bay was much less so at low, the factor which had so seriously disadvantaged his Spanish opponent.

'I'd suggest that's where we should anchor till the storm blows itself out. Tide will be full afore the first dog watch and it will be light till after eight bells.'

'You believe we should act so quickly.'

The ruddy countenance took on a troubled look. 'Milord, I believe the devil waits for no man, be he ever so high and holy.'

'The Spaniard?'

Given the work being carried out on the *Santa Leocadia*, she was not in a fit state to employ sail.

'We has boats enough to warp her through the channel.'

'Mr Pearce, it is a course I suggest we should follow, do you concur?' Responded to with a degree of hesitation, as the man asked was still pondering on his orders, Langholm added, 'I intend to follow Mr McAllister's advice.'

'It seems the safest way to act. I will return to *Hazard* and set things in motion.'

'Can I suggest you lead the way, being the vessel drawing the least water?'

Again, there was a slight feeling of discomfort, quickly dismissed by a man who knew he was sometimes too inclined to see questionable motives where none existed.

The first task was to take away those of his men still working aboard the Spanish frigate and issue orders to his premier, Isaac Hallowell. If the American wondered at the instructions, and the hesitation implied he did, it was well hidden by the alacrity with which he acted.

Those members of the crew who understood the duty were sent to the capstan, while the topman went aloft, as they always did, at an arrogant lick. Their manner of showing away underlined their certainty that they considered themselves superior beings. It was pleasing to see a couple of his young mids, Campbell and Livingston, previously very cautious, following them up the shrouds and doing so competently.

John Pearce, on the quarterdeck and stationery, could reflect happily on the difference between what he was observing now and that which had preceded it when he raised anchor on his last home landfall. At Falmouth, it had been enough to bring him to the blush for, with a crew of Quota Men new to the navy and few experienced hands, weighing had been cack-handed in the extreme. His discomfiture had been made worse by being under the eye of a crabbed Port Admiral, as well as, no doubt, a raft of his sneering subordinates.

Now, with the fortuitous addition of a draft of experienced sailors, plus novices who had learned a great deal in the intervening period, the whole act went smoothly. It was not perfect yet by some measure, but it was so much on the way to being so; John Pearce felt a surge of pride. He was aware Samuel Oliphant had come on deck, as usual struggling to stay out of everyone's way, he being no Jack Tar at all. In fact, the man was every inch the lubber and appeared proud of the fact.

Seemingly content merely to observe, which lasted until he saw the way the prow was aimed, Samuel Oliphant moved towards Pearce to enquire what was going on, as usual ignoring the protocol which barred approaching a commanding officer at such a time.

'I observe we are not putting to sea.'

'Good Lord,' Pearce responded with deep irony, 'We'll make a sailor of you yet.'

'Am I allowed to ask what we're about?'

It was with a sigh Pearce explained. Even if his relations with the man had improved since their first encounter, there was still a resentment at Oliphant's inability to grasp where *Hazard* went and how she got there, outside of the needs of a shared mission now complete, was none of his business.

'Which will impose a delay on my getting back to England.'

'I'm sure the nation will not mourn the loss of your presence for a day or two.'

'Dundas is going to require a fuller explanation of what we've achieved than the scrap of information we sent him. And that's before we engaged in a battle with a supposedly allied warship, something, as the Minister for War, he's going to have to explain to parliament. I daresay even you have thought through the potential ramifications.'

'Even me?'

'You know what I mean, Pearce.'

'Captain!' was barked enough to turn heads.

'Forgive me,' Oliphant said, with an air to imply he didn't mean it, 'I forgot.'

It had been a bone of contention from the very off – the need to remind Oliphant how he addressed Pearce in private was unacceptable on deck where Pearce's air of authority had to be maintained, this to a fellow who gave the impression he saw it as a mere conceit.

'Since you can add nothing to what we must do, I suggest you leave the deck.'

'I agree. I will be spared the nonsense of people shouting to each other who could perfectly well, on a vessel this size, whisper their commands.'

He was gone before Pearce could respond, ducking down the companionway as the shouts continued in what was far from a straightforward manoeuvre. It was necessary, on a gusting and increasingly irregular wind, to control the rate of sailing, as well as the doglegged course to be steered. There were moments when it looked as if it might not be as smooth as desired, but good seamanship from his officers and warrants saw HMS *Hazard* through the channel and into the safety and calm waters of the inner bay.

There they could watch as the crews of *Lively*'s boats hauled one way and then the other, also using their prows to push, until the Spaniard was in the straight part of the channel, where they shifted to a tow. His second lieutenant, Worricker, opined they were probably cursing Langholm for sending the Spanish captain and his crew ashore. It had been easier to do so than deal with such a quantity of prisoners, besides which their status as such was questionable.

Langholm brought his frigate through without trouble, for he commanded a crack and experienced crew, who seemed to have recovered quickly from the toil in the boats. Once behind the reef, which formed the northern arm of the channel, it was time to clew up the canvas so as to reduce the wind pressure on the sails, as the breakers grew in power. They were now pounding through the anchorage they had just left, hitting the inner bar to send aloft great spouts of white spume.

'So,' Oliphant asked, once both were in Pearce's cabin sharing toasted cheese and a glass of wine, 'What now?'

'We wait in safety till the storm blows itself out.'

Chapter Two

If the inner waters of the bay were calm, it did nothing to modify the scream of the wind through the rigging, which made for an uncomfortable night and nothing improved, quite the reverse, on the first hint of daylight. The sky was grey and full of scudding clouds, while it was obvious, outside the entrance to the outer bay, the decision not to risk putting to sea had been a wise one.

So, the work of the day could be carried out as normal. The swabbing and flogging dry of the decks went ahead as if there was nothing untoward – evaporating quickly in the hot wind. The hands were then piped to breakfast, none of which impacted John Pearce. He was busy writing up his logs, which included a comprehensive report of the action just engaged in, one he suspected might differ from Lord Langholm's.

He then visited the sick bay to talk to or sympathise with those suffering from a variety of wounds. Each one was discussed with Surgeon Cullen as to their chances and rate of recovery. It seemed most, if not all, were on the mend.

'Except Mr Moberly is still comatose, which I find especially worrying.'

This was said softly by the surgeon out of the earshot of those assisting him, and such concern was etched on his tired face. He had barely rested overnight while seeing to his charges, some of whom were noisy in their pain and distress and in need of tincture of laudanum to alleviate their suffering.

'The longer he fails to respond,' Cullen added, 'the less likely is the chance of a full recovery. I fear a severe fracture.'

The marine officer had taken a blow to the head on the lower deck of the *Santa Leocadia*, only surviving even more telling wounds by the swift action of a pair of his men. They had dragged him away from the line in which the Hazards were giving battle. At the forefront of the action, John Pearce had been furiously engaged, alongside the massive presence and fighting ability of his Irish friend Michael O'Hagan.

Recalling what had occurred subsequently and how it had ended, while being regaled with reports on the others, Pearce reckoned himself lucky to be alive and listening to the depressing news on Moberly. He also felt the need to remark on the strain Cullen was putting himself under.

'If you ask for the aid of *Lively*'s surgeon, I'm sure Lord Langholm would grant your wish.'

To which, the reply was brusque: 'I care to hang on to my brandy, sir, and use it on my patients.'

Cullen might not have been present the day before, but even if he had not observed his opposite number, he knew him to be too fond of the bottle. It was a common affliction in those who followed the naval surgeon's trade which, in the worst cases, could be more akin to a barber than anything medical. The sardonic smile, denoting acknowledgement, disappeared as the sound of a dull boom came through the scantlings, lifting both heads with expressions showing complete surprise.

'Gunfire?' Cullen asked, clearly confused. 'Surely not our own?'

He found himself addressing thin air, given his captain was already halfway up the companionway. Pearce came on deck just ahead of his officers to find his oldest midshipman with a telescope to his eye, which was trained on the high southern hills, part of an elevated arc of highlands enclosing the bay.

'Where away?' Pearce demanded as others appeared.

Maclehose replied by handing over the glass and pointing. 'There was smoke a moment past, but it has disappeared on the wind.'

'Definitely cannon?'

'A single discharge, sir,' the youngster said in his soft Caledonian burr. 'I watched the flight of the ball. It landed near yon reef I think, but with the water so disturbed, it was hard to see exactly where it landed.'

Jock the Sock, as he was known to the crew, was now pointing to the said reef and beyond it to the very troubled sea, just as a huge wave sent up another high curtain of white water. The boom of this striking nearly drowned out the sound of a second round of cannon fire, the smoke from the discharge just visible as it was whipped inland at speed. Even against a grey sky, the trajectory of the ball could be tracked and it proved the mid was right. If it disappeared into the spume, there was no doubt about the intended aim.

'The channel,' Pearce barked, before adding, 'get my boat crew assembled.'

Looking at his destination – the quarterdeck of HMS *Lively* – he could see it was crowded with the frigate's officers, all looking in the same direction as his own. They had come on deck with the same alacrity, while on the Spaniard all work had stopped. It was unnecessary to say, on all three decks, there was an air of surprise, and even more, an element of shock.

Two more salvoes were fired as Pearce crossed to *Lively*, the actual source hidden by it being located too high on the hilltop to be visible at sea level. Any ceremony on coming aboard was eschewed by what was happening, though given the look he got from Russell, Langholm's premier, as he joined the knot of officers, there was always the risk that the absence of the courtesy was deliberate. His glare was very similar to the one which had been aimed at him on first acquaintance and it was the opposite of friendly.

'Single piece from what I can make out,' Langholm muttered as Pearce joined him, the words hard to hear with the wind buffeting his ears.

'A field gun I would reckon, with not much in the way of weight of shot.'

'Interesting target, though.'

There was no need to elaborate, that being obvious.

'They'll be looking for the right powder charge to regularly hit the channel,' Pearce added.

'Near impossible to work out in this wind, wouldn't you say?'

'I would say, whoever is in command, would have been better waiting till the weather eased.'

'Which Mr McAllister suggests will not be any time soon, so I'm not so sure you have the right of it. With this windage, I see it as an invite to get out when we can.'

'With a serious risk of running afoul of the weather or the rocks.'

Pearce, as he replied, had to acknowledge Langholm made a telling point, even if, imagining himself in charge of a field gun and, under the circumstances, he would have held back. The trio of ships could not get through the dogleg of the channel at anything approaching speed, regardless of the weather. In fact, it would take an age. Plenty of time, with a lesser wind, to work out the proper combination of the weight of shot and powder to regularly hit the point of aim.

Not that such would stop them, and it was the realisation of this fact which made what had been suggested by Langholm valid. Even with plunging fire, which it would be from their present elevation, the amount of damage a single field gun could do to a sturdy wooden vessel would be minimal. Unless they used heated shot, a point he made.

'Are you suggesting we oblige them immediately?' Langholm asked.

There was, to Pearce, nothing sly in the suggestion, it being a straightforward enquiry. It was not accepted as such by the rest of Langholm's officers. Taking their cue from an openly sneering premier, they each managed a muffled scoff.

'No,' Pearce replied, 'but I would posit, if they have managed to place one cannon in such a position in forty-eight hours, there may be more on the way. So, we should not delay any longer than we have to. If they get a full battery in place, or even more than one, we might find exiting from the bay difficult, especially when we are unable to reply with anything other than swivels.'

Langholm nodded at what was also obvious, the weapon named at anything like long range being useless; while there was no way to so elevate the main deck cannon so they could impose a check on such a target. They might have to be lucky, but the Spaniards only had to do enough to disable the lead vessel and they would trap the rest, with their own captured frigate already damaged and likely to sail at nothing close to efficiency.

'They want their silver back.'

'But,' Pearce responded, his tone soft. 'They might prefer to see it at the bottom rather than allow us possession.'

'Then we must find a way to confound them.'

'Hear him.'

This enthusiastic cry came as a chorus from the knot of lieutenants and midshipmen behind him. Pearce saw it as sycophancy, which would come from having the offspring of a belted earl in command. Pearce wondered if any of them had made the connection between their captain's decision to let go the officers and crew of the *Santa Leocadia* and what was now happening. Not that he had disagreed with the deed: he would have had to accommodate a portion of them.

The Spanish officers had given their parole not to engage in any act of aggression, but it would be hypocrisy to call their present behaviour a breach if they were the ones doing the firing. They had, after all, been intercepted, boarded and captured by men who were, as far as they knew, still allies and had lost both their ship and cargo. Pearce could only imagine how the news of such losses would be received by their superiors. He could guess it would be far from comfortable.

'They only way to be sure of confounding them is to destroy the cannon.'

'Sound thinking Mr Pearce,' Langholm responded, for him somewhat animated, given his normal economical responses. 'So let us put our mind to how this can be achieved. I will ask Mr Russell to join us as we deliberate. Do you wish your premier to be likewise included?'

'If he is to be involved in any action, yes. I will send my boat back for him.'

Pearce returned to the cabin to find Russell present as Langholm made a request.

'We must send someone over to the *Santa Leocadia* to speed up the work, which has slackened considerably since the first cannon shot. We might have to raise some sail on her even if it risks carrying away a mast. I take it, Mr Pearce, you have no objection to one of my lieutenants issuing orders your men should crack on?'

Pearce looked at Russell then, for it would be he who would detail the person so employed, to say with some emphasis. 'I'm sure it will be carried out with the appropriate level of respect.' The resultant look did not provide any reassurance that he was correct.

It was obvious the only way to achieve what was required would involve a landing party, which had Pearce worried, given he had serious concerns about the way it was proposed it be carried out. Langholm was talking about a large combined force from *Lively* and *Hazard*. He also clearly saw the leadership falling to Russell as the frigate's premier.

It wasn't that Langholm was shy; it was a fact that responsible captains, of which John Pearce could hardly call himself one, usually delegated any such duties to their second in command. First because they were required to put the needs of the ship ahead of personal glory, but also any such accolade should go to an officer who might benefit from garnering some to themselves. The concomitant of which was he would send Isaac Hallowell, who would be under Russell's command.

He had no fear Hallowell would acquit himself badly, quite the reverse. What experience he had indicated there could be confusion in who was issuing orders and who'd be receiving them, which could lead to a less-than-perfect scenario. The action they were discussing would have to be undertaken in darkness, against an enemy in numbers of which they had no idea. This, in itself, set off another train of thought.

If it was the crew of the *Santa Leocadia*, they had totalled near to three hundred souls. True they had left without weapons, but if they had mustered a field gun, what else had they got hold of? If they had muskets, any approach up a steep hill being detected, many lives could be forfeited. What about swords and even farm implements. In close quarter fighting, they could be deadly.

'Can I say, Lord Langholm. The size of a force engaged in a full assault will require it to be substantial, and from both our vessels, thus it should be led by a commanding officer.' This had the normally lazy eyes showing genuine surprise as Pearce added. 'I do of course mean myself.'

'Which, milord,' Russell barked, the glare aimed at Pearce now undisguised, 'could be recorded under the heading of glory hunting.'

'I think you'll find, Mr Russell, I'm well sourced in such. And, if you will forgive me, I must ask if you have led a shore party in a night attack?'

'I have no doubt about my ability to do so.'

'Which tells me the answer is no.'

'And you are claiming you have?'

'I would hardly make the point if I had not and done so successfully.'

'This poses a dilemma, Pearce.'

The lack of a title of any kind, mister or captain, was telling. Langholm had ever been assiduous in the use of the proper honorifics. But Pearce was not to be deflected by a mere lack of manners for he'd drawn another conclusion.

'Indeed, I would suggest for any action to be a success, it would be best if the shore party was smaller and came from one vessel. At night, confusion is as much of a foe as an enemy so it is paramount any instruction is obeyed without question. The voice issuing orders must be one those required to act upon it recognise.'

Seeing hesitation, Pearce elaborated on the dangers, both those he had already thought on and a few more for good measure. All the time he was subject to a basilisk stare from Russell, who saw his thunder being stolen, which drove the man he clearly hated to contrive a solution.

'Added to which, an intention to attack regardless of what we might face with could be construed as folly. Would it not be best to send a small party to reconnoitre the situation? When we know what we are up against, a proper plan can be formulated. In what I propose, the wind will act as an aid, allowing a cautious approach in small numbers to be covered by the sound.'

'Russell?'

'I am happy to undertake any task you allot to me, milord.'

'Never doubted it man, but I think Mr Pearce has a point on numbers.' He had obviously arrived at the same conclusion as Pearce regarding those manning the cannon. 'Best we know what we must overcome before charging in, all guns blazing.'

A knock on the door brought in Hallowell, with Pearce speaking quickly, in order to avoid a reprise of everything so far covered. He also wanted to present a *fait accompli*, given that certain other things had occurred to him.

'We need a shore party Mr Hallowell, to set off as soon as it is dark. So, seek out a spot where we can land and choose twenty men to make up the number, which I will lead.'

The man was shocked at the abrupt nature of the orders, as well as wondering as well why he'd been obliged to boat over to hear them. But he had served with John Pearce and had been subject to his quixotic ways long enough to not question the fact. Nor did he, like Russell, and for the same reason of knowing his commander too well, question why the task was one his captain had decided to undertake himself.

'Aye aye, sir.'

'And they will need to apply the burnt cork.'

'Am I allowed to protest, milord?'

'Mr Russell,' Pearce responded, 'if you wish to join us, I would welcome your company.'

It was interesting to watch a man struggle with two conflicting notions, the first being his desire to partake of any action proposed. But to accept would put him under the command of John Pearce, even if, in time served as a lieutenant, he outranked him. But the man was a Master and Commander, which counted for more. Then there was the implied insult that he had no prior knowledge of what he would be doing, while Pearce obviously did. Being treated like a novice would be too galling.

'I'm content to take part in what will follow, a proper assault, and lead it if required.'

This was accompanied by a look at his own captain, one which implied he was letting him, and his men, down.

'I must catch Hallowell,' Pearce pronounced, rising from his chair and heading for the door.

He didn't hear Langholm as he said quietly. 'Don't be hasty with condemnation Russell. When it comes to people being killed, I much prefer to keep you whole. I cannot say the same for the officer who has just left us.'

As Pearce and Hallowell crossed to *Hazard*, the gun, which had been silent, opened up again, firing several rounds, clearly to pepper the disturbed waters around the channel. Overhead, some of the cloud was breaking up showing patches of clear blue sky, though it seemed to have no effect on either the wind or the amount of spume spilling over the bar. It did however allow for a clearer sight of the trajectory.

'Looks like they're getting the range, sir.'

'To which we would be subject.' The look of curiosity this engendered brought forth the reply, which had occurred to Pearce in the cabin and spurred his thinking. 'Who do you think would be delegated the task of getting through the channel first?'

'Us,' was Hallowell's reply after a second's consideration.

'Precisely and before that happens, I want to know exactly what we might face. At this distance and at such an elevation, all we can see is the smoke of discharge, so we can't be sure if they're ranging with one cannon or several.'

Back on board the first task was to get those he wanted back from the Spanish frigate, men he knew to be good fighters, as well as obedient to his commands. There were three members of the shore party who were self-selecting, there being no way his fellow Pelicans were going to allow John Pearce to go into danger without them coming along. Quite apart from their loyalty, they had leadership and fighting skills he had already seen in action on a similar target in the Mediterranean.

'Were we on *Hazard* volunteered, John-boy?' asked Michael O'Hagan, addressing him with easy familiarity, as he always did when others were out of earshot.

'In a manner of speaking, Michael.'

'Sure, I take that to mean it was you who did the volunteering.'

'You don't have to come along,' was the response, delivered in a querulous tone from a man who so hated to be so easily found out.

'Bejesus, have I not got to keep you whole. When you have the fine estate yon silver will gift you, I'll be looking for a place to take my ease and so will Charlie and Rufus.'

The pair mentioned were the others self-selected, men with whom he had been illegally pressed into the King's Navy. Only three years past, it seemed like another era entirely; so many things had happened in between. Much as he would be glad to have Charlie Taverner and Rufus Dommet along, there was no way he was about to openly admit it.

'And here's me thinking, with such a fine reward, I would finally be able to get rid of the lot of you.'

～

The idea Samuel Oliphant had anything to say on what was proposed might be a notion of his, but it was not one shared by John Pearce. In fact, his opinion was the complete opposite, and he now regretted telling him of what he intended and the steps already taken.

'You're again commenting on things which are none of your concern.'

'I have a worry you seem intent on getting yourself killed.'

'Something I would say, on past experience, you seemed better equipped to achieve than me. And I find, in light of your previous behaviour, your supposed concern for my welfare borders on hypocrisy.'

There was much truth in what Pearce was saying. Ever since he'd met and become involved with Oliphant, which he had good reason to believe was not even his real name, the term slippery was the one which described him best. He had a habit of keeping things to himself when danger threatened, which happened on both the missions in which they'd been engaged. He tended to keep hidden avenues which might ensure his survival, without much seeming concern for the life chances of the man accompanying him.

The protest was immediate. 'I'm depending on you to ensure I get my slice of the value of that silver.'

Why did Pearce see it as unconvincing? He had put Oliphant on his muster, so a share, admittedly not a great deal, when the prize money was distributed, would come to him automatically. Perhaps the man's expression belied the words or was it the tone, which led to a surprising conclusion: the notion Oliphant might actually care if he came to harm. In some way, the next words backed up such a view.

'To say you're wedded to risk is an understatement. I may not know much about the navy, but I do know other captains delegate the kind of task you propose to undertake to their inferiors. They do not risk their lives on hairbrained adventures. You're forever telling me how much faith you have in Hallowell, but I must say you rarely demonstrate it.'

The truth of both statements could not be denied, which led to the rejoinder Pearce saw as necessary, on this occasion, to observe things for himself. Then, ever so slightly embarrassed by being presented with the truth, he began to remove his blue coat.

'If you'll forgive me, I must get ready.'

CHAPTER THREE

Getting ashore would have to be undertaken without the employment of lights, for their use would alert the enemy to the approach. Pearce was not prepared to assume the Spaniards were at ease and feeling so secure that they would not have piquets in place on the shoreline. It was best to work on them being on high alert, especially as the warm wind seemed to be easing a fraction, though it was still blowing at gale force. The break up in the cloud cover was there, but intermittent at best, so even with evidence of such, being out at sea and heading their way was not something upon which to rely.

The sight of him in the afternoon, on deck with a telescope, he assumed would be taken as natural. Yet it required much more movement than strictly necessary so as to not be seen examining any particular area. Hallowell had identified a good spot on which to land, right off the beam, albeit the tiny strand was pebbles, and he was searching for two things: any sign of men to guard it as well as a path up the steep hillside. He sought the one used by humans, in the hope no shoreline was left untroubled by such a presence, if only for a quiet place to fish.

There was no sign of guards on the strand or anywhere near it; indeed the whole hillside seemed to be bereft of any human presence. In his imagination Pearce could conjure up other ways to negate an approach, trip wires and the like attached to bells, a good way to sound the alarm without the physical use of sentinels. If he thought on such tactics, worrying would make no difference and the risk just had to be accepted.

As the light began to fade, the cutter was loaded on the starboard side of *Hazard*, since this had to be carried out, in this latitude, even earlier than the usual hour of twilight due to the sky again being heavily overcast. If the approach had to be made under such conditions, it could only be when daylight was gone. But to get everything in place before setting off required enough light to see where they were putting their feet.

Much activity on the deck was also required, so those making up the shore party could get over the side and into the cutter without attracting attention. This amounted, to anyone observing and they would be, almost an air of impending mutiny, so great was the confusion. It was far from sure if the reaction from *Lively* was of any help; the men on their deck were seemingly as taken up with what was happening on *Hazard* as anyone might be from the heights: Did it demote authenticity or invite suspicion? There was no way to tell, so it was best ignored.

There was no uniform coat and hat for John Pearce as he made for the gangway. It was sailor's ducks and a kerseymere top, with a bandana round his head, which caused Michael O'Hagan to opine he looked almost human. Once in the boat and out of sight, the burnt cork could be applied to blacken faces, with white cloths tied round each neck. These would hopefully aid them in seeing the man ahead when moving in the dark.

Weapons loaded earlier through a gunport were distributed: clubs, tomahawks, short naval hangars plus, for a pair of marines, muskets, though they were not primed to avoid an accidental discharge. The hammer and spikes they'd brought along had been loaded more in hope than expectation that the chance might come to disable one or more field guns.

With only one night to observe the decks, Pearce had to assume the particular arrangement of the lights on his lower masts would not arouse comment ashore. A certain amount of the approach, which was no great distance, could be achieved by the use of a luminous compass. But a pair of special lanterns, set apart, rigged in such a way so that both were only visible if they held the right course, should get them to the desired part of the shore, in safety or not, depending on how much their foes had taken precautions.

One fact had not occurred to Pearce. The Spaniards up on the heights required light, not just to cook but to go about any tasks needing to be carried out. Coming out from the lee of *Hazard*, he saw, on the ridge above the point for which they were aiming, an extensive orange glow reflected off the cloud cover. This spoke of men in numbers, while the lack of a sight of a flame indicated their position was well behind the crest. For this he was thankful, given none of the glow from the flames spilled onto the rippling water of the bay.

Rowing had to be carried out softly, there being the risk of disturbed water which, if the sky suddenly cleared, might send up a flash of reflection. The only person to speak was Worricker, who was looking over the stern and using the shipboard lights to tell the man on the tiller of any adjustments to his course. Pearce was in the prow, looking into the inky darkness for any hint of sound or movement, it being the point of maximum danger. If anyone was going to suffer for his stratagems, it should first be him.

The cove and its stone beach had advantages, the first being it was sheltered from the wind, making the loud hiss on the pebbles caused by the rising or falling tide clearly audible. This acted like a measure of the distance to be covered, while it also meant, to an acute ear, that anyone seeking to come forward to challenge them at a rush would make a great deal of noise.

He was out of the cutter before the keel struck, with the freezing water up to his groin making him gasp. He grounded the boat in silence, the command already issued everyone else should stay aboard, with oars poised for a quick departure at any sign of danger. The noise of movement on the shingle applied as much to him as to anyone; so it sounded, in his ears, as if it would be heard in the port of Vigo, many miles down the coast.

The place must be in turmoil, it being the intended destination of the silver aboard the *Santa Leocadia*, so it was very likely that the gun fired today had come from there. Having made to the head of the beach with no sign of any piquets, he called for the others to follow, with Worricker and two men staying by the cutter.

'Lantern, Michael,' he called, once they were all safely up against a line of stunted trees.

As yet unlit, the catch had to be opened by feel, with only the striking flints providing a modicum of glim, to establish if it was safe to set the spark to the oil-soaked wick. It was a risk but, up against the vegetation, Pearce reckoned that the same elevation which hid the Spaniards from sight would act in reverse for them. The light allowed Pearce to search for the break in the trees he'd spotted from the deck, with no assurance of what he'd supposed to be the beginning of a path would turn out to be one..

A shaft of moonlight out in the bay passed over at a tremendous lick, lighting up the ships, the reflection off the water enough to aid Pearce in finding the spot he'd identified earlier. So, it was with some relief he pushed through and onto a hillside covered with dense gorse, this as the moonlight died away, the moving clouds again blocking it out.

'We'll have to wait,' he hissed.

It had been no part of Pearce's plan, it if could be so termed, to do so. Throughout the day he had thought, more than once, he was acting on the wing. His actions were based on hopes not facts; one being the lack of clarity in what he anticipated was a way to ascend the hillside. With no idea when a lantern, risky to use anyway, would be visible from the crest, it was too perilous to overuse and then only as a last resort.

'We need more breaks in the clouds before we can move freely.' There was no spoken question in response, their discipline holding well, but he was sure there was one, so he whispered. 'If we don't get any and we're here all night, it's back to the ship before dawn and think again, so get off your feet and rest awhile.'

⁓

What followed was frustratingly slow, causing them to move in fits and starts; no shaft of moon or starlight lasted more than a few minutes. The scudding clouds were racing across the sky and their spilled light did the same. It was a case of setting off when a gap appeared, which showed there was a path, albeit overgrown, and then getting as far as possible, only to hunker down again as the light disappeared.

Faintly, from out in the bay, came the sound of a ship's bell, which was better than having along a timepiece, though the sound was telling Pearce what they were about was taking too long for comfort. This led to the possibility, if the situation continued, of staying on shore throughout the next day, hard to contemplate given he'd not thought to bring any supplies, especially water.

There was no problem with direction; they just headed uphill as best they could, zig zagging one way then the other, using the reflected firelight to act as a beacon. But it was summer, hot and uncomfortable, made even more so by the strong wind, which did nothing to deter the biting insect's intent on extracting as much blood from the human party as possible. Once or twice, they disturbed nesting and resting birds, sending them squawking skywards, creating a sound that Pearce was convinced must be heard at a distance. Yet, if they caused alarm, there was no evidence of it.

One thing reassured him; discovery of their presence would not happen soundlessly. It would either be with a cry of alarm or a gun shot, depending on how far out the enemy had placed the sentinels and what arms they possessed. If he and his men were subject to fear and troublesome sounds, this applied in spades to any fellow stuck out ahead of his comrades, tasked to sit peering into the mostly stygian darkness and no doubt imagining horrific illusions.

In the end, it was the increasing reflected glow of the enemy fires which made quicker progress possible, while its strength acted as a good indication of the distance still to be covered. Yet this also required it be exploited with caution; if they could see more clearly, so could their possible opponents.

It was Charlie Taverner who put his mouth to Pearce's ear, to say he'd heard a coughing sound, his barely visible finger jabbing and pointing ahead. The next thing his captain saw was the obvious glint of a waving knife, the blade picking up the firelight. To the question posed, so quietly only Pearce heard it, there was no option to do anything but pat Charlie on the shoulder, with enough pressure to act as an encouragement to proceed.

In the silence to follow, Pearce was aware of the tightness in his gut and also of every little sound Charlie made as he slithered forward. Then it was silence and concern because, if he failed to find and silence what he thought might be a piquet, the position his party was in carried great danger. They were close to the crest, and so if the alarm was raised, flight was the only course of action. In the dark, to retreat at speed would be difficult, while it was no great prospect to contemplate trying to fight and hold off an enemy as they sought to slowly retire.

The query might be a soft one, but it was not in English and sounded anxious, which was soon followed by a muffled cry, and then the thudding sound, which could be the knife being employed. This was followed by a gurgling sound, and hope replaced fear as the noise of a less than fully cautious approach led him to believe Charlie had enjoyed success and the low hiss confirmed it.

'Got 'im, John. Might be the way ahead is clear.'

'Up to me to find out,' was the equally soft reply. 'We're close to the crest. Keep the others still and I'll go ahead.'

He had no idea Michael O'Hagan was close enough to hear. The sharp, breathy whisper told him otherwise. 'Not alone you won't, John-boy.'

This was no time to argue and, he knew from experience, to do so would probably be a waste. 'Silently Michael. Charlie, you are in charge. If it goes wrong, get back to the boat as fast as you can.'

'Won't be easy.'

'See if the lobsters can prime their muskets in this light. A couple of balls cracking past an ear will slow any pursuit. Can you see my white cloth, Michael?'

'I can.'

'Then let us move.' There followed the sound of muttering, to which Pearce responded with an impatient whisper. 'What are you about?'

'I'm begging St Patrick to see off any snakes, am I not.'

It was necessary to bite back any reply. This was no time to be telling Michael his religious superstitions were pointless. Instead, he got down to move forward, as Charlie had, on elbows and knees, acutely aware of every sound he was making, as well as those of the Irishman behind him. But at least he could see, which was testimony to the number of fires being continually fed over the crest, indicating a lot of people requiring light. Perhaps it was, as he had suggested to Langholm, the whole crew of the *Santa Leocadia*.

He knew he was only yards off with the sight of sparks flaring off unseasoned wood.

They were not rising high as they would on a still night but being blown away by the wind off the sea, probably even stronger at such a height than it felt down in the bay, to die out before they'd gone far. Finally, inching forward there was flame, being ferociously whipped inland. Pearce halted until Michael could join him, aware, as well as the crackling of flames, he could hear voices, the calling of what sounded like orders being the loudest.

'Time for the last few yards,' was imparted into an Irish ear.

There was no call for a reply and Michael did not provide one. Back on elbows and knees, Pearce used the way the gorse bushes were silhouetted against the flames to find an approach which would give him cover. Behind one he could part the branches to try and see what lay beyond. It was far from clear; the only obvious fact being that the gorse cover ran out as the barren top of the hill was revealed, as well as a whole host of moving figures illuminated by the orange glow.

In order to make out what was going on, and by the sound of it, there was a lot of activity, he needed to get on to his knees and risk his head being seen as he raised it for just a second. There was no certainty in what was revealed; it was too much of a blur, which meant repetition and the need to concentrate on what lay before him in sections, running from left to right.

The impression he got was off a substantial encampment, the white of tents quite far to the rear being the most obvious, with dozens if not hundreds of souls busy on a seeming multitude of tasks. But he spotted something which he knew required closer examination, and so, dropping down and removing his white neckerchief, he crawled under the bush to a point which took his head out into the open and what felt like bare rock. No one was looking in his direction; they were too busy making what they had fetched up to this hill top ready for employment. When he realised what it consisted of, his heart nearly stopped.

The scrabbling backwards was delayed, so he could take in the full extent of what he was observing. But the point came when Pearce needed to see no more, and sure, speed was essential; he passed Michael at a fast enough pace to make the man slow to follow. He kept going till he re-joined Charlie Taverner and the others, issuing a quick, if suppressed, order to get back to the boat and to eschew care in doing so.

It was as well, once they were away from the reflected glow, they had a patch of clear sky with which to see. This allowed the party to move, if not at speed, at least at a pace many times faster than the ascent. When they seemed to be about halfway down, with the light reflecting off the nearly still water below, bathing the hillside, Michael finally spoke. He made no attempt to lower his voice, asking what the hell Pearce had seen that had him in such a hellfire hurry. With the men now well spaced out, he had no need for titles.

'And John-boy, I'm not the only one to be a' wondering.'

If Pearce was tempted to reply, he was after all a man to be open with his crew, especially so with Michael, but caution made him hold back.

'From the rush, sure I take it not to be good.'

'It's not, but I'll wait till we're aboard to tell you.'

'So bad,' came with the same heavy breathing affecting his friend, 'your feart the rest of the lads might hear it.'

'Just keep moving. There's no time to waste.'

It was a journey which could not be made without mishap; nearly everyone fell at some time and far from silently, the man in command included. They were tripped by a root or a stone they could not see, and it was a tribute to his concern; no allowance was made when anyone cried out in pain. The only time a halt was called came when one loud cry hinted at a more serious result; indeed Pearce was half convinced he could hear the breaking of a bone.

The yell of deep distress was loud enough to alert both the Spaniards at the top of the hill, as well as Worricker and his two men on the strand. There was no need to tell Michael to help the unfortunate, but it was not provided without loud sounds of agony.

The Irishman, with scant gentility, hoisted one of the marines on to his shoulder, for it was he who had taken the tumble, and the pain of his jogging movement had the fellow pass out.

Finally, Pearce felt his feet begin to scrabble on the pebbles, his second lieutenant appearing as a black figure set against the water, in a pose which indicated he had taken out and was aiming both his pistols. This required an order to belay and help get everyone aboard at speed. It was only when he stopped and steadied his breathing, Pearce heard the sound of pursuit, and a glance backwards showed bobbing torches, as those he had spied upon came on at speed. Their clear intention was to ensure that if anything had been seen over the crest it would remain a secret.

It was a testament to the discipline his party had acquired, which showed in some of the Quota Men who, not weeks past, didn't know one end of an oar from another. The way they took up their sticks with alacrity, quick to obey Michael's order to row, was impressive and they were just as quick to get right the rhythm of employment.

The cutter sped away from the shore, with Worricker, taking careful aim, seeking to fell the first torch bearer fast approaching the edge of the beach. The question Pearce had raised, as to what weapons they might have, was answered by a ragged volley of musket fire. The only thing they hit was water, with the spurts rising on both sides of the boat until they were out of effective range.

'Head for *Lively*.'

'We've got a broken bone here, your honour, an' it sounded bad.'

'Which is unlikely to kill him.'

He nearly added that delay might kill them all, but again caution made him hold his tongue. It was testimony to the ingrained naval tradition that Michael called out *Hazard* as they approached the frigate. Pearce was shouting too as he was taken close to the battens lining the scantlings, telling whoever had the watch to rouse out their captain.

He arrived on the deck, which had gone from soporific to active in less than a minute, and brushing aside the duty officer he made for Langholm's cabin, ignoring the marine sentry seeking to bar his way as he burst in. The man was up and in a dressing gown, his fair hair tousled, evidence he'd been asleep.

'A hell fire commotion Mr Pearce and you in the guise of a pirate.' His attempt at *savoir faire* was blown away by what was said next, his voice speaking low to confine the exchange to between them. 'Thirty-two pounders?'

'A quartet of them, and being set on the reverse of the slope, their muzzles are elevated, so they will act like mortars. We'll be subjected to plunging fire as we go through yonder channel and from cannon that might even have the weight of shot to sink us. I would suggest, even if it's still dark, we must weigh immediately. I will certainly do so as soon as I get back aboard *Hazard*.'

'You intend to lead the way?' Langholm demanded, in a way which implied he would order such a course if he could do so.

'I do.'

It was the reply of a man already on his way out of the cabin. He did not add the notion he had arrived at in the boat, which was that the heavy cannons were not the same as those fired earlier in the day. So, they would not yet have the range, which would take several salvoes to find. Now, to be first out of Pontevedra Bay was the safest course and Spanish silver be damned.

Chapter Four

Much as they tried, getting the ships over their anchors could not be done in silence. The crews were accustomed to it being a noisy business and no number of commands for hush could ensure imposition. This was before the sky cleared once more to illuminate the sails just let loose from the yards and in the process of being sheeted home. Not that they gave them much steerage way: the very wind which had got them into the inner bay was now, being dead foul, set to keep them there.

Fortunately there was only one saving grace, one which had been obvious from the first sign of bad weather. The direction of the wind meant any Spanish vessels wanting to intercept them would struggle to get out of their west coast harbours. And given they had already established that Vigo, the base bordering Portugal, had no warships of any size berthed, the nearest danger looked to be some distance off. It lay far to the south at the main Spanish fleet base of Cadiz.

It was quickly obvious, even as they braced the yards right round, trying to access the exit channel under sail, even if the tide was fairly full, was to invite disaster. So, towing by boats seemed the only secure method of tackling the dangerous dogleg. All the while, as he stood frustrated at the slow progress, John Pearce was wondering what was going through the mind of Lord Langholm, still seemingly happy with him leading the way.

Positions reversed, would he not have wanted to ensure the safety of a frigate over the smaller HMS *Hazard*, perhaps even to get the *Santa Leocadia* out of danger first? Or was he waiting to assess the risk before moving, for even when told what they faced, he had not seen what had been gifted to his fellow captain. He could not but recall the activities which so alarmed him at the crest of the hill – men furiously constructing raised gun pits to increase the muzzle elevation of their heavy cannons and doing so with commendable proficiency.

He did not even begin to wonder how they'd managed to get such weapons to where they were such a potent threat, or from where they had come, most likely from the naval arsenal in Vigo. If British Tars could work miracles when shifting ordinance ashore, it would be stupid to assume the same skills were absent from the sailors of the Spanish Navy or the disgorged crew of the *Santa Leocadia*. But it was a feat to be admired for it must have taken an enormous amount of manual and bestial efforts to execute such a coup and get to the very top of the escarpment.

'It does however confirm they have nothing afloat close enough to effect the same outcome. If we can get to sea, all we face as a danger is the weather.'

A gloomy nod from his inferior officers underlined what was still a far from rosy prospect. 'Time to man the boats. Every man who can be spared to ply an oar. Mr Macklin, I reckon your lads to be the best in this area, so I will allot to you the task of one boat, while Mr Worricker commands the other.'

'Would I be allowed a suggestion, sir?' asked Macklin.

'Feel free to make any which you think will aid our aim.'

'If we could have assistance from the crew and boats of *Lively* it would speed our passage, with the promise to reverse matters once we are secure and at anchor. We could then combine again to bring out the Spaniard.'

'Capital thinking.'

Pearce reached out a hand to take Hallowell's speaking trumpet, proffered by a fellow who agreed it was a good suggestion. This he raised to call out to the frigate's deck, his request answered by

Lieutenant Russell in the negative, words less than clearly audible as they were whipped away by the wind.

'I have sent half our men to the *Santa Leocadia*. Given the pulling they have before them, I cannot say I favour asking them for more. I fear you must make your own way.'

There was a temptation to demand he rouse out Langholm, but it was put aside. For his lordship to countermand his premier on an open deck would not serve in the article of discipline, so he was unlikely to do so.

'We'll just have to hope our own efforts suffice, gentlemen.'

HMS *Hazard* was not short of boats, having acquired an extra pair off Brittany, but Pearce did lack the men to fully man them all. It was best to use the two largest and give them full crews rather than seek to employ everyone. Besides, he needed a certain number of men aboard to work the sails if they could be seen to aid forward progress.

It was hard to call what transpired such a thing, for the ship crept towards the exit at snail's pace, the wind acting as a brake on the hull. Not all of John Pearce's attention was on the dogleg channel, as much was aimed in the direction of the orange glow, still topping the barren crest. It had him wondering what was happening out of sight.

It did not last long. They were close to the narrows when the first heavy cannon fired, the flash of the discharge visible before the sound of the muzzle blast. It being still dark, even when the cloud cover was now broken, the trajectory of the ball was not visible, but its effect was. If it fell well short of its intended target, the huge plume of water thrown up was both clear and worrying, falling as it did within a cable's length from the neck of water they must get through.

This would be as visible to the gunners as it was to their enemies on all three slowly moving vessels, with HMS *Hazard* now well clear of the others. They were close enough to the bar to be deafened by the pounding of the waves against the rocks, with spume blown nearly as high as the water spout caused by the gunnery.

'Call in one of the boats, Mr Hallowell, we will put the men released on sweeps. They will serve to push us away from danger as well as aid our progress.'

The order was not reacted to with the usual alacrity, as the flash and boom of another ranging ball took everyone's attention for several seconds before it struck. It was not water this time, but solid rock, even if it was still well short of the actual channel. The sound of it striking overbore all the others assailing their ears.

'The wind will make aiming more difficult,' Pearce said, as much to reassure himself as anyone else. 'Oblige me by carrying out your orders.'

It was Worricker's cutter which was called in, to find, when they had secured their boat and got aboard, the sweeps were out and ready to be employed. To say the man in command was concerned was an understatement for the wind was not and had never been steady. The increase in hull pressure brought on by sudden gusts was his major fear, especially when he was required to make a slight alteration of course, which increased the pressure on his beam.

Macklin was out ahead acting as a tow, with Pearce tempted to call out to him to keep the head of the ship steady. But he put this aside, given that Macklin was a very experienced sailor who would not require to be told. Instead, he put the greater number of sweepers to starboard to both keep going forward and be ready to fend off if the wind took *Hazard* too close to the rocks.

The next ball from the hillside was enough to induce dread, landing as it did close enough for the wind-swept column of disturbed water to blow across and drench the forward part of the deck. Again, Pearce had to bite his tongue and resist the temptation to call for greater effort. There was not a man jack aboard who required to be reminded of the dangers they faced, and they were giving their all because of it.

'The rate of fire is slow, sir.'

'It is, Mr Hallowell, for they're ranging with one cannon. But when they've worked out the right quantity of powder to place their balls where they want them, we will be under the fire of four of the sods.'

'Was taking the lead such a good notion?'

Pearce looked over the stern to where HMS *Lively* was creeping along, its boats strung out in an arc ahead of its bow, to observe they had put the *Santa Leocadia* under tow as well, which naturally made progress near to negligible.

'I'm not sure Lord Langholm wished it so for reasons of kindness. But I would suggest, from what we have seen so far, he is going to find his exit a mite more dangerous than our own and that's bad enough.'

Pearce made his way forward from the quarterdeck to the bows. It was from there he would be able to see the difficulties with which they were going to be presented. None of the risks they faced were hidden, with the surging waves making sure very rock which might hole them was visible as long as the overhead cloud remained broken. With dawn only an hour away, there was a temptation to back the sails and wait, but those ranging shots were coming too close for Pearce to draw any comfort from a clearer sight of the perils they were about to encounter.

As if the thought was farther to the fact, all four thirty-two pounders opened up, the muzzle flashes merging into one whole, likewise the booming sound to follow. When they landed, it was in a bracket to hit both sides of the channel, though not the deep water itself. If it was inclined to induce hesitation, it could not be countenanced for the situation would not improve. If anything, it would deteriorate, with Pearce reckoning absolute accuracy was impossible. The gunners had to get lucky, but so did he and his crew to survive.

There was no choice but to ignore the guns, given worrying about them would serve no purpose. So, he leant out over the bowsprit, calling out the dangers he saw, and the same duty was carried out by his officers. In the lead cutter, Macklin's men were straining hard to keep *Hazard*'s bows from pointing right forward until they reached the point where the channel turned half left. This had him calling out, not that he could be heard doing so, for the larboard oars to be shipped. The aim was to turn the ship's head aided by the rudder. Macklin had carried out the correct manoeuvre anyway.

She came round, so slowly disaster was close; the bowsprit aiming at a body of badly eddying water, which spoke of hazards beneath the surface. Heart in mouth Pearce kept his eye on what could sink them, as orders behind him had the yards shifted to provide a bit of backing. Aided by the efforts of the oarsmen, this helped, in conjunction with much fending off with the sweeps, to keep them clear of the reef.

The action had to be reversed to traverse the next bend, both made under a now regular rate of fire, not thankfully one which matched King George's Navy, but steady nevertheless. The spume where they struck water swept over the whole deck, the noise where it was rock an ear-splitting crack. Now the sweeps to starboard had to be employed, as several men with feet planted strained to push *Hazard* into deeper water.

This was taking place as the first hint of daylight began to show as a grey tinge above the eastern hills. It was not something which was going to help Lord Langholm get both his frigate and his charge out without damage.

The next turn of the bow would take Pearce out into the open bay, but there was scant security there. Rolling waves were still powering in from the southwest and were about to hit his bows with an effect which would only become apparent when it occurred. It was time to risk all, for without forward motion, such a run of the sea could force them onto the rocks.

'All hands on the sweeps,' he shouted.

Pearce ran to take the end of one himself, right by Michael O'Hagan, mouthing a near-silent entreaty through lips now salt encrusted. He made an entreaty for the luck which had seen him survive many perils, to find a woman to love and to be the father of a child, as well as to get to and hold his present position.

'Would that be prayers I'm hearing, John-boy?' the Irishman gasped.

'To pagan gods, Michael, if to any gods at all,' Pearce panted.

'Then it's hell for you if we don't get clear.'

'Well at least I can get dry in the flames.'

The scrapping sound of wood on rock only made the entreaties, and no doubt Michael's prayers, more heartfelt, but there was no time or point in wondering how serious any damage might be. Survival depended on effort, not concern. It was with almost a sense of deliverance Pearce felt the bows lift on a wave, one which, coming in from the open sea, swung the bows to starboard to take them clear of danger.

Leaving his hold on the sweep, Pearce went to where Mr Williams stood on the quarterdeck, just as behind them, one of the four bracketing shots hit the actual channel – solid metal balls which might have gone right through *Hazard*'s deck and taken out her keel. If he felt luck had favoured him, he could not help but wonder what Langholm would make of such a sight.

'We need to get in the lee of the island, Mr Williams. And before you tell me, I'm aware of the dangers of the rock-strewn seabed.'

'We will still be in range of yonder cannon, sir.'

'I have to reckon they have bigger fish to fry than us. Can it be done?'

'It will mean a rate of backing and filling.'

'Do you feel able to oversee it?'

For a man normally nervous of his captain, the reply was firm. 'Aye, aye sir.'

'Then I leave it to you to see us anchored out of this damned wind.'

It took an age, though the increasing daylight was of help. It required the use of the sails to get a modicum of forward movement, quickly reversed, when necessary, by a swift backing of a scrap of canvas to slow the ship. The point at which success was achieved came suddenly, as the wind died away, if not to silence, to a level, in the lee of the island, which was tolerable to the ears.

'Mr Macklin, bring your men back aboard and a tot of rum for the whole ship's company is appropriate.' There was no cheering as would be common for such a grant; everyone was too exhausted. 'Mr Hallowell, once the grog is delivered, set the watches as normal and get the cook to light his coppers so the men can dry their clothing and be fed.'

Pearce made his way to his cabin to change his soaking garments; this done quickly so he could get back on deck and observe HMS *Lively*'s attempts to emulate what he'd just achieved. It was immediately obvious his intention was to tow the *Santa Leocadia* through. First, no doubt, on the grounds, if the Spaniard gunners had got the range, this could only improve. The thing hindering true accuracy, the wind acting on the round shot, might fall away, and there was some evidence it was moderating.

There was no pleasure in watching this attempt fail, though there was appreciation of the way Langholm's men were swift to react to the danger they faced. As soon as one round shot clipped the deck of the Spanish frigate, to take out a huge chuck of bulwark and a section of the deck, alteration was executed. The men towing the ship forward cast off their lines, rowing furiously to take up the cables hanging from the stern and get the vessel back into the deeper water of the inner bay.

At this point the gunnery ceased. Neither *Lively* nor the *Santa Leocadia* warranted powder and shot, which would be held back until they once more risked the channel. This was a point even Samuel Oliphant made when he came on deck, having spent the whole of the previous hours in his cot. He desired to see what was afoot now that *Hazard* was at anchor.

'They've stopped firing.'

'Conserving powder and shot for the real aim, which is to trap their own ship in the inner bay.'

'What will Langholm do now?' he asked.

'Perhaps wait until it's dark again. Try it when the gunners can't see as well as they can in daylight.'

'Not without risk.'

'No.'

'And if that fails?'

'You will observe I am not on the deck of HMS *Lively*, so no decision falls to me.'

'None yon silver will fall to you either if he can't get out. Even I know it's only a matter of time till we see the sails of a squadron of Spanish ships.'

'You know or have you once again consulted Mr Williams?'

Oliphant didn't reply, leaving Pearce to suspect that his guess was correct. His erstwhile companion had a habit of querying the master before he put forward any point, in the past usually a complaint, to the man in command. But that was by the by; more worrying was the fact that he was right.

'Langholm has no choice but to risk it and, if I were him, I'd get my ship out first and if necessary, leave the Spaniard behind.'

'What about the . . . ,' there was an interruption, swiftly responded to by John Pearce. 'Having shifted the cargo to his own holds.'

'Were you not of the opinion there were dangers in such a course?'

'I was, but things change. It's the lesser of two evils.'

Pearce moved away from Oliphant to again stare at the point on the top of the hills where he knew the Spanish cannon to be placed. There was no orange glow now, just, in full daylight, wisps of drifting smoke, probably fires for cooking, which left him to wonder what they were about and what plans they were making.

If the escape *Hazard* had just achieved had been exhausting, he knew, from his own experience, working a cannon over many hours was equally so. The gunners would be sleeping while they could but, as soon as either vessel still inside the bay showed any hint of seeking to brave the dogleg, they would be back on their weapons and firing.

The water where he was anchored was disturbed but nothing like that exposed to the run of the sea, which was evidence that the wind was still blowing strongly, so Langholm's task was as difficult as his own had been. What could he do to render it easier?

'Mr Campbell,' he called to the midshipman on watch. 'I will be in my cabin.'

<hr>

When Pearce emerged, once more dressed as a common seaman, it was to curious looks from the crew. This was made more so by the command to his stalwarts of the previous night's escapade to once more man the cutter. They were to take with them a couple of lit lanterns, doors firmly shut, as well as a barrel of turpentine.

At first, hugging the protected shore of the Island of Ons, they found progress easy, but this changed as they cleared the southern cape and were hit by the kind of waves which lifted the cutter's bow nearly above their heads. The course was a dangerous one too, right across the entrance to the outer roads. This meant steering into and then away from the run of the sea, until they could make a landfall.

Once ashore, it was a trek along a rocky and inhospitable coast, slithering over boulders green with seaweed slime, until they made it to a tiny sandy, wave-washed inlet. This allowed them to make some progress inland, and soon they were among the same kind of gorse and steep hillside which had so hampered their movements the night before. Pearce was moving ahead, feeling the bushes until he was satisfied.

'And what is it you were seeking?' asked Charlie Taverner, with a scowl to indicate how he felt about his captain's actions. The addition of a 'sir' was late in coming.

Pearce just grinned, then went to relieve the man carting the turpentine. Using a knife, he levered out the bung before walking across the hillside spilling out the contents. He then called for a lantern, tipping the flaming tallow from within on to the turps, the flames erupting with immediate effect.

'Best be on our way lads. I have no notion this spot will be comfortable afore long.'

And he was right. By the time they made it back to the cutter, the whole hillside was ablaze, the tinder dry gorse not only burning fiercely but also sending up a wall of smoke to sweep ahead of the fire driven by the wind. In time this began to billow over the crest where the Spaniards had their cannon and, very likely further back, shaded by trees, their powder magazine.

'I suggest breathing will become a mite hard up there, and who would want to be beside powder barrels when there's an inferno on the way?'

There were subsequent loud booms, as stores of powder went up. They would have been kept well away from the guns and probably

47

under trees which showed clear proof that Pearce had the right of it. Not that time was spent pondering on such matters; the boats were re-employed to help get both *Lively* and the *Santa Leocadia* through the channel. With the first sign the weather was truly moderating, preparations for getting to sea could be completed, though it was still wise to wait until the weather was, if not calm, far from the fury of the previous days.

'Gibraltar, Mr Pearce, I think. Given the extra damage to the *Santa Leocadia*, I now hesitate to risk her at sea for any length of time. Nor will I shift the cargo, given we are not the only ones who will benefit from a more benign sea, so who knows what we will face. I suggest we close with Lisbon in case of another storm but give Cadiz a very wide berth, do you concur?'

'I will be in your wake, sir.'

Chapter Five

It was most unusual for Edward Druce to notify his partner he'd be out of the office for close to the whole day, without confiding a reason for his extended absence. The thief-taker Walter Hodgson had been most insistent on the time he reckoned necessary, as well as the need for absolute discretion from the prize agent, regarding both the meeting and what was to be discussed.

The note Druce had received left him in gnawing doubt about what kind of conversation or revelation would require so much time. This did nothing to ease the anxiety which had, over the course of the last three years, become so pervasive it was the stuff of worrying possibilities as well as recurring nightmares.

Hodgson saw it as a possible endgame to an affair which had seen murder done, this causing an innocent man to nearly hang for a crime he did not commit. It had persuaded him to work against Druce, who had originally employed him and rewarded him handsomely over two years. The task he had been given, an odd one, was not to find a fellow called Cornelius Gherson.

At the very outset, even the description given to him was false, no doubt as an insurance against actual discovery. Gherson was not dark-haired, black-eyed, unbecoming and unprincipled. He was a near white blond with an absurdly handsome face, though his manner, on finally meeting, confirmed the last part of the portrayal. Hodgson had rarely met a fellow so lacking in either scruple or decency; he was a liar, a thief and a heartless and sequential seducer, yet he had worked to save him from the gallows.

Given the level of dishonesty from Druce, and this was not the sole example, he'd batted to and fro the notion of completely severing contact. Against such a notion was the idea of giving the whole affair one last shot. It had the aim of establishing a truth, one worthy of further pursuit, as well as a chance to see justice done. If a tissue of lies lay at the base of all his dealings with the man he was about to meet, this could only come about when everything had been revealed.

There was self-interest added to curiosity: to put the true culprit in the dock would bring recognition and could ensure prosperity but another reason had nothing to do with affluence. He had no idea if he'd become implicated in things which might come back to put him at risk, even to the point of his own life. This was not a comforting notion when one murder had definitely been committed and a second previously attempted.

He took a private upstairs room at the White Swan in Clerkenwell, his habitual haunt, so the two could talk without the need for discretion. No one would enter without knocking first, and this would only be a servant fetching refreshments. Hodgson paid out more than he normally would on wine, to match the high quality he had tasted in Druce's office. As well, he purchased a bottle of contraband French brandy on the grounds it might be necessary to stiffen a fellow he considered a weakling.

When Druce was shown up, it was immediately noted he was dressed as a normal man of business. That said, the way he was holding his cane had about it the idea it could double as a weapon, which was mightily amusing for someone who would surely shirk from anything in the physical line. The expression on his face was one to imply Hodgson had over-tested his indulgence.

'I see you took seriously my advice not to seek to disguise yourself.'

'This is damned inconvenient enough,' Druce growled, 'without me having to playact. I'm a busy man and have no time for such nonsense.'

'Rest assured, it's far from trivial.'

'I'd be obliged if you would state the nature of your note, the tone of which I found lacking in even a modicum of respect. Am I required to remind you, who is the employer in this association, as against who is the employee?'

The manner adopted told his host that Druce had come prepared to be firm, to play the superior and even to browbeat. When it came to playacting, this was as convincing as his previous absurd attempts at masquerade. On the previous meeting in this very tavern, he had donned a curious get up in the hope of appearing to fit in. Amusingly, it was one to attract the attention of the whole tap room instead of deflecting it. His manner now had to be bluff, pure and simple, which he could quickly puncture.

'You paid the bills sure enough, Mr Druce,' was imparted in an emollient tone, as a glass of the wine was poured and proffered. 'Or, would it be more accurate to say, you processed them on behalf of your brother-in-law, Alderman Denby Carruthers.'

The wine was waved away and bluster maintained, even if Druce must wonder how he knew.

'The manner in which I transact my business and for whom is beyond any requirement I owe to you.'

'It doesn't concern you that I know it was his money I was receiving and not your own?'

'Why should it?'

'Because I could be the only one to save you from the gallows.'

'What gibberish is this?'

The response was entirely undermined by the way, at the mention of a gibbet, the blood drained from the man's face. The wine glass was pushed forward once more and this time taken; it being evident that the hand doing the clutching was far from steady.

'Sit down Mr Druce and put your high horse back in the stable. We have a great deal to discuss and it will take time. I have ordered us some of the fine pies they serve here, which may help to steady you.'

It required a very gentle hand on the elbow to move a stunned Druce to the table, where, having removed his cane, he was manoeuvred into a seat.

'You surely must know the penalty for being an accessory to a capital crime,' Hodgson continued, without emphasis, as he sat down opposite. 'It is the same as for the actual commission. If the perpetrator of a murder gets the rope, so does anyone who aided and abetted him.'

'I have no idea what you're driving at.'

'Best we go back in time and see if your memory recovers. A young and vain scoundrel seduces a married woman in need of affection, only to fall foul of a much older husband who cannot live with the knowledge and the possible disgrace of cuckoldry.'

'Disgrace?' was defensive in tone.

'I admit to a certain degree of supposition, but I put this forward. Gherson seduced your brother-in-law's wife and he wanted satisfaction. You had little knowledge of his clerk, beyond his name, before you were innocent as a party in the attempt to murder him.'

Hodgson sat back and fixed a stiff-faced Druce with a slightly amused stare, in part to let him think, but more importantly to allow him to recall the way events had played out. The first approach by his brother-in-law had been to ask him to find the means to ostensibly give the said Gherson a sound beating. He would be unaware and would remain so of the real intention, which was to toss him into the raging Thames and certain death.

Yet, like the proverbial bad penny, Gherson had not only survived but turned up as clerk to Captain Ralph Barclay, an important naval client who had made a great deal of money in prize taking. He required the services of Ommaney and Druce to both secure his just rewards and to grow his fund, and the responsibility of keeping track of their efforts fell to Gherson. Druce, recognising the name as that of his brother-in-law's thieving clerk, saw an opportunity for extra profit plus a willing accomplice eager to line his own pocket.

How tangled had the skein become. A man that Denby Carruthers thought dead not only resurfaces but has become a means of nefarious gain. But the said brother-in-law, on discovering him still alive, a mystery as to how, since Druce would not have told him, is determined to find him and finish what he had begun. He was also willing to pay whatever it cost. So, he goes to the same fellow who provided hard bargains for the supposed beating and asks for help a second time.

'Had I known then what I know now, when you hired me not to find him, I doubt I would have taken the commission.'

'I have no proof you are better informed.'

'Be assured I am. You forget, I questioned Gherson in Newgate while he was awaiting trial. He told me the details of your underhand dealings as well as his being thrown off London Bridge and by whom.'

Comfortable with deception, Hodgson felt no compunction in attributing to Gherson the information, much of which had come from another source. He related how the louse had been dragged from the swirling waters around the bridge pillars by strong hands into a passing cutter, which saved his life. The men manning the boat were crew to the said Captain Barclay, on the way back to Sheerness, having pressed men for his frigate from a certain upriver tavern. It was his widow who had told Hodgson of a dripping Gherson, hauled on board, being added to the night's catch.

'How galling it must have been when Carruthers found out his attempt at disposal had failed.' The glass was emptied quickly while he waited, hoping to be enlightened. When it was not forthcoming, he said. 'More wine?'

This was declined. 'Then I'm bound to ask what would have happened if I'd actually found Gherson?'

'I've no idea.'

'I suppose there was a time when that could be said to be true. It does not, however, hold much water now. Even if you didn't know what happened on London Bridge, you were fully aware the search was not just to find but to harm him. But you needed the fellow, once he resurfaced, to stay safe and secure your illicit gains, did you not? It's fitting, in the end, you paid a high price for the deception.'

'You betrayed me,' was an outburst and a plaintive one. 'You worked for Barclay's widow while still taking my money.'

Hodgson responded with a belly-deep chuckle. The firm of Ommaney and Druce, on details provided to Hodgson by the very same Gherson, had been required to reimburse Mrs Barclay the full amount of their depredations, added to compound interest.

'For which I might, this day, make amends.'

The knock on the door stopped Druce from saying anything. It preceded the arrival of the said beef pies, along with steaming vegetables and two tankards of porter. Hodgson remarked, in a jocular tone, even good-quality wine was thin brew when faced with such hearty provender. As soon as the door closed behind the servers, he went back to the subject.

'The double game you were playing forced my hand, when what you were about became obvious. It left me no choice but to act against you and for Mrs Barclay because, in order to hide your frauds, you would have let Gherson hang for the foul and bloody murder of Catherine Carruthers.'

It was telling there was no attempt at denial, more anger at the outcome. 'I doubt you can guess at the cost of what you did.'

'I think I can, but the money you owed her to repay your depredations on her husband's account was not the concern. I acted to save an innocent man, one I actually despise, when you too knew, in your heart, he was not the culprit.'

'You cannot know that as a fact.'

'And the pair of villains you sent me in search of?' No reply was forthcoming, Druce was still processing what had gone before, as Hodgson insisted. 'Eat, sir.'

A fork was picked up and stabbed at the meat pie, but no food made it to the mouth before it was dropped, this as the thief-taker reflected on the next task with which he'd been charged. His investigations into the murder of Catherine Carruthers had turned up a pair of suspects, and so he'd employed a limner to execute hand-drawn likenesses. Druce, no doubt playing a double game when shown the drawings, had encouraged him to find and identify them.

But matters moved on when an unknown client of Druce claimed to have a ship he owned stolen from him. It had been purloined by a certain lieutenant in command of a brig, a fellow who had the gall to claim it and its cargo as a prize.

In order to prove ownership, he needed the papers of purchase, but these were in the hands of some erstwhile partner named Tolland, who was known to reside on the North Kent coast in a hamlet called Beltinge. Hodgson had been engaged to fetch them; on the face of it, this was a simple task, one in which he could extend his search for the unknown pair suspected of murdering Catherine Carruthers.

It proved anything but that. At the mere mention of the name Tolland, Hodgson, highly experienced in the pursuit of villainy, had sensed real danger. No one was willing to admit the existence of anyone so-called, this added to almost open aggression. Then, later in the day, the very drawings, executed as means to identify the suspected murderers, had been purloined from his satchel. The connection, given even the limited knowledge Hodgson already possessed, was obvious.

Druce listened with a graven countenance as Hodgson outlined the events of the curtailed stay in Beltinge, which had obliged him to get out of the village with haste, able to draw certain possible conclusions on the way. Not least that such a spot, on the coast of the River Thames with a beach at the base of high cliffs, provided an excellent location for smuggling.

'You will recall the faces of those two villainous types of whom I gave you a likeness?' Receiving no reply, he added. 'The ones presently in your desk drawer, men you seemed eager I should find.'

Hodgson wondered what was going on behind Druce's blank eyes sure there had been yet another devious purpose.

'I suspect one of them to be called Tolland, maybe both.' The name was repeated in a whisper in order to cover the shock. 'None other than the co-owner of the ship shared with the client you refused to name, which has to be your brother-in-law.'

'I think I'd best leave.'

He was halfway out of his chair before Hodgson's words stopped him. 'To rewrite your will, no doubt, which will be required by a man about to atone with his life for his sins. Walk out now and you may as well hang yourself for, if not, the state will do it for you. I reckon to have put a name to a face, one of the two men who were in a certain Covent Garden bagnio on the night Mrs Carruthers was murdered.'

There was a wait to see if any comment would be forthcoming, and with none, Hodgson continued.

'This was attested to by several people, including the owner, merely on the drawings being shown. One fellow turns out to be in a partnership with your brother-in-law, a man who had already tried to drown Gherson in the Thames.' Hodgson paused for a few seconds before adding. 'But I'm not telling you anything you don't already suspect or know, am I?'

'Tolland,' was spoken so softly it was hard to hear.

'Did you tell Carruthers where Gherson could be found?'

He didn't want to answer, but with Hodgson silent until he did there was no choice. 'I merely said he would be found drinking and whoring in a certain part of Covent Garden.'

'I suspect Carruthers told his wife, or made sure she knew, which is why she went there to find the man she loved. The poor woman was much deceived; Gherson did not care a jot for her. Her husband knew she would seek him out so, having located him through you, our two villains were sent to do their worst. I wonder if Carruthers had any idea what their worst meant.'

'I cannot believe he did.'

'There's really not much point in saying more, is there? And your pie is getting cold.'

It was embarrassing the way he began to weep, but Hodgson had seen much of this before – the felon realising his crimes were about to bring retribution and indulging in unmerited self-pity. So, he let the tears flow and concentrated on his own meal, until he judged it was time to speak again.

'I see the task now as ensuring those who killed or conspired in the murder of Mrs Carruthers are brought to justice, while those who were inveigled into criminality by error or omission do not join them on the gallows. You may cease your crying, Mr Druce, for that means you.' A pitiful nod, 'You're a dupe sir, and something of a weak fool. But you are no killer.'

'Most assuredly I'm not.'

'Except you must have guessed what Gherson's fate would be when you sent Carruthers after him.'

'I had no choice. And how was I to know of the devilish scheme Denby had hatched to see to them both?'

'You had, but the coward in you allowed you not to exercise it.'

'If you knew what the consequences would have been . . .'

'So, a life has to be sacrificed to save your comfort? I hope you do not wish this to be seen as anything other than despicable.'

'What was I to do? What am I to do?'

Hodgson had to hide his satisfaction. Druce was now exactly where he wanted him to be.

'You must work with me to place guilt where it belongs. The only way to prove it, as well as save your own hide, is to bring down your brother-in-law, which presents one great difficulty. If he suspects for a moment you're conspiring against him, how do you think he'll react?' The man gulped; he knew very well. 'But you have no choice but to do so if you wish to save your neck, a very uncomfortable place to be.'

'Surely,' came with a look of desperation, 'there has to be another way. What will be served by opening up matters about which no one any longer cares? You speak of saving my comfort. What of your own and what if this could be guaranteed?'

'You see the solution as buying my silence.' Druce was thrown by this. 'It takes no great intellect to reach such a conclusion, sir. But it also takes no great genius to conclude, for you, it will not serve.'

'How so?'

'You lack the means to buy me off, though I must point out, there is no sum of money which would have me accept. As for your proposing it, how long will it be before Carruthers, whom you would have to ask for the funds, sees you as the link to his criminal involvement?'

Hodgson left out one obvious fact. To be bought off would put him in the same position as Druce, one, unknowingly he might be in already.

'And how does a man of his stamp deal with such problems? He might have you done away with, just to ensure his own survival. If Gherson can be tossed into the Thames, in the expectation he's bound to drown, so can anyone.'

There was a need to see if Druce would get the point of the last words spoken, which brought Hodgson to the nub of the reasons he engineered this meeting, with the vital question.

'Does he know of my role in getting Gherson freed?'

'I doubt it,' came the reply, after careful consideration. 'He asked me to hire you to find Tolland, which would hardly be the case if he did.'

'There's another threat. I am near certain that the pair in those sketches you keep in your desk have already committed one murder and, by the look of them, it will not be the only one. They rely too much on the conspiracy surrounding Mrs Carruthers' murder not being investigated. But as soon as it is, and it must be, what then?'

'This Tolland?'

'Is resident in Beltinge, as you informed me.'

'And?'

'I would say he's a man unsafe to approach.'

'Do I take from that you didn't meet him?'

'Certain actions by others led me to believe it would be unwelcome. But there's no doubt he lives there. Tell me, Mr Druce, is there anything you find peculiar about the arrangements for buying this vessel Carruthers is so concerned about?'

Again, it was plain, he didn't want to answer.

'Because if there is, it would be to your advantage to tell me, which applies to everything in which he engaged you. I would not want there to be any gaps in my knowledge. I have to be sure I'm acting on certainties.'

It took a while, but Hodgson's look left him little room to equivocate. When he did speak, it was of the history of the whole affair, starting from the very day he'd supplied Denby Carruthers with the men tasked to deliver Gherson a beating, a couple of hard bargains from the Impress Service. Then there was the task of deceiving him and the putative search, followed by the absurdity of Carruthers's excuses regarding the stolen vessel.

'It all began with an honest mistake, Hodgson,' he insisted, seeking to exculpate himself. 'I naturally took Denby's side when he asked for my help, and why would I not. He's brother to my wife and was in misery, thanks to Gherson. The swine not only cuck-olded him under his own roof, he stole money to dress himself and parade around in finery, which did not fit his status.'

'I think you'll find Mrs Carruthers was so besotted that she gave him the money, no doubt another grievance Carruthers could not abide.'

'I still plead innocence of any foul intent on my part, but once drawn in…'

The claim, to Hodgson was feeble, but such was by the by, given the way the confrontation had worked out. He had a way to seal off any risk to himself, which sadly, could only be achieved by saving Druce, a man he now knew, without doubt, was unworthy of the effort.

'Your brother-in-law sees himself as untouchable, above the law in fact.'

'I doubt you know the extent of his reach. Being a member of the Council of Aldermen affords him contacts he can use to insulate himself from harm. And he is rich beyond the dreams of avarice.'

'Forgive me if I doubt the latter. I've never met a wealthy man who didn't hanker after more money.'

'You have not met him, Hodgson, so you have not been, as I have for years, on the receiving end of his arrogance.'

'It is necessary to turn such arrogance against him, so he must be induced to make the kind of mistake against which there is no defence. You must draw him into it and, perhaps, this co-owned ship can be the cause. It will link him to the actual perpetrators of the murder and from that there's no escape. If it is to work, you must play an active role.'

What little blood remained drained from his face, which was soon hidden as the tankard of ale was raised and tipped high.

'Think on this,' Hodgson drove home. 'You'll only save yourself by ditching him. He in the clutches of the law, and put there with your assistance, will ensure your survival.'

'What if he tells the law otherwise and claims me as an accomplice?'

'I take it there's nothing in writing to incriminate you?'

A shake of the head came only after the point was well thought-out. 'It was a private arrangement, of which no one knew the details, especially not my partner, even if he shared in the profits which accrued from Gherson's actions.'

'Your clerk knew who was paying my bill.'

Enlightenment dawned, which was odd; his clerk being the only other person Hodgson had dealt with. It could only be hoped the man would not pay a price for the disclosure of the true paymaster.

'Given the nature of this partnership in the ownership of a vessel, what makes you think they're engaged in honest endeavour?'

'This I had not considered.'

'So, tell me about this ship, everything.'

'I know only what was vouchsafed to me.'

'There may be something in this you do not realise as important.'

So Druce reprised the conversation he'd had. How his brother-in-law had gone to Greenwich and why, to look at the possibility of purchasing a second vessel only to end up sure the one for sale was already his. He then claimed an inability to prove it, given he didn't have any of the purchase papers, saying they were in the possession of this Jaleel Tolland.

'Which, by the way, I chose not to believe.'

Druce said this with a hint he had challenged Carruthers openly, which Hodgson supposed unlikely. The truth was likely that Carruthers had paid for the vessel but it was registered in Tolland's name. He seemed to be recovering some of his confidence as he related Denby's meeting, as well as the questioning of a peg-leg naval officer, who revealed the vessel had been had up by the navy, not the excise.

'One very odd fact did emerge. The officer reputed to have taken her was called John Pearce, which I suspect is a name not unknown to you.'

This did throw Hodgson. 'Are you sure it was the name used.'

'Denby was very sure of it. Apparently, the service has a low opinion of him, which will not be enhanced if what Denby believes is proven. But Pearce stands to profit greatly if the truth is not established.'

'Carruthers's truth.'

'I have little doubt it is the vessel he bought. If he were not so certain, why would he engage you to go and fetch the proof? Perhaps the answer lies with this Pearce fellow.'

Hodgson considered this for a moment before saying, 'I may have the means to find him.'

CHAPTER SIX

Admiral Adam Duncan was a strong believer in close blockade. But he had to acknowledge that a short and occasional spell in harbour, away from the unpredictable North Sea, for the sake of both his ships and their crews, was wise. So, leaving a squadron of frigates behind to mask the approaches to Amsterdam, he had withdrawn his line of battle ships from the Dutch coast, taking shelter from an anticipated northerly gale in the port of Harwich.

If it lacked a dockyard, the twin river estuary was still home to a shipbuilding facility, so could thus provide both a safe anchorage as well as replacement masts and cordage. These were necessary to ensure his vessels were ready for battle, one Duncan knew must be imminent. Harwich also had the advantage of closer proximity to the waters in which this fight would be joined, which did not apply to the main fleet anchorage in the River Thames.

Situated where silt from the River Medway flowed into the Thames, to form an anchorage on the Nore sandbank, it was too far off if the fleet of the so-called newly named Batavian Republic ventured out beyond the Island of Texel. They needed to be challenged and defeated before they could get out to the open Atlantic and sail on to where they could join with the French in Brest, providing a threat to the whole containment strategy of the Admiralty.

As usual, when any ship of war anchored, and it was naturally multiplied in numbers with a fleet, traders plus a large number of entertainers and whores in small boats set out from the shore. Their stated aim was to bring comfort and pleasure to the crews. The real intent was to relieve the crews of as much coin as could be extracted, while also pilfering anything which could be purloined by nimble fingers.

Jaleel Tolland, aboard HMS *Director*, was not alone in looking forward to such arrivals, though his motives were less to do with pleasure than the possibility of escape. His situation since the day John Pearce captured his ship had been bad, but it had gone downhill since then. His attempts to create mayhem aboard HMS *Bedford*, into which Pearce had decanted both him and his men, had been far from good: now it was ten times worse. Not only had he been separated from his brother Franklin and the majority of his crew of smugglers, he'd been shifted to a much worse berth aboard HMS *Director*. Tolland was now under the command of a captain named William Bligh, whose reputation for harsh discipline went before him.

None other than 'Breadfruit' Bligh of the infamous *Bounty* mutiny, he was a flogger of note, as well as a man with a nose for even a hint of dissent, added to the dread of a second rebellion. Thus, the chance to carry out the kind of games he'd planned to play aboard HMS *Bedford*, which would oblige his then-captain, Sir Thomas Byard, to seek repairs in a home port had been cut short. This was a pity, since it had included the killing of a bosun's mate to establish an atmosphere of dread throughout the crew, an action now wasted.

The only thing in Bligh's favour was his attitude to anchorage pleasures, given that some of his fellow captains would not allow a soul aboard their ship who was not navy. Bligh was one who saw the benefits of release, no doubt to compensate for the excessively tight way he oversaw his command at sea.

Of all the home ports in which to drop anchor, this was not the one Tolland would have favoured by choice. It lay well to the north of the River Thames, where he knew a whole host of people, men who would aid him, including fellow smugglers all along the tideway. Still, he had encountered people who ran contraband in and out of this estuary, fellow cargo runners who picked up their illicit goods, as did he, from the Flanders port of Gravelines.

As a group they were not overtly friendly or easily approachable, being the kind to hold themselves and their dealings close, careful even of their names being known. Nor were they committed visitors to the more raucous ale houses and whorehouses, earning a reputation as a stand-offish lot. Yet enough interactions had taken place for him to recognise them by sight and hopefully they him, without it being a cause for caution. The men from the south of the River Thames were not in competition with coastal Essex smugglers and never would be.

He had an idea of the area over which they would operate from long past, when he'd sailed on the coal barges coming to southern towns from the north. Harwich was a place he'd many times anchored to drop off a cargo or avoid foul weather. In harbour taverns, locals talked: the useless and indigenous, probably keen to pretend to knowledge that they could not truly possess.

Desirous to extract a pot of ale, they would hint at nefarious goings on, up and down the long beach running south from the town. It was a strand with flat marshland behind, one Tolland has sailed past and observed many times. This formed, to an older smuggling mind, a landscape perfect for the running of untaxed goods. It was a spot where it would be near impossible for the revenue men to get close without being spotted, well before they could take either the crew or cargo.

Other things he could deduce, like there had to be a place inland where they took the goods to store them before they were sold. He and his gang required the same, albeit back from the tops of the local cliffs, a feature which provided the same security as a long strand of beach. It was to such he must seek to make his way, the hope being he would be recognised as a face from Gravelines, one who presented no threat and could thus be offered assistance.

So, when the array of boats set out from the shore, Tolland, who'd been fruitlessly examining the deck of HMS *Adamant* for a sign of his brother Franklin, set a keen eye on a target which would suit his purpose. He aimed to get off the ship and into the town, which could only be done by a combination of luck, determination and ruthlessness.

It also had to be achieved in the face of people who knew every trick in the book, the ship's officers and marines. The latter were armed and instructed to use whatever force was necessary to prevent desertion. Even getting hold of a marlin spike, to use as a weapon, now tucked in his waistband, had been hard. The top was hidden by a short jacket into which he'd stuffed the very basic necessities, his razor, a bit of hard tack and a set of flints.

There was another thing to observe. Bligh was in his barge and on his way to the flagship, no doubt for one of Admiral Duncan's dinners, from which, him being a serious toper, he was likely to return in a state of inebriation. In the few weeks Tolland had been aboard, it had been obvious that Bligh was paying him special attention, no doubt alerted by his previous captain in *Bedford*. With Bligh absent, he felt his situation was marginally improved.

Even better was the departure of the warrants, excepting the bosun, as well as the ship's surgeon. With the master, carpenter and the sawbones gone, there were areas of the tween decks which would not be occupied by those who normally berthed there. Not that he'd be the only one to spot such a fact, but it could allow space to achieve his object and, once ashore, he backed himself to get clear of any pursuit.

Jaleel Tolland marked himself as a man who could avoid the crimps and traps set up to catch deserters and, if he failed to do so, was capable of the brutality required to deal with them. Once out of the port, he would not be safe, since being on a road, even for a short time, was dangerous for a running sailor. Those hoping to profit from turning him in were a lot less obvious than they would be in a port city: a seaman was the very opposite for, by their gait in a country setting, they stuck out a mile.

If he could find shelter with the Harwich smugglers, he would then try to contact Denby Carruthers and alert him to what had happened. He was sure whatever help was needed for both himself and his brother would be forthcoming, given they were engaged in a joint enterprise.

Carruthers might put up the money, but it was of no account when he could not sail a ship or recruit the kind of men needed to run contraband. Nor did he wonder why a man, already rich and powerful, was prepared to take such risks, even if the rewards for success were substantial. The financier was a gambler by nature, while his past actions had proved he was just as ruthless as any man who lived outside the law.

All tastes were catered for in those allowed aboard, whores of every stripe from overblown doxies to mere slips, girls who could hint at the possibility of virginity. There were fiddlers, music box players and jugglers, plus traders selling every kind of gimcrack trinket an inebriated sailor might be tempted to buy. And drunk they would be, either through hoarded grog or the illicit drink brought aboard by the traders, in spite of strict orders banning it. For all their supposed probity, marines were as partial to a slipped coin as any man, while those visiting were experts at both bribery and concealment.

There was no immediate need to join in the jollity, with a sense of pleasure and laxity quickly established by those who knew how to create the required atmosphere. The music was quick in coming, and carnality soon followed, the cheap-jacks moving swiftly to pass over their worthless objects, as souvenirs of the day, for ten times their true value. Tolland hung off for two bells of the four Bligh had allotted to this watch. He sought to produce the amused smile of the observer, which was hard given his usual crabbed manner, added to a countenance not noted for much other than habitual ferocity.

There was more than one of the type he was seeking – painted "ladies" so over-decorated with rouge and lip paint barely covering a trace of beard, which marked them out as cross-dressing males. They would perform as required, though often they were welcome just for their arch wit, screaming false tantrums and outrageous behaviour guaranteed to produce hilarity.

All being in full swing and time moving on, Tolland indicated to one such fellow, a substantial brute, that he wished for more than high-pitched amusement, his aim being fleshly pleasure. He nodded towards the companionway, which would take them down a deck to an area with a modicum of privacy, difficult to find on a ship with a crew of over five hundred men, added to officers both petty and commissioned, authority on the wander, to catch out anything forbidden, drink especially.

His destination, into which he was followed, was the screened off hovel occupied by the surgeon's loblolly boys, assistants who helped him administer various treatments, some of which required physical restraint. His fancy man slid in behind him, the grin on his stubbled face exaggerated by his painted lips and the provocative swing of his clutch bag. The look was soon removed by a right hook which, by the sound of it, broke his jaw.

It certainly felled the creature, his descent cushioned by Tolland's arms; hands were soon busy on his garments, hooks and buttons undone, taking off with care an elaborate pink gown with fluffy sleeves and many attached ribbons. Chosen for his size, which being far from meagre, the dress was voluminous enough to fit over Tolland's ducks, checked shirt and jacket. The carried bag revealed what could only be hoped for – the means to repair face paint and a small looking glass with which to apply it.

There was little care in what followed for Tolland had no time for perfection. Bligh might be lax in the article of ship visiting by the denizens of Harwich, but it was limited to one watch only. Eight bells would be the point when everyone not on the muster would be hustled back into their boats, many searched to ensure they were not departing with any small possessions belonging to the ship or the crew.

So, the application of rouge and coloured lip gloss was swift and haphazard, which in some ways provided verisimilitude. Such creatures as the comatose fellow, still out on the deck, were often roughly treated, part of their attraction to those so inclined being the ability to accept a degree of violence. Once he had pulled on the cheap brassy wig, Tolland passed back through the screen and, moving with highly exaggerated swaying hips, crossed the deck to take cover behind the companionway. There he came near to disturbing a pair heartily rutting in the gloom.

They were too occupied to care for him or his proximity, no doubt as aware time was not on their side. The seventh bells of the watch had gone while Tolland was seeking to disguise himself and transfer his few possessions to the bag. It was a guess as to when it was safe to move, with no surety when he did so that he could get to the entry port at the same time as it would become crowded. He also risked being spotted for who he was by the marines placed by the open gunports.

Given it always took time to clear the ship, he emerged on to a main deck full of the sound of bellowing from the unluckiest of the officers, those who would have to wait for their own run ashore and the concomitant pleasures. They had the task of getting this rabble off HMS *Director* in Bligh's allotted time.

Tolland joined the jostle, producing one or two high-pitched, throat-straining screams of protest for being hard pressed. In fact, he was the one doing the pushing and shoving, seeking to get to the crowded entry port. There was no way the order in which all had come board could be replicated on departure, for it was a melee. So, it was the first boat with space where, once seated, he bowed over and gagged, as if to imply he was a sufferer from sea sickness.

A fierce glare, when he occasionally looked up was in place to deter curiosity which, unbeknown the wearer, was made doubly effective by his slapdash face paints. If any aboard, a dozen in number, guessed at what he was about, they were not going to let on unless certain and that could never be. Good fortune had placed him in a craft with no one who had come out to the 74-gunner earlier with his victim, but there was still one threat to overcome. A section of marines from the flagship had been placed on the jetty, a double insurance against desertion.

Again, with several hired boats disgorging their loads, the jetty was crowded, forcing the arrivals to shuffle towards the line of marines. As he came close to the lobsters, Tolland surged forward with real force, which sent several of those coming ashore tumbling into the water. This produced the confusion that he needed to slip through a cordon, now part occupied in the measures needed to save folk from drowning. A stare from one marine was deflected by the blowing of a kiss, added to a come-hither look, responded to with a grimace of distaste.

The temptation to move fast had to be suppressed. Tolland actually turned to watch those still struggling in the water, as well as one dripping specimen already fetched ashore, all being roundly cursed by a marine lieutenant as useless clods. Only when he felt he'd stood long enough did he move off, aware, for all his tough nature, his heart was beating fast.

One danger had been overcome, but it was not yet safe. The navy paid well for returned deserters, so there were individuals hanging about on the quayside, trying to look disinterested when they were involved in close scrutiny of those come ashore. Performance was the only way to pass them, the swaying gait employed aboard the ship covering for the habitual one of a man who, by second nature, compensated for the movement of a heaving deck.

Like every seaport, the Harwich foreshore buildings, both warehouses and dwellings, were dissected by narrow alleys. Tolland disappeared into one of these, only to immediately hear behind him the sound of echoing footsteps. This had him cast a quick eye over his shoulder to assess the fellow who had followed him. He saw a burly cove in a tricorne hat, tipped back on his head, who had a swinging Billy club in one hand and a smirk on his face, which widened as his prey turned to face him, indicating the crimp was sure he had spotted easy profit.

A nod and a glance, aimed over Tolland's shoulder, was enough to indicate another fellow had shot up a similar alley to get behind him, so there was no time for subterfuge or an attempt to persuade this pair that they were mistaken. If they'd met violent hard bargains in their time, they had never come across the likes of Jaleel Tolland who tore open the dress he was wearing hauled the marlin spike out of his ducks, before rushing to take on the man who'd followed.

The first task was to slow the crimp, aided by his opponent stopping and taking up a defensive posture, sure that he and his confrere, now moving to join him, could do what was necessary. The speed with which Tolland closed induced surprise, as did the marlin spike which, being longer than a Billy club, got in the first blow. Tolland landed a straight jab into the midriff, which winded him and doubled the man over.

He hauled his head up and hit him hard then, not to knock him out but to turn him sideways enough to force him round. This was so he could get behind his back, scraping his own shoulders on the brick wall; so tight was the space. Simultaneously his teeth bit hard into the man's cheek to then wrench out a mouthful of bloody flesh.

The scream was ignored as an arm went round the neck, the marlin spike dropped so Tolland could use his other hand on the back of the head, a combination which, once applied with full twisting force, broke the fellow's neck. Holding a suddenly limp body, he glared as the second crimp, who with the body in the way could not get at this now obvious deserter, even if he too had a club.

'Not the first shit of a creature I has done in an' it won't be the last. So, if you're keen to meet your maker, stay where you are or come on. If not, best be on your toes, mate, 'cause I will need to kill you an' all, which I will do, even if I end up hanging at the yardarm. Now back off.'

As he let go of the body , Tolland bent with it to retrieve his marlin spike and then stepped over the crumpled corpse. The wig had gone in the struggle, and the crimp was faced with just the painted face. He began to back down the alley, followed slowly by the man he had hoped to take up, an individual snarling and spitting out the words of what fate awaited him, which was enough to have him turn and run.

The dress was ripped off then used to wipe off the rouge and face paint, made easier because Tolland was sweating. It took strength and scrabbling to get the coat off his lifeless victim and he was moving before he tried to put it on, the hand clutching it holding the tricorne hat as well as the marlin spike. The other end of the alley opened out into a wider, busier and cobbled street, which caused him to delay until he had donned the stolen clothing.

Then, hat pulled low, he crossed into another alley. Moving fast, he espied a church at the far end, across what looked like a main thoroughfare, and he shot across to get into the cool and silent interior. Kneeling at a pew, hands held up as if praying, he tried to calm his breathing. He needed to move on and quickly, without attracting attention, assuming the crimp who'd ran off had gone for help.

Exiting through a side door a couple of minutes later, still heading away from the shore, Tolland found himself in a grassy graveyard full of headstones and sarcophagi, the latter used to hide behind and surreptitiously watch out for pursuit. With no one obviously around, he took time to properly arrange both the coat and hat, the weapon being slid up his sleeve. Then with the air of a man with a purpose, he strode to the rear of the cemetery and on to an unmade road across which and still under construction lay a row of new houses.

A glance at the sun, beginning to sink in the southwest, was enough to indicate the direction is which he should head. This too was done head up, gaze firm and steps lengthened to disguise his nautical gait. As the evidence of habitation began to fade, he turned with his back to the golden orb. Its position and the increased cawing of gulls provided a sure indication that it would take him to the sought-for beach. He could be confident for the immediate moment he was clear of any more crimps and a navy which would barely register his escape.

Tolland was mistaken, his problem being he was too well known. Even if he'd only been aboard HMS *Director* for a matter of weeks, being such a hard-nosed and unpleasant bastard, he was notorious to all. So, when his moaning victim was discovered, and with the ship now cleared of the whores and hucksters even with a crew so large, it was not long before the officers established who was missing.

Soon there were more boats heading for the shore, given they knew how such news would be taken by their captain. These were manned by the 'reliables,' the kind of long-serving tars any captain trusted. When they sent men ashore as press gangs, to bolster the number of their crew, these were fellows who would relish the task and could be trusted themselves to return. The orders were simple: find that bastard Tolland and fetch him back aboard and, if he was a corpse, so much the better. It would save Bligh the trouble of hanging him.

CHAPTER SEVEN

John Pearce, on coming within sight of Gibraltar, hazy in the late summer sunshine, was afire to know if hostilities with Spain had already begun. The breaking dawn had found the trio of vessels sailing closer to the African shore than the Iberian, on a current to bring them in from the deep Atlantic, with John Pearce in the tops with his telescope, looking for signs of enemy activity. There was no doubt that they themselves would be sighted in a strait which, at its narrowest, was a shade over eight miles wide, while they would have already been under close examination from Tarifa.

For warships exiting the Mediterranean, the fortress of this coastal city was a thorn during wartime, given that the current required to get out to the Atlantic took them closer to the northern shore and its cannon. There was nothing to indicate activity of any kind now from either place, certainly not gunfire. The smoke of discharge, even from musketry, would possibly be visible at a distance, nor was there any sign of Spanish ship seeking to intercept them before they could anchor.

Indeed, the Rock, as it was generally known, looked as peaceful as it had on his last visit and nothing altered the impression as they changed course and the distance closed. Pearce was sure they would come under the examination of everyone in the garrison, including the Governor Sir David Rose. He would see, as had the Spaniards, that the two intact warships were cleared for action the guns run out and manned, ready to fight if need be.

Some might recognise HMS *Lively* as a previous visitor but, bringing up the rear, they would surely ponder on the name and commander of the much smaller 14-gun brig. Real interest would be reserved for the vessel they were escorting, another frigate and one showing a high degree of damage of the kind caused by sustained cannon fire. How would Gibraltar react to seeing, fluttering above the red and gold ensign of Spain, the union flag of their own nation, indicating the damaged vessel was rated an enemy prize? Was this yet legitimate? Had Spain declared war?

Deep interest would also be prevalent in the port of Algeciras, opposite the Rock on the eastern shore of the deep bight of Gibraltar Bay. There, if no declaration had been made, and all was still normal, and it seemed to be thus, the Spaniards would be just as curious. There was no doubt they would also be furious at what they would see as a deliberate insult to their nation and sovereign. Back on the quarterdeck, Pearce kept his telescope trained on the Spanish port, looking for the faintest sign of any aggressive intent. Curiously, given the time which had elapsed since taking the *Santa Leocadia*, the place seemed near to being asleep.

The usual ceremonies ensued as they closed the anchorage, with the warships saluting the governor's flag and the fortress responding to salute the approaching ships in great blasts of sound and smoke, to at least one floating observer – a total waste of powder. Following the act of anchoring inside the south mole, the signal went up calling for Lord Langholm to repair ashore and report. He asked, through a speaking trumpet, in what looked like a singular courtesy, for John Pearce to take one of his boats and join him.

On landing and arriving at Admiralty House, Lord Langholm was immediately closeted with Commodore Truscott, the naval C-in-C. Pearce was left in an outer chamber with little to do but to run his eye over what he could see of Gibraltar and its defences, formidable because they had to be. The island had been subjected to siege twice since being ceded to Britannia after the Treaty of Utrecht in 1713, which ended the War of the Spanish Succession.

It was a settlement that Madrid had never, and would never, accept, and they had done everything in their power to retake Gibraltar in the so-called Great Siege. This had been implemented in the year '79 and was not raised until three years had passed; the Dons were beaten off by the determination of the garrison, aided by the ships of the Royal Navy, who with supply kept both the inhabitants and the garrison from starvation as well as a lack of shot and gunpowder, which would have crippled the defender's cannon.

The town sat on a narrow strip of land to the west, set at the southern end of a sandy causeway, defended by formidable outworks. This, added to a combination of artillery and musketry, created a murderous killing zone, with no landward means by which it could be outflanked. The remainder of the Rock rose steeply to a pinnacle on the east, with the combined topography making it near impossible to capture.

Even if there were few places to try, attempts at landings by boat had been made on the scarce strands of beach. But these were backed with easily defendable and precipitous escarpments, rendering any such assault deadly, which left only bombardment and famine as the keys to success.

Such a tactic was not of much use against a defence which could not be cut off from resupply, as well as one in which shelter against shot and shell for the defending forces was plentiful due to a network of tunnels. Such ruminations were curtailed by an opening door and a soft, polite cough.

'Lieutenant Pearce, Commodore Truscott asks if you can join him now.'

As the Master and Commander of HMS *Hazard*, he was entitled to be addressed as captain; so was there a subtle insult there? Not a man to obsess about titles, Pearce was ever sensitive when it was lacking in naval folk, so he looked at the midshipman sent to fetch him to see if, in his expression, there was some clue.

The mutual stare was not held long enough to establish the truth one way or another, so he followed the youngster towards the inner sanctum at the same time as he became aware behind him, on the outside of the building, there was something of a commotion, with much shouting added to the rattle of coach wheels on the cobbles.

If there had been doubt about his standing, it evaporated as soon as he observed the glare on the face of the senior naval officer. Truscott was a man he had met briefly on his last visit and a person for whom he held little regard. There was no title at all when the commodore spoke; it was an abrupt and brittle 'Pearce,' delivered with a sour expression. As he felt his bile rise, it was overcome by the unannounced entry and a loud voice full of good cheer.

'Spotted you on your own quarterdeck, Pearce,' bellowed Sir David Rose, his florid, square, pugilist's face alight with bonhomie. 'Made me think of bad pennies.'

'It takes one to know one, Sir David.'

The head went back and the laugh was booming. 'Damn right, so I'm heartily glad to see you again.'

'I think it would be fitting, sir, to acknowledge Lord Langholm.'

This slightly acid comment from Truscott was delivered with some reservation, given he was very much junior to the governor, a Lieutenant General and Knight Commander of the Bath. It produced a harrumph from Sir David, who clearly did not welcome being checked, he having hurried to the naval headquarters to find out what was afoot.

'Forgive me Langholm, but I've not seen this brigand for a while, whereas you are near to a regular visitor these last six months.'

'An interesting appellation to attach to Mr Pearce, sir,' was the response. The curious look from the governor invited him to expand on the comment. 'I would say what he has been about recently might sail very close to banditry, matters on which I'm sure he is keen to enlighten you.'

'There is much to require explanation, not least the tale of the damaged Spaniard you have fetched in.'

'I have Lord Langholm's report, Sir David.' Truscott accompanied this by the waving of a sheaf of papers. 'Had you not seen fit to attend upon us, I would have been coming to see you. There are things here to require consideration.'

'But I have Truscott, so I'd be obliged with some kind of immediate justification. There are folk across the bay who, even if the rumours we have are correct, will be in a hellfire bate to see one of their ships brought to our anchorage in such a manner.'

Eager to know about the said rumours, Pearce's curiosity was cut off by what Langholm said next, with an air suggesting a lack of urgency.

'Mr Pearce, you may wish to provide the verbal justification regarding the taking of the *Santa Leocadia*.'

'Verbal justification? Would it not be merely a reprise of your written report, sir?'

'I sense there might be variations.'

The reply troubled Pearce, not just for the words but for the bland look on the man's face as he delivered them. He had about his lips a faint hint of humour, which was singularly inappropriate.

'Well Pearce?' demanded Truscott, who did not make any attempt to hide his distaste at having to enquire.

An immediate problem lay in the way he had come to be here, given he felt it unwise to be fully open about the mission upon which he had been engaged. To do so would invoke the name of Henry Dundas, the Minister for War, and he would not welcome being associated with something he wished kept secret. The fact Pearce, in the company of Samuel Oliphant, had uncovered the very thing they had been sent by him to find out must remain hidden, but the result could not.

'I fully expect, Sir David, if the Spanish First Minister has not already declared war, he will do so at some time in the not-too-distant future. This would stem from a treaty Godoy recently signed at the royal palace of San Ildefonso, one which obliges Spain to ally with France against us.'

'You're sure of this?'

'Absolutely certain, sir, just as I know you suspected he might be manoeuvring in such a direction when I last called here. If it was a possibility then, it's a certainty now. Hence the captured frigate, which goes by the name of the *Santa Leocadia*. Agreement with France has been reached, but no action was to be contemplated until she docked at Vigo, her holds full of Peruvian silver. The ingots are now, thanks to the joint actions of *Lively* and *Hazard*, held by the Royal Navy.'

'How did you come by such information?' Truscott demanded.

This again was worrying; surely Langholm had explained both verbally and in writing the how and why of the capture.

'A fortuitous coincidence, sir,' sounded feeble. 'I was on my way to the Mediterranean, with a message from the government for Sir John Jervis.'

'Message?' Truscott demanded. 'The way you say the word makes it sound verbal, not an official despatch.'

'It was and it explains my sailing under an Admiralty pennant.'

'Singular,' Truscott barked, 'but not germane to your previous statement. And I find it hard to believe anything so important would be entrusted to the likes of you.'

Seeing Pearce swell up to put Truscott in his place, for he knew very well why he was not loved in the King's Navy, Sir David intervened. 'Stick to your tale.'

Several deep breaths were required before he responded. 'As an aside, we were tasked to assess matters on the border between Spain and France, so we looked in on both Hendaye and San Sebastian.'

'We?'

It was Langholm who replied. 'Mr Pearce had along a civilian, a fellow called Oliphant, who was boated ashore off Lisbon, intent on going home on one of the postal packets. Rum sort to my mind.'

If he didn't have much time for Oliphant, Pearce was not about to have him traduced. 'Without his aid, Lord Langholm, we may never have uncovered Manuel Godoy's intention to desert the coalition.'

The tone of the response was lacking in respect and deliberately so, which had Truscott snarl. 'And by what alchemy did you a lowly officer like you unearth this?'

'Not witchcraft, sir, but solid information given to us by certain parties, people who have no love for Godoy or the Spanish Crown. We made contact with certain fellows who could provide the intelligence we sought.'

'They being?' Sir David asked.

'Members of the regional Basque *Cortes*. It was they who gave us the information regarding the *Santa Leocadia* and its cargo.'

'Why would they do such a thing?' Truscott demanded, 'And, more to the point, why would you believe it to be true?'

'It is a situation in which you would have had to have been present to appreciate their reasons. My colleague Oliphant is headed back to London and took with him a request, asking for assistance from Britain to aid them in seeking independence for the Basque region. It is one we assured them would meet with a favourable response.'

Pearce paused, which he assumed his listeners thought was to allow the point made to sink in, when, in truth, it was brought on by a degree of embarrassment. Both he and Oliphant were close to certain that no help for the Basques would be forthcoming. This had made Pearce, at least, glad the exchanges and verbal commitments made to these members of the *Cortes* had taken place in a darkness barely mitigated by the light of a fire.

'In return, they provided solid proof of Spanish intentions.'

'You can't pretend to be surprised, Truscott? We know Godoy has never liked the idea of being in a coalition which included us. I doubt he would ever have agrred to it if the French hadn't guillotined their king and queen.'

This point from Sir David Rose was acceded to with a grimace from the naval officer. Rose had worried and warned Whitehall that this might come about since Godoy had signed a treaty with France to end the so-called War of the Pyrenees. It brought to a close a conflict in which the Dons, after much initial success, had been comprehensively trounced by the mass levies of the Revolution.

Pearce then related how, in the treaty which followed, the French had reneged on a commitment to the Basques leaders, which was made while the war raged – people to whom they had promised autonomy from Madrid as a payment for their support. Feeling betrayed by the French, the Basques explained their willingness to provide information in the hope of attaining the same object with British aid.

'The Basques told us Godoy was waiting for the *Santa Leocadia*, so I set out to prevent it making its promised landfall. I was fortunate enough to meet and engage on the same enterprise Lord Langholm. Its capture will now be no mystery in Madrid, but the expected betrayal will be without the silver that they hoped they would have to fund it.'

'Have you established a value?' asked Sir David.

'Neither Lord Langholm nor I feel qualified to do so, but it will be a substantial sum. Enough to finance a war, it must be.'

'It won't finance a war, Pearce,' Sir David responded, with an avuncular smile. 'What you've done may, if you have the right of it, delay things for a while, but that's all. There will be another high-value cargo already on the way I shouldn't wonder. And, if not, Godoy will send ships to secure the funds he needs. And he needs deep pockets, especially for a siege of Gibraltar, the recovery of which is so dear to the Spanish heart. As ever, I expect it to be their primary objective.'

'You mentioned rumours, sir.'

'Conflicting ones, Pearce. Activity at San Roque, the place from which they launched their previous siege in '79. Hints of the concentration of artillery and infantry, as well as some ships being prepared in Cadiz. I asked our ambassador for confirmation, but he's failed to provide it.'

'It was, we were told, a secret treaty. I doubt it's known to anyone outside a tight group around Godoy.'

'Yet you found out,' Truscott barked, the obvious implication being he was gilding it.

Sir David pounced on that. 'You know Truscott, as well as I do, how hard it is to keep a secret in any court, never mind a Spanish one.'

'I suspect,' Pearce cut in, 'the Basques have high-placed sympathisers in Madrid.'

'While it appears, we lack the same.'

Truscott changed tack in the face of the governor's opinion. 'It does not seem to occur to you Pearce, by your actions, that you have given Madrid a *causus belli*, in short an excuse to do just as Sir David fears.'

Pearce was looking at the captain of HMS *Lively* when he replied to a very bellicose Truscott. 'Surely you mean our action, sir.'

'Yours are the ones to be examined.'

Langholm was looking at the ceiling, not prepared to catch any eye, which had Pearce wondering what he had said in his written report. The suspicion could not be avoided; for whatever John Pearce put forward verbally, it would not be the same.

'I'm happy to produce my logs for inspection,' was nothing more than prevarication.

Truscott smiled for the first time, but there was no warmth in it. 'Will they record your instruction to close with the *Santa Leocadia* and request they heave to before engaging in any aggressive action?'

'Something I recall distinctly ordering you to do,' Langholm added, finally looking at Pearce. 'You were to precede any act of interdiction with the said request and, if denied, to follow it with a shot across the bows.'

Sensing some kind of a trap, and given the question could not be answered by a simple yes or no, refuge was taken in a bit of quick thinking, as well as the employment of his singular status, while his tone was far from friendly.

'Lord Langholm, you are and never have been in a position to issue any orders to me. I would remind you of my Admiralty pennant.'

'Yet you agreed to this as a precursor of any aggressive action.'

'You have this in writing?'

'Don't deny it.'

'Which means the answer is no.'

Truscott butted in again. 'You cannot gainsay it would have been the proper way to behave?'

The man was right, but there was no way Pearce was going to acknowledge such a fact. Even if he had agreed with Langholm to employ it as an opening gambit, it failed to meet the actual circumstances on the day. Faced with a vessel that could blow *Hazard* to matchwood and with Langholm too far off to provide immediate aid did not permit of such a courtesy.

Tempted to explain, he decided to keep such facts to himself. He did so on the very good grounds that he had no idea what the future would hold, especially when Langholm was clearly playing some kind of game. Luckily Sir David was keen to get to the nub of the thing.

'Whatever the rights and wrongs of what you lot are arguing about, I am minded to concentrate on the contents of this Spanish frigate, plus the vessel itself, as the first order of business. Then, if what you say is true, I need to consider putting the garrison on a full war footing.' He turned his attention on to Pearce. 'Which means, do I believe what you're telling us is true?'

'I think, sir, you must ask yourself this. Would I have acted in such a high-handed manner if there was any doubt?'

'You expect anyone,' Truscott barked, 'to give credence to any word a man of your stripe would say.'

'Be thankful your rank protects you, sir. If it did not, I would be asking you to choose your weapon and a place at which to meet.'

About to deliver another insult, Truscott was stopped by the governor, who told him to be quiet. 'Pearce, you will accompany me to Government House, where you will explain how all this came about and in detail.'

'One fact of which you should be aware, sir, is this. The same information imparted to you, should already be known in London.'

'Government House now,' commanded Sir David. 'And Truscott, ensure the *Santa* whatever it's called is well guarded until I can decide what to do. Lord Langholm, I would suggest, to ensure it stays safe, your place should be aboard HMS *Lively*.'

That pricked his languor. Being senior, he was miffed at being so ordered, when John Pearce was to be permitted a private discussion with the governor.

CHAPTER EIGHT

Sir David exited the room with the same bustle with which he had arrived, forcing Pearce to shift in order to keep up the pace, which he maintained until they were both seated in his coach. About to speak, an upheld hand from the older man stopped any conversation. A meaningful glance was thrown at the fellow on the box, he being clearly either Spanish or a Gibraltarian. If the journey was made in silence, it was not one of long duration; how could it be in a possession not much larger than an aristocratic estate?

Outside Government House, crisp salutes from red-coated sentries greeted the pair, responded to by a lifted hat. Pearce was led to the gubernatorial office, with its panoramic view of half the colony and the bay. He was left for several minutes to twiddle his thumbs as his host disappeared without explanation, nothing being provided on his return either. Sir David was followed by a servant bringing port wine and anchovies, with Pearce invited to sit in silence until the liquid was delivered and poured. Only when the man departed, did Sir David speak.

'Chapter and verse, Pearce, and no more equivocation.'

'You're so sure there has been any, sir?'

'Have to be blind not to. There's clearly a difference between what you thought Langholm would report and what he relayed to Truscott. So, you'd best describe to me the action you engaged in as well as what led up to it.'

'Which would be made easier if I had sight of what Langholm did say.'

'Never happen.'

'Can you not demand to see it?'

'No, I can't. It's naval and will go to the Admiralty. My responsibilities, or should I say my powers, do not extend to poking an oar in there. Perhaps the senior salt who granted you your pennant can dig it out in time, not that it will do you much good. Once it's been read by those who excoriate your name, and it damns you, which I hesitate to doubt it will do, the dispatch will assume the stature of holy writ.'

There was a gleam in the governor's blue eyes when Pearce did not immediately respond. For all his bluff manner, which went with a rubicund countenance and a hearty bonhomie, he was no fool, which was proved by what came next.

'Though why some admiral would send you on such an undertaking as the one you describe escapes me.'

'You can hardly deny what the Dons get up to is of some concern to the navy.'

'Nor would I, but this has the smack of a political hand, not a watery one. So, I wonder if you're going to tell me what you've obviously kept from Truscott and Langholm.'

'Is it obvious?'

'I said no equivocation, did I not?'

'It would require you to be very discreet.'

'Which tells me I have the right of it, so think on this. Whatever Langholm has said, it will not be the only report carrying weight in London.'

'You'll pen one too?'

'Of course, I will and it will not go to the Admiralty.'

'We were acting on instructions from Henry Dundas,' came after a considered pause.

'To whom I owe my present appointment and to whom I report.'

It was a telling fact and one Pearce had not considered. It was pointless worrying about what the navy would think of his actions, for he could not, and did not, expect any favours from such a quarter. But a positive report to Dundas from the governor could not but be a good thing. Having observed his guest thinking for several seconds, Sir David added.

'So, start at the beginning and leave nothing out.'

'I'm not sure our Minister for War would be happy at my being fully open about everything.'

'He'll be a damn sight unhappier if I lose Gibraltar because you've held anything back.'

'You perceive a risk of that happening?'

'Just look at the history of the place, man. It's been besieged over a dozen times and taken by force more than once over the centuries. Everyone on the Rock lives with the prospect of such an outcome as a constant concern. Given it will not be yielded without a fight, what happens to the folk who live here and must endure a siege, even more if it falls?'

'We're surely beyond the age of sacking captured possessions.'

'Which is what the good folk of places like Lyon, Marseilles and Nantes thought before the damn Revolution and the guillotine arrived.'

Feeling as if he's been slightly naïve, Pearce changed the subject. 'In Truscott's chamber, you mentioned rumours.'

'No, no, Pearce, you first,' was issued like a command, with none of the previous affability.

So, he obliged, not without interruptions and shrewd questions. He outlined how the mission had come about, though there was no mention of the previous assignment which had taken him to Paris. Oliphant was described, with as much conviction as he could muster, as a man Dundas trusted, and one who had the required skills to get them both to where the information sought could be uncovered.

The need to observe matters in both Hendaye and San Sebastian were more fully explained, as well as the nature of the people who had provided the intelligence, with their rabid commitment to Basque independence and hatred of both Madrid and Paris.

'Easy to see why the French reneged, Sir David. Half the old Basque country, which is the one-time Kingdom of Navarre, lies over the border in France. They'd be inviting trouble in their own bailiwick.'

'By which I take it to mean you trust them?'

'Absolutely,' Pearce responded.

This was followed by a description of the action against the *Santa Leocadia*. Pearce outlined this in graphic detail so his listener, a soldier, would be afforded a comprehensive view of the problems faced. He also explained the very cogent reasons for not acting as Lord Langholm had suggested, as well as the dangers they had faced in hanging on to her.

'In order to get any kind of response, I would have had to close to within near pistol shot distance and would not be much further off if I had decided to put a shot across her bows.'

'Well within range of her superior cannon?'

'And the Spaniard had the wind.'

'Unwise.'

'So, I make no bones regarding our intention to block her off from Vigo and, once entry was no longer an option, this drew her into a pursuit in which the action was on terms more favourable to me.'

'Joined by *Lively*?'

'In time, yes.'

The governor nodded at the piqued tone of the response. 'Anything else?'

This was responded to with a shake of the head; what then happened in Pontravedra Bay and the escape from there had little bearing.

'Your rumours?' Pearce asked when he felt there was no more to say, only to find Sir David was no quicker to respond than he had been previously. He too thought through his words before speaking them.

'It's more than rumours, but they have to be kept under wraps in order to prevent alarm. What we worry about is kept within a very tight circle, just as we have to be discreet in what measures we undertake to strengthen the defences. Luckily, such action is ongoing ever since we took the place, so the building of new fortifications is taken as nothing exceptional. But alerting the soldiers can only be done when a threat is manifest and under way. It would never do to spook matters too early.'

Anything more, he explained, might see half the population seeking to leave. He went on to relate how it had taken three annual resupply fleets, each with a huge escort of line-of-battleships, to hold out in the Great Siege of '79.

At one point the navy had been required to evacuate over a thousand civilians to avoid famine, and it was a far from happy experience for those taken off. Too many sickened and died, either aboard the ships or in Portuguese hovels in which they were confined. So, those with the means and long memories would have a plan in place to get themselves out and their possessions with it.

'In short, we reside in a colony where morale is as important as batteries of cannon and strong fortifications.'

'Which are formidable.'

'So will be the forces ranged against us if Godoy again has the French on his side. Some of them will have been observing everything we do and pondering on new ways to overcome measures which cannot be kept secret.'

'Even tunnels?'

'They have to open out and become visible somewhere, man.'

This was delivered as if he was talking to a simpleton, so it was a somewhat abashed John Pearce who responded. 'Of course, and their worth in terms of defence can be established.'

A soft knock on the door brought in a redcoat lieutenant, which saved any further blushes. He handed over a flimsy to the governor; this was read and followed by a nod, which was taken as a dismissal. As the door closed, the information was imparted to Pearce.

'A fleet of half a dozen line-of-battleships, accompanied by frigates, weighed from Cadiz five days past, which our people say could be destined for Algeciras.'

'Is the information reliable?'

'We pay well to be kept abreast of such things, but it never can be wholly so. The Dons are well practiced at deception. It could be off to the Americas for more gold and silver.'

'Spying on an ally,' Pearce remarked with a wry smile.

'Coming from you, and after what you've just related, is sophistry indeed.'

'Do you receive similar intelligence from Minorca?'

Sir David knew the purpose of the question; the main Spanish battle fleet was anchored off Port Mahon and might be ready to join their confreres if they were headed for the anchorage across the bay.

'None, but they can be here in less than a week with a fair wind. On top of that, since the treaty ending the War of the Pyrenees, the Spanish troop movements have been a concern. What did you see on the border?'

'Few French troops were visible and, from what we could observe, no sign of any Spaniards at all.'

'We have to assume their main forces will have withdrawn following the peace. They may not move all the way to Andalusia, but what if they are south of Madrid? Their artillery may have come even further, as I mentioned earlier. They point to a concentration which can have only one purpose, to eventually threaten the Rock.

But I doubt they'll move their main force, assuming what you tell me of the treaty is correct, until they've been joined by the French.'

'Who, as I have informed you, have severely limited means in Roussillon. The army which beat the Dons has been sent to Italy.'

'The zealots in Paris are very good at conjuring up new armies, Pearce, while our own government is damn slow in getting fleets assembled and even more so at getting them to sea. The Rock can't be held without naval support, so I'm wondering if playing for time might be a sound tactic for us, just as it now seems to be for Godoy.'

The smile on the older man's face hinted at his meaning, which allowed Pearce to make the connection. 'Using the *Santa Leocadia*?'

'And the silver? The cargo would not be common knowledge and surprise is always a valuable ploy.'

'You're not thinking of handing it back?' Pearce protested.

'Got you there, did I not?' was accompanied by a broad grin, followed by a deep-throated laugh. 'No, we'll unload it after the sun goes down, so the Dons can't see what we're about. Then we'll invite them to recover their frigate, which is useless to us and of little value without we have a dockyard.'

'Which will lower the value of the capture, sir.'

'Don't be greedy, Pearce, but I'm going to agree with your earlier point. The arrival of the silver and its purpose would have to be a well-kept secret from their own people as well as us at any time, never mind the present. Even with the vessel in their harbour, will Madrid be willing to admit what it carried in its holds now it's lost? It points to something so confined as to be impossible now to be open about.'

Seeing Pearce pondering this, Sir David added. 'If I accept what you say is true, I also have to believe that Godoy will want to move at his own pace and in concert with the French. He cannot take the Rock without their support and they are clearly, by your information, not yet ready.'

'So, it's best not to stoke up national resentment.'

'Public clamour could oblige even a fellow like Godoy to respond.'

'And *Hazard?*'

'You have your orders, do you not, so you best obey them. But, if you call on me before you weigh, I'll show you the outline of what I intend to say.'

'Langholm?'

'Must also get away too, or he risks being trapped by the squadron from Cadiz, if what we're being told is fact and their aim is aggressive. The report I'll pen for Dundas, he will be tasked to take home and I've just sent to ask Truscott to issue him his orders.'

'He might take your report to the Admiralty first.'

'A strong possibility, and I don't doubt they know how to lift a wax seal and replace it without leaving a trace. But they will be obliged to pass it on to Dundas even if they do. With what I intend to say, if Langholm is intent on ditching you, it will sow doubts. To my mind, always assuming what you say is a factual account, you acted in the best interests of the nation and you must hope others see it in the same way. So, make up your wood, water and powder and be ready to weigh in the morning.'

'I need roundshot as well.'

'Get everything you need from Truscott and, if he dares to delay you, tell him I'll throw him in the lazaretto.'

'Can you do such a thing?'

'Not immediately, but I can if I declare martial law, which I would need to promulgate in order to put the garrison and the populace on full alert. Such an order also means no one can leave without my written permission, which renders it an act with perils attached. Only when I'm sure an attack is imminent, will I do so.'

'To avoid civil unrest?'

'Perhaps, but the locals fear the Spanish more than they dislike us, which will have them clamouring to be allowed to aid the defence. Now go and see to your needs while I begin to compose a missive which will keep you out of the tower.'

—◦—

Aboard HMS *Lively*, Captain Lord Langholm was closeted with John Russell, his first lieutenant, relating the bones of the meetings he just had with Truscott and Sir David Rose. There was a bond which made their relationship closer than that which normally existed between captain and premier. Russell was a scion of a cadet branch of the family of the Duke of Bedford; indeed he was namesake, so he could claim more than a trace of blue blood.

Yet the true strength of Russell's position was the fact that his aristocratic commander was a touch indecisive. For all his *sang froid* in public, he was less assured in private and thus depended on his premier more than most captains. This gave Russell a lever he could exploit and he did so for genuine reasons.

In the time they'd had since departing Pontevedra Bay, he had worked on his superior to bring him down from the elation he had manifested since the taking of the *Santa Leocadia*. He had done so with care, hinting at certain future problems without over-elaborating, while never forgetting to mention the silver and its value. It was there, but not yet in their grasp.

Over several days, he had become bolder. He had never been happy with the idea of cooperating with a person like John Pearce. So, Russell had many times repeated, for his captain, that such an association was not one to produce unbridled benefit and might do the precise opposite. He had claimed it to be a conclusion reached when he examined how it might be seen by those, and they were many and powerful, who would take any chance they could to damn the man in command of HMS *Hazard*.

Russell had begun by speculating on the action against the Spaniard, which could, by malicious minds, be seen as akin to piracy. Given the sums involved and the jealousy this would create, there would be many who would incline to such an interpretation. He pointed out such a capture, lauded in war and the source of a fabulous reward, might be seen in a different light, when executed against an allied warship.

Like water on a stone, he had first dented and then worn down Langholm's certainty that the action would be seen as justified and great wealth would automatically ensue. He had then alluded to the fact the information which had come aboard HMS *Lively* with Pearce and his distinctly slippery companion, Oliphant, was verbal. There was nothing in writing to back up their claim of Spanish duplicity, and no witness, he personally would trust, who could have verified their claims.

Finally, the time had arrived, before they expected to raise Gibraltar, to be more definite. It would be best for Lord Langholm to put in a report which allowed him, if asked, to deprecate the actions of John Pearce. It was best to do this in order he would not suffer from any opprobrium which might be headed the man's way. If there was none, then no harm would be done by being careful.

Langholm might be the scion of a noble Scottish family, but he was the fourth son and way off inheriting very much of a patrimony, or a title, which would go to his elder brother. Russell knew, for he was in the same boat, that both depended on the navy for their future well-being. In order to avoid any risk to their future career, it would be best to submit in writing a despatch which was equivocal.

'I don't say it is necessary to damn Pearce,' he had maintained, 'though I can think of a number of places where to do so might work to your advantage.'

'So, you reckon I should muddy the waters?'

Russell had heartily agreed with the conclusion drawn, delivered in a languid manner which disguised he was prey to doubts. They had then fallen to discussing how this might be achieved, which saw the original report rewritten, with caution for reputations in mind.

'As you know, sir,' had been Russell's final point, 'My future in the service is tied to your own. I hope, as you do, the rewards for the recent events will be forthcoming, but I see safety in a touch of evasion.'

Now Russell was hearing how varied had been the reactions of Truscott and the governor. This had him suggest that the opinion of a senior naval officer would outweigh anything from a bullock, however elevated. This got a nod from his captain, though it did not miss Russell's attention, and the man was plainly worried. He reassured himself, if they were being ordered back to Pompey, he had lots of time to stiffen his backbone.

—◁—

As soon as darkness fell, the harbour and mole were sealed off by redcoats and it was they who were tasked to shift the boxes of ingots; no one local was employed. Not because they were universally mistrusted, but because it took only one loose tongue to set going a tale which would speed round the colony and inevitably be heard over the causeway in La Linea. The Spaniards might guess at what was afoot, but that was very different from having certain knowledge.

Distraction was provided by the amount of lantern-lit activity on the decks of the two new arrivals, with some of the work being necessary, but the time taken added to the bustle and a degree of a bluff. The last act of the night was for Pearce to dine with Sir David, where what the governor would say was outlined in copious notes and his guest was invited to ensure the details of the action were accurate.

At first light, both *Hazard* and *Lively* put to sea, parting ways as soon as they reached the straits. There was, of course, an illusion of regret, with flags hoisted to wish a 'Happy Return' to the frigate. But John Pearce reckoned Langholm would be as content as he to be free of encumbrance, while he wished, given what the other man was going back to and from which he was sailing away, the position could have been reversed.

———

Two things John Pearce had determined upon without recourse to any orders. First his ship and crew should be able to impress, this added to the notion of not being caught out by any imputations of a lack of judgement. He was sailing into the orbit of Sir John Jervis, a man who had demonstrably shown a visceral loathing for his very name. Jervis was also the kind of admiral, a strict disciplinarian, inclined to act as independently and in any manner he saw fit. He would damn the views of a Board of Admiralty sitting a thousand miles away from any fighting.

He must be given no cause to exercise his irascibility on either HMS *Hazard* or the man in command. So, as soon as they cleared Gibraltar and the normal activities of the day had been carried out, Pearce got busy on sail drills, working everyone aboard to perfect the raising and taking in of canvas. This was at the expense of what he would also have liked to engage in, which was gunnery exercises. But when Jervis sighted the ship, and when she came into the lee of HMS *Victory*, it had to be done with perfection.

Even if he had no orders to do so, there was a second matter to see to, namely the present position and state of readiness of the Spanish fleet. This ensured his course took him south of the Balearics – the aim to close with their base at Port Mahon. On the east coast of Minorca, this put them a few days sailing from Jervis's

Mediterranean fleet, without being in the arc of any immediate action.

If their yards were crossed, with sails clewed up, and they had not been when he passed by on his way home to England, it meant they were ready to sail and possibly to pose an immediate threat. Sir David Rose's spies might believe those five sail of the line from Cadiz were intent on anchoring in Algeciras Bay, but there was another possibility. They might be sailing to reinforce Admiral Langara and his main battle fleet, to what end being moot: to fight or act to join with the French at Toulon in the hope of preventing Jervis exiting the inland sea.

Blessed with good weather, sunshine and a benign wind, added to a crew growing more efficient by the day, HMS *Hazard* was a delight to be aboard as she ate up the miles. The water creamed past her bows as she ploughed through what was a light and even swell. Pearce found he was happy, in a way he would not have anticipated in years past, even to the point where concerns for his private problems, or even dreams of great wealth, could be put to the back of his mind.

And, unlike the previous part of the voyage, the aim was simple. There were no worries about going ashore on to territory which was certainly hostile or visiting a place with dubious allies. There was no Samuel Oliphant to constantly question him and seek explanations for matters which were none of his concern.

He could even, without the bounds of his responsibilities, allow time for a few private conversations in his cabin with his Pelicans. Such meetings were, allegedly, about the various areas of the working of the ship, which Charlie and Rufus oversaw as watch captains. Michael O'Hagan fulfilled the role of Master at Arms.

It was by such means he could take the temperature of the crew, over and above what would be reported to him by Isaac Hallowell. Were the men content with the caveat tars of all stripes never were utterly so? Had the sailors brought aboard off Brittany melded with the Quota Men, lubbers all, foisted upon him by a malicious Admiralty? Was there laughter and shared jokes? Were there disputes? And, if yes, how serious? In general, the information gained was encouraging.

Time also had to be spent with his warrants, some pleasant, others less so. The bosun, Crocker, known to the crew as Crock of Shit, never ceased to leave Pearce gloomy, he being such a miserable sod. He clearly felt that being landed with such a commanding officer was some kind of personal affront. Williams continued to be cautious in any exchange, still smarting from the failure of his weather prediction while no one could be happy after listening to the moans of impending poverty from Porlock, the purser.

More cheering was Mr Low the gunner, who had quickly sensed that his captain had an ability to be treated as human, as well as having a sense of humour. So, he had taken to regaling him about the tribulations, much exaggerated, of having his wife aboard. She was indeed a formidable presence, both physically and, apparently, in mood, thus to be treated with respect even by the captain.

Towse was a competent carpenter, so any engagement with him was brisk and short, while Cullen had become a daily source of good news about a continually improving George Moberly. He was now conscious and taking portable soup dipped in hard tack, but not yet up to attending dinners where Pearce, in rotation, entertained his officers and midshipmen. But it was something which he would not be long in attending.

Guests were invited in two groups, which meant he got to know them better. Not least this applied to his acting lieutenant Macklin, now known to have a given name of Frank. He was an experienced seaman with long service in the merchant marine and perhaps more dubious adventures which he was disinclined to talk about. It was plain that he found the formality of a naval dinner hard to cope with on his first occasion, albeit he was a man at peace compared to the mids.

As was true in all things, Jock the Sock was the least stressed of the quartet, while both Campbell and Tennent, tongue tied and very dour in the case of the latter, seemed terrified of committing a gaffe, and so said very little. Campbell had at least lost his puppy fat and was now a leaner soul through being worked hard. Tennant had about him the gloom of the Scottish kirk, hardly surprising given a Calvinist-leaning minister for a father.

But it was the mite who brought out the paternal in John Pearce, a lad initially so shy and fearful, it had been necessary to encourage him to any duty, even the simplest. But he had grown in both confidence and, even if it was slow, in body. Allowed a glass or two of wine, he opened up to the point of the occasional attempt, usually a poor one, at a witty sally. It was easy for Pearce, in looking at Livingston, to imagine his own son might one day share his table and be as engaging.

He got to know all four best when he took them for fencing practice on the foredeck. Here was an area where he could not be bested in competence by anyone aboard, having been given lessons by a master of the craft in Paris. The formal way of fighting he took them through time after time. It might have the cadences of a dance, but it was a deadly one, which he was determined they should master.

It was also an activity which could not help but take him back to the happy time, after he and his father had arrived in Paris, having fled from England and a writ for seditious libel. A warm reception was extended to a known radical orator who shared the triple mantra of the Revolution. Inevitably this led to the dark and gloomy conclusion of what had transpired, with a regime which slowly and inexorably turned utterly murderous.

'You best ease up sometimes, John-boy,' was a whispered injunction from O'Hagan, who'd fetched some small beer to quench the thirst brought on by exertion. 'You're not duelling with the ghost of that shite Robespierre, are you now?'

It was a cause for some embarrassment to realise, as he looked over the soaked shirts and sweat-soaked faces of his mids, now like him quenching dry throats, what had happened. He had been thinking too hard about the excesses of the Revolution and the sins it had visited upon him and his father. Taking the ire these recollections produced out on lads too young for his sudden ferocity was wrong. But backing down he would not do.

'Assure me, Michael, when they cross swords with an enemy twice their age, he will go gentle and so will I. Anyway, it's time you took over from our gentlemanly pursuit and taught them the bruiser's way.'

If Pearce relished teaching formal fencing, he had an equal in the Irishman, for both men knew any fighting these lads might engage in was going to be no gentle parry and thrust. It was going to be cut or be cut, with the short and sharp blades of naval hangers, not the canvas sheathed of just-employed officer's swords. But that had great value, even so. The lesson from Pearce was how to anticipate an opponent's intentions, which applied in any fight, be it with weapons or without.

'Watch the eyes,' Pearce would shout as they contested with each other. 'Look for the dip of a shoulder, of the placement of the feet. Any deadly blow requires delivery to be carried out with balance and you must always maintain yours.'

With Michael it was the same, with the addition of brute force, also with guile for these youngsters. Even Maclehose, the tallest and strongest, as yet lacked the muscle to go toe to toe with a grown man. So, they were taught to always have the side of the body protected by one of their fellows, told to protect the flank of another and never to be drawn forward into isolation. If they saw a chance to land a punch, or an exposed groin, which would benefit from the placing of their foot, it was right not to hesitate. It was important to win: being a gentleman was of no account.

'For, sure, you'll be looking Jesus in the eyes if you do, hoping he'll pardon your sins.'

'Trying to turn them into papists,' was Charlie Taverner acid comment as, by habit, whenever the deity was mentioned, Michael crossed himself.

A cry from the masthead alerted all to the fact that the clouds hovering around the eastern hills of Minorca had been sighted, so it was time to don blue coats. The ship was brought round until they were on a northward course, aiming to bypass the entrance to the deep and narrow bay which formed Port Mahon. The guns were housed and, in all respects, HMS *Hazard* was showing peaceful intent.

But, if the Spanish were now enemies, it was dangerous. They were required to be close enough to gain something of value but far enough off to avoid the costal batteries on the bastion of *Punta Santa Carles*. They must also avoid those on the promontory further north, and the cannon packed outworks of the *Fortalesa di Mola*, it being unwise to venture too close to such a formidable fortress.

They would be doing so at the maximum speed of which HMS *Hazard* was capable, knowing its position did give a chance to see far up and into the deep anchorage. At the first hint of danger, it would be up helm and flee, with orders already put in place. But Pearce might at least have part of the answer he sought: Was every Spaniard now unquestionably a foe?

Pearce had an idea when they were hull up to the dangers they faced – one which had him call his officers to a quick conference. As always, the decision was his, but if he was possibly going to put the whole ship's company in greater danger, he felt it only right to share his thinking. Once explained, it led to the final comment, which was greeted with nods of agreement from men who were now fully cognoscente of the situation *vis-à-vis* the Spanish alliance.

'I think it gives us a chance of smoking where our Dons now are in terms of peace or war.'

So, the breaking out of the tricolour at the masthead, once they were in farthest range of the first bastion, was carried out with breaths held, not aided by an immediate discharge of black smoke from a single cannon. Exhalation was possible when no ball came as accompaniment, making it a perfunctory salute, which assumed a proper one must wait for the sight of Admiral Langara's flag.

'Acknowledge,' Pearce murmured, which was carried out immediately with a swivel. 'Are we ready to make the change?'

'Standing by, sir,' replied Livingston, his hands on the halyards.

'Am I allowed to posit, sir, it might still be a trap.'

'Mr Hallowell, I would despair if you did not.'

As ever, when everything was at risk, the only sounds were the wind whistling through the rigging and the pounding as the bows dipped before hitting the next oncoming wave. As they sailed on, the narrows of the entry to Port Mahon opened to reveal the masts of the Spanish battle fleet, Pearce looking aloft to where Worricker was sat in the tops.

'Yards crossed sir, sails fully rigged and many loosed to air, with boats and hoys loading supplies.'

There was no need to say the obvious. It appeared to be that the fleet could be preparing to put to sea, so Pearce quietly gave Livingston his orders. The tricolour came down with a rush, to be replaced with the union flag of Britannia, this carried out in the space of half a minute. It was testimony to the possible nerves of the man in command of the shore gunners, the first ball to be fired took not much longer.

By that time HMS *Hazard* had come round and was heading due east, happy to see the splash and water plume of the round shot land where they would have been, now with the worry they were within maximum range of the *Fortalesa di Mola*.

'Gunners are training round, sir,' came from aloft.

Worricker's information, even if anticipated, was acknowledged. Pearce was mentally calculating the time it would take to shift the muzzle aim of what he reckoned to be forty-two pounders. It would be no easy task given they weighed something approaching four tonnes. Anyone watching him would have seen his fingers moving as he counted off the seconds and, when the order to change course was issued, it came with a yell.

The new course, already worked out, was acknowledged by Williams and, swiftly on a south east heading, the result was as previously, and just as gratifying, as the yards were loosened, quickly swung into place then sheeted home to take the wind. The round shot disturbed plenty of seawater, but the target was no longer where it was supposed to be.

'We must crack on,' Pearce said in a quiet voice, as he realised the flaw in what had looked like a cunning ruse. 'I reckon we might have a couple of frigates in our wake as soon as they can be warped out of the narrows. They'll be seeking to find out who we truly are.'

'Do you think they could doubt it, sir?' Hallowell asked.

'If you can seek to fool folk with one flag, why not two?'

It took a few moments for his premier to see the sense of what Pearce was driving at. What they had just experienced was not definitive. 'Remember Spain and France have a truce, one which, for all we know, extends beyond their shared border. To then have us seeking to guy them with the switch of flag…'

'Seen to be trying tweaking their nose.'

Pearce grinned. 'A perfect summary, if somewhat lacking in stylishness. They're a proud lot, the Dons, I doubt they take to being guyed, especially by us.'

'We'll show them our heels, sir, the way *Hazard* is sailing.'

'Then let us see if we can squeeze out another knot or two. Mr Williams, we will change course to the north as soon as it is dark.'

'Then to Hallowell,' as he glanced at the sky. 'And we will darken the ship.'

CHAPTER NINE

Walter Hodgson had no qualms about calling on Emily Barclay, who had just moved from the abode of her friend, Doctor Heinrich Lutyens, to a house of her own, one not long built in Fitzroy Square. A handsome stucco-fronted dwelling with a spacious interior, it had to be remarked he was visiting a building site as much as a dwelling. Only the south side of the proposed square had been completed and the leases granted.

What was designated to be a grass-covered central park was now, early on a sunny morning, baked earth and would be mud when it rained. The Barclay abode, and those alongside it were, however, handsome dwellings, with arched fanlights over doors wide, solid and gleaming with fresh paint. These were framed by imposing lamps of shiny brass, set against walls of white-painted concrete.

His rap on the knocker was responded to by a liveried footman and, on entering, he could not but be impressed by the furnishings she had managed to acquire. The hallway contained two fine-looking silk-covered settles and a large round table, the top of which was polished walnut of high quality. In the middle stood a large vase – Italian by its design and dimensions – filled with flowers.

'Mr Hodgson,' Emily said in a warm tone, as she entered the drawing room into which he had been shown, one as yet sparsely furnished. 'To what do I owe your calling?'

'Would it not be enough to enquire as to how you are faring in your new house?'

'Fatigued rather than faring, sir. The builders are constantly required to return to put right those things not carried out properly in the construction.'

A gesture invited the thief-taker to sit in one of the only two chairs in the room, she occupying the other. Both were in sore need of repair – so worn was the original pink covering over uneven and patched padding – their state referred to with a grim expression.

'And when not so occupied, it is time spent at every auction house in London, seeking decent furnishings, which I do not need to tell you is a sore trial. To purchase new is to wait several months, if not over a year, for what I require to be made. And when it comes to the possessions of the sadly distressed, I am not the only one bidding in what can resemble a bear pit, so aggressive do the other buyers become.'

'You do not employ a factor to act on your behalf.'

'For the very good reason I am particular in my requirements and have no wish to send back what someone else supposes I might like. I do have some furnishing coming up from Somerset, where the competition is not so fierce.' She smiled. 'It is an area in which I can rely on my mother's taste. But I am remiss, some refreshments, perhaps? Tea?'

'No thank you, but I must enquire of young Adam. He is doing well, I trust?'

'He fatigues me even more since he started crawling, but I must also add nothing delights me as much as his endless mischief.'

Hodgson responded with a benign smile, while taking in the vision of a strikingly beautiful woman. She had matured a little since he'd last visited her, not so much physically, as in poise, but the fact of being the owner of her own house was probably part of the reason. The pinned-up auburn hair was held in place by a garnet-covered band, which showed a delightful swan-like neck and enough below to point to an engaging bosom, even if she was still obliged to still wear black. The face, slightly freckled around the nose, had a lively quality when conversing, which added to the impression of a person happy in her situation.

He had been tasked on his previous visit with seeing off the impecunious pleas of Cornelius Gherson, a man who'd become a bane in her life, an endeavour now successfully concluded. The menace was presently at sea in a transport vessel, bound for the Mediterranean with supplies for the fleet and, as far as Hodgson was concerned, with a decent hope he might fall overboard and drown.

Did she regret helping to prove Gherson's innocence in the matter of the murder of Catherine Carruthers, in which Hodgson had played a major investigative role? He would have liked to ask but it was, on two counts, inappropriate he should do so. First, the mere mention of the name would, he knew, stir deeply unpleasant memories regarding a man she loathed. Second, it was not the purpose of his calling.

'I've come to ask if you are in communication with, or know the whereabouts of, Lieutenant John Pearce.'

The stiffening of the shoulders was close to imperceptible. It would have been missed by anyone not wedded to the close observation of people's bodily reactions, a very necessary attribute in his trade. It was a subject on which he knew Mrs Barclay to be highly sensitive, yet he felt he should not be included in such reservations. Never acknowledged was the fact he knew very well that they were lovers, while holding a strong indication Pearce was the father of the child just mentioned. She could not surely be in doubt that he, a man so insightful, would in any way be fooled by the pretence they maintained.

Her reasons he could only surmise, but they were sound. The wealthy widow of a deceased naval captain could not have it said, if wishing to be accepted socially, she was an adulteress. Even less would be the notion that Captain Ralph Barclay was not the father of young Adam. Not only would she be ostracized if it became public, but the boy would carry the stigma for life.

'Why do you ask?'

If it was an obvious response, it was also one calculated to give her time to regain her composure.

'I have uncovered certain information which might present to him some future difficulties. I also feel, should my suspicions prove correct, his being warned would be to his advantage.'

'Am I to be privy to these difficulties?'

'Are you aware he intercepted a merchant vessel in the North Sea. It was one he claimed to be French, which was handed over to the naval authority in Ramsgate as a prize?' Seeing pursed lips and a negative headshake, Hodgson added. 'I am only asking and my motive, if indeed I have one, is to protect Lieutenant Pearce from what might be unpleasant repercussions.'

'You seem to imply he is in trouble of some kind.'

'I have no idea if that's the case, but information has come my way to cast doubt on the provenance of the captured vessel.' He was required to lie then, since he did not wish to be open and frank about Druce and Denby Carruthers. 'It may be the ship was a neutral.'

'The letter I received from Ramsgate made no mention of this. Such things as captured ships, of whatever designation, are not a subject on which he would communicate with me.'

'You have many other matters to discuss, which I understand.'

This got him a very direct look indeed and one not entirely friendly. But it was important she knew he was not fooled by her carapace of respectability. Hodgson cared not one jot for her past actions in relation to her marriage but, if he needed her cooperation, and he might, she had to know it was necessary to avoid subterfuge. Let it be unspoken, but not be treated as a secret.

'The person he would communicate in such a case would be his prize agent.'

'Who is?'

'Alexander Davidson. He has offices in High Holborn, which is something you could have found out by sending me a note.'

He'd sensed the change in her demeanour as it took place, a shift from openness to caution. This reminded him he was not only dealing with a woman of beauty, but one he knew to have a sharp mind.

'There are ramifications to the case which required me to ask for any information you may possess.'

'Mr Hodgson, Lieutenant Pearce is on a duty of which I know nothing. As of this moment, I have no idea of his whereabouts and I doubt even his prize agent is much better informed. He, like me, last had word of him from Falmouth, but I have had no indication he has heard anything since. Given what you do as an occupation, as well of the nature of the man we're discussing, I'm beginning to wonder if Lieutenant Pearce is indeed in some form of trouble. If he is, I would appreciate being told.'

'Did he mention his destination?'

'No.' was abrupt and so was what followed. 'And I asked you a question, to which I would appreciate an answer.'

It was time, once more, to avoid too much disclosure and his motive was protective. In a matter involving the people with whom he must deal , he could not divulge anything which might put her at risk. Weak-willed Druce, browbeaten by his brother-in-law, might easily let slip she had funded Gherson's defence, and Carruthers was not one to let such a thing pass. So, it was as much to avoid being open as indulging in a very long shot indeed, he asked his next question.

'Does the name Tolland mean anything to you?'

That did provoke a less-studied reaction, it was in fact very much the reverse. Her nostrils flared and the tone of her voice changed markedly. 'It means a great deal. It refers to a pair of smugglers, brothers, who tried to kill Lieutenant Pearce for a perceived theft, one of which he is wholly innocent.'

A hand went to his chin in a reflective gesture, really to cover for his shock, so it was several seconds before he could bring himself to say. 'You intrigue me.'

'While I do not know the details of the alleged theft, I do know there seems no way to convince them of John's...' There was a pause then at the slip of the tongue, followed by a hasty, 'Lieutenant Pearce has assured me he was not the culprit. I am bound to enquire as to why you asked.'

'The name came up in conversation on the subject of the neutral vessel.'

'Then let me assure you, Mr Hodgson, if those villains have anything to do with it, the vessel is no neutral. It is more likely to be engaged in the smuggling of contraband than any innocent pursuit.'

Hodgson stood, not in haste, but with studied calm, even if he felt the need to hurry away. 'I thank you for indulging me with your time, Mrs Barclay. I think I must call on Mr Davidson at his office and see if he can enlighten me as to the whereabouts of Lieutenant Pearce.'

'Mr Hodgson, sit down. It is obvious you are not being open with me, something I would not have said in our previous dealings and I require you to be so now. If the name Tolland has surfaced, with reference to the officer mentioned, and given I know something, albeit not everything of the association, you must tell me all.'

'If I was to say knowledge could put you at risk, would you desist?'

The sharp look made words unnecessary, so Hodgson sank back into his chair and, with a sigh, began to talk. He was unsure if the lack of response was due to her poise or a determination not to shudder at the depth of depravity being revealed. She required no details of the murder of Catherine Carruthers; those she knew already. But the possibility it might have been committed by the same pair who tried to kill her lover was enough to banish her calm demeanour.

'It was a case to set hares running, Mrs Barclay, from the very outset. The seeming involvement of Lieutenant Pearce does little to ease such a situation. It's very much the reverse. It concerns me your association to the person in question may bring problems to your door.'

'I cannot help but congratulate you on your discretion, Mr Hodgson,' came with a slight smile. 'But the manner in which you speak indicates to me it is not only you who have made a connection between us. That concerns me more than any threat from the Tollands.'

'It would be of some help if you were to tell me of everything you do know.'

'I'm obliged to ask for the purpose of your enquiries?'

'To see justice done, Mrs Barclay. And, I will confess, to protect myself from any untoward consequences of what I undertook on your behalf.'

There was a decent interval before she began to speak, slowly and deliberately, each word seemingly measured before being expressed, relating a tale which was as unlikely as it was astounding. If she was careful of her association with Pearce, she at least avoided outright pretence. It left him with the impression that the fellow was something of a booby, given the scheme he had fallen for should not have duped a mewling child. This was despite the well-known trope that sailors who might be competent at sea were fabled for being fools when ashore.

But it did establish another fact and a disturbing one. The Tollands had tried to exact revenge on him not once, but twice, which spoke of the kind of people for whom redress took precedence over all else. This made them an even greater potential threat to him, should his name ever become known, while doubling his concern. The woman before him should be kept as distant from the same as was possible.

'I see them, Mr Hodgson, as the blackest villains imaginable and the notion they may have had a hand in that poor woman's murder does not surprise me in the least. If you find you require extra resources to see them to the gallows, you may call upon me for the means.'

'Be assured I will do so, Mrs Barclay,' he lied, determined in his own mind never to cross her threshold again or at least to avoid doing so until the Tollands were beyond harming anyone. 'I would however ask you to pen a note to Mr Davidson asking if he will see me.'

'Gladly, if you think it will help.'

He could not avoid conjuring up the faces from the drawings he had carried and which had been stolen. He was now sure one served as a fair likeness of Jaleel Tolland, now established without peradventure, as a smuggler. No doubt now existed in his mind he was also one of the murderers of Catherine Carruthers, and so killing a woman was not a thing to trouble him. If it carried a personal risk, the man, and likely his brother as well, had to be found and rendered harmless as quickly as possible.

'I would be grateful to be kept informed, Mr Hodgson.'

'If I find anything you need to know, Mrs Barclay, I will drop you a line.'

***

Jaleel Tolland was faced with a seemingly endlessly flat landscape: marsh grass cut through by water-filled ditches, dotted with the odd farmhouse, the rare sight of a barn and a few isolated trees. It seemed ideal for the hiding of contraband, while also perfect as a place of concealment for the men who carried it out.

Once a cargo was landed and hidden away, they would not hang about but disperse to where they would appear as innocent locals. This rendered, for the excise, the task of apprehending them, if they'd been missed on the beach or in the act of transportation, near impossible.

A night spent in the open was made hard by the clear sky, inky and star-filled, sucking out the heat of the day. It was hard to sleep, with the creeping cold followed later by the damp of dawn dew, leaving Tolland feeling unrested. Still shivering, he washed his face and slaked his thirst in a water-filled ditch, having first seen his reflection in the still water. It was not a sight to inspire confidence, being unshaven and grimy, added to which, it had never, in the first place, been becoming.

There was no thought to move at speed for care had to be taken even in such open country. There would be folk about of a morning; there always were in a place poorly populated. Some would be cutting grass for animal feed, others out hunting with their dogs, who would be hard to spot as they sought to evade discovery by their prey. Indication of a presence would come from disturbed, ground-nesting birds or gulls and jackdaws gathering for a possible carrion feed.

He would trudge for a while and then stop, down on one knee, listening as well as looking for possible trouble, this as the sun rose in the sky, to make it necessary, when it reached its zenith, to remove his coat. The distant discharge of a weapon had him drop face down into the tall grass, the sound echoing through the still air: someone was out with a fowling piece seeking their supper. This had him rest for what must have been a good hour, enough to let whoever was employing the gun, and it was fired several times, meet his needs. He only moved on after a long period of silence.

Sometime later, the distant tower of a church, shimmering in the afternoon haze, came as the first indication of more than single human habitation. If there was a church, there would likely be a tavern, possibly even more than one nearby, for piety and dissolution went hand in hand.

But this village was on the way to somewhere and still too close to Harwich, so there were very likely people around he needed to avoid, the problem being the same as ever. It would be impossible to tell them from those he needed to provide help. If he was unsure of the names of the local smugglers, there was the hope, if he could find them, of a familiar face or two from Gravelines. He had no choice but to keep going and take a risk.

The sun was dipping in the southwest by the time he got close enough to plot his approach to what was a substantial village. With the church tower as his guide, he sought out the graveyard, a walled space which should be easy to approach. It was as well a spot where, of an afternoon, a solitary figure, hat in hand and head bowed, would seem natural. A cemetery also had headstones behind which it was possible to make discreet observations and even, if the need arose, to hide.

What he could make out of the village from the elevated position of the church, once he got there, labelled it as far from remarkable. He could see a couple of streets of houses, with paths leading to a few more substantial red brick dwellings, these backing on to the open country. The church itself, square, sturdy and built of stone, was a byway, which ended at the portico under which the resident divine could greet his parishioners. In one far corner, and of no concern to him once he saw himself ignored, a pair of diggers were busy scooping out a new burial plot.

Near one wall at the village end stood a large sarcophagus, inscribed with several names, all of one family from ancients to infants who had passed over, it said, into the hands of the Almighty.

This allowed him a reasonable view of the main street, which confirmed there was a coaching inn, a large timbre-framed, white-painted building, with an arch over the entrance. This would lead to the yard where passengers joined or alighted.

It was as if the gods willed it, as much as he did, the sound of a blasting horn announcing the imminent arrival of a stage coach. Before long, the hard packed mud on the street resounded to the pounding of six pairs of hooves, the conveyance itself coming into view. It took a slow swing to get it under the archway, where the horses would be freed from the traces, and replacements brought out to be harnessed.

There was a brief thought – stealing a horse might be a better bet than looking for his fellow smugglers – but it was one quickly put aside. There was no better way to set in motion a hue and cry. If one thing united a group of citizens, it was the theft of an animal on which all heavy work and movement, as well as income, depended.

Could this tavern be the place where the men he sought took their pleasure? If so, the task became how to get in and find a place to loiter without attracting attention. The presence of a coach, noisy travellers and working grooms provided the possible cover of bustle. It was not to be an opportunity likely to last; so he made a move, just as a quartet of very obvious sailors emerged from a dwelling further up the street.

He was back behind the sarcophagus in a flash, head raised and hat pulled low, able to recognise, at least two of his recent shipmates leading the party. They carried short naval hangers drawn and ready for use, being men known as trustworthy by Captain Bligh and not afraid to use a weapon. The hilt of one was employed on another door, the demand for entry clearly audible and, when it was opened, they pushed their way inside.

If they were this far inland, maybe as much as ten miles from the beach, it was possible they knew of what he'd done in Harwich.

Perhaps they'd been alerted by the crimp he'd chased off as to what he was wearing, and this to men who knew him by sight as well.

Was he safe where he was? Would it be best to get back onto the open marsh he'd so recently traversed and hide up from another night? Surely Bligh's gang would not hang about once they'd searched the village. Yet to move, when he had no idea if there were more than he could see, had its own risks.

In concentrating on what he now feared most, recapture and a certain rope, his antenna had slipped and he failed to hear, over the soft grass, what was a careful approach. The blow, albeit cushioned by the tricorne hat, was still enough to fell him, and Tolland first sank to his knees before canting sideways. The punch which followed was one as hard as he himself could deliver. As consciousness slowly faded, he heard a gravelly voice say.

'Tie him up and gag him. We'll leave the bugger where he lays till sun's gone down and those navy sods are on their way. Then we'll see if he's a' spying for the excise or just another tar a' running.'

'I say get rid is safest, Dob. Happen yon diggers could go a foot or two lower. Can't spill if he's under a layer of earth and a coffin.'

Tolland didn't hear any opinion on this as a course of action: he was out to the world.

CHAPTER TEN

If Walter Hodgson was reflecting on what he'd been told by Emily Barclay, he was glad so many loose ends seemed to come together. These thoughts stayed with him, a couple of days later, on his visit to the offices of Alexander Davidson, constantly driving home that he was in the middle of a real tangle of overlapping conspiracies. Also, in reflecting on what he knew, he had come to wonder, if the ship taken by Pearce was being sailed by the Tollands where were they.

He could not believe they were in their home village of Beltinge, for the very simple reason he might never have got out alive after he'd asked for Jaleel by name. At the very least, he would have faced questions as to why he was asking, and on whose behalf, which would likely have been a very painful experience.

People with a criminal bent, the kind that he had chased over the years, and the Tollands certainly, possessed such a thing, wished to stay in the shadows. Daylight was anathema and the pair had proved, given what he had been told by Emily Barclay, the notion of murder, up till then a strong suspicion, would trouble them not one jot. He reckoned if he had come face to face with either of them, he would have later been found a smashed body at the base of the Beltinge cliffs. He had a theory, but it was a very loose one.

'Thank you for seeing me, sir.'

There was much shuffling of briefs on Davidson's desk before the prize agent replied. Hodgson rated him a handsome cove, seemingly too young for the role he occupied, with ample if untidy fair hair over a boyish visage, added to what seemed an outgoing demeanour. When he spoke, the fact of him being Scottish, albeit well educated, was very evident.

'Mrs Barclay's note was pressing and indicates I should apologise for putting you off, sir. A case of mine was coming to a conclusion in the Admiralty Prize Court over the last two days, one which has been hanging on for three years now, so I was fully occupied. Now that you are here, how can I assist you?'

'I need to gain information regarding the whereabouts of Lieutenant John Pearce.'

The kindly look evaporated. 'And the purpose of this is?'

'I assure you it is to his advantage and Mrs Barclay would concur.' The look this received seemed to imply, easily said but insufficient to provoke disclosure. 'I take it you know about his recent capture in the North Sea?'

'If I do, I'm curious as to how you have become aware of it, since it has not yet been submitted for adjudication. The total value is, as yet, undetermined, given only the cargo and ship's stores, before an auction, have been laid out for previewing. But the hull, upperworks and cannon require the opinion of proper marine surveyor.'

'Can I ask if there will be any head money included for the crew?'

'A curious question, sir, if I may say so.'

'Surely one easy to answer.'

'You must understand Mr Hodgson, discretion in matters relating to any of my client accounts is essential.'

'Which I am bound to respect, sir. If I was to speculate the answer as being no, would it trouble you to confirm it?'

There was a long pause before Davidson responded, which was indeed only to indicate to Hodgson what he already suspected. To get this man to open up would be difficult, as it always was with lawyers. So, it was a case of asking such rhetorical questions, added to a modicum of bluff, to see if he could get to the things of which he was ignorant.

'I will agree only because Mrs Barclay said I should trust you.'

'The vessel was claimed as a captured French merchant vessel?' A nod was very slow in coming. 'If I was to tell you, there is a strong possibility that it was no such thing, what would you say?'

'I would be bound to ask why you feel you have enough information to make such a claim.'

'I am in possession of evidence to take it beyond mere speculation.'

The discreet knock preceded the entry of a fresh-faced clerk who spoke quietly into his employer's ear, which occasioned raised eyebrows. Davidson nodded to dismiss the lad and drummed his fingers on the desk for a moment.

'There is someone in the outer chamber I must see, Mr Hodgson. Please oblige me by waiting until I have dealt with the matter, since it may be germane to your enquiries.'

Left to his own devices, Hodgson looked around a well-appointed, if slightly untidy, office. His gaze then alighted on what would be, given the man's occupation and the nature of his clientele, something very necessary. One wall was devoted to a large naval battle scene, with several ships in action, all guns blazing, fighting and flags fluttering.

There was also a portrait of a rather severe old gent on another wall, the likeness indicating it was a relative, quite possibly a parent. Another, of a much younger and comely lady dressed in clothes long out of fashion, which tended to date it as executed some time past, hung opposite.

When Davidson returned, and he'd been gone for what seemed an age, it was with an open letter in his hand and an expression of deep study on his face. Once behind his desk, it was a while before he spoke.

'You have clearly come by certain information, sir, and I'm curious as to the source.'

'I have acted for Mrs Barclay in several matters, which require of me the same discretion you see as essential in relation to those who employ you. Suffice to say, I can confirm the vessel taken by John Pearce was no Frenchman. Indeed, I suspect it was a British vessel, one engaged in smuggling.'

'The taking of such vessels is the preserve of the excise.'

'Hardly a preserve, sir, if what I'm telling you is true.'

'And the question of head money?'

'If no sailors came with the capture, who is to say what is the true provenance? And this begs the question, given there had to be a crew, where are they?'

'Which imputes Captain Pearce, and I refer to him in his rank as a Master and Commander, is engaged in matters underhand and perhaps something more sinister.'

'If he is, I see it as my duty to protect him from the consequences.' This got him a very odd look, to which he replied he had his own pressing reasons. 'In order to do so, I am required to communicate with him directly. I need to know the full facts of whatever occurred and the fate of those who crewed the vessel, if possible, down to their names.'

Davidson picked up a small bell and rang it. This occasioned the opening of the door, through which was shown a tall fellow who examined Hodgson, and this immediately riled him, as if he was some kind of felon.

'Mr Hodgson, may I introduce you to Mr Samuel Oliphant.'

The thief-taker had to bite his tongue then, for standing over him and glaring was a fellow he had not seen for years and one he knew as Oliver Winthrop. The temptation to identify him by his true name was strong, but Hodgson had to resist it. Outside personal gratification, it would serve no purpose. He did also note the man was very much more tanned than he recalled, which suggested he had been somewhere warm.

'He may have information germane to your enquiries,' Davidson added.

'Which I would be most anxious to hear.'

'Where did you come across this tale of a false capture,' Oliphant barked, which was marked by the continuing glare.

It was the kind of treatment of which the man in receipt was not, and never had been, about to tolerate. He kept his own tone even and professional.

'May I suggest you sit down, Mr Oliphant.'

The glare evaporated immediately, with Hodgson realising it had been caused partly by fear: By what name would he be addressed? The last time Hodgson had seen him, was ten years past, when he'd been chasing lottery forgers. Not the sixpence and shilling petty thieves who worked the streets. He was in pursuit of those engaged in the kind of countrywide frauds designed to bring in large sums of illicit money.

Thievery of such a magnitude involved people prepared to do anything in order to protect their profits, so it was highly dangerous. It also relied on seemingly respectable individuals who could deal with the sums of money brought in – people who could pass it through a system which rendered any such transaction invisible.

There thus had to be a degree of political protection to deflect the enquiries undertaken by the likes of the man now taking a seat. So, it was perfectly possible the name just employed was his true appellation and the Winthrop identity a previous cover.

'It is in the nature of my trade, sir, of which I assume you've been appraised, to protect any source who provides me with information. Suffice to say, what I have told Mr Davidson is true to the point of being beyond discussion. I also assume he has brought you into the conversation because you have some information which might be relevant.'

'Mr Hodgson,' Davidson said, leaning forward over his desk. 'It must be the case anything said in this room, henceforth, has to be treated in the strictest confidence. I require your commitment to this being so.'

'You have my word and it is one I will keep, as long as silence does not put anyone for whom I am responsible at risk.' He turned to Oliphant, who was now looking slightly smug, which was irritating. It was time to chuck a large rock into his pool of seeming complacency. 'Does the name Tolland mean anything to you?'

'If it did . . . ,' caused no ripples.

'Not a response to get us very far.'

'I'm sure you have facts or are they suppositions, which might take us somewhere.'

The game being played was obvious; tell us what you know and we will either confirm or deny it. Much as he didn't want to take part, he suspected he must, because Davidson had become a bystander. The person he had to deal with now knew how to play this kind of game.

'The vessel is part owned by a Mr Denby Carruthers, who is a member of the City of London Court of Alderman.'

The name got a reaction from Davidson, a sucking in of breath, but a blank from Oliphant cum Winthrop. He looked curious, in the way one does, when what you are hearing makes no sense.

'Part owned?' Davidson enquired, seeking and failing to appear unconcerned.

'The other listed owner is a smuggler called Jaleel Tolland. Now I know you want to play your cards close to your chest, but both men named are capable of extreme violence and quite indiscriminate in its application.'

'Is this Carruthers any relation to the woman so recently murdered?' Oliphant ventured.

'Husband, while Tolland is one of a pair of brothers, whom I'm now convinced killed her on his behalf. Both would have been on board the vessel taken by Pearce and both are nowhere to be found.'

'I think you have nothing which with to concern yourself in that quarter.'

'I fear it is something which requires explanation.'

The slight smile was grating. 'You must take my word.'

'From a man I've only just met?' Hodgson asked.

The sarcasm hit home and the man Davidson called Oliphant clearly saw it as such. He and the prize agent exchanged a glance, one in receipt of a near imperceptible nod, which showed there had been a degree of prior discussion outside this room.

'Lieutenant Pearce gifted them to a fellow captain serving with Admiral Duncan, off the Texel. They will be aboard her or another vessel for the duration of the war.'

'Then it's time I tell you a tale scarcely credible in its idiocy. And at the centre is the very same John Pearce, who it seems to me has just excelled even that level of folly.'

The explanation was the same as the one provided by Emily Barclay and recounted; it sounded even more bizarre than it had when Hodgson was the listener – a plan to steal a cargo in Gravelines, one belonging to a fellow who'd been dunned, leading to a conclusion which beggared belief. He could hardly go on, it sounded so preposterous.

'It is an act which has caused the Tolland brothers to twice attempt to murder Pearce and, while I accept service in the navy comes with risks, I would not be relying on them to remove from this earth men so bent on vengeance.'

'Which you say is misplaced.'

'It is in the eye of the beholder, Mr Davidson, so they see it as just. And, by his subsequent actions, I would say Mr Pearce has done no more than confound his previous folly. If anything, he has increased the risk.'

They looked for further enlightenment but they sought such in vain for, in the scheme of things, it made no difference.

'It is one in which some means must be found to protect him from himself. So, gentlemen, perhaps I should leave you to absorb what you have learned today. I suggest we reconvene at another time to conjure up a solution. I can be found at the White Swan in Clerkenwell.'

'What's in this for you?' was an abrupt question from the present man of mystery.

'Justice, sir, and the need to see certain folk hang for the foul murder of a poor woman, whose only crime was misplaced passion.'

He was damned if he was going to admit that it was also for self-preservation. Everything he'd heard about the follies of John Pearce convinced him it was necessary to act, to avoid ending up in the same boat.

❧

Jaleel Tolland was still groggy when, roughly handled, he was thrown on the back of a cart before being covered with a tarpaulin. The route travelled was rutted to begin with, and increasingly so as they left what had to be the road used by the stage coach. They had moved on to farm tracks, with their 'passenger' wondering into whose hands he'd fallen. The greatest fear was the notion of being handed back to the navy, but there was little comfort in the idea he could be headed for another destination altogether.

Curiosity was heightened when the painful bumping ceased to be replaced by a smooth surface and the sound of wheels on gravel, something which continued for some time. Acute to any other noise, he heard voices, and then no more gravel but a surface still smooth, with a slight echo to the sounds as if he was within some kind of structure. There he lay, listening, hearing nothing for a while, until came the faint sound of what seemed to be several pairs of boots.

'Get him out,' came as a sharp command.

The tarpaulin was pulled away and he was hauled out feet first, with hands laid on to ensure he did not fall head first on to the ground those same mitts getting him upright to hold his arms behind his back. He then faced, when his eyes adjusted to the light of several large wall-mounted lanterns, a fellow dressed as a real gent. His coat of blue satin was worn over a buff waistcoat, holding in a protruding belly. Lowered eyes showed white doeskin breeches and gleaming silver buckled pumps.

'Take the gag off.'

Tolland raised his head to take a proper look at the face of a fellow well past his first youth. There were puffy bags under watery blue eyes and heavy jowls, all topped by a white and freshly pow-dered wig.

'Hold him tight, we have a hard bargain here, right enough. Your name, fellow?'

The voice was deep, but lacking anything approaching a country accent, and, on his breath, the smell was of wine.

'Tolland, Jaleel Tolland.'

'Running for the navy, I daresay you'll claim?'

This Tolland confirmed without adding more. He needed to know who he was dealing with before he would disclose his true purpose. This man had the air of the magistrate about him and, if it was the law, he was doomed.

'I doubt you'll own up to being what you really are, a spy?'

The question threw Tolland, but he was quick to cotton on to the last word and its implications. If they thought him a spy, what would a fellow so engaged be seeking to find out? It had to be something illegal and only one trade sprung to mind. No one who upheld the law would say such a thing.

'It will save you much pain if you're honest, for the men holding you are not of a gentle nature. Tough as you look to be, there is no man born who can withstand their ministrations when in search of the truth. Indeed, I find it impossible to stay and observe when they go about it. Too gory by far, but your true purpose you will admit, this I know for certain.'

'Am I allowed to know who I'm talking with, your honour,' was delivered with what was, for him, a rare grovelling tone.

Being polite seemed to have no effect, the response being a sharp, 'No.'

'Would I then be allowed to enquire, sir, if you've ever been across the water to Gravelines?'

The hand that struck him then, flat but delivered at speed, jerked his head sideways. Tolland rode the blow to face his assailant once more, a man no longer calm. His eyes blazed with anger and the voice reflected how he felt.

'You do not question me, cur. Own to spying and you will die swiftly, without pain. Deny it...'

If he then smiled, it was not with any trace of humour, nor did he feel the need to repeat what was in store. It was chilling enough to make a cast of the dice essential. 'I wondered if I might be fortunate enough to be addressing a fellow in my own trade, your honour.'

The words gave enough of a pause and engendered a degree of curiosity. This allowed Tolland to produce a grin of his own, albeit from a jaw aching from the heavy slap. 'Which be running contraband from the port just mentioned.'

'Condemned out of his own mouth, Baron,' was hissed by one of the men holding his arms.

The eyes flicked to the speaker, clearly unhappy. At what, the use of a title, something which might identify him? Again, being out with the law could be the only objection.

'Dobbin by name and with a horse's brain to match,'

Taking advantage of the distraction, Tolland spoke quickly. 'I am on the run from the navy, right enough, ship named *Director*. But my trade is smugglin' an', if there be any folk hereabouts who have sunk a tankard across yon water in Gravelines, they will know my face.'

'A plea I see as desperate.'

'If it be a lie, I'm a dead man. But I came here as a pressed man seeking succour.'

'Succour indeed?'

'To get back to my own hearth. Then I need to deal with the bugger who stole my ship and cargo, afore handing me over to the navy.' The man was curious enough, even if he was sneering, to leave space to add more. 'I work out of Beltinge on the south Thames shore, an' there's a name to me that might ring a bell or two.'

'I sense a quicksilver tongue.'

'An' I sense a man I might call a comrade, if I was to speak above my station.'

The countenance was bland again. 'Keep talking.'

Which Tolland did, even naming John Pearce as the navy bastard who'd caught him and stolen his ship. He left out their previous run-ins, for he needed his tale to be sharp, not a meander. He regaled the tricks employed to disguise the name of his vessel and admitted to his lack of an identifying flag, as well as the attempt to run, which failed.

'Common practice. I reckon you'd agree when on the French side of the water.'

'Why would the navy bother with the likes of what you describe?'

'I had doings with the Pearce sod afore. Reckon he saw me on deck and came after me personal. Nabbed me an' every man jack of my crew, including my dear brother. He then set us aboard a seventy-four blockading the Dutch coast. The bastard sailed away with my ship, crewed by his men, for only God knows where, but I reckon to line his own pocket.'

'A fine tale, fellow.'

'But a true one. Your lads may do their worst, but they get out of me only what I's said right now. Question is, do you want to do in one who might share the trade?'

'A conclusion you have arrived at without a shred of evidence.'

'You feart a spy. If I is right, then it can only be the excise to give concern.'

'And what would such creatures do, but fit up a man sent to spy with a fine tale, just like the one you claim to be true and one I take leave to doubt.'

'I drank with my lads in a tavern called the Auberge du Citadel, to give it it's French name. An' I reckon men from this part of the world might have done so too.'

This got a head shake from he who was high and mighty. 'What if you're a smuggler who's been taken up by the excise, who say to you, freedom is yours if you work for us. If you are as you say, you know who else plies the trade from ports such as Gravelines. So perhaps we are not the first to face your betrayal.'

If the words were delivered with no empathy, they were enough to tell Tolland he had the right of his previous assumption. But how to get this gent to believe him? It was in thinking of the nature of the fellow questioning him that set his mind in the right direction. This silk clad inquisitor was not of the type to soil his hands with the act of running contraband, so what was his role? In a previous bind, again brought about by John Pearce, one man had got him and his brother Franklin out of a hole. If it was a desperate throw, it was time to use the same ploy now.

'I have a partner to vouch for me.'

'If such a fool exists, he shows an excessive want of good sense.'

'He's a man of your stamp, your honour, I would hazard, a member of the London Council of Alderman, whose name you can check.'

This produced a sneer. 'I cannot believe a man of such stature would have dealing with the likes of you, who stinks of bilge water.'

'I will name him, even if it comes as a risk.'

His Lordship was intrigued enough to say. 'Go on.'

'Denby Carruthers.'

Even if he tried to hide it, the name registered, evidenced by a flicker of the eyelashes, followed by a slightly more pensive expression, before he looked away. 'If I would put you to the hot irons, I can only think a man of such standing would visit upon you a much worse fate.'

'A letter by Post Chaise can be in London and back afore much more than a whole day is gone. I beg you try it and I know, with my name affixed, Carruthers will pay for the delivery.'

The wait for a response was long and the expression unchanging, like a fellow at a card table with a good hand. 'Gag him and tie him to the cart.'

The instruction was obeyed swiftly. Tolland left with a rope round his neck, which was then lashed to a spoke on the wheel. But at least he had a brief sight of his surroundings, a large barn with stables at one end and vaguely illuminated by dim lanterns. The sight of a coach, its paintwork shining and reflecting the light spoke of prosperity.

'You will not speak or try to free yourself,' the silk-coated gent said. 'Shout and you will spook the horse, still in the shafts and the result will be the same. You will so tighten the rope it will strangle you.'

With a nod to the other pair, he moved away, to then convene with them and talk in soft voices Tolland could not overhear. Whatever was agreed was soon arrived at, one of his captors left behind to watch him, the gent and the one he reckoned called Dobbin departing.

'A drink would not go amiss, friend,' he called to one left behind. 'Ain't wet my lips since I made the graveyard.'

'Why, I'll nip to the nearest tavern and fetch you a jug of ale.'

'Water will suffice, which I take leave to suppose you have for the horses.'

'Creatures who rank higher than you right now.'

'It would be an act of mercy.'

'Then you've aimed your prayers wrong.'

'I was thinking, happen you have been to Gravelines.'

'Stop talking, or I'll haul on yon rope and finish you right off.'

'They know how to brew good ale, do Flanders folk, an' the ladies are right obliging. Something to hanker after I'd say.'

As an attempt to get some information, it was one doomed to fail. When he opened his mouth to keep trying, a club was produced. His goaler made a move towards him with the clear intent to employ it when a voice, rough and country, from a person not visible in the arc of the lanterns, stopped him.

'Back off, Nipper, I need a clear sight.'

There was no need to ask Tolland to look in his direction; to do so was instinctive but all he could see was a vague, featureless outline. In the silence to follow, Tolland held his desire to know who it was for as long as he could, until he found it impossible to not speak.

'I would ask you to step forward, friend. Don't seem fair, you clockin' me, when I can't see you.'

The response was the opposite. The shape faded from sight, to be replaced by another, again observing him in silence before disappearing, Dobbin emerging from the gloom.

'Happen you have said your name true.' Tolland's heart surged. 'Which don't mean you ain't what's suspected. Nipper, get the horse out the shafts and see it to a stall.'

'An' him?'

'We're to sling him in another, but tied up. And we're to feed the bugger, which is a waste, I say.'

CHAPTER ELEVEN

Davidson and Oliphant had talked long into the night after Walter Hodgson departed. This was hardly surprising as the news of the capture of the *Santa Leocadia* and its cargo were included in the discussion. Every time they sought to talk about what had happened in the North Sea or the inanity in Gravelines, the subject of the Spanish cargo was too tempting to avoid.

If the three separate tales were conflated, it sounded like it could be a litany of folly, though Oliphant could at least reassure Davidson of one fact: Henry Dundas had taken the recent one well. Indeed, his eye had lit up at the quantity of silver mentioned, but he was adamant that he wished the news to be kept confidential.

'Dundas told me the country is almost bereft of specie – no silver and even less gold. Too much has gone to our allies, who seem to be making a poor fist of its use. The French are trouncing us everywhere on land.'

'Hardly a secret, Oliphant. I myself have been putting a wee bit of coin aside.' Davidson added a sly look. 'According to rumour, a run on the bank is not out of the question.'

'So, the government, I suspect, will be grateful for such a cargo.'

Davidson knew what he was driving at; a quick decision by the Prize Court was possible, followed by a payout of a large portion of the sum in reward.

'I find it best not to get my hopes up, sir, and I say so from experience. The case I told our recent visitor of when he first entered my chambers concerns the late Captain Barclay. It has been three years under consideration and concerns a merchantman he took off the coast of Brittany in early '73, when the war was scarce weeks old. Now it is resolved in his favour or should I say that of his widow.'

Davidson paused before adding, 'It may interest you to know, one of the beneficiaries will be a certain unrated seaman called John Pearce, who is entitled to the princely sum of one pound, seven shillings and four pence.'

'It won't take that long surely?'

'The Gibraltar Prize Court is no more noted for haste than any other, and I must employ a deputy to act in the matter. This will lead to a great deal of correspondence which, of necessity, takes up time.'

'For such a sum, would it not be worthwhile to take up residence there?'

'No sir, not even for such a level of commission as you imply.' Seeing the look this produced, Davidson added, 'As any advocate will tell you, nothing is certain in law.'

Blissfully unaware matters may be unravelling at home, John Pearce was enjoying himself, albeit with the certain knowledge it was unlikely to last. Reckoned by Mr Williams to be a full day's sailing from Corsica, he was coming into the orbit of Sir John Jervis, so a warm welcome was not to be expected. But Pearce hoped the news he was bringing, added to his pennant, might protect him from much of the admiral's malice.

Time since Minorca had been spent in constant training, something his Quota Men, in the cold northern waters, had resented. But sunshine, blue sea and growing competence now had them, apart from a few diehards, coming to his orders with cheerful willingness. They sought, at every attempt, to improve the time taken for any action, most importantly in the article of gunnery, the time taken to run out and load the cannon from first order to completion. It was now closer to respectable.

Likewise, with Mr Moberly now fully recovered, boarding practice, which was always an activity to produce a degree of mayhem, was now not an occasion for moaning; it was full of laughter when something went awry. The crew had jelled well so there was now no way of telling one batch from another – this being the way of maritime existence. It was a life in which men moved from ship to ship and had to find their feet in a new setting. Pearce was certain there would be disputes, there always were, until the hierarchy and close companionships had been forged, but none to affect the running of the ship, which was his major concern.

It was time, he thought, for one more convivial dinner before the circumstances of everyone would change. There might be limits to what Jervis could inflict on HMS *Hazard*, but he was not a man known for constraint. So, Pearce had everyone crowd into his cabin despite the lack of space, officers and mids, for a hugger-mugger meal, leaving Mr Williams to con the ship. Well-wined himself, when looking around the red faces of his hot and equally imbibing guests, there was only one place he thought he could be more content – one several hundreds of miles in his wake.

He happily recalled, as the conversation flowed, the times Emily had sailed with him, first running from her husband and subsequently as a not-always-willing passenger. This led him to contemplate how matters would change when he made a happy return. Thanks to the Spanish silver, he would be a wealthy man and in no need of any assistance from what had been left to her by Ralph Barclay. It was an inheritance she was keen they should share, while he was adamant he wanted not a penny from the money left by a man he had loathed.

By the time he got home, her period of respectable widowhood, which he'd never understood as important, would be over, while his stature would be high. Thus, quick nuptials would be seen by society as a wise move on her part. She would be catching possibly London's most eligible bachelor before he fell under the spell of some other fortune-hunting female. Then he could set about a formal adoption of his son Adam, which would bring on a much-desired change of surname.

'I think, sir, Mr Livingston would be better off in his hammock.'

Dragged from his thoughts by Worricker, Pearce looked down the board to see the lad canted over, his head resting on the chest of Campbell, his fellow midshipman. He did not look to be in a much better state, which engendered much amusement from their seniors. Tennant, who was abstemious, as befitted a son of the kirk, was trying to be as cheerful as the company demanded, but there was too much of his parent for him to fully relax. Only Maclehose, and it was ever him who led the way, seemed able to fully participate in both drink and jollity.

'Mr Tennant,' Pearce called, 'I think it would be of benefit to call upon a couple of hands to aid Mr Livingston.'

Picking up the implication, the lad replied, 'I will happily see to his needs myself, sir.'

'You will require assistance, Sandy,' Maclehose cried, 'he looks comatose from where I'm sitting.'

'Send for O'Hagan,' Pearce suggested, 'he can carry the boy in one arm and, if need be, Mr Campbell under the other.'

'Aye, aye sir,' Tennant replied.

'And,' his captain added, seeing he'd missed the jest and remained unamused, 'if you feel the need to retire, you may do so.'

The exchange brought home to John Pearce certain responsibilities he had hitherto been able to ignore. Coming into the orbit of a fleet commander, this would alter. He wondered about Maclehose being set for an examination, to assess his suitability to be promoted to lieutenant. The youngster had shown great aptitude in every task he had been given and, while it might be premature, he should be aware it was possible, which would bend his mind to serious and bookish study.

The other person who might qualify, and would no doubt sail through an examination, was Frank Macklin. The problem being it was not his real name, while his present rating on the muster as

Master's Mate would not serve. As a sailor and leader, as well as a fellow who fitted in, he was every bit as competent as both Hallowell and Worricker. So much so, it was hard to recall a time when he had not been present and part of *Hazard's* crew. Despite his rating on the muster, he held the position of acting lieutenant, and it was time he had it confirmed.

It was the next morning before he could act upon such a thought and, in calling Macklin to attend upon him, he wondered how to propose the nature of his thinking. The man's real name was Deacon and in that there would be a background. A place of birth, parents, the wife he's admitted to on an offshore Irish island – none of which applied to his present designation. This was laid out after he assured Macklin it was to be a talk between equals, as well as his thinking on the matter, followed by the way he took on the conversation.

'It seems to me you must create a story of a life you have not lived.'

'Living the lie has not been hard aboard *Hazard* captain, but it might be difficult to sustain in another setting.'

'Which is why it must be well rehearsed in advance. I suggest it only as a cover for the questions that are bound to be asked. I also suggest it is best to stick as close to the true facts as are commensurate with the needs of the questions you will face . It is telling, even I know nothing of your past, for the very good reason you refuse to disclose it.'

'The reasons are sound,' was a response robustly delivered.

'Do you desire to leave all of your previous life behind?'

'Easy to say out here in the Mediterranean.'

'But not so easy in cooler climes, like the coastal waters off southern Ireland?'

There was no need for Macklin to admit that his name and face were known in places where lawbreaking had occurred; this had already been established by his previous silence. Pearce was left wondering, and not for the first time, at the depth of the wrong-doing. He was forced to conclude it must be serious, which made questionable what he was suggesting.

'You may have heard something of my previous life.'

'I know the name and nature of your sire, sir, having read his tracts on the plight of the poor.'

'Do you know we both ended up incarcerated for the contents.'

'Hinted at, I would admit to.'

More than just hints, Pearce reckoned. Ships were hotbeds of gossip and even more a source of rumour, which extended to the utterly fanciful, outdone only by superstition. Macklin would no more admit to what he'd heard about his captain than reveal any more about himself, which was to be admired rather than con-demned. The man was honourable, which had been proved in the way he had stood by the men with whom he'd come aboard, if you excused one outright rogue.

'Those in power called it sedition.'

'Those with much to lose would.'

'Prison is a sobering experience,' Pearce murmured, wondering, as he said it, if he was talking to a man who knew very well this was true. Indeed, there was an element of fishing in the remark. 'To say it alters a man's view on his fellow humans comes as an understatement.'

The pause for a telling response was wasted. As usual, when Macklin had no desire to reveal even his thinking, Pearce was met with a bland and non-committal expression. It was one which ensured nothing was given away.

'I state my opinion that you would make a good naval officer.' Did Macklin get the reason for the slight smile? Would he smoke John Pearce was far from sure the same could be applied to him? 'I blame myself for the lack of time you will be afforded to consider it, since we will be with the fleet shortly.'

'Next watch, I would say.'

'But I will tell you this. Out here, there is always a shortage of officers; indeed, it is often starved of seamen of all grades. Therefore, it is incumbent upon all captains to look for those who may warrant elevation. I cannot say for certain this will apply to you, but all I will tell you is you have an opportunity in the Mediterranean, which would not exist in home waters. I leave it to you to decide if you wish to take it.'

'Whatever I decide, sir, I thank you for your consideration.'

The change of expression, from cold to genuine gratitude, embarrassed John Pearce; this covered by a command to send to him Midshipman Maclehose, who would be a much easier prospect with whom to deal.

He was on deck from the moment the lookouts sighted Punta Mignola on the north coast of the island. The hours between this and the opening of the Bay of San Fiorenzo were spent making an already shipshape vessel so spick, you could eat off the planking. Jervis was a stickler for the cleanliness of every vessel within his command, a fact known to Pearce. This had him wonder how many captains, or even admirals, joining from home and content with common standards, had sailed into a proper roasting.

So, a cradle had been put over the side so the scantlings could be given a coat of paint. One of his Quota Men, who'd been a limner – as well as a drunkard he admitted – in life, was tasked with prettifying the figurehead. Others had hauled out canvas which was yet to be exposed to wind and weather, striking down that which had long lost its pristine whiteness, to become dun-coloured through exposure.

So, by the time the masts of the anchored fleet came into view, HMS *Hazard* was looking at her best and so was every officer on deck. All were sure there would be a telescope trained on them from the moment it was close enough to reveal anything. It may not be the man himself, but Jervis would have subordinates who knew and agreed with his ways. Hallowell was looking for HMS *Courageux*, captained by his Uncle Ben, a vessel he would want to visit once Pearce had seen Jervis.

'The admiral will wonder at our purpose, sir, will he not?'

His premier was merely referring to a query already proposed by him, that it would be a good idea to raise such a message, given that they were indeed bringing information.

'Undoubtedly, Mr Hallowell, and I for one revel in the notion of his ignorance. Let our pennant suffice to keep him wondering.'

Any vessel of *Hazard*'s size, joining a fleet, would normally be carrying despatches, so would fly a flag to say so. But John Pearce's information, being verbal, required no such forewarning. Hallowell's point had been denied for a very good reason by the man who would be called aboard HMS *Victory* to report. Anything which might wrong-foot Jervis, even slightly, was to the good, while it was also necessary to establish that he enjoyed a degree of independence.

Examination was a two-way affair, and Pearce was not the only one taken with the state of the line-of-battleships. They had been out here for a long time, and it showed in both the caked nature of the paint on their planking, which boded ill for the state of the decks and masts, while clewed-up sails would hide their worn condition.

'Flagship has made our number, sir. Captain repair aboard.'

'I'm surprised they could dig it out,' was Pearce's acid response.

But there it would be in the list of His Majesty's Ships and Vessels with annual supplements. He'd known this was coming for a long time, and nothing had convinced him it was something to be looked forward to. The man he was about to face had sent him home from this very station the year before, he suspected, with a message, one which said he should not be employed in any capacity by the King's Navy. Jervis had reckoned without Henry Dundas and his power as Minister for War, so he was in for a shock.

He heard Hallowell order his boat and crew to be made ready, in his mind rehearsing the words he would use to put Jervis in his place. But, by the time he was in it and being rowed towards the flagship, such thoughts had been put aside. With a face familiar to many on the ships which had been out here for years, Jervis would surely know by now who was coming. He had his men and ship to consider, so indulging in a personal vendetta was unwise. Best be courteous.

This was an attitude which was adopted on coming aboard, to be greeted by the premier with all the ceremony afforded to a captain. The squeal of the bosun's whistle, a small file of smart marines he was obliged to inspect, while complimenting their officer on their dress and deportment. Then he was led towards the admiral's cabin, only to find, in the outer part and waiting for him, the Captain of the Fleet.

'Calder,' was imparted brusquely, his rank and position added. 'I am charged to enquire what is your business?'

This was an unusual greeting in more than one respect. The lack of civility was no surprise, but not to see the C-in-C in such a situation was surely deliberate and intended as a snub. It was a message to say, for Jervis to engage with him personally was beneath his dignity.

'You will have seen my pennant, sir.'

'I have.'

'And so, I assume, has Admiral Jervis.'

'Which is no concern of yours.'

It took an effort, with his temper rising, for Pearce to keep his anger in check, but he wasn't having it. 'He does not fear, by being impolite to me, he is insulting their Lordships of the Admiralty?'

'You board a vessel where no such insult is present.'

'Then please tell Admiral Jervis I demand to see him personally.'

'Demand, sir! It would serve you well to recall your rank.'

'While it would serve the admiral well to reflect, if I carry no despatches, but fly such a pennant, there has to be a reason. I have for him a verbal message, and it is for his ears only. What he then does with it is his business.'

'Your tone is offensive.'

'Who's blacking the pot and who the kettle?'

'I ask again what is your reason for being here?'

'I repeat, I have a verbal message for him, from the Minster for War, which I will deliver and not through an intermediary, however elevated such a person sees himself. It is one in which I would posit the safety of the entire fleet is at stake.'

'What nonsense is this!'

There was no need for Pearce to turn to face the voice in order to recognise the speaker. In its harsh tone and barking delivery, it was one he knew only too well.

'Do I detect someone's been listening at the door.'

'Damn you, sir.'

'Something you have done already, Sir John, which is why I did not anticipate a warm welcome.'

'You're about as welcome as a turd in my soup.'

'Elegantly put,' was Pearce's reply when he turned to face Jervis, 'but then you always did have a gift for a turn of phrase.'

The sarcasm clearly went right over the older man's head, not difficult given he was a good six inches shorter than the source of delivery. Jervis had a face to match his irascible nature, one which lent itself to annoyance, with its pointed nose, ruddy cheeks and the mouth of a pinchpenny.

'Your problem is, Sir John, I am the bearer of information which you are going to be obliged to listen to.'

'You dare command me?'

'Perhaps advise would serve better and it is something, since you will know with your eavesdropping, I will only impart in private.'

'Strikes me, Calder, the people running the navy have lost their wits, in giving this degenerate a ship. A berth in the bilge of a prison hulk would serve him better.'

'It hurts me to say so, Sir John, but he has mentioned whom the message is from and it is a name to demand attention.'

'From thief-takers, perhaps. When it comes to corruption, Dundas has no rivals.'

'An opinion I will take comfort in delivering to him when we next meet.'

'The man is in no doubt of my low estimation, so feel free. But you will speak not only to me but to Captain Calder, to whom I would, in any case, pass on what you have to say.'

'Then I suggest the inner sanctum.'

'Here will suffice.'

'Then the marine sentry should be sent away to a place where he cannot hear.'

Jervis, after a pause, consented with a nod. He knew what Pearce said would be all over the ship in an hour if he stayed, so they waited till he'd gone.

'Well, what is this vital information?'

Given it really made no difference to him, Pearce obliged, relating his tale to an initially sceptical pair, showing an air of disbelief which faded as he added telling details of how and why he and Langholm have come to the decision to intercept the Spaniard. Eyebrows twitched at the mention of the cargo of silver, but it seemed both men were seemingly determined to avoid any obvious reaction which might hint at either praise or envy.

The supporting rumours circulating in Gibraltar, added to Sir David Rose's intelligence about Spanish fleet movements, struck a deep chord, the whole adding up to a pressing problem. The fact the Spaniards intended to declare war on Britannia and would, if they decided to strike, do so at a time of their own choosing.

'If I may be allowed to advance an opinion, and it is one backed up by Sir David Rose, the action of Lord Langholm and myself in interdicting said cargo has imposed a delay on the plans of Chief Minister Godoy, but it is no more than that.'

The statement got him a jaundiced look, but it was also clear Jervis was rendered concerned, much as he tried to hide it. For all the support he enjoyed at home, such would evaporate in a blink if he lost a fleet. Pearce wondered if the spectre of Byng troubled even an admiral as highly regarded as he. If it did, he was not alone; every senior officer in the service feared the disgrace of being shot by a firing squad on their own quarterdeck, for no other reason than to avoid embarrassment for a government needing a scapegoat.

'Calder,' he growled, indicating his inner cabin and to Pearce, 'You, wait here.'

'I would prefer to do so aboard my own ship.'

Jervis lost it then, his face becoming so suffused with blood he looked to risk an apoplexy, while his verbal response could be heard at the masthead. 'Damn you, sir, do as I say! As for your ship, the command hangs by a thread, so learn to mind your manners.'

'My pennant. . . '

'Can be cut down if I so will it. And don't think I fear Whitehall, which is a thousand miles away and powerless.'

He was gone before Pearce could reply, to be left with a glare from Calder, just before he too entered the inner cabin, the door firmly shut.

CHAPTER TWELVE

John Pearce felt slightly foolish looking at the closed door, while wondering what he and Calder were discussing. There was frustration at not knowing the situation of a fleet he'd only just joined, while wondering how it would be affected by the news he'd brought. Also, was the warning just issued timely or something to merely be taken into consideration? Having stood like this for several minutes, he decided whatever Jervis ordered he would move, but reckoned it wiser to stay aboard *Victory*.

The remark about his pennant being at the admiral's discretion had struck home, reminding him of how much he valued the independence it provided, something he would miss. Also, if Jervis could remove such a flag, could he also remove him from command, with no one having the authority to countermand such an order?

More worrying was the fact that he could carry out a repeat of his previous manoeuvre and send him home, possibly again on a transport. It was not a welcome prospect because, as a voyage, with the Spanish looking to become enemies, it had become ten times riskier, and this was not the worst the man could do.

As he made his way out to fresh air and the quarterdeck, some very unpleasant scenarios played out in his imagination: the scary notion of him being stuck with some hard horse commanding officer, aboard a seventy-four and at the bottom of the pecking order. Given the time served, this could probably make him the most junior lieutenant in a wardroom unlikely to be overly friendly.

As a fate, it was something he'd managed to avoid since his promotion and it was a prospect he dreaded, especially if he was exposed to malice and condescension by his peers.

Pearce knew he would not be able to stand it and, with his temper, it would probably end in him either challenging a fellow officer to a duel or chucking in his commission. If that was not a vision to bring joy, what would it mean for his Pelicans?

They would survive, because they were the sort to do so, but he would have broken, for him, a pledge. It was one never stated to Michael, Charlie and Rufus, but a bond he held to with real conviction, to always be there to protect them from the worst the navy could do. It was to save him from his own folly they'd ended up as volunteers. And this was after he'd got them the freedom from being pressed seamen provided by exemption certificates.

Of course, Emily would be pleased and perhaps, with what he and Langholm had taken out of the *Santa Leocadia*, he would have the means to buy them out of the service. With the last thought filling his mind, he found he could smile at the Officer of the Watch. He then informed him, if the admiral wished his presence, he was aboard and would respond as soon as his attendance was required.

Having checked there was little chance of the *Victory*'s captain using the windward side of the deck, he made his way there to look over the assembled ships, an inspection which drove home the sorry state most were in, and this was obvious even at a distance. Closer inspection would, he knew, reveal much worse: repairs to bulwarks, wounded masts and frayed rigging, for practically every vessel had suffered battle damage.

Added to this the Mediterranean was not a benign sea, but prone to tempests which put huge strain on the very construction of a wooden ship of war, so scantlings would spring leaks, while various timbers would seek to part from those to which they were joined.

Then there was rot, playing on the very material in which Britannia professed so much pride.

An amusing thought occurred to Pearce, words he mentally put in the mouth of his late father. The Wooden Walls of Old England were like the nation itself, impressive at a distance but, when closely examined, riddled with the smell of rot and in a state of corruption.

⁓

Inside the great cabin, the conversation was about to move on from the news Pearce had brought to the man himself. The previous talk had come to the conclusion, if the Dons were set to desert the coalition, but had made no move to do so, no immediate action was required, and Jervis would ensure they were prevented from joining up with the French warships at present locked up in Toulon. He still felt able to defeat any single fleet he met in open battle, while acknowledging, if he was not reinforced, it was a situation which could only deteriorate.

The real worry he had was not nautical; it was the continued success, on land, of the French General Bonaparte. He had taken most of Lombardy and knocked Piedmont out of the war, to then become engaged in a seemingly endless series of battles with the Austrians. Now, as far as Jervis knew, their main forces were locked up in the fortress of Mantua, south of the Tyrol, and awaiting relief.

The French then moved south to threaten the Grand Duchy of Tuscany, in particular Leghorn. The port, Livorno to the Italians, had been the main source of revictualing for the fleet. It also served as a city in which both officers and trusted members of his crews could relieve the boredom of tedious blockade. This entailed, if the French did not venture out to sea, being at anchor in San Fiorenzo Bay.

There had also been a thriving, if small, English community ever ready to entertain them in their homes, as well as at arranged entertainments. Such pleasures were now denied to them, for the enemy struck in a lightning advance. It was only by luck Captain Freemantle had got away with people who were now refugees, some in no more than the clothes on their backs. There were now families and officials accommodated on various vessels throughout the fleet.

It was the task of the frigates of the Inshore Squadron to warn of the need to weigh for a contest, which would only be necessary if the French sailed out of Toulon. They had done so before, only to scuttle back home and, if they could, avoid a fight. In this they'd been unsuccessful, but they had never been brought to a battle which would be conclusive, so remained a threat requiring to be contained.

Bonaparte, so much of a nobody a couple of years previously, seemed unstoppable in two things: in his conquest of Europe's richest provinces and cities as well as in his ability to plunder the stupendous wealth they had accrued over centuries. He had taken gold and treasures from the northern Austrian provinces, even more from the Papal States: How much money and precious objects had the Pope surrendered to keep him out of Rome?

This was not the real concern. The loss of Leghorn left the Mediterranean fleet dependant on Genoa for supplies and, as a source of such, given their leanings towards, or fear of the French and Revolution, they had never truly been reliable. Their claim to be neutral was a fig leaf in which they sought to appease the French who maintained a diplomatic mission in the city.

This official did everything he could to impede supplies of fresh meat, fruit and vegetables to Jervis's fleet, so the men were not confined to the kind of diet which rendered them costive. The port was even open to their warships and Nelson had, on more than one occasion, proposed cutting out any frigate found in the harbour, only to have it denied to him by whichever admiral was in command.

'I'm surprised you didn't react to his tale of the Spanish silver, Calder. It sounds like the sod has got his hands on a fortune to match the one taken out of *Hermione*.'

'A name which has dogged me since I was midshipman, sir, and frankly I'm sick of having to relate how much money I was paid when she was taken and how it came about.'

'A tidy sum, I recall.'

As an invitation, it was one for Calder to avoid, which had him change the subject, a fact not lost on his superior.

'Pearce, sir.'

'What the devil was Dundas thinking of, giving such a man a ship. And what dolts at the Admiralty agreed to it.'

There was a sigh in the delivery, for Jervis was ever damning the politicians at home, while never acknowledging he was as political as they. As a member of parliament, he'd supported Pitt and still continued to do so, through the long Regency crisis, though he had ploughed a different furrow on other matters. As he liked to say, and repeatedly so, he was, in that bearpit, his own man.

'We can only suspect Dundas had sound reasons, sir, and their Lordships declined to challenge them.'

This attempt at tact was wasted, allowing Jervis to exercise his bile. Not short on a naturally high colour, this was enough to turn what was rouge to something akin to scarlet, while his energetic cursing was wont to add a degree of spittle to the occasion.

'He's the worst of your race, Calder. There's nothing so deceitful as a Scots lawyer, and Dundas raises the chicanery to a higher bar than any man I know. His finger is in every pie, and he is forever pulling out the plums for his own pocket. I'm sure he deliberately gets Billy Pitt sozzled so he can exercise his wiles. The pair rarely turn up in the house before they've sunk four bottles.'

Jervis did not see any hypocrisy in then picking up a goblet of wine and draining it, before pushing it towards his Captain of the

Fleet for a refill. If Calder too was a Scotsman, there was no trace of a revealing accent in his gentle remonstrance, he having been raised and educated in Kent.

'It would be a bad idea to upset him, sir.'

'Damn me, I'd keelhaul him if I could.'

For all the response, Jervis knew what Calder was hinting at. They had no way of knowing the reasons why the Minister of War had seen fit to gift Pearce a ship, especially a flyer like the class of brig in which he'd arrived. It hinted at deep waters in which it was dangerous to fish, for the power the man wielded could not be in doubt. Dundas controlled the entire block of Scottish votes in parliament, at a time when the Tory faction and Billy Pitt's majority was a slim one. Indeed, it was also dependant on the support of a body of Whigs led by the Duke of Portland.

These were two groups who could not be ignored when it came to handing out important commands, like who was given the major battle fleets in the Channel and the Mediterranean. The Sea Lords would seek the best man for the task but, always in need of money for an ever-expanding number of ships, they would temper their choices. It was wise to keep one eye on the naval estimates coming before parliament.

The most egregious example of a political choice had been Hotham, the man who'd preceded Jervis, as he in turn had succeeded Lord Hood. A competent fleet commander, Hood too was a political appointee, who'd been sacrificed to meet the wishes of Hotham's partisan, the Duke of Portland. These two men had no need to discuss the dangers of upsetting apple carts in Whitehall.

'It might be best just to send Pearce home with your next despatches, which would acknowledge you have received the intelligence he fetched out. If he's potential trouble, it would be the safest way to deal with him.'

'No.' Another swig emptied his goblet, this carried out with a degree of defiance, almost childish in its expression. 'The good of the navy does not permit of such a course and the first thing to go will be that damned pennant. If it came through the manoeuvring of Dundas, the sod has no right to it. I've damn good mind to disrate him and put the bugger before the mast, never mind remove him from his command?'

'There is a double risk in taking either away.'

'The king?'

'His Majesty might struggle with his wits, sir, but as of what we last heard, he has long periods of lucidity. Since he personally promoted Pearce to lieutenant. . . '

'I know, Calder, I know. But it offends me and anyone with a belief in the service. There's a proper way to the quarterdeck, and it has been flouted. It must be made plain no favour can be shown to anyone who circumvents the proper path of promotion.'

'At the risk of increasing your ire, sir, I have to point out, Pearce has enjoyed some telling successes in this very theatre under both your predecessors. It's the cause, I know, of jealousy in many a wardroom if his name comes up. Lord Hood seemed to favour him and even Hotham gifted him chances to distinguish himself, though it's rumoured he loathed his very name.'

'Opportunities which could just as easily have fallen to a more deserving officer.'

'Given what he has told us about his latest escapade, it will raise the level of the particular vice just mentioned to new levels, and I speak from experience. Folk may slap your back and heartily congratulate you for a prize money windfall, as they did to me. But I reckon half would just as soon have stabbed me out of envy. I would also counsel that a man so well rewarded, as he will be, becomes a different kettle of fish to a relatively impecunious officer.'

'You're not seriously suggesting I should worry on such an account.'

'Sir, I am saying it is unwise to risk it becoming a concern.'

'I won't send him home, and I'm going to have his damned pennant regardless of what you might say. His flying it is a travesty and, while he has it, he can cock a snook at me and I won't have it.'

The last part of the sentence saw the table slammed and the goblet, thankfully once more emptied, nearly go overboard, which was only prevented by a quick grab from Calder.

'You intend to put him under your command?'

'I do.'

'Then we must find a way to employ him.'

'Whatever you think of, make sure it's perilous in the extreme. Let's see if the damned good fortune you mention is due to run out.'

'Are you suggesting I deliberately put him in harm's way, sir?

'Of course not,' came with as much sincerity as Jervis could muster, which was not a great deal.

—————

'My pennant was granted by the Admiralty; Captain Calder and the admiral does not have the right to deprive me of it.'

'A case to be made in London, not out here. Take my advice, Lieutenant Pearce, and accept what cannot be gainsaid. If you continue to refuse, he will send a company of marines to strip both you and your crew out of the ship. Then, where you and they will go is in the lap of the gods?'

The demand had been made with none of the Jervis ire, indeed Calder had been polite, acting as the reluctant bearer of bad news. There was no way of knowing if this was genuine or whether he was dealing with an accomplished dissembler, but the threat was telling. Applied to him alone, he would have refused. But the old sod would love nothing more than to break up his crew and distribute them round the fleet, thus enhancing his reputation as a martinet.

'I am bound to ask what then happens?'

'You will come under the command of Sir John, and he will direct you to where you can be of most use.'

'Not a prospect in which I place much faith.'

'Which I would take as ingratitude, given I had to argue hard and long to get this.'

This got Calder a keen look. 'Why?'

'The job of an executive officer is sometimes to protect his C-in-C from himself, Mr Pearce and you may take what I say as a confidence. Repeat it, and I will see you back before the mast and you may bleat till the cows come home, but it will be so.'

The hint of anger only came at the end of the response, but the scowl accompanying it said more than the words.

'Your first task will be to carry despatches to Commodore Nelson, who is cruising off the coast of Genoa and Savoy, seeking to keep the French out of their ports. We need to find out if he's making any progress in slowing supplies to the Bonaparte menace. Now go back aboard *Hazard*, take down the damned pennant and replace with the flag of an Admiral of the White. I will send over your orders presently and you will weigh immediately.'

The crossing to *Hazard* was not of long duration, but it did provide time for John Pearce to consider an alternative course. If he was being sent away, what was to stop him, once out of sight of HMS *Victory*, replacing his pennant and sailing due east? It was a tempting prospect, a spit in the eye to Jervis, which did not last to the point where the bosun's whistle blew to welcome him back on board.

Regardless of the consequences for him, such an act would impact on those he commanded, putting them, in naval terms, beyond the pale. Hallowell and Worricker were committed to the navy, and he doubted any sum of prize money would serve to alter this. Perhaps Macklin would be too if he could wipe the facts of his past. The four mids he'd been gifted by Dundas would be even more desirous of the same, given they would not be in receipt of reward enough to make abandonment of the service worthwhile.

There was also the chance such an act would be seen as unlawful, at least in the eyes of the navy, more likely to back Jervis than the reprobate who'd disobeyed him. Would this impact on his warrants too? They were men seeking to make their way in the service, no doubt dreaming of life in a ship-of-the-line instead of a brig. What about the crew, not least his Pelicans? Any amount of retribution would be visited upon them. In obeying him, could they even stand accused of mutiny?

When it came to a life eased by a large amount of money, Pearce knew the same applied to him as it did to his officers. In his various envisioned future scenarios, the life of a country gentleman had not figured at all. He would say yes to a fine house and all the accoutrements which went with it. But it still smacked of stagnation, the very thing he had been determined to avoid even before the capture of the Spaniard.

It was, and still would be, the main bone of contention between him and Emily, she being one to favour domestic bliss over his need for a degree of excitement. And how could it be otherwise? His life had always been peripatetic, as his father took him, a boy growing into a youth, all over the country. He travelled the roads in old Adam's company, as he preached his radical alternative to the present state of grinding poverty for the majority of his fellow citizens.

If he craved a family and a place called home, something he'd never had in his life, at least beyond the point of his mother dying, which he could scarce remember, then it was not something to which he wanted to be tied. Pearce was honest enough to admit to the fraudulence of such a position, the sheer selfishness which had him put his desires ahead of those of the woman he loved.

'Welcome aboard, sir,' came from a premier who could not hide his curiosity.

'Mr Hallowell, strike our pennant and replace it with the flag of Admiral Jervis. We are about to be in receipt of orders so I fear you will have to put aside your desire to call upon your uncle for the moment.'

They all stiffened except Moberly, already at attention before his marines, all of them, no doubt, wondering what this portended. Pearce, still in the depth of ruminations on his and their future, did not want to talk about it, at least not to the whole assembled crew.

'I'll be in my cabin, but I wish you to make preparations to weigh so we can do so as soon as our orders come from the flagship.'

'Aye, aye, sir,' was put forward in expectation of an explanation.

None was forthcoming; all Hallowell had was a sight of the back of John Pearce. Once in his cabin, hat and sword taken off, chair occupied, he gratefully poured the coffee his servant had prepared on seeing him approach.

'Derwent.'

'Sir?'

'Please ask the Master at Arms to attend upon me.'

The half a second of delay got his steward a look, one which hurried him out of the cabin. Pearce needed someone to talk to, and it could not be one of his officers. Even if he trusted them in their duties, this did not apply to his private life. This left only one person, who was punctilious on arrival in the way he greeted his captain. Only when Derwent was sent away, did Michael O'Hagan accept the offer to sit down, declining to accept a drink which was not to his taste.

'I'm not exactly at a stand, Michael, but I am in need of a board on which to sound out my thinking.'

'Which sure tells me, John-boy, meeting with this admiral went as well as you did with the last pair.'

The weight of his concerns seemed to be lifted merely by the truth of the remark, which made Pearce chuckle. It was such a relief to be in the presence of someone with whom pretence was impossible. O'Hagan knew him too well, and he was also a good listener, as his friend reprised the thoughts he'd gnawed on in the boat, to find his fears echoed.

'I reckon the tar's expression to be shoal water and a foul wind.'

'And my relationship with Emily, what of that?' came when this too was revealed.

'Jesus only knows, John-boy, you're one to judge poorly those who scarcely deserve it. Who did the good lady marry if it were not a navy man? Barclay was a bastard I will give you, but he was a blue coat for certain?'

'I don't follow.'

'We're all short on sense at some time. If she wed a sailor, she was set for a life of long partings, was she not? Holy Mary, you'll be havin' the best of both worlds, a warm hearth when you come home and all the joy you get from risking your life, your soul havin' gone adrift a long while past.'

The sight of Michael crossing himself when he named the Virgin did not, for once, provoke irritation but a smile.

'And you?'

'Jesus, someone had to keep you whole, John-boy. It's my penance to be the poor sod needing to see to it.'

The orders were not long in coming to join Commodore Nelson and HMS *Captain*, with various rendezvous points listed, the places where his manoeuvrings took his squadron. So, the orders were issued to shape a course for Genoa, the scene of his most pressing activity. As the tops of Jervis's fleet dipped below the horizon, John Pearce felt his old sense of exhilaration return at the possibility of action.

If anyone could provide such, it was Horatio Nelson.

In the great cabin of HMS *Victory*, Sir John Jervis was penning a personal letter, which would be copied to people he held to share similar opinions to himself. The superscription would say it was from him, while on the inside it would tell the recipient the subject was a matter of the gravest concern. Many were senior naval officers, but there were also politicians and even some members of the royal court. In it he outlined what he saw as cogent reasons why a way should be found to stop John Pearce from benefiting, in any way, from the capture of the *Santa Leocadia*.

'I'd rather see the sod in hell than in comfort' were the words he mouthed before calling to his senior clerk to make copies to which he would add the superscription. 'And be discreet, no gossiping.'

'Me, sir?'

'Take that look of innocence off your face at once. You'd sell your mother for a guinea.'

'If you wish, sir.'

The next composition, which would go in the same batch, was private and addressed to the Minster for War, and this required more careful consideration. If Pearce was his man, damning the sod would hardly serve, so he merely asked for permission to hang on to his services rather than send him home, while he hoped such an act found favour. In a sense, it was to cover himself.

Having no idea of the depth of the association or what plans Dundas had for his emissary, it was best to be cautious with a man who had garnered so much power. It was also necessary to make a fair copy and mark it as sent, with the date of despatch attended by the use of a special seal. That way, Dundas could not deny receipt: after all he and Pearce were both damned Scotsmen and no doubt joined at the hip, with corruption as the bone marrow.

CHAPTER THIRTEEN

Denby Carruthers was back in his own city residence, after months imposing himself on his sister and brother-in-law, a move undertaken to avoid the amount of importuning he had been subjected to as husband to a cruelly and bloodily murdered Catherine Carruthers. The case and manner of her death was one to set the scurrilous pamphleteers of Grub Street furiously scratching their quill and running their printing presses. When the suspected murderer, Cornelius Gherson, was acquitted, it did nothing to quell what should have been a nine-day wonder, but things had moved on. Other scandals took the limelight, leaving him free to work from his own property.

As an alderman and hugely successful businessman, Carruthers was in receipt of a great deal of correspondence throughout the working day. Added to this were personal messengers from those with whom he contracted regular business, with an equal amount going out to the same. Thus, the knocker and pull bell on the part of his dwelling that he used as an office, separate from the actual house, were in constant use.

This was no cause to be remarked upon by the master of the house, being taken in and dealt with by Golding, his live-in senior clerk, the third he'd employed since that snake Gherson had occupied the role. The one with the name Tolland by the seal was unusual in that it was neither. The fellow who delivered it was no post boy and no payment was asked for, so it was put in the desk tray holding offers of insurance contracts.

Carruthers was a member of several syndicates, and the same tray held requests to part-fund outgoing cargoes from London. These were destined for ports various, which took no account of the frequent speculative schemes, all potentially fabulously profitable, in which he was invited to participate and was inclined to decline.

Picked up with a touch of irritation, given it appeared to have been misplaced, the name leapt up at him. It had Carruthers furiously slicing at the seal, unfolding it to find a message written in a hand determined to disguise the person who compiled it. The writing was a series of stiffly executed capital letters, which merely asked if he knew of a fellow called Jaleel Tolland. The rest informed him, if the answer was in the affirmative, that the man who'd carried out the delivery would call by to collect it. He was not to be questioned; otherwise all future communication would cease.

There was little choice but to consider what this could portend, but no enlightenment came from such peregrinations, so he had to ponder it might be some kind of hoax. But who could perpetrate such a thing? Who knew such a name could be linked to his own? The only candidate to come to mind was Edward Druce, and he was too much of a lily liver to ever conjure up any kind of jest. There was, of course, the thief-taker Hodgson, whom Druce had finally admitted he had employed, but as far as Carruthers knew, the man was in ignorance of his name.

He rang the bell to summon his clerk, demanding an explanation of how it had come to be in the wrong tray; the excuses were mumbled but the explanation of its arrival was explained. He then, after a period of reflection, gave him instructions to make his way to the Bow Street Courthouse and engage one of the runners.

'Find their quarters, which are in the basement. I need the services of one of those good fellows for the day. Use my name and merely state the rewards will be as before.'

'The task, sir.'

He held up the letter. 'This says the fellow from whom you took possession is due to return for a verbal answer. It is to be in the affirmative, yes, and no more. The Bow Street fellow is to take station so he can watch our front door. At a signal from you, one you must arrange, he will follow this strange messenger, and then report back to me.'

Once his clerk had gone, Denby Carruthers mulled on the nature of the service he sought and from whom. The Bow Street Runners, blind Sir John Fielding's own special body of thief-catchers, were said to be honest and upright fellows, beyond corruption. The man seeking a service today knew better: for a coin, they could be bent to the will of people such as he.

—◦—

Jaleel Tolland was not a man for introspection, it being a word and sentiment which was entirely outside his thinking and had been so ever since his youth. Also, for many years now, he had been too busy for such things, as there would always be some upcoming problem requiring a solution. Smuggling trips to plan, pre-selling cargoes or taking orders for specific goods, all the while ensuring his vessel was sound and had all necessary things to set sail. It had to be to cross one of the least predictable seas in creation, on a journey which could last a couple of days or a fortnight.

Even aboard the vessels he'd so recently been obliged to crew, ways to get to where he was had occupied his every waking thought and if he'd required some form of comfort, then it was a thing easy to come by and a service to be bought. Now he had nothing to do and it was mighty strange.

He was being well cared for in the article of food and drink, with a pail of hot water provided so he could wash. That said, the notion he might be permitted his razor and strop was met with derision, the former being a weapon. Brooding on John Pearce and the revenge he would take only got him so far, so he went to recalling the more distant past.

Childhood in Rotherhithe began as idyllic, with the freedom of the Thames mudbanks as his playground, until he recalled the hard knocks taken from both parents as well as the hunger which seemed a constant. His mother was a more violent beater than an occasional visitor who claimed to be his father, though it seemed every time he called, he left behind his seed.

This resulted in regular pregnancies, a dent to the already scrimping and scraping family income, a noisy interlude of infant wailing, soon followed by a burial. Only one other child, his brother Franklin, whom he cherished, had survived to become a toddler.

As soon as he was old enough, Jaleel was put aboard a Newcastle collier as a ship's boy, the lowest of the low, where kindness was an absent commodity, with vicious payback for petty transgressions commonplace. Time and growing prowess with his fists saw to the brutishness of the crew, with Jaleel becoming the beater not the beaten. This position he occupied with no sympathy at all for those who now filled the place he had so hated. He gave out as good as he had received.

And then, nearing manhood, physically strong through endless toil with heavy sacks of coal, he was snatched in the wide Thames Estuary. Tolland was taken aboard a seriously shorthanded vessel in foul weather, only to discover it was a smuggler when out of sight of land. They quickly showed him the knife, which would slice his gullet if he failed to help them sail to the Flanders coast.

He did smile when he recalled going from fear of his losing life to a fear he might lose the life on offer. It came after they'd landed their second cargo and the whole crew was gathered in a ramshackle and isolated farmhouse. Preceded by dire warnings about holding his tongue, coins were placed in his palm, more money than he had ever previously seen. If it didn't amount to much, given his future successes, it seemed a king's ransom to a lad of seventeen years, who had hoarded over a decade the few copper coins he had ever been gifted.

'I'd be more 'n willing to serve again,' had been his response.

The leader, the man who had doled out coins to all, looked around the gathered crew at the suggestion. They were hard-looking men, made more menacing in appearance by the way the table lanterns underlit their faces, to see how it was taken. The process of threatening him had, over no more than ten days on water, changed into a sort of adoption, which included taking him ashore in Flanders and including him in their pleasures.

A couple had set out to get him so drunk he could no longer walk, to then cause great jollity by repeatedly ducking him in the horse trough to sober him up. Another, on finding him a virgin, had taken care to see to that rite of passage, only to regret his indulgence when the lad begged for near constant recurrence. But the mood here and now was what counted and it seemed, from a faint murmur, to be in the positive.

'Then we best find somewhere round these parts to lay your head, so's I can find you when we next sail.'

'It'll be a warm and heavin' bosom, I'll wager,' produced chuckles.

'Am I permitted to know where I am, your honour?'

'Conyer Creek, lad, where the excise don't dare come sniffin,' lest they wish to lose their nose.'

He'd been watched, they'd have been fools not to, but gradually acceptance turned to respect as he became increasingly important in the shipboard hierarchy. Young Jaleel grew to become the man who enforced chastisement, for he was engaged in a rough trade. There was always someone seeking to steal your goods or dob you into the excise. The former had to be fought, to the death, if need be, and the latter eliminated, a correction in which Jaleel Tolland took genuine pleasure.

He had been more careful than his peers, who could not hang on to a coin if there was pleasure to be bought. He hoarded as much money as he could, without being seen as a pinchpenny, his aim to buy his own boat – the first a far from sound cutter. He and Franklin, now grown old enough, had set off for Gravelines with every penny Jaleel still possessed, to haggle for goods enough to fill it. They then had to endure a near disaster and drowning by the elements on their return journey.

'But profit I turned,' Tolland said, his clenched hand repeatedly slamming the wooden wall of his stall. 'And I did so hand over hand, till that bastard Pearce stole my ship and cargo.'

'What's you on about,' came from Dobbin, his head leaning over the bottom half of the stall door.

'Cursing fate, friend,' Tolland replied, essaying an attempt at a sincere smile.

'Won't do you much good, mate. Likely it be sealed by now.'

Tolland could not see the substantial house to which the barn was adjoined. Four square and in mellow red brick, the upper floor frontage ran to ten windows, with more attic dormers above. The size of those on the ground floor, and the parterre before it, spoke of spacious apartments in the abode of a wealthy man and indeed it was so.

Sir Bertram, 8th Baron Tendring, was entertaining, though suffering would have described it better. He was listening to the pleas of a naval lieutenant for aid in finding and bringing to justice a late member of the crew of his vessel, HMS *Director*.

'Captain Bligh is most desirous of his speedy return, Sir Bertram, so an example can be made of him, one which will have an effect on the civilian population as much as the fleet. We wish them to consider any benign attitude they might have for deserters is misplaced, given it can lead to the foul murder of one of their own.'

'But have you not already instituted a search? I'm told your men were all over the district not more than a day past.'

'With a lack of local knowledge, sir, any search can only be partial.'

'The fellow's name?'

'Tolland, Jaleel Tolland, though we doubt he'd own to it. He murdered a man trying to apprehend him and return him to the ship.'

'No doubt for a reward,' was a response larded with a modicum of distaste: no one loved a crimp.

Tendring walked over to one of the floor-to-ceiling windows, to look out over his courtyard and drive and beyond to the tree-studded deer park. With his back to the naval officer, he allowed himself a smile. The cryptic note to London now appeared superfluous but he was still glad he had sent it. He was now sure Carruthers would recognise the name and be, he hoped, troubled by it.

'Lieutenant . . . Sorry, I've misplaced your name.'

'Sutton, sir, second in *Director.*'

'All I can do is alert the various watchmen in the district. I will instruct them to ask around, for they will know of anyone who might provide shelter for a navy man on the run. More than such aid, I would suggest, can only come from the Yeomanry, and they are based in Colchester.'

'I doubt I have the time to rouse them out before Admiral Duncan orders us to weigh.' The officer opened a folder he was holding and produced a paper. 'I have here a physical description of the miscreant, Sir Bertram, which I hope you will have copied and circulated.'

'Is there anything more, lieutenant?'

'No, sir.' Sutton got the hint. 'So, I will wish you good day.'

The fellow who rang the Carruthers's bell did not say a word when the door was opened, waiting for the affirmation or rejection regarding the letter he'd delivered earlier. With the name confirmed, he left immediately, the slight gesture by the clerk setting the runner on his tail. It required all the man's experience to stay with him in the crowded city, which ended up in a coffee shop, hard by Smithfield Meat Market.

The odour of blood and rotting meat was strong, as were the cries of the porters as they strode alone with whole sides of beef or the carcass of a porker on their heads. Thus, the smell of roasting coffee once indoors was welcome. The quarry, having raided the rack for one of the latest journals, took a seat and placed an order for what became a pot of coffee. There he sat sipping and reading.

Since he was moonlighting, the man set to tail him had only a limited amount of time when he could justify being away from his proper place of employment. Unbeknown to him, the message had already been passed on, one as silent as all which had preceded it. No more than a nod to another fellow unknown to anyone else, the man had risen and left the coffee shop before the pot of the brew had been delivered to the watched table.

So, there was no choice for the Bow Street Runner but to do likewise, to grab a journal and order a pot of his own, a newspaper over which he could keep his eye on his quarry. No man is ever unsure of the time in the City of London, with the regular ringing of church bells to tell the hour as each quarter went by, with each peal rendering the Bow Street man less and less comfortable.

In the end he was relieved by his quarry for, having let his guard slip for a second, something in the journal having engaged his full attention, he raised his eyes to find the man standing over him, a slight smile on his face.

'Best go back from whence you came friend and make up a place to where you followed me. I will take my leave now and, should you try to keep up the chase, I'll use the meat market to lose you.'

And he was gone, before the runner could vacate his seat and dash for the door, to look over a packed street, in which there was no sign of his quarry.

—◁▷—

'Bellamy's Coffee House by Smithfield, your honour,' was what he reported. 'Sat hugger-mugger with a half a dozen coves and deep talking they were. Trouble is, when they broke up, they went their separate ways an' I had no idea who to follow. Went back and asked if they was known. All I got was the notion they was like to be stock jobbers, planning a fraud.'

If it was unsatisfactory, the man still had to be rewarded. It was necessary to keep such fellows as the one reporting to him on side and, in reality, he and his like came cheap.

'Recall me to your comrades.'

—◁▷—

It was a full day later when Tolland again met the nabob who had questioned him, this time in daylight.

'So, it seems you are who you say you are, which obliges me to accept as true your tale of how you lost your ship. It seems there's a villainous streak in even the most supposedly upright of people.'

'He won't be upright if I come across him.'

'Not your first trip I suppose, made a few.'

'Half a dozen this last twelve month and many more afore that.'

'I'm curious to discover how you became associated with a fellow like Denby Carruthers?'

'I needed a ship. He fancied a bit of risk an' high reward for his speculation.'

'I would be happier with a great deal more than that.'

Not youthful, slightly puffy and ruddy enough to hint at the bottle, the man exuded, in his carriage, demeanour and wardrobe, long-standing wealth and the assurance of his social position. When he spoke, there was no attempt at putting passion in his words. The voice was even, well-paced, deep in timbre and carrying the certainty with it, any questions he asked, would naturally be satisfied.

As he had previously, Tolland had to moderate his normal rasping and intemperate mode of speech; he needed this cove, but he also had to lay down a marker he was no supplicant now. That flick of the eyebrows in their previous exchange, which he reckoned himself lucky to have spotted, was paying dividends.

'I might not see it as bein' in my favour to be too open.'

Jaleel Tolland was trying it on. He needed to get on level terms with this Baron whatever he was called. Perhaps not equality, but to a level where he could use information to gain insight into who was holding him and what plan, if any, they now had.

'I've had a visitor from HMS *Director*, a lieutenant called Sutton. I take it you know the name. He was most desirous of taking you back on board. Perhaps you'd like me to oblige him? I can send a rider to fetch him.'

Sir Bertram produced the same slight, humourless smile he'd employed on the night of Tolland's capture. 'I therefore think it is very much in your favour to be open with me.'

'There's not much more to tell. We has a business arrangement, whereby I was to sail the ship and he was to fund the matter and help shift the cargo I bring back.'

'He must have provided more. And before you answer, consider I might know of how such trades are carried out.'

'You tellin' me you're in the game?'

'I give leave to doubt you have not concluded such already. And I've never found it advantageous to treat a man of your stripe as a fool. Perhaps there's more profit to be had than either of you presently enjoy.'

Tolland, for obvious reasons, was not about to say what he thought, which was he couldn't see how. Carruthers had access to the society of London, with money dripping off a huge and concentrated body of well-heeled folk. However high and mighty this fellow before might think himself, he was in the country not a town. He lived in a place where, if there was wealth, it was dispersed and thus obvious.

'Might be of interest, right enough. You suggestin' we might trade together.'

'Perhaps we could find some mutual points of interest. But let's untie you first and attend to some other needs. I fear I cannot see you anywhere other than in this barn and you cannot come and go from here. The house servants might talk and the navy has circulated a description. I think you would own to being easily recognisable.' Sir Bertram wanted to say he was such an ugly and unpleasant looking bugger he would stick out a mile. 'But let us converse further when we have had a little more time to think on what I have said.'

'Fair enough.'

He was a few steps away before he turned, just as Dobbin was undoing the ropes binding Tolland's hands. 'Did you come across Carruthers's wife in your dealings with him?'

'Never met the lady,' was abrupt, too much so that it provoked a surprise reaction.

'Interesting case, wouldn't you say, with the fellow originally charged, the clerk who claims to be cuckolder to his master, having been acquitted. It makes me wonder who is the real culprit, for surely there must be one.'

'Daresay time will see the truth out.'

'Do you think so?'

Then he was gone, leaving Jaleel Tolland wondering where the last question had come from, as well as his own foolish reaction. It might have relaxed him some to know the man who asked had his own conundrum. Having established the truth of Tolland's existence, he was thinking of how to exploit it and coming up with no real conclusion.

CHAPTER FOURTEEN

Pearce found Nelson several miles south of Genoa, a small squadron consisting of a couple of frigates, several sloops and the like, dominated by the bulk of the seventy-four-gun HMS *Captain*. The signal to repair aboard was a mere formality, as *Hazard* was now showing a pennant, which denoted she was carrying despatches. So, the cutter was in the water in double quick time to be smartly rowed towards the commodore's vessel.

Welcomed aboard by Lieutenant Edward Berry, who'd come as premier from Nelson's previous ship, HMS *Agamemnon*, he was spared the usual disdain; this was a mark of Nelson's officers, and such behaviour, in his case, was seen as diminishing of both their ship and personal standing. His welcome by the man in command was the opposite of what he usually faced from men of high rank.

'Why, Mr Pearce, this is a very pleasant surprise.'

'For us both, sir. I trust I find you well.'

Too late, he realised, it was the wrong thing to say to a man for whom his ailments were a constant source of concern. On cue, the ubiquitous large handkerchief was produced and the nose loudly blown, this before the various afflictions from which he was suffering were listed. Not least, and in fact real, was the eye damaged by pebble splinters at the Siege of Bastia, far from healed and worse now than when inflicted. It was, Nelson complained, still subject to an unsatisfied claim he should be compensated by the government for the wound.

'And operations, sir?' Was interposed in a brief pause.

'Worse than my health, Pearce. Bonaparte is unstoppable, which I lay at the door of our allies, who lack vigour.'

The list of military misery followed, hardly required since the man being informed was not entirely in ignorance; Piedmont soundly defeated and gone from the alliance, Sardinia suing for peace, with Naples likely to follow. More serious was the loss of Tuscany, while the titular overlords of the province, the Austrians, despite the odd small victory, were being comprehensively and regularly out-manoeuvred by the French, to be drawn into battles they usually lost.

'And I have my doubts about Spain.'

'I fear they are well placed, sir.'

The invitation to continue meant the tale of Godoy's intentions was provided, as well as the action to intercept the *Santa Leocadia* and why, which for once was heartily and fulsomely praised.

'Whatever questions may arise, and they will be some, I would have done likewise with such ingrates. Hesitation in war is a curse, when being bold might bring the reward we both seek and require.' The mood settled to pensive. 'I think you will understand my frustration at recent events, Pearce, the inability to have any meaningful effect on the land campaign. You'll join me for dinner, of course.'

'Thank you, sir.'

By the time dinner was served, Pearce had been entertained by Lieutenant Berry in the wardroom, so was already mellow with wine when the tureen appeared. Nelson was his usual expansive self, volubly expounding ideas on how to both bring an enemy fleet to battle and defeat it, with boldness as the watchword. But he wished to be active on land as well.

'And another innovation I have recommended to their Lordships is the need for each fleet to bear with it a full battalion of marines, equipped to operate ashore without waiting for army boneheads to agree on a course of action. The trouble Lord Hood had with the bullocks over Bastia was enough to grind a man's teeth to powder.'

'Fully equipped, sir?' asked Pearce, who could see the notion being proposed was far from straightforward; in fact, it tended towards the truly complicated.

'With their own field artillery and supply train, added to the kind of boats, and enough of them, to get the whole ashore in short order. Thus, we could act quickly to confound a fellow like Bonaparte, able to swiftly disembark our own men on any shore which is suitable for a landing. I do not exaggerate when I say, such a force, last year, available for use on the beaches to the west of Genoa, might have imposed a severe check on the French route of supply, perhaps enough to stop their advance.'

He had been ashore on the very coast being discussed the year before and for the very same very purpose, albeit not in battalion strength. The force of which he'd been part was soon obliged to get off again in some rush and disorder, so Pearce had serious doubts about both amphibious operations and marine efficiency.

Added to which, given Bonaparte and his generals were usually victorious over much larger forces, a battalion of marines set ashore might be more of a liability than an asset. They would probably require swift re-embarkation. It , however, would have been impolitic to say so to such an enthusiastic partisan of the notion.

'Do you know what was in the dispatches you fetched aboard, Mr Pearce?'

'No sir.' It was even less polite to say Sir John Jervis was more like to entrust such information to the fellow who sluiced out his privy.

'Well first, and this will disappoint you, *Hazard* is to return immediately to the fleet.'

He was right there: Pearce had been hoping he might be attached to Nelson's squadron, first because something was always happening with him in command. But more important, he would be away from the basilisk eye of the crusty old bastard in *Victory*.

Seeing him obviously crestfallen, there appeared a twinkle in the good Nelson eye. 'The other instruction is for me and concerns the Island of Capraja.'

'Which I had off my starboard beam on the way here, sir. I cannot say I saw anything to excite interest.'

'It is home to a nest of vipers who call themselves privateers and they are tolerated if not positively enabled by those snakes in Genoa. They allowed them to skulk in their port, from which they could not sail with me offshore, so they have been given use of the island as a base for their depredations.'

Pearce had to smile, and he noted Edward Berry was seeking to hide his. The sailor servant employed by the commodore, who was not noted for acceptable manners, had kept his goblet well supplied, and it was beginning to show. Taciturn in the extreme, the servitor was an improvement on his predecessor, a noted drunk. The new fellow was a Norfolk lad – many of Nelson's crew were – of stunted growth and uncouth manner. Once more, Nelson would have folk wondering why, with any man in the fleet to choose from, he had ended up with such a specimen.

'Sir Gilbert Elliot wants them cleared out, to stop their preying on the trade of his Corsicans.'

The 'his' was taken as strange, until Pearce recalled that the Corsicans had asked for and been granted special status under the British Crown, opting to come under the protection of King George. Elliot was thus a Viceroy, though it had to be doubted how much control he exercised over such a famously fractious race.

'Now it strikes me, Pearce, since you will be passing Capraja in any case, it would be a pity not to try a bout with the privateers who use it. I am told they are as bloodthirsty a crew as you could conjure up, so they require to be cleared out. In the morning, I'll shift my flag to *Minerve* and I invite you to join us, in what should be a hot little action.'

Pearce should have said no. It would infuriate Jervis, which is why he said yes.

—◦—

'No parleying gentlemen, we sail in and sink as many of their boats as we can by gunfire, and then board what remains and set them alight. As to the crews. . . '

'They'll run for the shore, sir,' the answer came from George Cockburn, captain of the frigate *Minerve*, a handsome forty-gunner, taken from the French after the siege of Calvi.

'They may well Cockburn, where they will languish and hopefully starve.' He looked from him to Pearce. 'I know we would profit by taking their boats, but we cannot crew what we already possess and, in terms of value, they are not worth the trouble. Dawn tomorrow and we go in with the sun at our back. Mr. Pearce, you draw the least water under your keel, so the inshore work I leave to you, though Captain Cockburn will support you with his boats.'

The early hours of darkness were spent in preparation – weapons were chosen, with those needing a better blade put to the grinding wheel. If Cockburn was of the opinion the privateer crews would run, Pearce was not so sure, for he'd had dealings with them in Leghorn, even gifting them men from Tolland's old crew. Their boats were both their home as well as their livelihood, so they would likely fight, not flee.

The bay of Porto Vecchio, the only town on the island, was a good small vessel harbour, protected from anything but a gale from the Alps by a jutting promontory, so the approach was from the northeast. *Minerve* would take station across the entrance to the bay and begin a bombardment aimed at the berthed vessels. The fact not all would be present – some would be out hunting prey – would just have to be accepted. She would then have to stand off drawing too much under her keel to enter what was shoal water.

With hopefully anyone aboard thrown into confusion, *Hazard* would then work in for close action. The aim was to drive any privateers away from their vessels so the work of destruction could begin, the frigates' boats joining as soon as they could. Numerous as these pests might be, they would thus be heavily outnumbered by the navy.

The first flaw in the plan was revealed in the grey morning light, as a string of ships of varying sizes stretched across the mouth of the bay. It was a distance Pearce calculated at something below five hundred yards, and they were fully manned. Privateers did not carry heavy or plentiful ordinance, their few cannons tended to be small, designed to precede rapid boarding rather than do serious damage. Their aim was the possession of both the vessel and its cargo, so inflicting impairment on their quarry merely reduced the rewards.

'Would I be right in assuming that they knew we were coming, sir?'

'The only possible explanation, Mr Hallowell. I would guess Viceroy Elliot's activities and aims are not as secure as he supposed.'

'They won't stop us surely, though the notion may be to make us question the value of the operation.'

Pearce laughed. 'Then I suspect they have no idea who they're dealing with.'

'Signal from flag to come about, sir.'

'Thank you, Mr Livingston. Acknowledge.'

Having been sailing on a parallel course to *Minerve*, they swung away in a wide arc as the frigate also changed course. But not for long, she too came about to take her across the mouth of the bay and, in the increasing light, with the sun now up, they could see her starboard cannon being run out.

'Our friends are in for a drubbing,' Pearce opined.

'What they're about scarcely makes sense, sir.'

'I agree. I wonder if they thought with such a show, we would be tempted to parley rather than just attack.'

'And perhaps allow then to sail their ships for Genoa?'

'Possibly. The island belongs to the city, and Nelson is convinced they could scarce operate from here without some kind of nod from the Doge or his officials.'

'New signal, sir. Engage the enemy more closely.'

Whatever had been their original intention, the privateers opened up first; it now being clear action was about to be joined. They peppered the waters ahead of *Minerve*, a rippling salvo running from ship to ship along the line, which, if it was far from effective, argued for some controlling brain seeking to send a message.

'So much for Captain Cockburn's opinion they would flee.'

A query from Hallowell got a quick shake of the head. A senior officer's opinion, vouchsafed in private, was not for discussion, and Pearce had to remind himself to take more care when mouthing his thoughts. HMS *Hazard* had come about again and, without specific instructions this left him free, he was sure, to act as he saw fit. It was the Nelson way to give his subordinates the freedom to make their own decisions.

'Take us across the stern of *Minerve* and run out and load the bow chasers. Mr Moberly, your marines to the tops please, ready to supress any resistance. Mr Williams, down to topsails if you please and, once set, everyone not required on deck to repair below. It would be foolish, now they seemed determined to fight, to assume we may not face grapeshot and musket fire as we seek to break their line.'

The opening salvo from the frigate had Pearce turn a telescope on to the quarterdeck and there he was, Nelson, dwarfed by the much taller Cockburn, a glass to his good eye as he watched the effect. Using only upper-deck eighteen pounders, the frigate did massive damage to what were flimsy vessels, wooden splinters flying in all directions, with a couple of masts going by the board. It also created an immediate gap in their strung-out line, as one or two swung away, the cables holding them to their neighbours coming apart.

Once the forward cannon had been loaded and run out, Pearce ordered the crews to take shelter behind the bulwarks. He then reiterated his orders to include the quarterdeck, still fully manned, which he saw as foolish. As the man in command, he had to be there and so did the men on the wheel. But he had no need for a signal midshipman and lieutenants who subscribed to the theory to take shelter made them appear shy.

'Gentlemen, get below and organise your boarders. I want them up on deck and ready to go over the side in short order. There will be no time for delay in trying to organise them. It is going to be pell-mell work and with fury, added to as much noise as you can muster. And, be advised, they will face men who do this for a living, so it will be warm work.'

'Your weapons, your honour.'

The soft Irish voice was reassuring, and so was the way Michael ignored the order he too should go below. All this got was a smile and he took station behind his friend. If the approach was silent on the deck of HMS *Hazard*, as well as on *Minerve*, who'd backed her sails and begun to load crew into her boats, it was not up ahead. The screaming insults, faint but growing louder as the gap closed, were interrupted by the occasional sound of a fired off musket, useless at the range.

Pearce was fixated on the gap he intended to run through, the one created by the frigate's cannon, his gaze fixed on the deck of the southernmost vessel, which was still manned, though not, he thought, in the original numbers.

'Bows chasers,' he called. 'I need the deck dead ahead cleared, so fire as soon as you bear.'

'Which will make you a target, John-boy,' was a whisper.

'I'm one already,' Pearce replied, pointing to his opposite number who stood still with a telescope to his eye. 'Mr Moberly, yonder fellow holding the glass up ahead. See if you can make him dance a bit when he comes in range.'

'Will a lively reel do, sir.'

'It will serve fine.'

Pearce moved over to the wheel, to quietly instruct the men manning it where to aim the prow, nothing more than a tweak of a half of a degree. Moberly did indeed make his man hop, as his marines put their musket balls gouging into the deck. It was enough to shift him well back and crouching, which might well have saved his life.

As the bowsprit lined up with the selected deck, the two bow chasers fired in turn, aiming to employ the start of the down roll, so the balls would at least strike wood if they could not sweep the deck. They hit the scantlings halfway between waterline and the rail, sending up the whole section of the ship, the flimsy bulwark literally disappearing in a mass of exploding wood.

'Boarders on deck,' Pearce yelled.

This saw his crew, led by both officers and mids, pour up the companionways and head for the side. If most of them were thus occupied, it was not all in what was an action much practised in the previous weeks. There were still enough to let fly the sheets as *Hazard* closed with the first vessel their captain wanted taken. The wheel was then spun in such a fashion as to take most of the way off the ship, so when they came alongside, it was with a crunch but minimal damage; padded fenders having been thrown over ahead of contact.

If it seemed like previous rehearsed boardings, it ceased to be so very quickly. The sound of shouting was overtaken by the clash of weapons and the screams of fear or the pain or wounds. Pearce, with Michael at his heels, was quick to join in, slashing his way forward to get into the front of the line, which became a space in which movement was constricted, more dangerous than the freedom to swing at will.

Barely registering its presence, he stepped over a comatose body in a short blue jacket, being too busy forcing back his opponent, a dark-skinned fellow already bearing a long scar on his face. But he lacked nothing in determination and had not a sword, but a curved knife with a length of blade, serrated on one side, not much shorter than the naval hanger with which he was faced.

It was the axe with which Michael was wont to do battle that did for him, a sweeping blow coming over Pearce's shoulder that literally removed his forearm, blade and all. This produced a stunned look of surprise, before Michael's next sweep of the axe cut into his neck. Pearce had a moment to step back and avoid the fount of blood, bending down to grab the short blue collar and drag the youngster away from the fighting line, with a shouted command to get him back aboard *Hazard*. He had no time to see it obeyed or ignored; he had to get back into the fight.

It was warm work on a day beginning to feel the heat of the sun and their opponents fought well. But slowly and surely the privateers were driven back until continued fighting could only result in death. The clatter of dropping weapons replaced metal on metal, inducing a pause in which Pearce could assess what to do next, his attention taken by the sounds of fighting on other decks.

And there he was, in the thick of it, the blond, near white, hair come loose, the only thing truly visible as Nelson, surrounded by the men from *Minerve*, did battle with a fervour to match any of his confreres. The boats had come in between two privateer vessels, and there was the tall figure of George Cockburn. He was swinging what Pearce thought to be a Scottish claymore, doing real damage to opponents who seemed determined to stay out of its wide and deadly arc.

It could not last, so Cockburn's prediction, if late in coming, was fulfilled. The way the privateer line had been constructed gave them access to the shore and they took it. Bodies poured on to land and headed for the ramshackle buildings and drawn up fishing boats which formed the frontage of the port. The sound of their departure diminished, to leave an unnatural silence. Nor did they stop, making their way down the gaps between the fishing huts to head for the hills central to the island.

'I give you joy, Mr Pearce, we have done good service this day.' Someone had given Nelson his hat, and he was waving it from another captured deck. 'And now I think it is time for the combustibles.'

'Not afore we search to see if there's anything worth a coin,' came from a chest-heaving Charlie Taverner. 'There's bound to be stuff about these buggers have pinched.'

'Half an hour, Charlie, and use the time to set the faggots as well.'

The men of *Hazard* took their cue from Charlie, so there was much shifting of bundles from the still intact ships, with items being pocketed. But the other work progressed too, so as soon as the searching was over, the privateer ships were set ablaze. Nelson signalled farewell to HMS *Hazard*, she on her way back to San Fiorenzo Bay and the fleet. Pearce had in his possession a letter from the commodore for Sir John Jervis, relating how he had been diverted, as well as to what purpose and, he was told, praise for his sterling service.

'With luck,' was said in the privacy of his cabin, 'The old goat will choke on it.'

The mood he had of possible future pleasure was spoiled by Cullen, who came to tell him that they had lost young Mr Campbell, whom Pearce now knew to be the one he had dragged clear. His head had been stoven by a club, so there was a burial to be prepared and a letter to be composed to the lad's parents in Argyll. It had to be one in which his bravery was praised and his loss to the navy mourned.

Had he been an excellent officer in the making? There was no way of knowing if this was true, but convention dictated his relatives be told so in order to ease their grief.

CHAPTER FIFTEEN

A new set of orders for John Pearce and HMS *Hazard* was delivered as he dropped anchor, brought by boat from the flagship by a mere midshipman. This rather spoiled his intention to upset Jervis by detailing, in his report, the attack on Capraja, his part in it as well as the successful outcome. He hoped that the old sod would be furious, but it was less of an anticipated pleasure now as he would not be witness to Jervis's discomfort.

'You're to be denied your family reunion once more, Mr Hallowell. Please ask Mr Williams to shape us a course for Bastia.'

There was not much more imparted than he should report to the Viceroy Sir Gilbert Elliot, who would give him instructions as to the duties in which he should be employed. The firing of a signal gun as the ship was made ready was accompanied by the flags carrying *Hazard*'s number, this soon followed by an order to weigh. It was something he took great pleasure in ignoring until the message was repeated – the change of flags accompanied by a blast of black powder.

So, it was a reverse of his course, to take him once more through the channel between Capraja, Elba and the main island, until the stone walls protecting the city of Bastia, overseen by the twin spires of the waterfront cathedral, came into view. This time, the required salute was for the Viceroy, replied to by the fortress batteries acknowledging Jervis's flag. The harbour was fit only for fishing boats, though it did have within it an armed cutter flying navy flags. HMS *Hazard* tied up on the outer side of the mole.

Dressed in his best uniform and scraper, clothing never worn except when required for formal occasions, Pearce went ashore, passing the armed cutter, which had signally failed to react in any way to his arrival. Aware it was a lieutenant's command, and a very junior one at that, he was surprised the man in charge was not at least on deck to acknowledge his passing, as an act of camaraderie, if not respect.

There was a party of bullocks lined up where the mole met the quayside, with an officer to welcome him, which meant Pearce was presented with what was a depressing sight. All the red uniform coats showed how long these soldiers had been doing service under a bleaching sun. They had faded to the point of being nearer pink in colour, while the rankers webbing showed it to be severely frayed.

The salute was however crisp, both in the raised-to-the-lips sword and the combined moves of the muskets, both responded to by a raised hat. To this was added Pearce's name, rank and the name of the vessel he commanded.

'Lieutenant Vickery, 65th Foot. Welcome to Bastia, sir.'

To inspect such a unit, which he was invited to do, was to pretend all was as it should be when it was not, and Pearce was forced to keep his eyes level, so as not to take in the worn boots and breeches, quite a few showing patches on the knees.

'Fine body of men, Lieutenant Vickery.'

This was something Pearce could say with a modicum of conviction for, if their kit was in poor condition, the men, from their corporal to the dozen troopers, looked to be well fed, reasonably fit and disciplined. Their gaze was steady and aimed at a point over his head.

'Have you been on this duty for long?'

'Came ashore for the siege, Mr Pearce,' Vickery replied, 'and I have been here ever since, to hold the city and provide a guard for Sir Gilbert and his family.'

About to show surprise that the man had his family along, Pearce bit his tongue, there being no point in starting out with what might be reported as a discourtesy. Indicating he had completed his inspection, Vickery ordered his men to fall out. This had them disperse to a small stone building, obviously a guard house for the port which was cool inside.

'If you will follow me, sir, I will take you to the fortress.'

It was a steep climb, hardly a surprise since the place was on a hill; this backed by dense green mountains, high enough to keep a wisp of cloud around their summit. It was warm in the narrow streets, though the high building provided welcome shade from a sun close to its zenith. It was thus no surprise that the streets were quiet.

The entrance to the fortified section of the town, which enclosed many buildings, showed the damage it had sustained from being besieged, with great chunks of missing masonry; this inflicted by the navy cannon brought ashore for bombardment. He could imagine Nelson here, peering across the glacis before the main gate and revelling in the task of trying to breech the walls. This would be until a ball striking loose stones sent one to ricochet and damage his eye.

The cool of the deep barbican gatehouse opened up into a spacious quadrangle, with both barracks and stabling along the outer walls. Vickery led him to a sturdy and extensive building, with an elaborate motif above double doors, a cross with two standing griffins, one on each side. The building was stone at the base and had probably been a citadel in olden times. The section above looked less martial, being ochre painted with rows of windows overlooking the extensive square.

Above flew two flags, the Moor in profile of Corsica, alongside the flag of Britannia. To enter the doorway was to come upon a more ordered world of cool air, a spacious hallway, polished wooden flooring and good furnishings in what had obviously been domesticated from what would have been bare stone. There was, as well, an army major, sat at a desk, who wore a coat of such pristine scarlet it looked as if it has never seen daylight.

'May I introduce Lieutenant Pearce, sir.'

'Thank you, Mr Vickery. You may return to your duties. Major Warburton at your service, lieutenant.'

The contrast between the pair extended way beyond the state of their uniforms. Vickery was young and looked as if a good meal would not go amiss, while this captain was close to corpulent. The main buttons on his buff waistcoat showed signs of strain, while a rubicund face indicated that it might have seen more of the outdoors than his coat.

'I have orders from Admiral Jervis to report to the Viceroy, sir.'

'Which will have to wait. He and his good lady have retired for their afternoon repose, a local habit they have taken to since coming to Italy.' A Hunter timepiece was produced from a waistcoat pocket. 'He will be up and about at four of the clock.'

Pearce had to contain a smile: he had fond memories of having taken to a siesta with Emily, while they were stuck in Palermo and he recalled sleep was not always the prime purpose. Inducing discomfort, it was a thought necessary to put aside, so he asked Warburton about the somnolent armed cutter he'd passed by on the way.

'Now there's a fellow who likes his cot, though he must be forgiven I suppose, for being more active at night than during the day.'

Pearce had begun to think of his dinner, which would likely be prepared whether he was aboard or not. Indeed, he fully expected Derwent, his servant, would have gone ashore to seek fresh produce as was common when the ship was in port.

Aware of the time and unwilling to wait, he decided to return to *Hazard* and, on the way, call on whoever commanded the cutter. The fellow must, since he was clearly stationed here, have some notion of the tasks the Viceroy would have in mind for the new arrival.

'I have matters I must attend to pertaining to my own duties, sir, so please inform Sir Gilbert I will call on him at five of the clock, if that is convenient.'

Was that a look of relief on the bullock's face, the notion he might have had to entertain Pearce for several hours while Sir Gilbert Elliot slept.

'We all have duties to attend to, do we not?'

'Until later, sir.'

Unlike the narrow streets, the large quadrangle of the inner fortress was not only open to a good deal of the sunshine, but also its walls tended to trap the air. So, Pearce emerged to a bit of furnace-like heat, which had him hurry for the narrow alleys, only to find that the high sun was now able to strike the cobbles and dazzle the eyes. There was a bit of a forgiving breeze when he emerged on to the quayside, which had him contemplate, since he was hot, bypassing the cutter and making straight for *Hazard*, where he could strip off and enjoy a cooling swim.

This he put aside as he came to the side of the vessel, having observed on her stern the name HMS *Teme*, to detect a deck, which was as empty of humanity as it had been on his way to see the Viceroy. With a deck nearly level with the mole, he crossed a flattish gangway to drop on to the planking, deliberately making a noise, which provoked no reaction. What was noticeable was the rather disordered state of the deck and the planking also being less than freshly holystoned.

Having served himself aboard such a small vessel, he knew there would be a severely cramped cabin at the base of the short companionway. This he headed for, dropping a few steps to the door which would lead to the quarters of the man in command. To his rear, the sound of snoring was very evident and, in what was gloomy from lack of light, he could just make out tightly packed and occupied hammocks.

'Damn me,' he said softly to himself, 'the whole crew's asleep.'

An ear to the door produced no sound, so he took hold of and lifted the latch to ease it open. The body in the cot was also asleep, flat on its back and naked, with an open gunport providing both light and a minimal draught of air. It was with as much mischief as ire, Pearce said in a loud voice.

'I have taken your ship, sir, without so much as a fist shown to my face, so if you have your sword to hand, I'll have that as well.'

There was no a sitting up in surprise, just a low moan as the eyes opened and the mouth performed a fish like search for air. Having moved to overlook the fellow, Pearce found himself above a pair of sleep-filled blue eyes, orbs which went from surprise to a look of utter dread, this followed by a terrified scream. If the man so rudely woken was in a state of shock, so was the man who'd caused it to happen.

'Burns?'

Another scream followed, as did the hands pushed out to ward off any closer approach, accompanied by a garbled plea to be left alone. This was followed by a stream of gibberish which sounded very much like a plea to the Almighty that he be spared. The sound had at least woken one of the crew who appeared at the open door, and, seeing a strange officer, spoke in a whisper.

'It be best to leave him alone, your honour, with him having his troubled dreams. He has his demons.'

'Leave him alone? I'm more inclined to drag him out of his cot and chuck him over the side.'

'Pearce,' was a weak and hoarse murmur, as the fellow at the door withdrew from this furious-faced visitor.

'The very same and I am put to wonder how I got to the side of your damn cot without so much as an anchor watch to stop me. Every man jack aboard is asleep.'

'I....' Whatever Burns wanted to say wouldn't come; he was fishing for air again.

'Get up, sir, get dressed and meet me on deck in two minutes.'

If John Pearce wondered, at that point, if he was in a position to issue orders, it did not stop him from doing so. He repeated 'two minutes,' then stomped out and up the companionway. The time he waited was used for a more thorough inspection of the deck and rigging, none of which met the required standard expected by the navy, never mind Sir John Jervis.

He was breathing heavier than his situation demanded, for the very simple reason, if there was one name which could make his blood boil, it was that of Toby Burns. He was Emily's cowardly nephew who had been a midshipman aboard HMS *Brilliant*, the frigate into which Pearce and his Pelicans had been pressed. Nor could he even think of the little sod without conjuring up the face of Ralph Barclay, who might be dead, but such a fact did nothing to mitigate his hatred of the man.

'All hands on deck!' he yelled, 'and twelve of the lash for the last to show.'

As it was, Toby Burns was the one to emerge first, in his shirt and yet to be fully done up breeches, carrying over his arm a faded blue coat.

'You, sir, are improperly dressed,' was shouted, as heads began to appear, rubbing sleep from their eyes and blinking in the strong sunlight. 'Go to your normal stations.'

If they looked at this martinet with loathing, it had no effect on the man berating them. He was more taken with the pig's ear Toby Burns was making of getting his breeches done up and his coat on. He'd clearly forgotten his hat.

Whatever rank Burns had, John Pearce had been gazetted before him, so he set out to make the little bastard's life a misery. He demanded he look at the deck and rigging, ropes hanging loose, in the case of the latter and wanted to know if it was seen as satisfactory. He pointed out in a carrying voice the deck was a disgrace, while what lay about it begged to be seen to be believed. It was all done in a voice so loud that locals began to gather.

'It would have been dealt with this afternoon,' was stuttered, and the man speaking was shaking. 'When the crew was rested and the sun was going down.'

'Rested, sir,' was barked. 'You should be arrested. And it would not surprise me to find you confined and disrated were Sir John Jervis to pay you a visit. And where, sir, is your damned hat?'

Not being a natural bully, Pearce, when he turned away from Burns to look at his crew, was struck by the faces too slow to wipe away the expressions of true hate. It was a look he had not seen since the North Sea and it troubled him.

'Mr Burns, had you been awake you would have seen me arrive in Bastia, but you were not. I intend to go back aboard my ship and partake of my dinner, after which I have an appointment with the Viceroy. If it is still light, I will inspect your ship on the way back, if not, I will do so in the morning.'

'We sail as soon as it is dark, sir.'

Slightly nonplussed, Pearce was left to wonder why Burns was being so obsequious, especially in front of his crew, who would hardly respect him for allowing himself to be browbeaten. That was until he recalled what a weakling he was, a groveller of the first order, as well as a turd who had claimed success in a glorious exploit, which was in truth earned by the man shouting at him.

He wanted to ask why he went out at night, more a time for fishermen to sail than a warship, however small, but his dignity would not allow it. Then he recalled what Warburton had said about the cutter being active at night. Slightly at a loss, he said.

'I have told you of my intentions, and I must also tell you I will write a report on how well you react.'

This said, he stomped across the gangplank and headed for *Hazard*.

—◦—

Dinner could not be a leisurely affair. Taken at three and with an appointment at five, it was somewhat rushed so, with a slightly discomfited belly, John Pearce made his way back to see the Viceroy. He deliberately ignored what was happening on *Teme*, albeit he registered the hive of activity, which could hardly be missed. As he strode on, he imagined the looks which were being aimed at his back, which now troubled him not one jot.

It still being hot, the interior hallway he had visited earlier came as a welcome relief, though the earlier silence had gone, it was now a seeming play area for what had to be some of the Elliot offspring. There was a girl, the oldest and in early teen years, along with two younger boys. There being no sign of Warburton, he was obliged to ask the girl for the whereabouts of her father. Directed up the wide staircase and to his left, he found before him an open door, within which sat a man at a desk, quill in hand and busy. Assuming a clerk, Pearce asked for the Viceroy.

'Am I permitted to enquire who's asking?'

'Lieutenant Pearce, Master and Commander of HMS *Hazard*.'

'Oh aye, Warburton told me you'd come in.'

'Sir Gilbert,' was a tenuous enquiry.

'The very same.'

Which had Pearce look around the spacious study, which was empty of humanity bar the man to whom he was talking. He, on closer inspection, looked quite patrician, with a fine forehead hinting at intelligence, a trait also present in the bright eyes and firm chin.

'Am I allowed to remark on the lack of ceremony, never mind precautions, given your rank, sir?'

'Rank,' was a hoot. A fine bauble and no doubt I'd be a cringed to on another station. 'But here. . . '

The nature of here was left unfinished, with Pearce pointing out who had sent him. 'And, it seems, I am to take my instructions directly from you.'

'Pull up a chair, Pearce, or I'll crick my neck.' This done, Sir Gilbert fixed him with a strange look. 'I mark your name, sir, and detect a trace of a Scottish accent.'

'It's where I was born, sir.'

'Pearce, eh?' he asked, before checking the spelling.

Knowing what was coming, the man so addressed had stiffened in anticipation, aware he was going to have to, as he had so often done in the past, defend his father.

'I met a man of the same name in the Edinburgh home of Davy Hume. As lively a fellow in discussion as it's ever been my pleasure to meet.'

'That would have been my father, Adam,' came out as a tentative reply. Where was this leading to?

'Och aye, I now see a bit of a likeness, though you're taller by far.'

'He was something of a pupil to David Hume.'

'As was I, young man. Myself and my brother were sent to learn from him when he resided in Paris, we being just past twelve years old. Do you know Paris?'

Not wishing to admit he knew it well and way, he said, 'It's where my father is buried.'

'That's sad to hear. While I could not agree with much of what he propounded, I found I could respect him. He did not, as so many men do, lack for sincerity. Still, that is something we can delve deeper into on another day. I believe you're here for a purpose.'

'Which is?'

'To help me keep hold of Corsica, which I have to tell you, will be no easy task.'

'I believe they can be difficult to deal with.'

'Laddie, you don't know the half of it. They are proud and they never forget or forgive a slight, which is dangerous when a man is easily offended and always carries a knife. There are two factions on the island, but in truth there are dozens. It's more like our home-land north of Perth in its clannishness. But for us, it is those who supported our taking responsibility for the island as against those who preferred, or should I say prospered, when it was in the hands of the French.'

'Forgive me, but that sounds like a task for soldiers not sailors.'

'Which would be true if those inclined to the French were all on the island, but they're not. They are in Italy, and we have been trying to stop them from coming back, not with much success, as hard as Mr Burns seems to try. But he commands one wee ship on a long coastline and is very young for such a task.'

There was room for discomfort as Pearce recalled his actions of the early afternoon, but it had to be kept hidden as Sir Gilbert added,

'It is to be hoped with a second vessel, we can put more of a stopper on their game.' At which point the children burst in to mob their indulgent father, who managed to say. 'You'd best stay for dinner, so you can meet my wife, the true Viceroy of Corsica.'

The last bit was said with a twinkle in the eye.

Chapter Sixteen

Given there was a limited amount of time before dinner, Pearce declined to return to HMS *Hazard*, which also put paid to his threatened inspection of Burns and his armed cutter. Instead, he joined Sir Gilbert on a walk about the town, a constitutional promenade the Viceroy took in the cooler evening, seeking, as he said, to feel the mood of the people. They required an escort of two musket-bearing soldiers, which said a great deal, while it was impossible not to notice the occasional glare thrown in their direction.

Just as telling was the indifference of the majority of the citizens, though Gilbert made a point of emphasising Bastia, having been the place from which the French had exercised their power, was the most Francophone part of the island and had been the same for the Genoese before they upped sticks.

'There are many from around this part of Corsica who prospered and were far from happy to see the French booted out by Lord Hood.'

'Do they not do equally well out of us?'

'No they do not. I may be called Viceroy, Lieutenant, but I can hardly be said to rule and I do not have much in the way of largesse at my disposal. I represent His Majesty it is true, but it's more a convenience to the rulers of Corsica rather than any notion of King George being their monarch. They want the protection afforded by the British Crown and the Royal Navy, so will play lip service to the fiction of being an associate of the British Crown.'

'So, this is the centre of resistance?'

'It's on the eastern shore, closest to Italy and it's a fact, if you hold Bastia as well as Calvi, no one else can claim to control Corsica.'

During the walk Pearce was treated to a potted history of the island, a subject of which he was not entirely in ignorance; how could anyone be who had served in the Mediterranean for any length of time? But in-depth knowledge was different and Elliot went back all the way to the original fight for independence from Genoa which resulted in two separate governments. The Genoese held the important coastal fortified towns, but they could not control a hinterland in which it was far from safe for them to venture. So, they left it alone, which allowed for an independent Corsican parliament to be set up in Corte, a town in the central mountains.

'You will have heard of Pasquale Paoli?'

'Who has not, sir?'

The famous Corsican patriot first came to prominence fighting Genoa, being the prime mover in setting up the Corte government. Gilbert related how he'd written a constitution, been elected president and led an army he was appointed to command by the executive council, a body of which he was also the chief magistrate. He then conducted a proper and successful war against his Italian overlords.

In danger of losing control of the island, Genoa ceded it to France, but the locals were no more willing to be subjects of King Louis than the Doge. Fighting Genoa, Paoli held the upper hand, but he and his far from professional army were left dealing with a much more powerful, numerous and determined enemy. This made defeat in battle certain. It thus came to pass, meaning Paoli was forced to flee to London, where he was lionised as a freedom fighter against a great tyranny.

'On the grounds, my father posited, anyone opposing Catholic France was a friend to Britannia.'

'Then Adam had the right of it,' came with an Elliot chuckle. 'The Revolution brought him home, but to a less than united polity. Many leading families, like the Buonaparte clan, championed the zealots in Paris. Indeed, one of their number, Lucien, was a deputy in the National Assembly.'

One of the swarthy locals they passed spat on the ground, which Gilbert ignored, obliging Pearce to do the same. Besides, there was no guarantee it had been aimed at the Viceroy as an insult. He just kept talking.

'Families like the Buonapartes saw themselves as the best people to rule the island and were not inclined towards such foibles as parliaments or elections. Ultra-nationalists were keen to spread the Revolution as well as determined to annexe Sardinia and managed to persuade the executive council to back the plan, despite Paoli's strong resistance.'

As told, there was deep cunning in the way the old man had dealt with this proposed conquest. Still in command of the army, Paoli appointed his son to lead the Corsican forces. He then secretly made sure the Sardinians were made aware of their intentions, so their inferior forces were in place and concentrated to frustrate any invasion.

A furious Napoleon Buonaparte, at that time a mere captain of artillery in the French Army, the same fellow who was doing so much damage to the coalition cause now, assumed command. But, due to sickness and desertion it was too late to retrieve the situation, so it ended in a fiasco.

'The wily old fox ensured failure, only to be accused of being a traitor.'

'Easy to see why,' Pearce opined, not sure if he was such a hero after all.

'But the man was being pragmatic, lieutenant. He needed British support to secure the fortified towns the French had taken over from Genoa. He had no means of doing so without our aid, while Piedmont was on our side fighting the Revolution. Sardinia being a possession of their king, it was necessary for the Corsicans to fail.'

'So, Napoleon turned against Paoli.'

'Lieutenant, neither he nor his brood were ever in favour of the old man. They sought to replace him more than once and I don't doubt they had plans to eliminate him and his entire family. It was seen by London as best to pension him off and have him take up residence back in Britain.'

'Who took over?'

'A fellow called Pozo di Borgo, but his authority will never enjoy the state achieved by Paoli, so he had trouble controlling the various factions. I suspect, these days, meetings of the executive council are akin to the Tower of Babel.'

'Which begs the obvious question, what of Buonaparte?'

'His arrogance was his undoing. He was seen as a tyrant in the making, so managed to unite the oddest alliance to act against him, both supporters of independence and royalists, who hate each other. He was obliged, as were his family, to flee to avoid being strung up, women included. When people take against you on this island, they are not inclined to show mercy for anyone, male, female or even a babe in arms.'

'I take it those who agreed with him are the folk causing you trouble now?'

'Exactly so, and French successes on the mainland are giving them encouragement, doubly galling as they are being achieved by him in particular. Those who chose exile when we took over see him as a saviour, so are now returning in numbers.'

The Viceroy explained that such people were no more capable of taking fortified towns like Bastia than any of their predecessors. They had nothing, in the face of cannon fire, with which to assault defensive walls. The worry was a surprise attack from within, from the very streets of Bastia, so all efforts were bent to ensuring this was made difficult, if not impossible.

'So, we keep a tight watch on the arsenal and I'm happy to say it is one policy effectively pursued by the government in Corte. This means they must bring in weapons and the means to fire them. Stopping any trafficking of such to within the walls is our major concern.'

'I take it coming out to engage them is not possible.'

'Not, Mr Pearce, without we bring back the soldiers who departed after the French surrender. And even if I am no soldier, I would hesitate to campaign in a wild country such as this. The French paid a high price to chase Paoli out.'

'How many men do you have now?'

'A single company of the 65th Foot and they are no longer at full strength, plus a number of artillerymen to man the cannon on the walls. There's a similar-sized garrison at Calvi and two full regiments at San Fiorenzo, one of which would, in truth, be better employed here. But the soldiers obey their own perceived problems and I have limited power to have them meet mine.'

'Lord Hood had the same difficulty.'

'Indeed, he did. But I fear we may be approaching a point of crisis. Those who want us off the island are now concentrating in and around Bastia. I fear that they might come to outnumber the men we have to contain them.'

'Surely they're not all boating over from the mainland?'

'No, there's a strong body here and, of course, there are the opportunists who sense the way the wind is blowing. But significant numbers do and they are the ones most likely to press for action. It is also true that the greater their number, the more they recruit to their cause.'

'Can you not be reinforced?'

'The garrison in Calvi is fairly secure, but not so much that they can be depleted, while the army insists Jervis needs the soldiers at

San Fiorenzo to protect his anchorage. I fear we must make do here with what we have.'

Further conversation underlined how the man now leading the Corsican parliament was, in stature, no match for Paoli, so found it difficult to stir the kind of support he enjoyed. This made it easier for an opposition to agitate for the return of French rule, though they too had split into factions to further complicate matters.

Elliot had to deal with warring groups of royalists agitating for the return of the Bourbon monarchy, as well as revolutionaries who were supporters of the Paris Directory. There was a party who would welcome back Genoa and combinations of everything in between. A section of the populace valued independence under the British Crown but, when it came to taking action to preserve it, they seemed supine compared to those just mentioned.

'I cannot say I would put faith in any of them,' Gilbert sighed.

'It sounds as if you have more enemies than friends, sir.'

'Without the ability to know, on a daily basis, which is which.'

Their perambulations had brought them back to the main fortress gate, the discussion having moved on to the means by which Gilbert was trying to stop the influx from the Italian mainland. This, in essence, came down to a nightly patrol, if the weather was suitable, by HMS *Teme*, given it was in the hours of darkness and on a benign sea, the one-time exiles made the crossing.

There was a temptation to ask Gilbert for an opinion on both Burns and his ship. Where they being effective and if yes how much so? If not, why not? But he had a disinclination to air naval matters even with a Viceroy to whom he was seconded. Besides, there was also a telling fact; Gilbert might not have an opinion worth much in such an area and this left only one option.

'Then I need to see for myself how he goes about the duty, sir. So given the hour I must decline your dinner invitation and join Mr Burns aboard his vessel, which I suspect will set sail shortly.'

'As you wish, but take the invitation as an open one. You may dine with us on any evening you choose, since we keep a relatively open table. Lady Gilbert will appreciate the company, particularly as you're a fresh face and no doubt full of tales she's never heard.'

Pearce was obliged to hurry, given the early hour at which darkness fell in the Mediterranean and it was as well he did, finding Burns preparing to weigh. His arrival was not taken with anything approaching pleasure, quite the reverse. Toby Burns looked as if he wanted to object, while the crew, on deck and going about the tasks necessary to get *Teme* to sea, threw obvious glares in his direction. Pearce felt obliged to challenge them in a like manner, to stare them down.

'I am here only to observe, Mr Burns,' was imparted in a loud voice. 'I leave you to command and I will not interfere.'

This said, he took up station just ahead of the stern sweep, adding. 'All I ask is you carry out your duties as you normally would.'

Was Toby Burns nervous or just still useless? Watching him issue commands, Pearce could not miss the tremulous tone in his voice, nor the lack of swift application which came from his crew. They knew what they were about but, to the man observing, it seemed that they took a damned long time to go about it. This took Pearce back once more to the time of their original meeting.

Midshipman Burns was not a figure to attract much notice aboard HMS *Brilliant*. He had certainly failed to register with a man concentrating on surviving, in what had turned out to be an extremely dangerous situation. Peril, and there was no shortage of such from just being a novice aboard a navy warship, came from several sources, the first being the captain. It seemed Barclay had marked John Pearce out as in need of special attention, but he was not alone.

There was a malicious drummer boy, added to the ship's bully, both determined to cause him harm. As if this was not bad enough, there was Barclay's young and striking wife, to whom the eye of a young, well set and, from his time in Paris, practised seducer was irresistibly drawn. He had to wonder what such a beauty was doing wed to such a crab apple of a husband. It was a curiosity which brought retribution down on his head.

Burns only really mattered when the party, of which he was a member, ended up stranded on the Brittany shore, for it was there his endemic ineptness showed itself. There had to be a modicum of sympathy for a fellow so young, thrown into a position where he was supposed to lead grown men, most of whom were, to him, total strangers.

But the way the little shit had behaved, even after a long time and much water under the keel, still rankled with John Pearce. The real pity was he had managed, subsequently, to sink to even greater depths of mendacity, which made Pearce wonder how he had ever been made lieutenant. He himself would have struggled with an examination; in the case of Toby Burns it would have floored the sod.

They were exiting the tiny harbour at the same time as numerous fishing boats, mainly small and singly manned by a lone local. They would seek their catch by line, but coming along also were couple of larger boats, manned by two or three crew, who would use nets. The one thing they all had in common was some form of illumination, a single lantern on a stern staff for the small boats, the same fore and aft for the others.

HMS *Teme* had her lanterns rigged and lit, to illuminate the quarterdeck and forepeak, these much larger than those of the fishing fleet. Once at sea, the sails were set to take what wind on which they could sail, so there was not much activity on deck. Pearce realised a number of matters of which he was in ignorance and silently berated himself for not seeing to it before coming aboard. Loath to ask, he had no choice.

'Mr Burns, I wonder would you oblige me with some charts of the local waters.'

So hesitant was he, it was as if he'd asked him to recite a Shakespeare play verbatim, evidence of the endemic inability to swiftly react to any request. It stood as proof, his abiding feature, natural confusion, had not yet deserted him. He actually blinked before sending someone to fetch the charts, and these were handed to Pearce, who spread them over the sweep rudder, right under one of the lamps.

At least he had been given the charts which mattered, which were of a large enough scale to show both the island of Elba and the Italian coast. But it was the opposite shore which took most of his attention. It showed, running south of Bastia, a long and narrow sandbar enclosing a trapped body of seawater. The conclusion he reached was swift; it was a place he would have to inspect in daylight.

They had obviously reached the point at which they usually came about, for the orders were issued to do so. It was carried out in an easy fashion, *Teme* swinging in a wide arc, both the sweep and sail employed and shifted to bring her on to a northerly course, sailing on a slight swell. Burns in captain mode, stood just by the sole mast as this well-worn manoeuvre was carried out, a telescope to his eye.

What could he see? It would not be much on a night when the cloud cover had increased? It was more a studied pose than anything useful, for all he would pick up would be the numerous dots of lanterns by which they were surrounded. Most were stationary, necessary when line fishing, while the one or two in motion, trailing their nets, were inching along, easily identified by their twin lanterns.

Towards Elba, the local fishermen from the island were similarly occupied, which led to the conclusion how easy it would be to slip in among such a flotilla and creep towards the Corsican shore. It would have to be in the larger type of boat, the aim not to fish, but to smuggle bodies ashore, which would allow for greater numbers aboard.

And, at some point, the lanterns, which made such fellows anonymous, could be doused, rendering them invisible on a night like this. What was Toby Burns doing, sailing along with his own larger and easily identifiable lanterns showing, so anyone making such an attempt knew just where the one vessel they had to avoid lay?

Constrained by his own promise not to interfere, Pearce had to wonder if it was stupidity or deliberate. Toby Burns had shown himself to be a true coward on the one occasion he had been exposed to danger in the company of the Pelicans. He had later demonstrated the morals of a venomous snake, though to equate him to such a creature was to do an injustice to the reptile. Thus, the notion he was avoiding trouble and potential conflict could not be discounted.

The ritual of coming about was repeated twice before the fishermen began to head for shore, each seeking to be the first to land their catch and get the best price. It being still dark, it had to be the best time to sneak a party of exiles ashore, given the hour before dawn was a time when anyone set to watch for such arrivals would be at their lowest ebb.

Burns went through the ritual of running out his pair of guns at the approach of dawn, there being no clearing for action on the good grounds that there was nothing to clear and nowhere to put it if you did. It was like watching an act in dumb show, which had Pearce wonder if the same applied to him on HMS *Hazard*. He could only hope he did not come across as such an obvious poseur.

In daylight the cutter bore up for Bastia, in what was now a near empty sea, most of the fishing fleet having long made harbour. What vessels were now out, the early morning traders, were larger, tartanes mainly and designed to carry cargo between the islands and the mainland. Leaning on a bulwark, Pearce examined the approaching shoreline, noting it was rocky north of the city. But the long bar to the south was invitingly sandy before, at a fair distance, the shoreline turned to rocks once more.

Monk-like silence was maintained until HMS *Teme* was secured to bollards on the inner wall of the mole. At this point Pearce thanked Burns and departed, walking swiftly to find his own ship being given its daily clean. The fact that he emerged from his cabin, after not much more than a minute or two, wrapped in a towel caused no surprise. He was obliged, given their location, to discreetly lower himself into the water rather than execute a dive, where he struck out to take pleasure in its cooling embrace.

Aboard, Michael O'Hagan appeared on deck with two buckets of fresh water, while in the cabin, the smell of roasting coffee filled the air. He came back aboard as the hands were piped to breakfast, knowing his own would be ready once he was dressed. Following the meal, he would snatch a couple of hours of sleep.

'May I suggest lieutenant, if you wish to ride out, you do so in the presence of my wife, who takes a horse out just after dawn when it is still cool. She knows the country around Bastia as well as any local.'

Pearce accepted the implication that it was too late in the day. Whatever he had got from his swim had not lasted past his walk to see Sir Gilbert, so he was again uncomfortably aware how hot he was under his coat. He was also conscious of how little time he had if the Viceroy was going to take to his bed throughout the high heat of midday.

'In which case I will do so in the morning, if your wife has no objection.'

'Anna will not mind company of that I can assure you. So, I press you to attend dinner tonight to confirm the arrangement, unless you're going out with Mr Burns again.'

'No, I think dinner will be a better use of my time.' The remark got a look, which implied it posed a question, to which Pearce responded. 'Does Mr Burns report to you what success he has enjoyed?'

'He tells me how impossible it is to pick out which vessels might be carrying people instead of engaging in fishing.'

'I take it you have patrols ashore?''

'We do what we can with too few men to be truly effective. But they do have very occasional successes, always leading to a violent confrontation, which has burdened us with several casualties. Those who wish us gone are well armed and far from shy of the employment of weapons. If the Corsicans cannot agree on who should govern them or how it should be constituted, they are all, to a man, doughty fighters. It is a matter upon which Major Warburton will happily regale you, though it is Vickery and his inferiors who carry out the actual duty.'

'Then, with your permission, I will speak with both. Now, if you will forgive me, I must go back to my ship and issue some orders.'

'We dine at seven.'

'Until then, sir.'

The walk back was just as uncomfortable, but he did note not everybody on *Teme* was, as they had been the day before, asleep. There were men on deck idly tidying the ship, coiling ropes and moving various objects, an activity he was sure they only begun to undertake when they sighted him coming off the quayside. It was something he chose to ignore.

Once aboard, he checked Derwent had bought some of the fresh fish brought in that morning. He then sent an invitation to Hallowell, Worricker Macklin and Moberly to join him, reminding himself not to eat too much; he would be at the Gilberts board later. Sat at table eating fresh Turbot, he regaled all four with what he had witnessed the previous night. He also related what he had been told by the Viceroy, as well as his suspicions of the deliberate avoidance of action.

'It's impossible to be sure, but I know the officer in question well enough to consider it a possibility. But what I am certain of is this. His present mode of operation will yield him nothing for, with his lanterns lit, he might as well fly a signal to state his position.'

'If I may say so, sir,' Moberly interjected, 'that is a serious accusation to lay against the reputation of a fellow officer.'

'There are any number of people who will ask if I deserve my rank and position, while I hope my actions at least give them pause. With the fellow in question, I have no doubts of his unfitness for command.'

The reference to his background, rarely if ever mentioned, caused all his officers a degree of embarrassment, which meant they could not, for several awkward seconds, look him in the eye.

'However, it is what's to be done about it which is paramount. I want you, apart from Mr Hallowell, out in our boats tonight, without lights to alert *Teme* to your presence. I need you to row among the fishing fleet to see if anything presents itself. It will also be of interest if he uncovers your presence, for I'm curious to know what he would do about it.'

'They're bound to be observed by the fishermen,' opined Hallowell.

'Which is of no concern, but there may be others. So, you will each carry a pair of marines. Mr Moberly you will detail the men and I leave it to you if you join a boat or stay aboard.'

'I will be out, sir, rest assured.'

'Good. If you uncover anything suspicious, do not risk your lives, for you are likely to be outnumbered by people, whom I'm told, could be well armed and are certainly determined. At best, seek to drive anyone you suspect away from the shore, but make sure you put the safety of yourselves and the crew first.'

Seeing the reaction Pearce had to add, 'Gentlemen that is an order. We, like everyone else, are out fishing. The object is to gain information which will allow me to formulate some kind of plan which might work, for what is happening now is not.'

Alone, Pearce penned a letter, not sure if it was a missive he would send or hold back, for it was addressed to Jervis. In it he asked for permission to remove Toby Burns from the command of HMS *Teme* and replace him with Isaac Hallowell. He then began another addressed to Emily Barclay, in which he informed her of the presence of her nephew, with the information he had, in no discernible way, changed from the ball of slime he had been previously.

The rest was an update of his situation, with the addition of deep words of affection for both her and Adam, as well as his wish to be by their side.

--~--

The arrival of HMS *Lively* at Spithead was wont to evince more curiosity in the Port Admiral's quarters than surprise. For all anyone knew, Langholm should still be on his station, sailing between the Bay of Biscay and Lisbon to intercept enemy privateers. Nothing he made, in the report he delivered, hinted at anything untoward, though the haste with which he claimed the need to travel to London did.

He was in the coach before the day was out, and the despatches he carried from both Truscott and Sir David Rose were in his satchel. If he knew the contents of the former, the mystery of the latter he would have to wait to see it revealed. It was a matter of great interest, since he saw his primary purpose now as self-protection. He would have his share of the silver if it was going, but if there was fault for the firing on an allied vessel, he knew where and upon whom he wished it to securely rest.

CHAPTER SEVENTEEN

Several things were established at the Viceroy's dinner, the first being Lady Elliot was an engaging conversationalist, while Major Warburton was a bore and, to John Pearce's way of thinking, somewhat derelict in his duty. Having set a permanent guard on the road from San Fiorenzo, plus another on the wide track to the south, Warburton took no part in nightly patrols.

This had his naval counterpart wonder what he was doing here, only for Pearce to realise, with a bit of a blush, he was in the same boat, or not if you thought about it. He reassured himself with the notion this was a one off, whereas it was clear that the soldier was disinclined to venture out on such a lowly duty at any time.

Warburton complained his depleted numbers obliged him to confine his patrols to small bodies of men, no more than half a dozen in number and they were insufficient to cover the area required. There was the shoreline close to the walls, of course, but he also had to detail men to patrol the routes into the city, with only one which could be termed a road.

For the rest it was tracks, some well-established, others more for donkeys than humans, the latter numerous and impossible to completely close off. It was more the hope to deter than any attempt to seal off nocturnal access to Bastia. Warburton obviously knew, even if it made him splutter at the thought, the men they were seeking to interdict were likely running rings round his soldiers.

'Damned cunning the Corsicans, Pearce, it's in their blood. Inclined to kill each other as much as an enemy. Wholly unreliable when it came to backing us up in the fighting we undertook on their behalf. Left us to take Bastia almost without lifting a finger, don't you know.'

This being imparted with the air of a man who had undertaken the task single-handed, when the army had been damned slow to even arrive, pricked Pearce to respond with the acid comment, it was as well the navy was there.

'Point taken. Did a sterling job in assisting us, I am obliged to admit.'

'How are you with horses, Lieutenant Pearce?'

Their hostess asked this in a deliberate attempt to change the subject, she having observed her frowning naval guest being about to put Warburton in his place. Pearce had heard enough about the siege to know, without the navy, their cannon and marines, Bastia would still be in French hands.

'I admit to not riding regularly, Lady Elliot. What sailor can? But I can claim to have, from memory, a reasonable seat.'

'Which you may need, sir,' she chuckled. 'The local mounts take their cue from the local menfolk, who are touchy in the extreme.'

No longer in her first youth, Pearce could see the beauty she had once been, while her demeanour was engaging and had probably been so when she was young and at her most attractive. Her relationship with her husband was one of mutual regard and, if she agreed with him about his difficulties in representing His Majesty to the Corsicans, she made it quite clear how much she admired them. This was something of a snub to Warburton.

'One cannot, in my opinion, fault independence of spirit, in an equine or any other creature.'

The growl in the army throat was as good as saying 'Poppycock.'

'I wonder, Major Warburton,' Pearce asked, 'if I would be allowed to go out with one of your patrols on another night?'

'Can't see it will do much good, sir, but I have no objection.'

'Tomorrow night, then?'

'Best speak with Vickery and he'll set you up. I leave the details to him.'

'The art of delegation,' Pearce replied in a deeply sardonic tone. It went right over the soldier's head because he took it as a compliment.

Anna Elliot moved the conversation on from the talk of night patrols to the subjects closest to the hearts of those at the table – the prospects of further French victories in northern Italy, which might mean Naples pulling out of the coalition. More pressing, how Britannia would deal with the desertion of Spain, if what John Pearce had told them was to come to pass. There was also the perennial question: Could the men now running France survive, or would they too, like so many of their predecessors, fall to the guillotine?

'They will endure,' Sir Gilbert ventured, 'as long as Buonaparte is sending back chests full of gold and the treasures of the Italian city states. If he fails, I suspect they will soon follow.'

'To be replaced by what, sir?'

'A man with a sword, lieutenant, as all such upheavals do in the end. We had Cromwell remember.'

'And eventually a royal restoration,' was advanced by John Pearce with a tone of improbability.

'I would advise you not to wager against a return of the Bourbon monarchy,' Elliot said firmly. 'It may take a decade or two, but I see it as a prospect. People generally tire of radicalism.'

'I think you know what my father would say to what you call a prospect.'

'And what did Adam say about the Revolution?'

This had a slightly waspish tone, which came as a surprise from a man who'd spoken of the Pearce parent, if not with outright enthusiasm, at least with respect. The son replied in kind, making no attempt to soften his tone.

'He welcomed it, and then vocally deplored the way it developed, which, sad to say, cost him his life.'

'Forgive me,' was a quick response, accompanied by a sad look. 'I have been impolite.'

Being so genuine, Pearce could only smile and nod.

'My husband told me something of your father, lieutenant. He sounded an interesting man, even if I'm far from sure I would have agreed with his notions of how society should be organised.'

'You would decline the chance to vote, Lady Elliot, the universal right for women to do so as well as men, being one of his aims?'

'The notion is so novel that I cannot countenance how I would answer you. Perhaps when we ride out tomorrow, you can tell me more of his ideas. Who knows where we can find common ground, something we should all seek? Are not our present disorders a consequence of a failure to do so?'

'Fault of the damned French,' harrumphed Warburton. 'Never did trust them.'

The morning air was still and pleasantly cool. Pearce, coatless and comfortable in a shirt and loose sailor's ducks, shared in the appreciation of what his hostess so clearly enjoyed on a daily basis – a sense of freedom from the chores of her husband's office, for they were without an escort of any kind. The landscape was dramatic, with the air full of the smell of the herbs damp from the morning dew.

They made their way through clumps of tough gorse, the mounts doing so mostly without recourse to the reins, on a path rising ever higher into the hills behind Bastia, to provide a panoramic vista over the deep blue sea. Occasionally they passed peasants leading loaded donkeys, obviously the main means of transport for goods locally, heading for the town and the market to sell the produce with which the animals were burdened.

The subject of Adam Pearce and his radical ideas were fully explored, as she gently extracted from the son those points on which he and old Adam had come, over time, to disagree. There was no mention of the fact they'd suffered a spell in prison, where exposure to the dregs of society had seriously altered the younger Pearce's thinking.

From such an experience he had declined to still hold to the possibility of improving the lot of the mass of humanity. He did add, however, one of his father's main contentions, which was that poverty exaggerated what were common modes of behaviour. In other words, the rich, as well as those in the middle of those two states, were just as venal as the lowest rookery dweller.

They began to discuss the previous occupiers of Corsica, Lady Elliot going all the way back to the Greeks and Carthaginians, about whom she was knowledgeable, admitting it was a subject she had put effort into learning since her arrival. She talked of the Punic Wars with the kind of detail which made it seem as if she had been present at the time, to then allude to their displacement of the previous occupiers by the Romans. Finally, she alluded to the lack of the kind of remains so common in other parts of their far-flung empire, as an example of the spirit which animated the local inhabitants.

'There is scant evidence they were ever here, for there are few temples of the kind so prevalent in Italy and Sicily, certainly none inland.'

'Places you have visited, I assume?'

'Who could not, when fortunate enough to be in such proximity. It tells you that not even mighty Rome ever entirely subjugated the people of the island and I doubt the French would have fared any better. It is possible to suggest they might even come, in future, to regret taking over Corsica.'

Pearce was only half listening by this time, his attention now focused on what these heights revealed. The obvious fact being that all the advantage when it came to sneaking bodies and arms ashore lay with the exiles, and this was especially true if they had local support. Army patrols, and he assumed they were static, had to get into position in daylight and, even if they chose to try and do so at night, they would require torchlight. Both would reveal their position to anyone watching from these heights.

The kind of scrub they had ridden through, thick and thorny bushes mixed with clumps of stunted trees, made it an easy place to hide as well as to send signals by lantern, invisible to those lower down the hillside. Anyone at sea could be advised what to avoid when choosing a place to land. This made it likely that any encounters with Warburton's patrols had been by accident.

Lady Elliot had her spot for rest, a place where there was a modicum of shade, grazing for the mounts and rocks on which to sit and eat the fruit she had brought along. They watched as the sun rose high, to change the colour of the sea from deep blue to a pale azure. Pearce was studying the way the waves broke on the shore, not much on what was a calm day.

But it showed him how few places to the north of the city were suitable for a safe landing. He also observed that there were several small inlets, with sandy beaches, to the south, but they seemed to be backed by steep hills. This left the narrow spit of sand running down from Bastia as the obvious spot to choose, because any piquet placed there, lacking vegetation, would be obvious.

There was a body of water to cross, probably too deep to wade, which could only be done by boats but where would an interloper go then? He reckoned even the dimmest military mind, and Warburton looked to possess one, would seal off the exit at the north, nearest to the city.

'What do they call the water down there inside the sandbar?'

'In Italian it is called La Stagna di Biguglia. Etang is the name in French.'

'The latter I should know?'

'You have French?'

After this being acknowledged, the ride back was taken up with a conversation conducted entirely in that language, with tales of a long-gone Paris, visited and wondered at by a newlywed Anne Elliot. Pearce responded with stories of the city as it became, before the horror of the *Terror* took hold. If he talked of salons and the wit and erudition of those who frequented them, he left out the numerous romantic liaisons, on more than one occasion, this had led to.

He also related how, in the service, fluency in the language had brought him certain advantages as well as problems, the second the object of much amusement, given the way he related the stories. If he looked and sounded amused, in memory, it was less so, given he could recall the dangers such ability exposed him to, none of which was allowed to show.

Once Lady Elliot was thanked and the horse handed over to the stables, he retrieved his uniform coat and hat then went to have a talk with Lieutenant Vickery. Thus, he laid the ground for him to join one of the patrols, in fact the one the soldier would himself lead that night. Then it was time to make his way back to *Hazard* to receive a report from his officers not pleased to find them still abed.

'Since we only required an anchor watch, sir, I didn't think you'd object to giving them a couple of hours extra rest.'

'And I don't Mr Hallowell, but I reckon they have enjoyed enough. Coffee in my cabin in twenty minutes.'

The first thing established was the ease with which the boats had managed to avoid being sighted by HMS *Teme*. The easily spotted lanterns, which had so troubled Pearce the night before, were much more of a beacon to avoid when in a darkened boat. Macklin had ended up with the impression the armed cutter sailed the same course every night they were at sea. There was no sign of any manoeuvring or position changing by the fishermen to avoid it.

'They are thus safe from being rammed and tipped into the water.'

'How do they know their position in the dark?' asked Moberly who'd been with Worricker.

'I think you'll find Mr Moberly, those who fish the same waters night after night, know where they are, perhaps by sheer instinct. Then there is long habit and an intimate knowledge of the stars. Remember they do so in numbers, so each man out with line or net, will have a stated claim to a patch of water and the Lord help anyone who strays. It is probably one going back in their family line for an age, passed down from father to son and fiercely protected.'

'You speak, I sense, of what you know?' Pearce commented.

'It's the way of island life, sir, be it off the Southern Irish coast or here in the Med.'

Which reminded Pearce of where Macklin had said he hailed from and gave credence to his statement.

'We certainly gave one or two of them a fright,' Hallowell chuckled. 'I reckon some of your fisherfolk thought us ghosts.'

Which was not hard to imagine? The use of oars in the *Hazard*'s boats would have been minimal, barely enough to provide forward motion, with the crew ordered to be silent. On another partly cloudy night, they would many times have been invisible until in near touching distance.

'You say one or two,' asked Pearce. 'Not all?'

It was Worricker who answered in the affirmative. When his course and choice of location was revealed, it put him on the outer southern area in which the fishing fleet operated, making sense of his point. Those coming from Italy would not sail through the middle of the numerous fishing boats. They would make their way round the outer edge to avoid detection, and it would not be to the rocky northern shore.

'And time their dash when *Teme* was well away from their course,' concluded Pearce.

'The weather has suited them the last two nights, sir, but it will not always be so.'

Hallowell's point was acknowledged, which brought home to John Pearce a question he had never got round to asking: Did Toby Burns sail every night, excepting those in which the weather was unsuitable, and there would be a number of those? And at what level did he decide it to be unsafe, he not being one to brave the storm?

'Did you observe any signals from the shore?' asked Pearce, well aware he had issued no instructions they should do so, which was remiss.

The negative answer lay in the blank stares, which had him wonder if they were thinking the same as he. The explanation, of what he had concluded on his morning ride, was responded to with nods leading to a shared conclusion. This seemed to underline that the Pearce opinion on the behaviour of Toby Burns was the accurate one.

The way to confound incoming boats, and it had to be accepted they might not be active even on every suitable night, was to take up a position in a darkened ship. Then, those aboard could look out for signals from the shore; these being the alert they needed to attempt an interception. A small beacon, and it could be a burning one, would be visible well out to sea, while even a decent-sized blinking lantern would show. It would certainly be of more potent effect, once most of the distance had been covered.

'To tell them what?' asked Pearce rhetorically. 'If the soldiers have placed piquets and where they are, thus how to avoid them, given, and I'm assuming a point here, they vary their routes and locations.'

The thought that occurred to Pearce then harked back to his walk with the Viceroy. Sir Gilbert had said the people he feared were concentrating around Bastia with the aim of taking the place from within. This, if he had not actually stated it, threatened him, his family as well as Warburton's men.

Then there was the smuggling in of weapons, which surely had some bearing on where they would choose to come ashore. Muskets in quantity were heavy, barrels of powder without which they were useless even more so. There could be lead too, for the casting of musket balls; none of this was a problem afloat, but a burden once on land.

He ordered more coffee in order to let these thoughts develop, while idly taking in the fact that his guests felt free to talk among themselves while he was silent. This he found reassuring, knowing there were captains who would only allow their underlings to speak in their presence when spoken to. It was generally the sign of an unhappy ship.

Pearce sought to put himself in the place of those Burns had been sent here to stop. He imagined a warm night and, at this time of year, coming into autumn, they were generally sticky. The last thing anyone would wish for was a heavy load and miles to travel, while at the same time having to watch out for those sent out to stop them.

There would surely be comrades ashore, able to send signals that it was safe to attempt a landing. Warburton had spoken of narrow tracks and of the occasional surprise firefight, which indicated the system was not impermeable. So, the less distance anyone had to travel on foot, the less the effort. In his mind's eye he conjured up what he'd observed that morning, the beaches to the south of Bastia, the rocks to the north. But more importantly he thought of the spit of sand enclosing the Stagna di Biguglia, by his reckoning, some eight or nine miles in length.

If he had a limited knowledge of how smugglers went about their trade, he had one experience to fall back on, albeit one which was not a fond memory, quite the reverse. When he, along with Michael, Charlie and Rufus, had been party to such a thing, it was obvious that the landfall was made in a regular spot. It was not random, it was organised and had to be, for it took many bodies to shift a full cargo of contraband.

He would be out again tonight, but could he persuade Lieutenant Vickery what he wanted to do was different to the activity in which the army man would usually engage? Would he indulge John Pearce, who thought he might propose a possible solution to the problem? He could only hope so.

CHAPTER EIGHTEEN

Time spent with Lieutenant Vickery, before the men going out on patrol were paraded, told Pearce a great deal about the constraints under which the regiment laboured, not aided by an indolent commanding officer like Warburton. Vickery was careful in his language, there being no outright condemnation. But he had a way of imparting the facts of his duties, which left little doubt it was a burden laid almost entirely upon him.

The pair spent some time as the map covering one wall and the permanent dispositions were explained. Pearce enquired about the density of the vegetation at various marked points, denoting the places at which the watches could be deployed. These were never the same two nights running, but Vickery acknowledged that to get to any of them in secret was, for the reasons Pearce had already imagined, impossible.

The most salient fact to him were the wide and numerous gaps left, whatever they did. The soldiers were spread very thin, with one party sent to guard the rocky northern shore. The rest were allotted places in the concealment provided by the trees and bushes which hemmed in the various tracks.

Vickery, when asked, readily admitted that, excepting the exits north of the Stagna di Biguglia, they never took up positions on the narrow spit of sand. There was no cover and, more importantly, there was no option to withdraw without losses by superior force if threatened.

When it came to lack of numbers, he referred to the siege and its aftermath, of the sickness which had afflicted the troops, more than decimating their strength. The French surrender, in reality brought on by a lack of ammunition for their cannon rather than force, came at a fortuitous time.

The Recoats, thinned by disease, would have been hard pressed to mount any assault which would stand a reasonable chance of success. It was the naval cannon, blasting a breech in the curtain wall, added to their inability to withstand any subsequent assault, which saw the white flag raised and the garrison depart. The 65th regiment was left behind, while the remnants of the army, sick included, marched back to San Fiorenzo.

'The company has not been at full complement since before it fell. Also, we were seriously deficient in officers at the end, having lost several to fever and previous sorties. Two of the remainder of my mess have been killed since.'

'Fighting Corsicans?'

'In one case, yes. We lost Ensign Porter in an encounter in the maquis.'

A query from Pearce established that this was the name the locals gave to the dense and difficult to fight in vegetation. This was a feature of any part of the island above the treeline, a place where Vickery maintained one could hide an army. The ensign had been leading a patrol, which he took beyond what was considered safe, only to fall victim to an ambush. It had cost him his life along with three of his party, another couple sustaining wounds enough to render them ineffective.

'The price of seeking fame and glory, Mr Pearce.'

'You said two officers?'

'Captain Wroe fell to a knife one night in the town, when out on his own.'

The temptation to ask what he was doing out alone in darkness, in a place where the British had known enemies, had to be resisted. There could be any number of reasons, while the way Vickery imparted the fact, with a slight shake of the head to indicate folly, did not invite enquiry. He had to conclude that the man could have just been unlucky.

What these losses did do was leave the regiment short of men to command the troops they led, especially when split into small packets, which resulted in much responsibility falling on his two sergeants and a quartet of corporals. Relating this to some of the army boneheads he'd encountered, and the navy had its fair share, led Pearce to suspect the ordinary rankers were probably grateful at not being led by officers.

'If we do find trouble, we are generally outnumbered, so it's only our discipline, by which I mean the ability to retire in good order, which mitigates the risks we take.'

One of the sergeants appeared at the door to Vickery's quarters to say the men were on parade and awaiting his inspection. This had the lieutenant stand, don his hat, tug at his faded uniform coat, to then indicate he would be along presently.

'Bit of a farce, Mr Pearce, which you will recall from the day you berthed. The men are clad in close to rags. Been promised new uniforms for months, but they never arrive and the wear on our musket barrels is beginning to be a problem. We are of no use lest we practice and Major Warburton has insisted we must desist.'

Pearce couldn't resist it. 'Major Warburton is a man of strong opinions, I have found. He also seems to have no trouble keeping red the colour of his coat.'

'Captain Wroe's best, with the rank badges changed. If you look closely, you'll see some careful repair at the back.'

'I think I might take your word for it.'

Pearce picked up his pistols and jammed them in his belt, slinging a cartouche over his shoulder. They emerged to find Michael O'Hagan leaning against the wall, a short blue jacket over his shoulder. It was a position he chose to maintain when the officers appeared, until a look from Pearce had him pull himself up into a semblance of respect.

'I hope you do not object, I fetched along a fellow whom I trust to watch my back.'

Even far from fully stretched, O'Hagan towered over the army man and gave a good head to Pearce as well. Vickery took in both the weight and the width of shoulder and nodded.

'Best he waits here.'

With the quadrangle acting as a barrack square, the men, at a quick count, thirty plus in number, were lined up where the castle walls provided some shade. Pearce had already been told that there was a twenty-man piquet camped by the road which led over the mountains, while another guarded the most frequently used track to the south. This, at one time part of an old Roman road, ran all the way to Bonifacio at the base of Corsica with Sardinia in plain view across the straits.

Both piquets were kept within striking distance of Bastia so they could be supported, if necessary. They also had instructions to avoid becoming exposed and with orders to withdraw if severely threatened. They would then be able to reinforce the garrison, the security of the walls of Bastia being paramount. There were also the men he'd first seen on the mole, while there were bound to be, in such a climate, a number of sick, not including the wounded.

Men were acting as guards and sentinels, dotted around the walls and the various doorways, not forgetting the main entrance in addition to the men manning the cannon. So, a quick calculation put the total strength at around a hundred and fifty effectives, which underlined the peril in which they operated. No one, from the Viceroy down, knew what they faced in the number of their potential enemies. They could only surmise that their strength was increasing while the garrison would likely be diminishing.

'We have assurances from Corte, should we be threatened with uncontainable force, there are militias there in numbers who will come rushing to our aid.'

'I'm bound to enquire, Mr Vickery, having seen the terrain and the point you made regarding the lack of roads, how long they would take to get here?'

'By their own calculation,' came with a wry grin, 'faster than the crow can fly.'

'I'm sure you mean pigs.'

On sight of their officer, the men were brought to noisy attention, at which point Major Warburton appeared from within the main building, blinking in the strong sunlight in which it was bathed. Acknowledging a salute from Vickery, he marched swiftly towards the right marker, where a sergeant joined him, to walk a couple of paces behind, as he went down the line. The inspection was perfunctory, the major not bothering to notice the defects of the uniforms and there were many. Once he reached the end of the line, he turned and passed his inferior officer, returning the salute and adding.

'Carry on, Mr Vickery.'

Then he was gone, back through the door and out of the baking sun.

'I sense the major's inherited coat will hold its colour for a long time,' Pearce posited.

He was in receipt of a rather embarrassed grin and a nod, before the order was issued for the men to fall out. The patrol leaders were called to Vickery's quarters to ensure each knew their allotted duty.

'Lieutenant Pearce and the fellow he has fetched along will accompany us. And the watchword for tonight is hazard.'

—◆—

Late afternoon and a lack of wind seemed to hold the heat, promising an uncomfortable hike. Having exited the main fortress gate and crossed the glacis, the company split up: five men under a corporal heading for the rocky shore to the north. The rest headed in the opposite direction, as quickly as possible, finding vegetation by which they could partly hide their onward movements. Much swatting away of annoying and buzzing insects was necessary.

At intervals, Vickery silently indicated to a selected group, who then set out to find a place to act as a base, their first task being to load their muskets. By the time they reached the last point indicated by Vickery, darkness was falling. Without knowing exactly where he was, Pearce was aware they were nowhere near the southern end of the Stagna. Thus, a great deal of water lay beyond the point chosen, which meant a sizeable body of the spit was unguarded.

'Do you ever go further?'

There was just enough light remaining to see the pained expression on Vickery's face. The answer, imparted quietly once he was sure none of his men could hear, told Pearce Warburton has forbidden it. To do so would place his men too far away from support or the ability to get back to the safety of the walls.

'He is adamant we cannot afford further losses. Now I must ask if you wish to remain with this detail or accompany me. I must check the sections covering the tracks where we dropped them off to ensure they are carrying out their duty.'

'You have to go back the way we came?'

'I'll end up here finally. Then we will cease operations for tonight and fall back on the fortress.'

'I am minded to go a bit further.'

'I cannot, nor do I wish to command you to desist, Mr Pearce. Just remember the watchword when you return.'

'It's one I'm hardly likely to forget.'

'We generally pull back at the first hint of dawn. You'll espy it as the grey light tops the Apennines.'

'I will seek to do so with you, but I would ask you not to wait if I fail to return in time.'

Vickery's tone, hitherto friendly, took on a sharper edge. 'I won't, sir. To do so might increase the risk to the men I lead.'

'Michael, with me.'

There was not much between the pair and the still, unruffled water of the Stagna, Michael following Pearce till they reached the edge, there to pick up the faintest zephyr.

'Jesus, a breath of air at last.'

'Added to starlight and a rising moon.'

Right now, this was a yellowish orb, low on the horizon, its colour created by the trapped heat and air-held dust. This was yet to dissipate into the night sky, on this occasion, near to cloudless. It would turn to icy white as it rose to spread its glow, which could reveal anything afloat on water, the surface of which would be turned to a sheet of silver. But right now, the most obvious lights were the large fore and aft lanterns on HMS *Teme*.

'Jesus,' Michael said, crossing himself as he always did when he invoked the deity. 'He might as well fire off blue lights, the little gobshite.'

'The same conclusion I came to when I was out there with him.'

Given he trusted Michael absolutely, no one more so, added to the fact that the Irishman had experienced the way Toby Burns behaved in Brittany, Pearce had no hesitation in being open. He related what he had suggested to the officers in his cabin, something he would never share with the rest of the lower deck, Charlie and Rufus possibly excepted if the circumstances merited it.

It was odd looking back and thinking of those he'd been pressed with, to reflect, in some senses, that Burns had taken men who hardly knew each other and, by his actions, or lack of them, turned them into a group who bonded and came to identify themselves as the Pelicans.

'We're going to be walking on soft sand Michael, so I suggest we carry our boots and paddle our way down the edge of this water. It will be pleasant on the feet.'

'Sure, do they run to snakes hereabouts?'

Tempted to say you and snakes, Pearce replied in a jocular tone. 'I'm told St Patrick passed this way when heading for Ireland and practised his craft here, so you're safe.'

The thud on his shoulder was much less than the blow the Irishman could deliver, but the man on the receiving end knew it would be a bruise when examined. O'Hagan was not keen on jokes about snakes or his country's patron saint.

Pearce was right about the water. Hot feet cooled quickly and any aches of wear were eased as they paddled along. Pearce reckoned, for the moment and on the inner part of the Stagna, they would be invisible against the backdrop of trees and bushes. It would not last; the rising moon would soon be too strong.

'You're walking with your head down; are we looking for something, John-boy?'

'Boats or a sign that they've been dragged out of the water.'

'Jesus, a fine idea when it's dark.'

'There's a small tidal rise and fall on yonder seashore, none at all inside the spit, lest there's storm water, which we have not had for days. People coming ashore from a distance can only do it with decent-sized boats, for it's not safe to be out in open water with anything flimsy. It would be hell to near impossible dragging them over a sandbar, don't you reckon.'

'So?'

'What if there are other craft already on the inner side, which would mean just trading one for another.'

'I'd be thinkin', since I know you too well John Pearce, there's more to be told.'

He had to supress the temptation to laugh at what was the palpable truth. So, he explained his thinking about moving guns and powder, as well as human cargo. The fact men could use tracks inland to get to where they were going. But what if they had a load to carry, with the chance, slim he had to admit, of running into a group of Vickery's men.

'It's not a chance I would take.'

'And the good Lord knows how many of those there are, John-boy. Are you telling me we're going to take on these you talk of in numbers?'

'Never in life. We have boats out, as we did last night. From them we will get a signal if there's any danger.'

The ripple of light across the eastern sky was faint but unmistakable, though no sound came with it. It was enough to stop John Pearce and have him peer out to sea, seeking to calculate the reaction of those out fishing. If the locals knew where to drop a hook, they also had the ability to read the weather as it affected them. At first there was no discernible reaction, but a second stronger flash of lightning, showing the silhouette of the tops of the distant Italian mountains, was bound to cause concern.

'Comin' our way, do you reckon, John-boy?'

'Hard to tell Michael.' The air had gone still, the very faint breeze no longer fanning their cheeks as he added. 'Let's keep moving.'

Which they did, and for some time, till the first proper streak showed – a bolt shooting earthwards out of clouds briefly illuminated, the strike invisible. It was difficult to tell if the boats were moving at first, but as the lanterns began to converge, it was obvious they were abandoning their night's work. Sat still, in an open boat, was no place to be in, when deadly bolts were being discharged from the heavens.

'I hope our boats take their cue from the locals.'

Pearce had no sooner expressed this wish when two blue flashes appeared out to sea, the faint sound of musket fire taking several seconds to reach their ears.

'Our lads, John-boy?'

'How would I know?'

The answer was quick in coming, for there was a response. This time it looked like many more muskets being discharged, the aim of the shot, judging by the muzzle flashes, in the opposite direction to the first pair. This indicated one of *Hazard*'s boats had spotted a potential target and, in strict contravention of orders, had opened fire, which produced a string of curses.

It took a while, but the more numerous weapons were reloaded and fired. Pearce was praying Worricker, for he supposed it to be him, had the crew of his boat rowing like men possessed. They would need to do so to get out of danger, which given the poor range of the standard musket, as well as one fired off a moving deck, should not take too long.

It was then the distant sky lit up, with a whole array of streaks erupting from the now visible cloud cover, accompanied by a swish of cooler air. More, it momentarily lit the seascape, turning the surface of the water white, but also showing both the boats which had exchanged gunfire. One was heading north, with just the faintest vision of splashing from plied oars, the other stationary. From this came a third salvo, no flashes this time, for the overhead light was too strong, while out beyond them bolts of lightning were beginning to strike water.

'Jesus, that sod is moving fast,' Michael whispered as a strong gust of cool wind ruffled their shirts.

He crossed himself, this coinciding with the return of darkness, no more than a momentary interlude until the next flashes appeared, soon followed by the first deafening clap of thunder. Stock still,

Pearce and Michael watched until these became continuous, preceded by endless bolts raining down to pepper the sea, showing the fishing fleet, which had abandoned its nights work, crowding round the entrance to the harbour.

'Will they come on or. . . ?'

There was no need to finish as a lantern light appeared briefly, soon washed out by lightning. Whoever was in the craft had to be intent on sneaking ashore but had a real dilemma. They were closer to the Corsican shore than they were to wherever they'd set out from, but getting to land was no longer possible in secret, a point made by Pearce.

'With all running for their lives, they'd be best to do the same,' Michael concluded.

What triggered the explosion neither Pearce nor Michael would ever know – a bolt of lightning striking a powder barrel perhaps, someone dropping a lantern, or an accidental discharge of a musket when in the middle of loading. All they knew for certain was that the size of the detonation was enough to blow the craft apart and, within moments, to set light to its timbers.

This time, when Michael crossed himself, no words accompanied the gesture. It was a silent way of wishing for the souls of the dead to be taken into God's embrace. Then the heavens opened, sheets of rain falling as a wall of water, turned white every so often by the continuing lightning. The torrent began to extinguish the still burning parts of the wreck and soon there was no more sign of its presence.

'I would say we'd best be gone, John-boy.'

There was no audible reply. John Pearce was already moving fast.

CHAPTER NINETEEN

The storm from which they sought safety was the precursor of three days of bad weather, with high winds and seas rough enough to force HMS *Hazard* away from the mole, to ride it out in the deep water between Bastia and the Island of Pianosa. For all the discomfort this entailed, John Pearce might have been prey to even greater disquiet had he been back in England. There he was a subject of discussion in numerous locations, one being Downing Street.

With the despatch from Sir David Rose delivered and digested, the First Lord of the Treasury and his right-hand helpmeet, Henry Dundas, had to come up with a way to react to the questionable actions undertaken by Pearce and Langholm. Even at the most positive reckoning, they could not deny it was bordering on illegality.

The information vouchsafed to them by Samuel Oliphant, about Spanish intentions, had been confined within a tight circle of trusted government ministers, the type not given to gossip and of those there were too many. The last thing the country required, at a sensitive time in the political firmament, was stories of possible Spanish duplicity.

Oliphant had been questioned closely to ensure the evidence he had come home with was accurate. Luckily, he had the plea from the Basque *Cortes* to back up his story. If accepted, it pointed to Godoy playing a deep game. He would be manoeuvring so as to be in a commanding position when the French were ready to back him and the time came to act. Another question was just as pressing: Had Pearce got the message of impending danger to where it needed to be?

'Sir David assured us he sailed with twenty-four hours,' Dundas reminded his friend. 'It should be he faces no danger yet, as far as we know, from Spain. So, I think we can assume Jervis has been informed, and he will react as he sees fit.'

Pitt replied with no great enthusiasm, given the time it took for despatches to reach Whitehall from the Mediterranean; indeed his mood was gloomy. 'As usual, we are obliged to be patient.'

The overarching air of the Prime Minister's pessimism was based on a sound footing, which had little to do with Jervis. Austria was struggling against the French in northern Italy. It had got to the point where, according to the latest news, they faced an outright defeat, which would knock them too out of the war. There was no reliance being placed on Naples, though the kingdom was still begging for subsidies from the British Exchequer to keep their ships and army fit for battle.

'And a damn lot of use they are if they're declining to actually fight.'

The truth was, while their ships had ably supported Hood in the past, their army was more a mirage than a force to be reckoned with. With Napoleon rampaging unchecked, they had marched north with banners flying and trumpets blowing, led by King Ferdinand, moronic by reputation and reckoned to be on the verge of insanity.

Having come up against the French, they had promptly melted away, their sovereign leading the rout with the same level of enthusiasm with which he had led the advance. He was home long before his army, so the only thing keeping the kingdom from invasion was the lack of French forces, too occupied with fighting Austria, to exploit their weakness.

There was another telling reason for dejection. Pitt was under a great deal of political pressure. None of the coalition put together to contain the Revolution three years previously would lift a finger without British gold, and Britannia had run out. The opposition were baying for peace, claiming there was a risk of national bankruptcy, and it was true. There was a shortage of the means necessary to back up the currency.

There was also abroad a continuing fear of a French invasion, and the only thing to prevent it were the fleets covering both Brest and the Texel. This was leading to people withdrawing their deposits, converting banknotes for the gold which backed up its value, and this was in very short supply. Their fears would not be eased by the worries for the Mediterranean.

Dundas, despite what he took to be the truth of Spanish intentions, still had their ambassador pleading for a subsidy in gold for Madrid, so their fleet could participate in the war. The best slant which he could be put on this was telling: the poor dupe of an envoy had no idea regarding the manoeuvres of Spain's First Minister or the secret Treaty of San Ildefonso.

'If Godoy delays long enough, and his man presses hard enough, we may have to give him back his silver. Mind, Sir David Rose has serious doubts they will admit to its loss.'

'Let's hope he has the right of it, Henry. We cannot reward Langholm and Pearce and give in to Spain with the same cargo. We may even need it to shore up the bank. It's something to which we are going to have to find a solution and one which serves the national interest.'

'Speaking of Pearce, we both know how high he stands in the estimation of the navy. We can safely assume the Admiralty, with Langholm's return, have as much information as do we. Will some of the salts seek to use it to damn him? In doing so, who knows where it will lead?'

For the first time Pitt allowed himself a bit of a smile. 'I have some hope such a difficulty has been taken care of.'

On receipt of the report submitted by Lord Langholm, it had taken several days to arrange an examination by the Board of the Admiralty. It was now in session, with the man who'd written it in an anteroom, waiting to be questioned. There was also, and this would be kept hidden from everyone outside, a copy of the alternative and positive appreciation penned by the Governor of Gibraltar.

Even the men in the room were not privy to everything in the case they had been called to examine, having no knowledge of the prior discussions their First Lord had engaged in with William Pitt. The Prime Minister wanted an outcome which promised the least level of public speculation. And even Earl Spenser was not informed of everything, for instance, the fact that John Pearce had been on a secret mission initiated by Henry Dundas. But he had been given a remit and was determined to adhere to it.

'Gentlemen, I must first remind you we are here to discuss the actions of the two officers involved in the taking of the *Santa Leocadia*. Other matters are beyond our sphere of responsibility and will, in time, fall to others to adjudicate upon.'

All were aware, Spenser, who chaired the board as First Lord, was referring to what the Spaniard was carrying and its purpose, as related by Langholm. Being a political appointee, he was less than fully knowledgeable regarding matters to do with the sea, but three of the other half-dozen men in the room were sailors, so he did not lack for professional advice. As a plus, he had Mr Stephens, the long-serving board secretary and a member of parliament, who had been involved with naval business for decades.

'In which case we must address the fact that there are significant differences in the two accounts. I submit both cannot be accurate.'

This was put forward by Charles Pybus, the newest member of the board, as well as the youngest. A barrister and a recently elected MP, he had shone in the house with several erudite speeches which had impressed the Tory benches. Pybus was a personal appointee of

William Pitt, who was known to rate him highly, not a view unanimously shared by those with whom he was deliberating.

'Sir David Rose is adamant,' Earl Spenser conceded, 'Pearce acted properly, given the information at his disposal. Langholm, as we can see from his report, has reservations.'

'Sir David was not present on the day in question, so what he says will have come from Pearce,' bellowed Rear Admiral Lord Seymour, who was slightly deaf. 'I, for one, would believe Langholm over an imposter like Pearce. The day he got his promotion was a black one for the navy.'

'I think we must confine that particular event to history,' Spenser replied wearily, it being a complaint aired more than once before the meeting could be called, and not just by Seymour.

The sailor tapped the papers on the table. 'Before us sits a golden chance to be rid of the man, to get him in front of a court and drum him out of the service.'

'Surely a silver opportunity, admiral?'

The jest from Pybus was not taken well and got him a black look from the sailor as well as a warning one from the chair, but Seymour then went on to drive home the point: it was outside their remit.

'You may see it as humorous, sir, but I can assure you of one fact. You will struggle to find a serving officer who thinks it funny. I see it as a sign of His Majesty's disordered mind he issued the order for the man to be ranked a lieutenant without going through the proper examination.'

'Hear him.'

This call of agreement came from Admiral Young, another naval lord, not long back from the Med, where he'd served under the now discredited Hotham. He was a fellow of few words and less than rigid opinions, being something of a weathervane. He was very likely to vote whichever way he saw the wind blowing.

'I have heard the story,' Pybus essayed. 'And I seem to remember it was awarded to Pearce for conspicuous bravery.'

'A quality of which the navy, sir, is not short,' Seymour insisted. 'We'll get nothing but approval if we use Langholm's report to sanction Pearce. The man is a hot-headed menace and deserves the stocks.'

'Surely, any Court Martial would have to sit while the Dons are still our allies.'

'My information is,' Spenser said cautiously, 'time for such does not exist.'

This, which Pitt would likely have preferred be withheld, either raised eyebrows or led to a degree of chin stroking. The man who'd said it felt the need to ensure it was not taken as an established fact.

'I will add that it is subject to a high degree of speculation.'

'Can we not send out to Jervis and let him handle it. I rate him as reliable in the matter of Pearce, having heard him more than once curse the man's name.'

This suggestion came from Captain James Gambier, a sleek and well-fed looking officer, known to be highly competent, albeit a religious zealot. He was prone to press upon people improving tracts, advising them to seek God's good grace. His other demand was, for the sake of their souls, they should foreswear drink. This made him unpopular to the men of the lower deck, wedded, as they were, to their daily issue of grog.

'Did he not write to the board when he sent Pearce home, saying he should be denied employment?' Gambier added.

'Which would surely mean sending Lord Langholm back.'

In saying this Charles Pybus got confused looks from the salts, which had him add, he now tapping the documents before him, 'I'm assuming we are talking about an attempt to unearth which of these two accounts is accurate. This requires both officers to testify and to do so in the same room.'

'We could bury the despatch from Sir David Rose?' Young suggested.

The implication was obvious: pack the court with the right officers, supress evidence and the verdict would be the one required by the service.

'I would remind you all,' Earl Spenser insisted, 'we are not supposed to be aware of his opinion. I stress again, knowledge of the document is highly confidential.'

'As high as his opinion of Pearce,' commented Pybus.

'I sense a serious level of risk here.'

All eyes turned to Phillip Stephens, with his elephantine knowledge of what had gone on before in the King's Navy, not least the number and outcome of too frequent Courts Martial. Obviously, an officer faced one if he lost a ship or demonstrated cowardice, which was to be expected. But no action, even that initiated by admirals, went without what amounted to an enquiry into their conduct, especially when anything smacked of a reverse. Not even a victory would necessarily save them from examination.

Officers sought to clear their name when they felt they'd been slighted or accused of being tardy in the execution of their duty. A number of the captains present at the Glorious First of June had demanded Admiral Lord Howe rewrite his after-action despatch. They required him to remove the implication they had been shy of putting their ships in danger. Such disputes were the bane of the service.

'It is always best to assume,' Stephens added, 'any officer being examined can mount a reasonable defence for his behaviour and must be permitted to do so. He will not meekly accept he is guilty of acting inappropriately. This means a full trial and one, given the nature of the case before us, we would struggle to keep from becoming a public event. Given the reasons he had for his actions, and assuming they are made public, it could result in Pearce becoming a national hero.'

Pybus could not resist a jibe. 'A status I thought he already enjoyed.'

'Only in certain quarters,' Seymour responded briskly, 'and they are wholly mistaken in their opinion.'

Nevertheless, the prospect brought on gloomy headshakes from the sailors, who knew Stephens to have the right of it. The ordinary citizens of Britain would not care if the Spaniard was supposed to be an ally and, in truth, it was a situation most would not even begin to comprehend. Madrid had been an enemy too many times, so, for the ignorant, which was the mass of the populace, it was as if the Armada had happened yesterday.

'Which is the nub of it,' Earl Spenser concluded. 'But an allied frigate was attacked and taken by a pair of our vessels. I remind you of why we are here. Do we, as a board, approve of such behaviour and, if not, how do we act on it.'

'Reading Langholm's report,' Pybus added, 'and comparing it to the other, leads me to wonder if he is merely covering his own back. He may wish to do so in case the whole affair backfires and both officers are faced with a rebuke.'

Seymour was quick on that. 'While I read it as Langholm acting properly, I support him, for instance, in giving no credence to Pearce's Admiralty pennant.'

'Hardly an act the board on which we sit on should agree with.'

This was posited by the seventh member, Lord Arden, who had yet to speak on the matter, being a habitual listener rather than a talker.

'It was issued as a convenience to the Minister for War,' Admiral Seymour growled, 'and one I distinctly recall, it did not, at the time, have my approval. We had no idea who it had been granted to, this being left at his discretion.'

'As the senior officer present, Langholm should have assumed responsibility and intercepted the *Santa Leocadia* himself.'

'Things at sea are rarely so simple, Mr Pybus. There are sound reasons why it fell to Pearce.'

The look of impatience from Lord Seymour was obvious. The older man was clearly annoyed in being obliged to explain what Langholm was seeking to do, splitting his ships to cover as much of the approaches to Vigo as possible. He then reminded them of the stated aim, as laid out in Lord Langholm's report. Whichever one sighted him first should peacefully intercept the Spaniard and ask to inspect his cargo, this allowing time for the other warship to join.

'If he had declined to back his sails, the instruction was to then put a shot across his bows. With time taken and now facing both *Lively* and *Hazard*, the man would have been a fool to refuse. Instead, Pearce, we are told, stood off and allowed, perhaps even encouraged his adversary, to alter course and make for the bay in which he was overcome. As I see it, Pearce broke a clear agreement, and then went out of his way to initiate a clash.'

'Did he though?' asked Pybus.

Seymour picked up the relevant report and raised both it and his already loud voice even more.

'Langholm admits he was too far off to exercise control and stop him deliberately drawing the Spaniard into a fight.'

The barrister was not to be drawn into a loud rejoinder. His tone was, to the admiral, annoyingly calm. 'Yet the same fellow admits to doubts about who was first to fire their cannon. The truth, he maintains, that it was the *Santa Leocadia* was only confirmed, he insists, by Pearce himself, after the vessel had been overcome.'

'With such a man, he could have good grounds to believe he was not being fed the truth. And he would hardly ask the man who'd just offered up his sword in surrender, before being given leave to clear the ship. It may be, and I incline towards this view, the Spanish frigate was a victim of Lieutenant Pearce's greed.'

'Is it not possible,' Pybus suggested, 'the Spaniard could have fired first, if what he was engaged in was questionable? Such an act then implies he knew the purpose for which the cargo was intended. So, he would not have submitted to any request to heave to before he could get to the safety of Vigo.'

'You're clearly not a sailor, Mr Pybus.'

The remark stung and got a sharp and icy rebuke. 'No sir, I am not. But neither am I inclined to reach conclusions which merely fit a prior prejudice.'

'I resent the implication, sir.'

'Gentlemen please,' their chairman said, 'we are here to decide if we wish to, on the basis of Lord Langholm's submission, initiate a case against Lieutenant Pearce for acting both beyond his orders and the interests of the nation. This will require us to immediately recall him to London to face a court. It will also be necessary to put Lord Langholm and his ship on a duty which allows us to call him to the same hearing when we wish.'

'Given the time it will take,' Stephens interjected, 'it will be impossible to avoid talk of the reasons becoming common knowledge. While it may please the fleet, I wonder if it would not be wise to consider the wider implications.'

Seymour slapped the table, which earned him a frown from his fellow peer. 'I say it must be done, or the opportunity to put right a serious wrong will be forfeit.'

The discussion went round the table with many questions and few answers which could be said to be definitive. But it was clear Seymour, with Gambier and Young, minded to support him wanted to use the opportunity to damn and remove John Pearce. Charles Pybus was playing the defence advocate for him and, to the naval minds, a devil's one.

'We're talking of a fortune here,' Gambier remarked, which got a frown from the First Lord, who wished to keep the silver out of the discussion. 'The service will erupt if Pearce sees a penny of it.'

'But will happily grant the same to Lord Langholm.'

Gambier was quick to say where he saw the variance. 'It's the difference, Mr Pybus, between a highly regarded naval officer and a jumped-up spawn of Lucifer.'

'Let's have Langholm in,' the First Lord said, knowing an impasse had been reached. 'And see what he has to say.'

Langholm, questioned, merely repeated what he had said in his report, though it had to be noted his answers were somewhat lacking in spontaneity. Each enquiry was carefully considered before he replied to Charles Pybus, the behaviour of a fellow seeking to bestride two horses. He made the point, once Langholm, an oath of secrecy regarding the whole affair underlined, had left to many warm words from the naval board members.

The First Lord brought the meeting to a vote, with the caveat it was a matter which might require to be revisited. The sailors voted for Pearce to be accused, with Pybus and Stephens adamant it should at the very least be deferred, but if pressed, they would vote against. In the end, it fell to the near-silent Lord Arden to cast his vote.

'Is it not one man's word against another? Which means we would be required to call not only both captains, but all their officers and warrants along with their logs. If, as we are told, Spain is about to defect, I can imagine the uproar which would ensue for staging a trial against a man who set out to prevent it from being successful.'

'Who also set out to enrich himself,' Seymour cried out.

'Nevertheless, I would vote for a delay and, if Spain acts as has been predicted, I would agree with Mr Stephens. The game is not worth the candle. So, it is in that direction I will cast my vote.'

'Which leaves me,' Earl Spenser said, 'since we are tied, with the casting vote and I incline towards the same view as expressed by Lord Arden.'

He did not add that such a decision would please the First Lord of the Treasury, the decision communicated to William Pitt and Henry Dundas within the hour.

'You see, Henry, not only could Spenser see the point, but we had our secret weapon in Stephens.'

'What did you offer him, Billy,' was posited with a sly grin.

'Nothing I feel obliged to act upon, it was so vague.'

The third meeting was taking place in the offices of Alexander Davidson. The subject under discussion had nothing to do with Spanish frigates and silver; indeed one of the participants was in ignorance of their very existence. Walter Hodgson had been called in by Davidson on the matter of Jaleel Tolland's ship and what to do about it. The rest was none of his business.

'Admitting the vessel in question was taken illegally will not serve,' the prize agent insisted. 'My client will be in just as much hot water whether it surfaces in another way.'

'And a touch poorer.'

'I hope you do not consider my thinking it will have the same effect on me, and so colours what advice I give.'

It was clear from the expression of Hodgson's face he was reserving judgement on the point, but he was not unaware of the complications of sorting out what was a terrible mess.

'My sole aim,' Davidson continued, 'is to protect Lieutenant Pearce from himself, for I must admit I find his actions reprehensible in the extreme. I realise I am asking you to participate in what amounts to a fraud and understand you may wish to decline.'

'I have my own reasons for wanting to see the matter quietly settled, Mr Davidson. So, in the scale of felony, I suggest to you, there are those with a great deal more dirt on their hands than will stick to mine.'

There was, to his mind, only one way to proceed; first to frighten Denby Carruthers into abandoning any notion of claiming ownership of the vessel. The way to achieve such an outcome was to let it be known that his involvement in smuggling would be made public. The question was how.

'At least we don't have to worry about the Tolland brothers,' Hodgson said with what was close to breezy confidence. 'The navy will keep them till the peace and, as of this moment, I cannot see such a thing coming about.'

Chapter Twenty

Sir Bertram Tendring, beside the warmth of the fire, and with his dogs laying at his feet, was going over the steps he intended to take. The matter had been touch and go, whether to help Jaleel Tolland journey to London. The alternative was to throw his carcase, tied up and bloody, into the pig sty, where the porkers would make a meal of him. Ever a man who showed care before moving from thought to action, he was examining his intentions to ensure that there were no flaws.

A substantial landowner and local worthy, he possessed and ran several farms in what was varied husbandry, an inheritance built up by his forebearers over several centuries. The running was not undertaken personally of course, but he was the controlling spirit. His farm workers sowed and reaped wheat, grew peas and winter vegetables, while others ran the stud, or raised cattle, sheep, pigs and geese. He had an interest in a fish curing works and owned a lime kiln, the latter being a business he had added to his legacy.

Much of what he produced was sold locally, but a city the size of London, added to the prices which could be charged there, sucked in produce from all the counties on its borders. The Baron supplied many London markets with the things he produced, shipping them by sailing barge from the private dock he'd acquired, originally laid out to shift lime from the kiln, the wharf being the reason for the purchase.

The estate, grown in a piecemeal fashion, was now spread over much of mid and north Essex, and it was a valuable one. This showed in the possessions he owned and the social and business life he led, not least as a Justice of the Peace. He was powerful enough to decline the office of Lord Lieutenant, without giving offence to the crown and was, amongst other things, a director of the East India Company.

Such a role required time to be spent in London at the Company's Leadenhall Street offices. He was required to attend meetings, to discuss strategies, such as fighting off the continual efforts of William Pitt's government to exercise control over the South Asian monopoly. Contact with government supporters was essential – people who needed to be detached from their allegiance on particularly egregious bills, usually with a bribe. There was, as well, the party of Charles James Fox, the politician who led the opposition. At least he and his adherents came, if not free, for the price of a good dinner.

Both political Westminster and the trading City of London consisted of a constrained and somewhat incestuous world, which was why the name of Denby Carruthers had struck a chord. He did enough business with the company to merit attention, though Tendring was not fond of the man, finding him to be too abrasive. Nevertheless, when they met, Tendring was unfailingly polite, for profit dictated all his actions both as a director and farm owner. It was the same for his clandestine business of running contraband.

As the owner of broad acres, few in the city would believe how his father, in the past, had sailed close to ruin. No one who farmed would show the least surprise, they being in an occupation fraught with risk. With bad harvests, lack of or too much rain, blight by pests, diseases in animals, many with no known cure, the propensity for loss was high. Smuggling, once taken to, had alleviated the ups and downs of his inheritance.

As a man who had to be seen as upstanding, it was one thing to fetch in contraband, another to sell it, so nothing brought ashore in clandestine cargo went to local buyers. Every load of produce shipped from his kiln dock, every herd of animals or flock of geese taken to London, carried with it part of his contraband cargo. In the Great Wen, it was exchanged for money or, in some cases, influence.

More hands-on in the running of untaxed goods than he was on the plough or the pitchfork, left no one for him to talk to when a problem in this area required to be solved. Farming was very different, a case of endless discussion, while smuggling was one of lonely contemplation. He had only one partial outlet, the man who oversaw his warehouse in London. He earned significant commission on the goods he shifted to Sir Bertram's contacts in the capital. Yet, for security, even he would not have been included in these ruminations.

It was the difficulties his agent had so recently encountered in shifting goods that had set his thoughts in motion, the struggle to move items previously and eagerly bought, which was at the core of his concerns. Someone was undercutting his prices and stealing his customers, which was reducing the gains to be had.

More importantly, it was making it slower to shift his cargoes, and this impacted on those who sailed his deep-water vessels. They did not do it for love, and there was a point, admittedly not anywhere near yet reached, where expenditure might exceed income and render the business unviable.

'So, it smells as if it could be you Carruthers,' a remark which had one of his hounds raise its head.

He certainly had the contacts, given he and Sir Bertram moved in the same circles, and there was no doubt he had the money to fund such an enterprise. A look at a map of the Thames placed Beltinge, which he guessed to be the landing place for Tolland's cargoes, as much closer to the market in which they were competing.

'And so, your costs are lower.' The dog pulled itself up and came to rest its chin on his master's knee, earning a rub behind the ear, thus to become the recipient of the words to follow. 'Left to carry on, you could ruin my trade, so we must hunt you down and put a stop to your games.'

Which only left the question and there was no easy answer. 'How?'

As the solution began to form, Sir Bertram would have been much comforted to know the person on whom he was cogitating was equally troubled.

—◆—

'I'm beginning to wonder if this Hodgson fellow you employ is capable of finding anyone.'

'He came to me highly recommended, Denby.'

'Then I should ignore any more of the same, from whosoever gave you his name.'

Edward Druce had to keep his hands below the level of his desk, for he could not be sure, if in view, they would not shake. In his drawer was a note from Walter Hodgson, one he now wished he had immediately destroyed. In very few words, it confirmed to him Jaleel Tolland was a known smuggler, who worked with a brother called Franklin, the obvious conclusion being they were in league with his brother-in-law.

The final sentence was the one to scare him to the marrow. It stated that there was now no doubt, in the thief-taker's mind, the pair had murdered Denby's wife and would have done so at his specific request. He concluded by advising him to be careful and to especially keep the Hodgson name out of any conversation.

If his brother-in-law could have observed his heartbeat, he would have been in no doubt of the degree of terror animating Edward Druce. His dread was simple; that a connection would be revealed by an inadvertent word, one which would expose to Denby the machinations in which he was involved. But speak he had to and he could only hope not to commit a gaff which, he reckoned, could cost him his life.

'He established and informed me your Tolland fellow did indeed live in Beltinge.'

'Yet he didn't meet with him.'

'I have to say Denby, and it troubles me, it was as if he did not wish to be found.'

He waited for a blast of invective as a response, one which did not come. Instead, Denby Carruthers was pensive, and it was a full half minute before he spoke and surprisingly softly.

'Edward, what you say troubles me. It makes me wonder if I may be the object of a clever fraud.'

'By Tolland?'

'In league with this Pearce fellow.'

Druce should not have laughed, but as a combination in crime, it was so unlikely, he could not help himself.

'I cannot think what you find so amusing. I stand to lose a substantial sum of money if I cannot prove, the vessel at Greenwich, is my property.'

'Sorry.' Druce hoped he sounded sincere, though it was hard, just as was what he followed with. 'So, you're suggesting they were working hand in hand to rob you?'

The old Denby quickly resurfaced and he growled. 'Have I not just said the very thing?'

It was necessary to act as if he took the proposition seriously, when he thought it nonsense. But the other thought was equally troubling and, if not entirely new, of a depth never before considered. Ever since he had been betrayed by his wife, Denby, usually a balanced and astute individual, had seemed to act beyond what could be considered reasonable. Yes, he had the right to be wounded and react, but to seek to kill Gherson bordered on the unhinged.

Matters had gone from bad to worse since Druce had first been engaged to find the miscreant. The constant agitation for news, when he had to pretend there was none, created scenes in which his brother-in-law seemed, in his cursing frustration, to part from reason. If Hodgson was right and he had conspired with Tolland to kill both Catherine and her lover, was it the action of a man with a firm grip on his sanity? And now this!

'I'm curious to see how this could be arranged,' he finally said.

'Then you are lacking in sense because to me the way to manage it is obvious. They make a rendezvous out at sea. And there my supposed partner and co-owner hands Pearce the ship, for which I have paid. Pearce then fetches it into Ramsgate and declares it a French prize.'

'But the cargo?' was, from Druce, an attempt to get back on an even keel.

Denby's face now had a look which hinted he could discern deep cunning. 'They see forfeiture, which is as nothing compared to the value of the ship, as a price worth paying.'

'And given there are no papers. . . ' was an attempt to get back in his good books.

'And no sign of a crew, either, which is even more suspicious. Easy to throw the documents overboard and for the Tollands and their men to disappear, which they appear to have done.'

'You will have to enlighten me to what end?' Druce asked.

He was unconvinced, but prepared to pretend the possibility existed, if for no other reason than to keep his brother-in-law from digging in the other directions. If he ever found out how he had been cheated, there was now only one way Druce could see him reacting.

'When it is put up for sale, the money goes to Pearce. He could then split it with Tolland, who would surface when the deed is done.'

If Druce thought the notion ridiculous, he was not aware of the enigmatic note his brother-in-law had received, the one which had set this train of thought in motion. The fact Carruthers didn't trust the Tolland brothers was not a point to make: he was not much given to trusting anyone.

'I take it you have no information on John Pearce?' was advanced tentatively, in being a safe way to steer.

'That's what makes me even more suspicious. I have good contacts at the Admiralty, so I assume he is at sea. But if he is, no one I spoke to could find any trace of orders detailing where he was to go. It's as if he too, having touched at Ramsgate, has disappeared.'

The notion of some kind of fraud was farcical, so much so it was difficult to keep a straight face. But this was soon forced upon him as he contemplated what he was dealing with and what was at risk. The other was to wonder where this farrago was leading, given all experience told him Denby was not the one to just cut his losses, which was implicit in the words to follow.

'I sense from what you tell me Edward, Tolland may, for the moment, be beyond my reach. I would fear to beard him if he were not if what I suspect is true. He's not a man to approach without you being in sufficient company or armed well enough to contain him.'

'How the devil did you become involved with him?'

'It was something of an act of charity, Edward,' was waved away as a folly. 'But let's put Tolland aside.'

'If you wish.'

'This Pearce fellow, what do we know of him? Very little and this must be corrected. I have limited faith in your thief-taker but put him on to the name and see what he can turn up. It may be he has an Achilles Heel we could exploit and it could be the key to restitution of my property.'

'Denby, you have expended so much on this, would it not be better to desist.'

Druce was well aware it was a brave thing to say, but it seemed necessary. The only weakness Pearce had, as far as he knew, was his relationship with Emily Barclay. She might have cost the firm a great deal of money, but he baulked at the idea of naming her to his relative, which would put her at risk. He was quick to regret his reticence, for Carruthers was on his feet in a flash, his face like thunder and his bark full of spittle.

'If you ever had to start from nothing and earn your own money, Druce, instead of imposing on me for loan after loan, you would take a different attitude. Now do as I say, or relation or not, I will call in my advances and this time I will brook no delay. You have a week to come up with what I need or contemplate a room in a debtor's gaol.'

He left behind, on departure, a man shaking from head to foot and it took a long time for the trembling to subside. There was only one person to contact, and it was Hodgson, not a course which would bring resolution, but he was beyond even contemplating challenging his brother-in-law. The threat he had feared most, in some senses greater than the one to his life, had just been issued.

It was time for the thief-taker to act and bring closure to the whole affair. If he dared to demure, he would find out that Denby Carruthers already knew his name and would soon be informed of where to find him. Time for Hodgson to share the risk he seemed keen to see loaded on to anyone but himself.

It wasn't long before the prize agent, wallowing in self-pity, took recourse to the decanter, gulping down the first glass of claret and immediately pouring a refill. The wine taken over to his desk, he sat down, but there was no sipping, while the depth of his misery increased with consumption.

By the time the wine was gone, he had reached the point where he imagined himself in rags, trying to survive amongst the dregs in the Marshalsea prison, and it would be in a crowded common cell: private rooms cost money and where were such funds to come from?

The tears pricking his eyes, as these images flashed before him, soon began to flow as Druce reprised how he had been duped into everything, acts of kindness which led to his being where he was now. His brother-in-law had lied to him; Gherson had betrayed his trust, while Hodgson had actively worked to undermine his position, both financially and personally.

It was the last which gnawed most at his gut so, quill in hand, he began to write to the thief-taker, telling him he must act and do so quickly or else. His name was known to Denby Carruthers and soon, if he did not find the means to save his benefactor – it was an indication of the mental deception of which he was capable, he saw himself as such – he would have no choice but to look to his own security.

Only the fear of too quick a retaliation stopped him from adding the action he would take. Hodgson might guess at his aim of alerting Denby to both his part in the Gherson acquittal and the fact that he habitually took his food and drink in the White Swan. He would not guess the rest. Having had to correspond with Emily Barclay over the way her late husband's account had been handled, he knew very well where she lived.

She was the link to John Pearce as well as the woman who had funded Gherson's defence, the key to getting Denby off his back. Whatever had taken place, the fantasy just expounded or another reason, Pearce was steeped in some kind of deception and the way to him was through her.

If nothing had been done to save him from ruin in the next seven days, and Denby looked set to follow through with his threat, it was something of which he would inform his brother-in-law, regardless of the consequences.

❦

'It seems to me, Tolland, if your tale is to be believed, you are, at this moment, without a ship.'

'Take it as true, your honour.'

The tone of respect, not at all normal, was necessary. He needed whatever crumbs this nabob could throw his way, while he had to think of him so, since no one would put a name to the man. Tolland reckoned him titled by the way his man Dobbin had addressed him, but this didn't get him very far. And what he was saying now? What was it leading up to?

'Trust I know enough about keeping those who buy untaxed goods happy. An interruption to supply is not good for business.'

'There be a fact,' was said with a feeling of deep suspicion.

'So, I would suggest some of the cargo you lost, the more common articles such as tea and brandy, have already found buyers. Are people now wondering what has happened to the goods that they may well have already paid for.'

'Not my side of the bargain. I deliver to my partner. . . .'

'Carruthers?'

A nod since there was no point in denying it. 'He sees to the shifting end. I just deliver to a warehouse he owns.'

'We operate in a trade which carries risks, do we not?' Another nod. 'Which is why I hold in stock enough contraband to cover for unfortunate events. Week long storms, the loss of a ship and the like.'

'You offering to sell some?'

'I knew you'd get my drift. One of my ships set sail last night. The men who looked you over in the barn were here to receive their instructions. So, I anticipate my stock level will be enhanced, weather permitting, in around a week.'

'Which be dead money if it ain't shifted quick, not as easy in the country as the Wen.'

'Sharp, as I suspected.'

'I ain't no novice at the game. If anything, it be Carruthers who's in need of a wet nurse.'

'Which may mean he is presently in an uncomfortable position.'

'One you're offering to ease?'

'As long as certain precautions are observed. I am willing to send you to London. . .'

'If I go, it must be to Beltinge. Happy to go from there to the Wen, which means, from there, I'll be in London town in less than a day.'

'And how do you propose to get across the river?'

'I know folk on the north shore who will boat me over the estuary.' An enquiring look had him add, 'There's another band I know of in Shoebury. Done trade with them afore.'

'Very well,' came after a long pause for consideration. 'You must have in your head a list of the cargo you had in your holds. Give it to me and I will see if I can match some of it, perhaps most even. I will give you a price for supply and undertake delivery to wheresoever I'm instructed, as long as I reckon it secure.'

'How?'

'Do you really expect me to tell you the secrets of my business?'

There ensued another pause, a few moments of mutual stare. Tendring seemed slightly amused, while Tolland was seeking to work out how this nabob could shift goods to London, reasoning it could only be done by sea, if for no other reason than weight.

'I think we're done,' he was obliged to concede.

'Good. But you will leave this barn blindfolded and remain so until you are far enough off to have no idea of the precise location. Nor will you know the name of myself nor my residence.'

'Then how do I say agreement, if there be one?'

Tolland was thinking for all his grand manner, this puffed-up fellow was not as clever as he thought. It would take him a day in the locality to find out. There could not be many folks in these parts as well found as he. It was as though the man before him read his mind.

'I think you'll find this a dangerous place for anyone who even sniffs of being a deserter or an excise spy. And strangers stick out, especially those who bring reward in coin, either from the navy or myself.'

'I have no mind to hang about.'

'As to agreement, it will not come from you, but from Carruthers, since he is the man financing your trade.'

'Which tell me you know how to find him.'

'It is never hard to find an Alderman of the City of London.'

He'd known right off the name had been recognised, a fact Tolland had to stop himself from blurting out. To do so would be mere showing away and serve no purpose. He would accept what was on offer because there was no choice or, if there was one, it was not likely to be an agreeable experience.

'You will be travelling with a cartload of wheat, some of the sacks used to keep you hidden until you are well away from the men from your ship. Who knows, they may well still be out hunting.'

'When do I go?'

'When you have given me a list of the things you lost. They will be what Carruthers requires and quickly. The cart is ready for you as soon as I have it and you will go from the back of the barn and out of sight of the house.'

'Then what happens.'

'When you meet with Carruthers, he will have already been appraised of the fact you are on your way and to be expected. You will then explain what is on offer, while he will have the choice to either accept or decline. If it is the former, we can take matters from there.'

CHAPTER TWENTY-ONE

Sir Bertram had already worked out a plan to put a stopper on the activities of Denby Carruthers and had even taken steps to carry it out. With Harwich as a busy port, and military garrison towns like Colchester on the route to London, coach communications, with several companies competing for trade, were excellent and so was the postal service. This was thanks to several newly built turnpike roads, regular stage coaches, with changes of horses and coachmen so the conveyances could keep going through daylight hours.

Carruthers, still in a black mood after his blast at Druce, returned home to find he'd been in receipt of a gift. A firkin-sized barrel sat by his desk, with the name Baron Otard, dated 1775, as well as the words Chateau du Cognac burnt into the side of the cask. Along with it was a folded note saying it was gift from a friend, but it was couched in the same writing as the previous mysterious missive regarding Tolland. Golding, quizzed, related that it had come in a like manner to the previous communication.

'The same, fellow, sir, who called before. Handed them over with the note and a letter and then departed.'

'And he again left no name? Did you bother to demand one?'

'No, sir, there seemed no point.'

About to bawl Golding out, Carruthers had to hold back. Things of such a mysterious nature were very troubling, which meant neither anger nor worry could be allowed to show. He held up the letter.

'One of my fellow syndicate members showing appreciation, I suppose.'

A cold look said he was not about to be enlightened as to whom it might be, so his clerk took the hint and left. The seal, plain red wax, was quickly broken to reveal once more the same style of writing. It told him Jaleel Tolland would soon be with him to explain the gift and the purpose.

'Purpose? What in the name of damnation does that mean?'

Even in possession of a very devious mind and his recent reference to conspiracies, regardless of how long he gnawed on possibilities, none presented themselves. But he did know Hodgson had failed to locate Tolland. Was it possible he was at the hub of some intrigue to do him down or cheat him?

Despite what he'd said to Druce, he had flirted with the idea of seeking him out personally, travelling to Beltinge, to beard him and demand an explanation. What stopped him, he convinced himself, were the words that Tolland will soon be with you. The question his brother-in-law had posed, regarding their association being odd, came to mind. This caused Carruthers to recall Tolland was a man with a propensity for getting himself into difficulties. Had he done so again?

He had been obliged to rescue both the brothers from incarceration on a hulk off Portsmouth, one used to house men who would be supplied to the fleet. Carruthers also recalled he had never been afforded a proper explanation of how they had come to be in such a predicament.

He only knew it had cost him golden guineas to get them released, so they could man a ship he'd already purchased. His largesse had paid dividends of course, half a dozen profitably run cargoes, the proceeds of which were in a chest in his cellar.

Since disposing of his wife, he had taken pleasure, of a night, when not socially engaged, in counting his money. Not his wealth, for that was in Bank of England notes. But there was a beauty to cash in gold and silver, especially money illicitly come by, which afforded him an almost sensual pleasure.

As for the other kind of pleasure, it could be found and paid for at his favourite high-class house of pleasure in Arlington Street. It had been a trying day, with much work before his meeting with Druce added to several queries as to the failure to deliver the expected and paid-for goods. And now he had this to worry about, so he felt the need to take his mind off a conundrum he had no means of solving.

The place to find distraction from troubling thoughts was just off Piccadilly. Arlington Street would provide him with food, drink, music and the company of some of the prettiest and cleanest ladies of pleasure in London.

'Golding,' he yelled, 'call me a hack.'

—◦—

Walter Hodgson didn't get the Druce note until two days later. If he was a regular at the White Swan, there were other watering holes he was inclined to frequent, places where, in the past, he had met and spoken with those who shared his profession. Chasing felons was a business where competition had always been stiff but was getting harder since the setting up of the Bow Street Runners. This tended to cut out the juiciest cases for Hodgson and his kind, grounds for complaint and moans of impending penury.

He was looking for a way to tip Denby Carruthers off balance, a way to let him know his nefarious activities were not the secret he thought them to be. So, in hinting to those of his own occupation, and suggest was all he could do, it was possible to set going a rumour. This speculated the well-known alderman was not the paragon he professed to be; indeed, he had a dark secret.

It was a certainty those with whom he spoke would want more. They were seekers of snippets of information by trade. Hodgson spoke with each one alone, to hint he would go further with them than anyone else, because he knew he could trust them. This one word was enough to get a response, soon followed by a look around to ensure no one else had heard or seen Hodgson's lips move. By such means, a drip feed of incomplete bits, he sought to harness the power of gossip, which he'd used in the past to flush out those of whom he had been in pursuit.

His suggestions, never anything definite, planted in the right ears, had an effect. Each of his peers always sought to indicate or boast that they had knowledge their competitors did not possess. Being, by nature, a tight-lipped bunch meant, when oddments of information did slip out, they gained a credence open admission would never attain. It was a long game, but one which suited him.

So, the note handed to him when he returned to the White Swan, once read, was a shock. It was simply the last thing which would serve, and it did not take long to work out the various ways in which Druce might betray him. If Carruthers knew his name, he had already done so, but what else could he reveal?

Tell of his part in uncovering the evidence of Gherson's inno-cence? There was little doubt how that would play with the man who had determined to see him hang. Did Carruthers have anyone other than the Tolland brothers to do his dirty work? The fact he might not was a chance Hodgson was unwilling to risk.

He had to see Druce and stiffen the man's spine, which was going to be difficult, given he hardly possessed one, so he set off at once. It turned out to be a frustrating encounter, especially at first, when the prize agent refused to see him. It took a threat to engage in violence to overturn this and finally to beard him in his office. There his first words made Hodgson's blood boil.

'If you have not come to tell me you have evidence to place the real culprit in the dock, with not the least chance of an acquittal, I have nothing to say to you.'

'Your brother-in-law is not the only one who can find footpads to do his bidding.'

'You dare threaten me.'

Hodgson threw his note back at him. 'What is this, if not a threat to me?'

'I have been given seven days to satisfy Denby's demands and two have already gone.'

'What demands?'

'A means by which he will get back what belongs to him. If I do not comply, I'm ruined.'

'I'm minded to go to Bow Street now and call upon Blind John. It would be of interest for him to hear what you have been up to. Fraud, accessory to bodily harm and then foul murder.'

With Druce visibly shrinking before him, in truth slipping down his seat, Hodgson dropped his harsh tone. 'I don't think you're in a position to refuse to answer my question. Demands imply more than one.'

He was too feeble a creature to hold out or was it a vivid imagination, feeling a tightening rope round his neck, just before the point where it either snapped his spinal cord or began to choke the life out of him. Out came the garbled theory of Pearce being in a criminal conspiracy with the Tollands, which was too absurd. How many times had the brothers tried to kill him?

'And how does he intend to deal with this?'

'I don't know.'

'I sense you do but are unwilling to say. Do so, or I'm off to Bow Street, the cells of which you will be in before an hour has passed.'

'He will make Pearce pay.'

'I don't know how, given the man is at present a thousand miles away.'

It was then the notion dawned. 'But those he cares for are here in London.' Druce could not look at him. 'What have you done?'

The pleading tone was sickening. 'I'm facing ruin and that woman has played a major role, so let her face the consequences. The money I would have used to pay off Denby is now in her possession. May she choke on it.'

'What a pathetic creature you are. And to think I was doing my best to keep you from the hangman.'

Hodgson stepped round the deck, pushing Druce aside, to reach into the drawer which he hoped held the original drawings made of the Tolland brothers. They were there, so he grabbed them before storming out, slamming the door behind him. He did not hear, since it was thick mahogany, Druce plead they still had five days.

The journey for Jaleel Tolland was comfortable to begin with, laying on sacks of grain, with cloth of the same to cover him if Dobbin, for it was he on the box seat with a boy to aid him, said he needed to hide from view. This was rare, but it was a good idea it should happen at the turnpike toll booths through which they passed. Also, when they heard the blowing horn of one of the many approaching mail coaches, coming in either direction, there would be passengers on the roof who could see into the cart.

Sleep had been taken at the side of the road, with food from the box on which Dobbin sat. They ate cured ham and cheese, with bread which would soon turn as hard as ship's biscuit, all washed down with water from the wells they passed. It was a lot less comfortable off such highways on the so-called country roads. On these it came down to how well each section was locally maintained, and this had to be variable.

Mud in winter and rutted when they dried out in summer, these byways had set the cart bucking and swaying. All the way to Shoebury, it had been tracks for farmers, their animals and any priest looking after multiple parishes and needing to walk between them. It took four days to get to the point where the Shoebury shore had become visible, Tolland dropping off to make his way to where he knew he would get help.

It looked to be a flat and desolate landscape but, as ever on a coast, there was habitation, for it was one of the shoulders of the wide Thames Estuary. There was fishing of course, but a vital feature was a long flat beach perfect for landing contraband, while the inland marsh shared with many a place for the trade, a clear sight of any impending danger.

The house to which he had made his way was one he knew well, there being cooperation over the estuary by people who made their living in the same way. The Shoebury smugglers, like all of their brethren along the North Thames shore, had their own markets for untaxed goods, so they never troubled those across the water. It was very much the reverse too, given the fickle nature of weather in the North Sea.

Rather than competition, there was a helping hand, as well as a warning if there were excise cutters about, the danger for a ship coming in from Flanders being a beacon fire on the shore. Sitting round a blazing indoor hearth, he had supped mead with men he knew well. They were grizzled folk who endured a hard life and, all bar the shouting, Jaleel Tolland knew he was home. Talk was shared memories, of dangers faced and traps avoided, stories told many times before, but listened to as if fresh. It came with a promise, if the wind was kindly, he would be by his own fire on the morrow.

And he was, put ashore at the base of Beltinge cliffs, those who brought him declining a return of hospitality so they could fish for their supper on the way home. So, carrying nothing, for he had nothing, he ascended the steep track up to the Tally Ho Tavern, where he was greeted like a returning hero.

Pressed with ale by the keeper and a coterie of his mates, Tolland was happy, till one let slip that some cove, a stranger, had come asking after him weeks passed. The description meant nothing, so he professed not to be concerned until the tavern keeper produced two drawings. One was very like him, the other, given a deep scar on the cheek, was unmistakeably his younger brother Franklin.

'Where'd you get these?'

'They was in his satchel. When I found them, I reckoned it might be a fellow looking to have someone up, which would be harder if they was filched.'

'You reckon him to be after me and Franklin?'

'Can't say for sure, Jaleel, but if he was carrying those. . . '

'What happened to him?'

'Scared off he was. Bought a spavined nag and lit out afore first light, likely for Herne Bay.'

'Get anywhere near my house?'

'How could he, when we denied the name.'

'Asked for by name, was we?'

'It were you Jaleel. Never raised Franklin. Said he had information which would be to your profit.'

'Well,' Jaleel said, pretending to be unconcerned once more, 'he's long gone now, so let's have another wet afore I go home and scrape my chin. I need to get some clothes an' all, for I've been in this lot too long.'

'Smells like it,' joked one wag.

The mood of bonhomie evaporated, the ale pot was slammed down and it was the Jaleel Tolland of old who surfaced, a man to have a care around. 'Happen your nose be a bit too near to your arse, mate.'

'Sorry, Jaleel.'

It wasn't far to the house he now called home, one of the only two decent-sized buildings in what was a ramshackle hamlet, close to the church and Rectory, the only other dwellings of size. This belonged to his brother for, hereabouts, they were kingpins. He was thinking all the way, which continued when he had let himself in and got a fire going to heat water.

He could not place who might be after him and why, especially as described, even if there was much in his background justifying a pursuit, and this lasted till a possibility occurred. It was good the locals had clammed up, but was it Denby Carruthers who knew where he lived, knew what he looked like and could have had the drawings made, but why?

The best interpretation he could put on this was his trying to find out what had happened to him and his ship, for they would be seen as well overdue. At first it made sense, but why the drawings, when the man who came looking, as described, was nothing like Carruthers, yet had asked after him by name?

There was a smell to it which didn't appeal but, if it was Carruthers, he would find out soon, for he had no intention of hanging about. He was a man Tolland needed to see and in short order to find out if the bugger was playing some game and one which would bring danger. If not, was he willing to trade with Essex?

Within the hour he had armed himself, as he usually did, with a knife. The drawings from the Tally Ho he tucked inside his coat and he was soon on his way to Canterbury. There he would board a coach for London, which ran every hour between Dover and Charing Cross.

To Hodgson, the notion of depending on rumour had failed, which meant time only allowed for drastic measures. He went by his lodgings and fetched out his pistol and the means to discharge it. The next stop at the White Swan provided him with quill, ink and paper. Once he'd penned his letter, a lawyer who drank there provided him with a length of red ribbon. With this, he made a roll of both the letter and the drawings, so it now looked very similar to a legal brief.

It was nearing the end of the business day, so he took a hack through the still bustling streets of the city to Devonshire Square, where Carruthers both lived and owned extensive warehousing. His abode was a substantial house in the Queen Anne style, with a separate entrance used as an office. It was a building which spoke of his wealth as well as his position on the Council of Aldermen.

In a deep warehouse doorway, Hodgson loaded and primed his pistol. Then, with it now hidden inside his coat, but with one hand on the butt, he pulled on the bell above the brass plate announcing the side door as Carruthers's place of business. This had the clerk, Golding, unlatch it, albeit with the inside chain engaged, so it only opened a fraction.

'Your employer, I need to see him.'

'He's not at home and has ceased activity for the day.'

'When do you expect him back?'

'I have no idea. And I'm obliged to ask what business you have with him?'

With the pistol butt getting warm in his hand, causing it to sweat, Hodgson was at a stand. Could he afford to wait until the next day? Would Druce hold out till then or crawl to his brother-in-law to seek to save his miserable life. Would Hodgson's threats drive him to act as the only way to survive?

'Can I ask your position?' was politely expressed.

'I am senior clerk to Mr Carruthers,' came with an element of pomposity.

'A trusted servant then?'

'A cut above a servant, sir!' was a stern rebuttal.

'Forgive me. I wonder if I can entrust this to you. As you will see by the ribbon, it's a legal document, one your master needs to act upon swiftly, for there is much riding on it.'

Hodgson was struggling to keep a desperate note out of his voice. He had another task to perform, to hire some men to stand guard on Emily Barclay's front door. So, he was reassured when Golding, in a slightly grand manner, informed him of his duty. He was tasked to take in all correspondence and place it in the right tray, according to the various interests in which his employer engaged.

'Then I entrust it to you and, I repeat, it requires a quick response.'

The inner chain was released and the document handed over. Golding, unseen by the thief-taker, was as good as his word. The tied bundle was placed in the centre of his employer's desk, a sign that it required to be acted upon immediately.

It was less than an hour later when the mysterious messenger, who had called twice before, rang the bell again. This time the exchange was silent, a sealed document was handed over, the man leaving as soon as it was in Golding's hand. Unsure if he was doing the right thing, the clerk placed it beside the recently delivered brief.

He then went back to his room to wonder if any of the maids in the main house might be willing to use the connecting door, to accept an invitation to share wine with him.

━ ⌒ ━

It was never fully established what happened in and around the house in Devonshire Square that evening. The only certainty was that the annexe contained two bloodied bodies with numerous stab wounds, while in the street outside, a rough looking cove, who looked to be the sailorly type, had expired from a set of wounds inflicted by a gun. It was known Alderman Denby Carruthers was a victim of the bloodied knife found on the cobbles, as was the man in the hallway outside his office, later found out to be his senior clerk.

It was the same house from which had come the murdered Catherine Carruthers, which had been much more than a nine-day wonder. So, the denizens of Grub Street, quick on the scene, were already composing their penny pamphlets. They would hit the streets of London the next day and those writing and printing them had a field day when it came to speculation.

The late wife had expired in the company of a known lover, so was the fellow in the street another of her paramours? Had it been a bloody confrontation between this fellow and an enraged husband? Was the woman who'd been seen as more sinned against than a sinner, no better than a whore? The other story to gain traction was a dispute over money, but who owed what to whom was left to the devices of individual creators.

Details of fantastic sums going missing were a staple of such tracts, and it was known that Denby Carruthers had dripped with wealth. But what was the meaning of the blood-stained drawings found in the hands of the creature with the two gunshot wounds, one of which showed a fair likeness to the victim. And who was the other fellow with the deep scar, for there was a trace of a family resemblance.

Those first on the scene, the servants of the domestic part of the household, were quick to recover from their trembling terror, willing to be in receipt of a bit of copper coin to relate what they knew. This being next to nothing, much invention was the order of the day. That was before they realised, they no longer had an employer.

So, it was best to look to their own needs and purloin some of the more easily carried or quick to hide objects. Sold, it might help to keep them from the gutter until they could find another place. They needed to act quickly, before the scene could be examined by the City of London Constable elected to this ward or the arrival of the Justice of the Peace or the City Marshal. By the time they arrived, the house servants gave a fair representation of grief for a man they heartily detested.

Two pistols were on the floor, one beside Carruthers hand, the other a fair distance away, both sniffed and pronounced as having been discharged. None of those called to the scene of the crime had been elected or appointed to a position requiring much in the way of expertise. Because of this, the marshal sent to Bow Street for assistance from the more experienced men, those employed by Blind John Fielding, the Westminster magistrate.

By the time Edward Druce and Denby Carruthers's sister arrived, the day had gone, so many candles were required to be lit, which turned more gruesome a scene already drenched in blood. The sight of her dead brother, from whom much of the blood had leaked, caused Druce's wife to faint, so she had to be carried to one of the bedrooms in the main house.

It was an understatement to say her husband was having trouble hiding his relief, but the impression he created was one to bring praise, being of stoical manhood in the face of tragedy. Papers were examined with his permission, which included a crudely written list of items, which looked very much like a peacetime cargo from across the Channel. Tea, brandy, tobacco, silks, French scents and Calais lace, all items with a price much more neatly appended for bales, casks and weight of beverages.

The letter with it, in a clear and educated hand, was addressed to someone called Jaleel Tolland, and it laid out how much the unnamed buyer was willing to pay for the goods listed. There was also Hodgson's letter, unsigned but dated, which alluded to actions by Carruthers of a less than upright nature, which made no sense. Brief and addressed to the man himself, it merely said he should have a care. There were people who knew enough of his actions to bring him down, men who would do so in order to save themselves. It ended with the statement, 'You know of whom I speak.'

'What utter nonsense,' Druce postulated with high and manufactured dudgeon. 'Jealous rivals, I would suspect.'

Nothing in the many documents subsequently examined led to any conclusions about what had caused these deaths, but Druce found it harder to be so impassive when a copy of Denby's will was discovered. Dated before the murder of his wife, it left everything to his sister, which in effect, as her husband meant, in terms of control, him.

Hidden elation turned to suppressed anger when a recent codicil laid a duty upon the executor of the will. It named a city lawyer who was tasked to ensure the former alderman's inheritance was to be placed under the total control of his sister.

—◦—

Walter Hodgson was just as nonplussed as anyone at the way matters had evolved. His sole aim had been to frighten Carruthers and maybe, with the addition of the drawings, create a rift between him and the unnamed people he'd alluded to. This, he hoped, would stop him from taking any precipitate action and allow him time to let his original plan, of employing rumour, to bear fruit.

A degree of enlightenment dawned when a new and elaborate pamphlet appeared two days later, priced at sixpence. It showed the face of Jaleel Tolland, while a smaller one of Franklin asked for information. He was left to wonder who, at Bow Street, had pocketed money to allow them to be copied.

There would be people who would recognise them both, not least the owner of the Long Acre Bagnio in which Catherine Carruthers had been murdered. It had been from her memory they had been created. Then there was the fellow who had executed the drawings at Walter Hodgson's behest.

It was necessary to visit and advise them that no good would come to by being open. There was no need to say the same to Edward Druce; he would never admit to having seen them before while, in and around Beltinge, no one would, by habit, ever admit to their ever having resided there.

———

'While the outcome is not one any decent person would wish, it seems that it might remove a burden on John Pearce. It's an ill wind, eh?'

Alexander Davidson seemed to be sincere in his opinion, and Walter Hodgson had to hide his own feelings, which were of relief. He could be assured Edward Druce would be silent on anything to do with his involvement in his brother-in-law's nefarious affairs and he'd advised those he needed to act likewise. They would do so as people who had no faith that the law meant justice: it was a blunt weapon just as likely to sweep up the innocent as the guilty.

Pearce would get his prize money from Carruthers's ship and cargo, because there was now no one to question it as a valid claim. The one who could as far as he knew, was still stuck off the Dutch coast and the whole thing would be done and dusted before the navy set him free. With Carruthers gone, the threat to himself had evaporated, so it was time for Hodgson to trawl round his old haunts to look for some felons to pursue.

Davidson paid him handsomely for the admittedly small amount of time expended on the case. Or he thought so, until rumour began to seep out of the capture of a cargo of Spanish silver and the possible identities of those who had taken it. This coincided with the news that Spain had signed a secret treaty with Revolutionary France and was now an enemy of Britannia.

CHAPTER TWENTY-TWO

If the conditions were far from clement – there was little possibility of landing illicit cargoes – it was still possible for John Pearce to be rowed ashore, his first task to make a silent visit to HMS *Teme*, now a much more shipshape vessel than when first seen. On another day he borrowed a horse and enjoyed a ride out with Lady Elliot, good company to a man who liked women and found them easy to converse with. She was also a person who seemed to relish the occasional downpour as much as the summer sun.

The following day he took one out on his own, in order to work out how those he needed to stop had gone about their gun running, as well as how they would react to what had occurred before the storm broke. He also surveyed the coast south of the Stagna di Biguglia, it being a feature he avoided for now, given he reckoned to have worked out how it was used.

What he did find was endless beach backed by thick vegetation, so dense at times, both he and his horse had some difficulty in navigating a way through to where it might thin. This proved so arduous, he felt obliged to get onto the sand and stay there in order to make progress, until this was halted by the mouth of a river, one he found too deep to cross.

Yet again there was a sandbar, one which acted like a hook, making the egress a narrow channel at the northern point. Was it wide enough to allow entry to the kind of trading vessels used locally? The only question being the depth of water for a ship's keel. Pearce then dismounted and walked his mount up the north bank to where the undergrowth did thin. This revealed a point at which the summer flow, even aided by the recent rains, could be forded. His own re-mounted crossing barely reached the knees of his horse.

That it was used at such was evident in the narrow track open-ings, suitable for donkeys, on both banks. To the north it appeared much more depressed and trampled upon than on the south, which applied as well to the nearby undergrowth. The temptation to follow it back to Bastia, where it must surely take him, was strong. But, with the thoughts he was having, he had to consider the possibility of being observed doing so. To his mind, this looked like a perfect place to land a not too heavy cargo and a place from which the heavier items could be moved by animals.

The ride back along the beach was an occasion for much pen-sive reflection, which established in Pearce's mind the thoughts he'd already had about how the opposition conducted their operations. If he were smuggling things ashore, some too heavy to carry, would not two points for a landing be better than one? If a signal could be sent out to sea, it could bear more than one message, to say which spot was the one to use? Against that it could be messaged in advance. In no time a plan began to form in his mind.

Once the weather eased and without informing the soldiers, he landed much of his crew, including marines, to search the waters from the southern end of the Stagna, up to the point at which Vickery had set his most extended piquet. The task was to find and destroy any craft he suspected the insurgents must have hidden in the inshore woodland. This turned out to be warm and sticky work, on a day the sun was out again, drying the soaked ground, creating a thin mist which would disperse as the day progressed.

HMS *Hazard* lay just offshore, her cannon very obviously pok-ing out of the gunports and swivels manned, the latter elevated enough to fire grapeshot over the heads of their own men, which would decimate anyone who chose to interfere. Worricker was sat in the tops, ranging with his telescope, to alert them to any approaching danger.

The craft were there, but expertly hidden, individually, at various points inland, not grouped, as Pearce had supposed. This led to a lengthier search than anticipated, made more so by the clever way they had been camouflaged using branches and leaves from nearby trees. Flat-bottomed craft, they were perfect for the shallow waters they needed to traverse. But it was noted that the bottoms were filled with water from the downpours of the previous days, indicating they'd not been employed since the thunderstorm.

Macklin proposed a notion to the sound of axes stoving in each one the men had uncovered, 'Without rain, sir, they would have to come and cut fresh branches every day. At this time of year and with the sun out, anything cut and leafy would turn brown within hours.'

'Which means, weather permitting, they are either numerous or active on a nightly basis.'

He did not add his thoughts as this might not be the only landing place.

'If they're around now, sir, they will know what we're doing.'

'Oh, they're about alright,' Pearce replied, a hand by habit easing one of the pistols in his belt. 'I doubt we can move in these parts without someone knowing our location. Their safety depends upon it.'

As he did so he looked to where they might be, wasted, since the density of the so-called hillside maquis made it impossible to see anyone who had no desire to be spotted. In his mind's eye, he visualised how it all worked in the Stagna. Given a signal it was safe to do so, a reasonable-sized sailing ship, like a tartane, would gently ground on the outer strand, to immediately begin unloading what they carried, humans included.

Their confreres ashore would have pushed their craft down to the water's edge, ready to quickly cross the Stagna and take on board what had been landed. As Warburton's patrols, still in darkness and nowhere nearby in any case, were withdrawing back to the safety of Bastia, they would be behind them, gently rowing their load closer to the city. Once by the outskirts, men and cargo could be taken ashore and hidden in the dwellings outside the walls. The flat-bottomed boats would then be brought back to where they could be concealed.

He was also thinking if Toby Burns had half a brain, he would have come to the same conclusion. Instead, he'd wasted his time ploughing back and forth, lit up like a Roman candle, acting as part beacon to those coming in from the mainland. Warburton was just as purblind, so equally guilty, for not properly employing HMS *Teme* to interfere with the incursions. But given what he'd deduced in the last couple of days, the major was now the man Pearce had to see.

'I'll take the cutter back to the city, Mr Macklin. When you think you're done here, ask Mr Hallowell to take up our berth at the mole.'

Sat in the thwarts of his cutter, Pearce was mentally working out how to act next, based on many of the judgements previously arrived at. He could not imagine the insurgents would desist for the loss of their easiest means of movement, of which they would find out soon if they did not already know. But they were bound to be more cautious, even before the occurrences of four days past. The exchange of musket fire alone, for which Worricker had been given a roasting, just before the thunderstorm, would have told them things had changed.

This begged a question he'd already considered: Did they have communication with their supporters not on the island? With trading vessels plying between Italy and Corsica on a daily basis, he had to assume it to be so. Which meant they would have heard of the arrival of HMS *Hazard* without knowing it was under the

command of a more active officer than the one they'd hitherto managed to avoid.

But this would no longer be the case, and it would be passed on
to those organising the shipments. So, it was incumbent on him,
as well as the soldiers to work out how to confound the new set of
circumstances. Stagna boats now destroyed, they would have to land
their cargoes at a different location, and he was now sure he knew
where it lay.

He first explained his thinking and what he'd observed to the
soldier. There might exist an infinite number of landing places on
a shore, with many miles of open beach, but he rated what he had
seen as near impassable. He drove home the most important point:
the less work involved in transporting whatever they brought ashore
the better. Moving it by water was the easiest, but he and his crew
had just destroyed the most convenient method.

'The longer they are moving what they smuggle ashore the more
vulnerable they are, so the shortest route is the best. Not much further south, there is the mouth of the River Golo. I'm hoping, after
the rain we've had, the waters are running with just enough flow to
allow a narrow access at the outmost point of a sandbar, but it matters not that they are too shallow. After all, they have been landing
on a sandbar at the Stagna.'

Pearce waited for a comment, one which might imply Warburton
had taken cognisance of what he was saying. He waited in vain.

'I suggest it as a spot they will now have to use to bring in what
they require. Even from the sandbar, both items can be shipped to
a point where they can load the weightier items on to donkeys. If it
is not as weak as it should be at this time of the year, they might be
able to sail or pole the ship inland. I would appreciate your thoughts
on the matter.'

'Thoughts?' Warburton enquired, as though it was an alien
concept.

'I would suggest,' Pearce responded patiently, 'the insurgents have had a good run at their game. So, we must assume much of the men and arms they require are already ashore. For all we know they may be close to seeking to evict us. Thus, stopping their game is more urgent than previously.'

'Fair point,' was conceded, but nothing followed.

Pearce had to ask if the major could suggest any other location on the shoreline which might serve their purpose, to get a blank look.

'I'm sure your reconnaissance would have pinpointed the kind of ground they would need.'

'I'll send for Vickery. If anyone knows, he will.'

Tempted to ask if Warburton had tried to recce himself, Pearce demurred: he was fairly sure he knew the answer, so he waited while a soldier servant was sent to fetch the lieutenant. The two men, who had nothing in common which would engender small talk, were left sitting in silence, with John Pearce wondering if the major was assessing him. He was certainly doing some measuring himself.

Any judgement from this complacent bullock would be unlikely to consist of unmitigated admiration. It was the way of the endemically buck passing, inept and idle, to see anyone who sought to burden them with the need for a decision, or a requirement to act, as a damn nuisance. And it made no odds what colour of coat they wore.

The depressing concomitant was the thought of how many generals and admirals fitted the mould, for incompetents had a way of rising in the ranks of military organisations. They did this by dint of never being caught out, either by disagreement with a superior or any act entailing risk which could be pinned to their name. Even better if a failure could be blamed on someone else. There was another method, the Burns way: claim credit of the actions of another, provided, of course, they were a success.

Vickery arrived and was punctilious in the way he greeted his superior, which did get a grunt of satisfaction from the major, followed by an invitation the lieutenant should pull up a chair.

'Mr Pearce and I were just pondering on what the damn Corsicans will get up to next.'

'I think it might be an idea to bring Mr Vickery up to date on what action I took this morning, sir, and what we have just been discussing.'

'Good idea, carry on.'

Pearce was left to reprise everything he'd told Warburton, as well as his thinking. This he did with the fat face across the desk nodding sagely, for all the world as if he'd participated in the destruction of the boats. But the point was made: the Stagna di Biguglia would no longer be suitable for smuggling in arms and men.

Vickery, when the next question arose, proved he had undertaken a task his superior had signally failed to do. He'd reconnoitred the coast to both the south and north of Bastia, so he was able to confirm that the latter was unsuitable for landing anything. This applied not only to the shoreline, but also to the very rough ground and dense undergrowth which formed a deep mass bordering the shore.

'Wherever they land, it will be necessary, if we wish to confound them, to catch them in the act. I would like to try my theory regarding the Golo Estuary, and I want to take some of your men to ensure, if I'm right, we can inflict a serious check.'

'Distance, Mr Pearce,' Warburton objected. 'I cannot leave the fortress undefended.'

'You have the navy here, Major. We can move your men much farther and faster than they can travel on foot.'

'A good point, sir,' got Vickery a look which was not one of unblemished approbation.

'It requires careful consideration, lieutenant,' Warburton grunted, leaving two men to wonder which one he was addressing.

Sensing evasion, Pearce was quick to speak. 'Which I'm sure it will be given by Sir Gilbert, when it's proposed to him.'

This brought on what was, by far, the quickest of the major's reactions. 'Never a good idea to go asking civilians about military matters.'

'I was thinking of asking him about the matter of survival. If this insurgency is not nipped in the bud, and it's possible we are already too late to stop it, there seems to me no way of containing it before it becomes a threat we cannot handle.'

'Within these walls,' came the smug rejoinder, 'we can hold. I've told you, the Corsicans, whatever party they adhere to, cannot breach stone walls. They don't have a decent bit of artillery to their name.'

'I do believe sir, or was it you Mr Vickery who reminded me, the French garrison were starved out?' Sensing the man still dissatisfied, Pearce added, 'I feel it's my duty to put the matter to the Viceroy and I will do so.'

Which was as good a way of any to say, I'm not army, I'm navy, so I will plot my own course.

— ~ —

The question of how to react to the recent events put Sir Gilbert Elliot on the horns of a dilemma. In his position, Warburton was the man in whom he was obliged to place his trust, he being in command of the military support, charged to both hold Bastia and protect him and his family. So, it took a great deal of tact to back John Pearce, without actually saying so.

'Can we say the situation has changed in the last week, major?' If Warburton expected to be allowed to give his view, he never got the chance; the Viceroy's pause was too brief. 'I must say I incline to the view it has, if only because those who oppose us will now be fully aware of the means we have acquired to stop them.'

'As long as we hold the fortified part of the city, they cannot evict us.'

'For which we must be grateful. But do we not cut a poor figure, as part of the governance of the island, relying on walls outwith of which we have no influence.'

'Would I be right in assuming,' Pearce asked, 'there are people hereabouts, and in numbers, who are not wedded to the notion of the return of French rule?'

'Lieutenant, the island has been batted back and forth too much these last fifty years. My guess is that the majority of the population would side with anyone who could bring peace and stability.'

There was an underlying point being made. He had the will and desire to bring such a state about, but lacked the means to do so. The best he could achieve was to hold to the present *status quo* and hope time provided him with a workable solution or a real and numerous army.

'Then,' Pearce responded, 'would not a serious check on the Francophones persuade those people to side with yourself and Corte?'

'It might,' was cautiously conceded.

'Then I cannot see how we can refuse to give it a try. Tonight, there will be a new moon, which will barely provide any light and the wind, such as it is, is from the east. So, it presents a perfect opportunity, for both ourselves and those who oppose us. They too will want to take advantage of such conditions, given the time and material they so recently lost. I suggest this will take them to the south of the Stagna di Biguglia, and we should be there to meet them.'

Warburton did not want to agree, but backed into such a corner, the soldier had no choice, though he had enough guile to avoid leaving himself exposed.

'As long as I have the means to hold the walls, I will consent, an opinion which I would like to be put on record with both you, Sir Gilbert, and my superiors.'

'Then, with your permission,' Pearce pronounced, with a hard look at the vacillating soldier, 'I will sound out Mr Vickery, whom I assume you will detail to help me.'

Sir Gilbert Elliot had to hurriedly pick up a letter from his desk and stare at it to hide his reaction to the stinging but cunning rebuke Pearce had just delivered. It seemed wasted on Warburton, who merely nodded his assent.

Appraised of what was proposed, Vickery demonstrated a positivity which cheered John Pearce. Even if it was only brought about by a change to his boring routine, such a duty was welcome. He agreed to supply eight muskets to back up the navy's marines, naturally the most accomplished with the weapon, with the caveat he would want to command them.

He also readily agreed to the notion that widely spaced beacons should be lit on the battlements of the fortress and kept going through the night to provide fixed points of reference for boats. They would be out at sea, in the dark and in need of such lights to mark their position relative to the shore .

There was very little to do in the article of planning, once he and Mr Williams had plotted the places at which the various requirements of the operation would be met. This included the point of disembarkation, added to a calculation for the amount of drift a line of boats would experience on the prevailing current. This could be corrected, using the fortress beacons.

Vickery assured Pearce, having been afloat before, the chosen men required little instruction on the factors which were essential when embarking at sea. To enter the craft with care, to spread themselves evenly, to ensure their loaded muskets, without bayonets, were pointing skywards, the last being to do exactly what they were told by whoever was in command.

Having called a conference, it was interesting to see how folk reacted to the presence of Toby Burns, not least the Pelicans. They were on deck, probably deliberately, to glare at him as he came up the gangplank. The speed with which he made for the main cabin demonstrated his fear they might do him harm. Little did he realise how the notion appealed.

With everyone gathered, Pearce was obliged to introduce the unprepossessing little toad, ranging carefully across the assembled faces to see their reactions, which were, to say the least, mixed. The mids, in ignorance, were polite, but expressionless, perhaps wondering at his lack of anything approaching presence. The lieutenants, including Moberly, stood stiffly formal: having heard the opinion of their commanding officer, they did not want to be too friendly.

It was not really a conference, more an issuing of orders. The means to convey them to where they needed to be would require the boats of both vessels and they would be roped together to ensure that they followed the course set by the lead boat. Burns would command his cutter and the men from his ship who crewed it, while *Hazard*'s officers and midshipmen would be in charge of the rest, including those from *Teme*.

Pearce, in the lead cutter, would be with Lieutenant Moberly, his marines and the makings of a boarding party of ten men, to include, as usual, his Pelicans. He would also take a rocket tube, pre-loaded with a blue light. Midshipman Maclehose, in *Teme*'s jolly boat, would supervise the employment of another rocket tube, firing flares off regularly. When the action was joined, the attacking parties needed to see what they were doing.

'We will go out with the fishing fleet, as HMS *Teme* was wont to do, with her lanterns blazing away. For once, we will do likewise; I want the people we are after to know our position, which will ensure they come nowhere near.'

Burns did blush, proving he knew very well it was a rebuke for his past behaviour. Others produced a series of coughs, of varying kinds, to cover their own, no doubt, unflattering thoughts.

'Once it is dark and we are in the position already worked out, we will disembark our half-dozen bullocks into their boat. I admonish you to look after them, since I will have to account to their commanding officer for any losses, and I would hate it to be from drowning. From then on, we wait. I am convinced anyone aiming to land men and guns off the shore will not do so without some signal to assure them it is safe to do so.'

The question, what if you're wrong, hung in the air, and Pearce waited to see if anyone would ask it. When they remained silent, he did so himself.

'I cannot see into the minds of the men we are required to stop, nor am I possessed of a crystal ball. As ever, we proceed on assumptions, which is likely to be true of every action in which you will engage.'

There was a temptation to take them through the thought process which had got him to this point, but he chose silence. Explanation could provoke confusion rather than clarity, as each step in his deductions was examined. He was in command, so it was his task to give orders and take risks. If it went well, they would praise his sagacity: if not they could indulge in as much, 'I suspected as much,' as they liked. Because, if nothing transpired tonight, the whole thing would be repeated every time conditions were favourable.

'I will have with me a lantern, which will remain shaded until required. On sighting any form of signal from the shore, I will flash it once to set our course due east to close the Golo Estuary. There you will take up your positions and cast off the towing lines.'

Seeing Burns nervously pulling his thumbs as he examined the chart, as others committed the details to memory, Pearce felt it wise to add more.

'The weather conditions could hardly be more favourable, given the light haze overhead. We will get no help from a new moon, but there should be sufficient starlight playing on it to reflect the waters of the Golo. We, at sea level, should be invisible against the dark of the shore.'

A pause allowed this to be acknowledged.

'Soft calls will be required to take up your positions, but it is imperative, once it is achieved, there be no talking, with oars only to be employed to hold your boats steady and to correct drift. If they are planning to be active tonight, they will have compatriots heading for the shore to aid them. Lieutenant Vickery's men will have their muskets ready to employ, and they are to do so as soon as they get sight of a target.'

'When and if the signal is sent aloft and the musketry has had the hoped-for effect, close with the target, discharge your weapons and shoot to kill, a request which will also apply to the bullocks. I want the side cleared of opposition. From my cutter we will seek to board and will look for support as soon as other boats can provide it.'

With a last look around the assembled faces, most keen to be active, only Toby Burns still looking pensive, he sent them about their duties. In the empty cabin, it was impossible not to reflect on the myriad things which could go wrong, just as to do so was pointless.

CHAPTER TWENTY-THREE

Vickery arrived on the mole with his men all, Pearce was glad to see, carrying their rolled-up cloaks, which being grey would ensure invisibility in the dark. This would apply to his marines and the whole of the crew taking part, given they too had been ordered to dress appropriately for the conditions. There was a chance some local, spotting a squad of soldiers coming aboard, might wonder at what was afoot, and they might even have the means to contact those who would be anticipating a landing.

It was a peril which had to be accepted, but he got them off the deck and below as quickly as possible. Pearce then gave the order to weigh before taking Vickery to his cabin. There he outlined his plan, adding the need, on sight of the blue light and a target, for a rapid response with volley fire.

'At the risk of stating the obvious, it's essential your men pause long enough to take aim. Any kind of movement on a boat will alter its trim, so no one must discharge their weapon until the craft has settled.'

The look Vickery gave him, allied to the lack of acknowledgement, told Pearce he was doing that very thing.

'It might be an advantage if you men could get some sleep, given we may be out most of the night. They can do so on deck, once we're away from the shore.'

Matters could not have progressed better from then on. HMS *Hazard* departed, heading out to sea in light airs, on a slight swell, behind the mass of fishing boats. This, nevertheless, as he'd expected, had the bullocks feeling poorly, but no allowance could be made for the affliction. They sailed on as darkness fell, very much replicating the course taken by HMS *Teme,* Williams hunched over his charts, measuring instruments busy, log cast regularly, until he gave the signal to heave to.

Well away from those fishing, the soldiers were put into the boats, to be followed by the sailors. Once in his cutter, Pearce gave the order to haul away, leaving Macklin to sail the ship on the up and down course, which meant things, at a distance, would appear normal. Sat with a luminous compass in his hand, Pearce was aware the time was fast approaching when he would find out if his plan was sound. With no land signal it would end up as a total waste, which made it impossible not to imagine a certain amount of ridicule.

This, he believed, would not come from his own officers, for he felt he had their respect. No doubt he would get an understanding nod from Elliot, but Warburton would certainly scoff, while the notion Toby Burns would laugh behind his back was one to have him curse under his breath.

'Fire onshore, sir,' came from Michael O'Hagan. 'High up in the hills.'

It was so faint, it hardly qualified for the description, barely made more so when Pearce aimed his telescope to enlarge the image. Such a blaze could be anything from shepherds worried about wolves to hunters cooking freshly caught game. Then it disappeared for a second, only to reappear, this repeated twice.

'Undoubtedly a signal,' was said with relief.

On command, the boats began to ply their oars, this executed without haste, until the collective rhythm had been established to ensure smooth progress. Pearce had his eye on the angle of the Bastia beacons so, even if he would have admitted to a certain amount of guesswork, the moment they were almost lined up to look as one, told him they were very close inshore.

Sure enough, there was the faint silver streak of the river, picking up what light came from above and a blessing, it was slightly south of his position, along with the gentle hiss of waves breaking on a shore. A soft call stilled the oars, the line to Hallowell's boat going slack, the sign he should back his oars, an action which, in turn, would pass the message down the line. If the others acted as instructed, they should cover the entrance to the estuary without being silhouetted against waters of the river.

Once more, there was nothing to do but wait, with Pearce prey once more to the same anxieties he'd had out at sea. What if nothing happened and no vessel appeared – this a thought growing as time ran on, the only positive being his injunctions about noise was being obeyed. He could easily have thought himself and his cutter to be alone, until a flash of light from the shore, lasting no more than a couple of seconds, lifted his mood. No fire this time, but a sizeable lantern.

'Damn me, I was right.'

This he whispered to Moberly, before berating himself for breaking his own order, to then wonder if the other boats had spotted what he had seen. There was no way to tell and no way to know if it was, for certain, what he hoped, nor how long it would be before anything else showed.

The wait was interminable, again raising doubts, it being easy to conjure up explanations for the things he'd seen so far which made his mood positive. Even more troubling, the time came when the first hint of a dawn grey tipped the sky behind the Apennines. This, as time dragged on, would nullify his whole strategy.

Then it came, a sail blocking out a section of the milky sky, obvious from his low elevation and with it, the realisation that in his long list of assumptions had forgotten one every important factor. The insurgents would require daylight to unload any cargo, something near impossible to do by torchlight, unless you wished to take the risk of illuminating a stretch of shore in a way visible for miles.

Thankfully it was still dark at sea level, so he gave the order for which his marine officer was waiting. 'Let's form a huddle, Mr Moberly.'

The quartet of marines formed a sort of circle, enough to cut off any light when the lantern was unshaded. This also enclosed the rocket tube, at the base of which lay a piece of wetted sail, there to absorb and kill any flame. The pulled lantern door showed ghoul-like faces before it was quickly shut, only being open long enough to allow a spare bit of slow match to be ignited. Pearce then set the glowing tip to the actual rocket fuse, one kept as short as possible, the fizzing sparkle of which, when it took, was much harder to conceal.

He got himself as far as possible from the tube as the rocket went off, emitting a streak of bright orange flame from the base, to set sizzling the wetted canvas. The projectile shot skywards, its line of flight visible before it turned to a star burst, illuminating the seascape as well as the shoreline in ghostly blue. And there was what Pearce had hoped and prayed for, the clear sight of a tartane, with its large triangular foresail and a cross jack rigged mainsail. It also revealed an excessively and dangerously low freeboard, and with it the numerous, startled white faces on its crowded deck.

There was a moment when Pearce registered the amount of human cargo; many more bodies than Pearce had thought they would face and so heavy, it was risky in the extreme in any kind of sea. There followed a momentary pause, to question if he had the numbers to do what was required. But these Corsicans were unprepared: the bullocks from the garrison were not and it was they who decided the issue.

Vickery's sharp eyes had spotted the fizzing fuse, meaning the soldier's muskets were up and ready with their boat steady when needed. They had enough faint light to take aim and, at short range, do damage to human flesh when duly executed. On Pearce's boat, with oars immediately employed as per his orders, it was closing, even before the firework burst. The man on the helm was aiming for the side of a ship and a deck barely above head height, made more so by the way those aboard began to edge over to the side to shout insults.

Moberly and his marines had not blasted off. With admirable discipline they waited for a command from their officer. As soon as it was forthcoming, they let fly, at point blank range, at targets each man had selected, with the firing making nervous anyone forced to face it. The purpose was to maim certainly but also to drive anyone who remained away from the side, which would help get the boarders on to the deck.

As the cutter scraped along the side, with oars quickly boated, an O'Hagan hand grabbed the bulwark now bereft of faces, so both were moving at the same pace, which, in truth, was snail-like. Those who leapt for the side, John Pearce included, scrabbled up the short planking to get a leg over the bulwark, to be followed by another, as a mate below gave them the extra push needed to get the whole body over. Pearce shouted that they should keep their heads down to avoid the pistol fire coming from the boats rushing in support.

'Michael, the wheel,' Pearce gasped as the Irishman joined him. He then discharged his pistols at a mass of bodies, so crowded on the foredeck, there was little space in between, making it impossible to miss flesh. Then it was time to employ his sword as a pair of the enemy came forward to fight, their progress halted by what was happening to their rear. Hallowell and Worricker had seen the cutter heading for the stern and so aimed their boats at the prow.

As another star shell burst overhead, Pearce had time to grab a couple of marlin spikes and pull them from their seating. Luck had this release one corner of the cross jack, a mainsail more suited to a square rigger, but effective with a following wind. Not now, it was flapping and useless, and so what little way the tartane had evaporated. The pressure on her still drawing foresail took her head round, which meant she was coming beam on to the shore. More importantly it made it impossible to steer the ship for the narrow entrance to the river, making it more likely that she would ground on the sandbar.

There was no time to register such a possibility, he being immediately required to employ his short naval hangar, not in attack but defence, with thankfully, the numbers facing him, being so numerous, they seemed to be getting in each other's way. But the pair out ahead came on making it necessary to take several rapid backward steps, with him wondering where his support had gone.

The long silver blades of the bayonets flashed by on either side, thrust forward by a pair of marines, till the muzzles were well past his body. And effective they were, piercing both his attackers, if not fatally, then enough to arrest forward movement. Reacting to this rendered their own weapons momentarily useless, with Pearce using the seconds he was gifted well.

Skipping forward, he sliced at the neck of one, to produce a fount of blood, this immediately followed by a classic fencer lunge, to drive the point of his sword at the chest of the other. Being a cutting weapon, this only served to check forward movement, but a following slash at the sword arm cut through both cloth and flesh rendering it useless. The hilt was then employed to brain his opponent.

Most of the fighting was taking place well forward, as the Corsicans tried to stop the rest of men from *Hazard* boarding over the bows. Pistols were going off, as well the odd musket, ragged fire, for these insurgents had been caught cold, so near their landing place and sure of success, they appeared overconfident.

As the rest of his boarding party went by, Pearce turned to look to where he'd sent Michael, the task for the Irishman being to take possession of the steerage, and he was afforded the time to do so.

Moberly had his men, with reloaded muskets lined up, before ordering them to advance. Ghostly figures in the light, their officer had
his pistol in one hand, sword pointing forward in the other.

On command all five weapons were discharged into the mass
of bodies, again at point blank range. Moberly then led them at a
rush, their bayonets doing good service, as did the officer's flashing
blade. Charlie Taverner and Rufus Dommet, sturdy fighters now,
were right behind them, swords swinging and curses audible as they
led the rest of the Hazards into the fight.

The combination drove their opponents back, a bayonet enjoying far greater reach than a sword, especially since, with the guns
already discharged, no time had been afforded to their opposition
for reloading. So much did the fear of the bayonets increase the
mass crowding into the bows, it made it hard for them to employ
their own weapons, even knives. It had their captain reckon, despite
the massive odds against it, confusion would see him on the verge
of taking possession.

The way the tartane heeled had him stagger and reach for something to prevent a fall, a necessity to everyone on board, of whatever
stripe. Once he'd recovered his balance, he peered aft to see Michael
O'Hagan, a spectral figure in the available light, in some difficulty.
If he had taken control of the wheel, he clearly lacked that of the
vessel for, with arms looped through the spokes, it appeared to be
supporting him.

Closing, Pearce saw two stretched out bodies at his feet, but he
was obviously wounded, this proved as he made it to his side, to find
blood dripping from a head wound. There was no time and no point
in enquiring if he could move, so Pearce rushed to the side, to call
down for help. As was common, a pair had stayed aboard to keep
the boat alongside, in case boarding had to be abandoned.

As he leant over, even in the increasing daylight, Maclehose sent
up another flare which, bursting high above, showed a stationary

boat some way off. Not only was it a cutter, but it was fully manned. With only two such crafts employed this night it took no great wit to guess who was in command.

'Burns, you little shit, get that damned boat alongside now.'

Pearce was sure the lips didn't move, but it was indicative of the sod's authority, or lack of it, the oars did, whoever was coxswain choosing to act without a word from his own commander. Still in the same position, head over the side, Pearce heard Moberly's voice and what he said was far from welcome.

'Sir, the current and lack of a mainsail has had the ship broach. Very soon she'll be side on to the shore, on the sandbar or stuck in the shallows. There are numbers we cannot contain on this deck, without we are reinforced, which our opponent will be by the men ashore.'

'The others?'

'Hold the forepeak but will not do so for long.'

With *Teme*'s cutter alongside now, he called down. 'We have a badly wounded sailor on the deck and I need him in my boat. Burns, get up here and, by damn, you will join in the fight if I have to drag you to it. Make sure you bring a blade, because you're going to need it. Mr Moberly with me.'

Moving towards the bow Pearce came up against the backs of the men who had boarded with him, including Charlie and Rufus and they were fighting hard. They had formed a line across the deck so those opposing them could not get past, not least because of the jabbing marine bayonets. His height allowed him to see other backs, rebels from over the water who were engaged against the bulk of the crew from *Hazard*.

The men before him would be tiring, it was inevitable, which was no state to be in when retreat was becoming necessary. This applied especially against men who would be fresh to the fray, driven home when he could see now what Moberly was talking about. The numbers on the sandbar to which the ship was slowly drifting towards dwarfed even the crowd on the tartane. They had to withdraw.

Forcing his way into the middle of the line, between his two Pelicans, he began a furious assault, in doing so ignoring his own rule never to get isolated. Only that his act fired up his own men, giving them renewed spirit, saving him from being skewered or clubbed to the ground.

'Hazards,' he yelled, hoping his voice would carry over the din. 'Take to your boats.'

He was later to thank Moberly handsomely for his actions, undertaken without instructions. Michael O'Hagan having been lowered over the side, the marine took command of the crew from *Teme*, ordering them to get on deck with their weapons. He then grabbed Toby Burns by the collar of his uniform coat, to drag him up on deck, then physically thrusting him into the fighting line.

The Temes entry into the fight was used to replace his tiring marines. These new arrivals being fresh, alongside Pearce, still in a fighting frenzy, began to drive their opponents into a huddle, if only by one of two strakes. They, in turn, pressed on the backs of those of their confreres fighting in the forepeak, inducing alarm. This brought a lull in their efforts, then a degree of confusion.

Pressure eased, Hallowell and Worricker began to get their men back into their boats, quickly done because of the tartane being so low in the water, they being the last to go. Even so, many landed in a heap or badly, while a couple required an oar pushed their way to avoid them drowning. This, of course, left Pearce and his cohort fighting greater numbers, the only blessing the lack of room for everyone to get at them. Even so the pressure began to tell so it was necessary to give ground until Moberly shouted.

'Captain, pull back.'

There was no time to argue nor was there time to stop Burns from simply turning and running, so as to get ahead. The scrub found himself facing a line of marines, muskets raised and aimed, their officer with pistol thrust forward, and this saved him. If Moberly had not been intent on his manoeuvre, with the inability to use his sword, he might have run the coward through.

There was also Vickery to thank. Having seen the boarding being abandoned, he had asked for his boat and men to be alongside. With reloaded muskets, they took station amidships, where the side was so close to the water, a standing soldier could aim at the deck. So, those facing Pearce and his men, as they rapidly disengaged, were faced with two lines of muskets, one to starboard, the other right in front of them. Even with many more bodies than musket balls, it takes a brave man, or a fool, to face certain death, and these rebellious Corsicans were neither.

Joining Moberly, the marine informed his captain that it was his intention to hold his fire and only order a discharge if presented with no alternative. 'But I fear, if you agree, we must give them their ship.'

'The bitterest of pills.'

'Best taken, sir.'

'Mr Vickery, can you hear me?'

'Clearly.'

'It is my intention to withdraw myself and my men to our boats.'

Pearce then did an immediate translation into French, which revealed what must have been present from the very beginning. Something of a leader, who only needed to take half a step forward to mark him out. No words came, but Pearce was sure he could see a hint of a smile which conveyed a message of an impending and unpleasant fate.

As if to drive home the point, men began to clamber over the forepeak, dripping water from wading through the shallows, a sure indication for the boarders the situation would not improve. The

Temes being the last to board, they were the last to depart, but Charlie Taverner and Rufus stayed with Pearce until it was just them and the marines on deck.

'Time for you to go, sir,' said the marine softly.

'I think not,' was the reply from a man who doubted these rebels were the type to take prisoners. 'I'll take your pistol, which will tell the fellow who has stepped away from the crowd, I will seek to kill him before he can take me. But you embark and, Mr Moberly, that is an order.'

The boom of cannon fire preceded the effect and took everyone's attention, both in its noise and the twin plumes of water, in truth way too far off to be threatening. But Macklin, unbidden, was bringing in HMS *Hazard*, to affect a situation Pearce thought himself unlikely to survive.

His only hope, and a forlorn one, was his ability to swim. Could he rush to the side and throw himself over before he could be taken, something he might possibly achieve once everyone else was off. In shallow water he would be at the mercy of objects thrown and possibly pistols fired, but it might give him a slim chance.

Did those two cannon balls change everything?

'Fall out and get aboard. You too, Charlie, and take Rufus.'

'Pelicans stick together, d'you not know Pearce,' was the response, one which probably shocked Moberly.

'Well, there's one in the cutter badly needs looking after, so you'd be better by his side than mine. Besides, have you ever known me not to have a plan? When everyone is off and oars working, shout Pelican.'

As they reluctantly complied, Pearce called. 'Mr Vickery, I should tell your boat crew to dip their oars, though it would do no harm to keep those muskets aimed at the deck from a reasonable range.'

'You're sure.'

Another salvo from *Hazard* made any answer superfluous. Pearce, who'd never taken his eyes off the man he thought to be a leader, had seen the change of expression the cannon balls had caused. No half smile now, more a slightly troubled look as he worked through the ramifications. He might not have a crystal ball, but he reckoned to be able to guess what his opponent was thinking.

With the estuary gone as a point of entry, anything they had aboard, humans included would have to be taken over the side or forepeak of a vessel which had run aground. Very likely, with a well-armed warship closing, it would have to be abandoned, but getting bodies ashore trumped any other consideration.

The French was accented by being local to Corsica, but the offer was plain. Pearce could go, if he undertook to allow them to get off the tartane without interference. Both his expression and his language changed with the discharge of two more 4-pounder balls, even if they hit the sea too far off to do any damage.

He turned his back and issued a stream of incomprehensible orders, in what had to be Corsican, which produced a degree of mayhem. Any men coming aboard abruptly dropped back into the water, soon to be followed in a disorderly manner by those the tartane had been carrying.

No one was any longer looking at a confused Pearce unable for several seconds to make sense of what he was seeing with his own eyes. But realising he no longer mattered, he ran for the side and dived over.

Chapter Twenty-Four

'The vessel was carrying only human cargo, which leads me to deduce, Sir Gilbert, the rebellious may have on the island all the firepower they think they require. They might, as well, feel they have the men too.'

'Which will never be enough, Pearce,' Warburton bellowed, 'which I seem to recall I have told you several times.'

'Which I would accept, if I was certain that you knew all you needed to know of their plans.'

'They can plan till doomsday, but without siege weaponry they will never overcome the walls of Bastia.'

'It is of course, your choice, sir.' Elliot acknowledged this to be the case with a nod, one which told John Pearce he had yet to make up his mind. 'But I would be happier if you and your family took up temporary residence in the governor's palace on Elba.'

'What a superb notion, Pearce. . . '

'Lieutenant Pearce, was a sharp rejoinder, to what was clearly sarcasm, 'unless you too wished to be addressed without your rank.'

'Damned touchy, what? I merely wish to point out you speak of an island from which may have come half the people we've trying to stop.'

'I doubt it is any longer, Major. And besides is it not home to several thousand French Royalists who took refuge there?'

'It is,' Elliot acknowledged.

'So,' Pearce added, 'All the rebels who resided on Elba, and I assume there must be some, are now, by my reckoning, here in Corsica. It is something those tasked with protecting you have singularly failed to stop.'

The implied rebuke was ignored as Pearce addressed the governor directly.

'Sir Gilbert, I was sent here to act under your instructions and will do so. But I wish you to know I see my misgivings as sound. The man I faced on the deck of that vessel was working out how to kill me without I put a ball in him first. Lieutenant Macklin. . . '

'Acting I believe,' Warburton interjected, still smarting from being quite properly rebuked in the article of manners.

Tempted to respond by pointing out Macklin was doing a damn sight better job in the capacity as an acting naval officer than Warburton was doing as a real army one, he held his tongue. It would serve no purpose, and his real concern was to emphasise his worries, brought on by what he had seen and the clear impression it had created.

The fact the Corsicans had abandoned the grounded ship came as no surprise given, once inspected, there was no cargo other than the men who had so crowded the deck. In the post-action analysis, in which Pearce had taken soundings from his boarders as well as their officers, the poor fighting abilities of their opponents had been remarked upon by all.

'Meet 'em on a deck any day,' had been Charlie Taverners's opinion. 'Known women who's better battlers.'

In Pearce's cabin, the men who had led the action were no less surprised to be alive than their captain. It was reckoned they should never have been afforded a chance to board against such numbers, never mind being able to stay and contest the deck. To the man listening, it indicated whoever had been in command, the man who had called on them to get ashore as quickly as possible, had some knowledge of the standard of those he led.

Which was not to say they had lacked worthy opponents: it normally took four to begin an even contest with Michael O'Hagan. But against two, he had ended up in Surgeon Cullen's sickbay with a dozen stitches to his head, openly admitting he had struggled. The pair Pearce had first met, rendered vulnerable by bayonets, then finished off, had not only initially fought well, but had appeared eager to do so.

Still, if the remainder were of a different stamp, why were they being fetched over: Was it merely sheer numbers? It never did to assume this as the solution to a successful contest. History was littered with examples of small, disciplined forces defeating larger armies, entities more difficult to control. Whatever, in Pearce's mind, it smacked of an approaching endgame and, if it was, he wanted the Elliot family somewhere safer than behind the walls of Bastia.

'Sir Gilbert, it would not serve for you to be confined by a siege.'

'I seem to be addressing thin air, sir!' was a proper shout, with flushed cheeks to go with it.

'Major, contain you temper,' Elliot responded calmly.

'Which I find hard, Sir Gilbert. I too have been charged with a responsibility, which is to both hold the city and guard your person, duties I feel certain I can fulfil. I have explained why to Mr. Pearce on numerous occasions, but my words do not seem to have penetrated his skull. The citadel cannot be taken without artillery.'

'Can the harbour, Major?'

'If it is, the area can be bombarded into rubble.'

'Very helpful when you run out of food. The Francophones don't need to do anything, other than wait to starve you out. The walls you're so certain of will become a prison, not a place of safety.'

'We can call on support.'

'The kind of support, from both Corte and San Fiorenzo, which has been so singularly lacking up till now. And do I have to establish for you what is at risk?'

'I think,' Sir Gilbert said, finally taking a full part. 'If you are required to surrender Major Warburton, it will be to exit with your honour unblemished, your arms as well, while leaving your cannon behind.'

'I say it won't happen.'

'The problem for me? Well perhaps, I'll let Lieutenant Pearce enunciate it.'

'Sir Gilbert would be required to surrender the island, on behalf of His Majesty King George.'

'Which I would feel obliged to refuse to do.'

'Which is why Elba would be safer,' Pearce added. 'All that will be needed is enough of your men major, to provide a guard, since they will not be required to undertake any other duties. The navy will undertake to keep Sir Gilbert and his family from any surprises and to evacuate them to San Fiorenzo should it become necessary.'

'Necessary?'

'Brought on by your being in difficulties here in Bastia.'

The major produced a crafty look, one to presage an excuse. 'If I gift you the men you want, I will lose my ability to send out patrols.'

'Since they're achieving precisely nothing, I cannot see what harm it will do.' Seeing to the plump poltroon swell up in indignation, Pearce added, 'And the navy will, of course, continue to monitor access by sea.'

'I still think it is madness.'

'I'm sorry, Major Warburton, but to my mind Lieutenant Pearce has made a compelling case. In the end, you are responsible to the Horse Guards. I am responsible to my sovereign, and my duties do not extend to shrinking his patrimony.' He looked to John Pearce. 'I will have Lady Elliot get herself and the children ready for departure.'

Warburton was not prepared to give up so easily. 'I'm not sure my duties allow me to provide you with a guard detail, without consulting my superiors.'

'Duly noted, major, and I will record in my report.'

This was imparted without any emphasis, but the implicit danger was plain. In future, any decisions made by anyone present would come under examination. Did Warburton want to face such an enquiry and admit he had declined to meet one of his stated responsibilities?

'I will get my ship ready to accommodate you, sir.'

'Is that really necessary for such a short crossing?'

'I see it as my duty to ensure however short it is, it should be comfortable. I will also send up a party to move your possessions.'

'Thank you'

'Might I suggest, sir, you take initially only what you require for your immediate needs. Leave the rest to be picked up tomorrow.'

'So, you're going to be dining a real aristo, John-boy.'

'Got Derwent in a real state of terror.'

'Sure, that old man of yours will be turning in his grave.'

'It's called courtesy, Michael, and you should engage with it sometime. Anyway, how's the head.'

'Mending, for sure.'

There had been two on the wheel, not the one O'Hagan had supposed and he had failed to see the second who had crowned him with what was later found to be a metal bar. He still paid for it with his life, but Michael was sure in the subsequent struggle had lasted any time, he would not have survived, as his vision blurred and his blood drained.

'Then I best go and don my best. No duties, till you are fully recovered.'

There was one task to perform before the arrival of the Elliot family, which was to have a private session with Toby Burns who had done his best to avoid him since his display of outright cowardice.

'Is it not an oddity, people see me as a disgrace to the service when there are examples such as yourself to act as comparison?'

'I had sound reasons for my actions.'

'Which you will, no doubt, be given a chance to explain. But for now, you will carry out a duty at which not even you could fail. I require you to take this despatch to Admiral Jervis, explaining why we will be evacuating Sir Gilbert and his family to Portoferraio.'

It also contained a report on the recent actions undertaken, but he was not going to tell Burns, given his behaviour or lack of same, had some prominence. There was deep satisfaction in what he had to say next.

'You are to weigh immediately. Now be so good as to get out of my cabin and off my ship.'

━━⌣━━

The dinner over which Derwent had fussed went off smoothly, the fare being fresh and the cooking skills for such being minimal. The conversation took great care to avoid any discussion of the reasons for departure, remaining stoically one of shared memories. The Elliots, once ashore in the handsome town of Portoferraio, were lodged in a governor's palace built to accommodate a Medici. It showed in its sumptuous interior, which became a new playground for the youngsters.

Pearce spent his days, turning to three weeks, patrolling the intervening channel, constantly aware he may have jumped the gun in moving the Elliots. In Bastia nothing happened, and this was replicated on all of the islands he could see on his excursions. Boat patrols were sent out at night, mixing with the fishing fleet but to no affect, other than to provide a good diet for the crew, especially the officers of HMS *Hazard*.

The waters were full of the sight of sails on what were busy trade routes, but a Man O' War carried a very different top hamper to a merchantman, so the sight of one approaching from the north had Pearce change course to meet it. He soon realised it was of a size best avoided, but as yet he had no knowledge of nationality, until the time came when its flags could be identified. Soon after, so was the hull.

'Welcome board *Captain*, Mr Pearce.'

'Commodore.'

Which was as cheerful as their exchange would get; Nelson had come with news which John Pearce had anticipated since he arrived in San Fiorenzo Bay to face the crusty old bastard who so hated him.

'Spain has finally declared war and given the French have Leghorn, it cripples our ability to remain supplied. Genoa is shut to us and if we do not show care, so might be the Straits of Gibraltar, given the news which arrived from there. Rear Admiral Mann, who was supposed to await us or to re-join Jervis, as was seen fit, has taken his four sail-of-the-line home.'

There was no need to elaborate: four ships down on what Jervis thought he had and the risk to the rest was obvious.

'Thus, we must give up the Mediterranean.'

'And Corsica?'

'With Spain as an enemy, we cannot hold it. I have a copy of a communication which will upset them even more. It tells them His Majesty's government can no longer offer them the benefits of the British constitution. I fear they will need to find the means to fight their own battles.'

'Which will sadden Sir Gilbert and especially, I suspect, his Vicereine.'

'I will do my best to cheer them, for it is my duty to take them on board.'

'And the garrison in Bastia?'

'Them too, though you might oblige me by taking the officers in *Hazard*.'

Pearce was given the task of getting the bullocks from Bastia into boats at first light, and he made sure Warburton found himself in one from HMS *Captain*. The thought of being stuck in his small cabin with that man was not to be borne and, if Nelson complained, he would merely plead an error.

It was equally depressing that no attempt was made to interfere in the evacuation. Those who had threatened previously were about to get what they wanted. Possession of the most powerful defensive bastion on the island and were going to get it without a shot fired. Yet there was no sign of jubilation: for the majority of the citizenry, what had been a peaceful presence was departing and none knew what would follow.

—✦—

The arrival in San Fiorenzo Bay was, as usual, an occasion for much banging of guns, with Pearce getting Hallowell away to his uncle's ship before, as he put it, the miserable old sod on *Victory* came up with some duty which did not oblige him to see *Hazard* from his stern gallery.

Pearce wondered if he would be summoned and it duly came, after Nelson had been aboard for some time, having boated over the Elliots for the far more capacious three-decker. Quite apart from room, ranked as a Viceroy until King George removed it, his position entitled him to the best the fleet could offer. The surprise for John Pearce was to be shown into the admiral's cabin, where he was greeted with a growl.

'You never cease to play the rascal, do you, Pearce?'

Which earned the flippant reply: 'I see it as my bounden duty to disturb the peace of mind accorded to senior officers.'

As expected, the remark went down like a lead balloon; Jervis's face going to that level of red suffusion which his visitor hoped might be fatal. The admiral picked up a set of papers and began to study them, but in such a way, Pearce saw as mere showing away. He knew exactly what they contained.

'I daresay you will have an excuse for endangering at least half of your crew on a hare-brained escapade.' Jervis looked up with a positively evil glint in his eye. 'I refer to your stupid plan to board a vessel while certain you would be outnumbered and would be unlikely to hold the deck. You quite deliberately, no doubt in your endless search for personal glory, endangered the life of every man you led.'

'I initiated an action, sir, which had a fair chance of success. It only became apparent what we faced when we sent up a rocket, by which time we were committed.'

'I have reports which say different.'

'Then you have clearly not read mine.'

'Oh, I've been through them, of course, which would be a cause for laughter if I did not know better.'

Pearce could guess what lay at the root of this; it had to be Toby Burns. But why would a shrewd fighting man like Jervis believe a word anyone like Burns would say. A whole raft of thoughts can spin through a mind in no time at all, and it struck Pearce that Jervis had given Burns HMS *Teme*. This had made no sense on coming across the bugger and thinking on it, neither did it make sense now.

'I find it hard to believe, if you've read my report, you will take as gospel anything reported to you from Toby Burns.'

'With whom you have something of a history.'

'Not one of fond recollection. He is a scrub and a coward.'

The voice rose to match the high colour. 'You choose to traduce the name of a gallant officer?'

'Gallant?' was shouted so loud it went through several bulkheads and was heard by the object of the conversation who was close enough to be snooping.

'Don't you dare raise your voice in my cabin.'

'I will do so when you claim as gallant a liar, a perjurer, an officer so inept, so shy, his men probably despise him. He is also one who had to be dragged into a fight which could have seen many of his fellow tars slaughtered.'

'For which you bear responsibility,' was imparted by an admiral who had got his fury under control. 'Do not then question the motives of an officer, one I personally appointed, with a modicum of sense, at least enough to know when sacrifice is useless.'

'You have never failed to hate me, Jervis, but I never rated you mad.'

'We will let a court decide if it is you or I who is mad.'

'A court?'

'Will be convened to examine your actions.'

'To which you will appoint the officers.'

The smile was vulpine. 'Never fear, I will be fair. Now get back to your ship and prepare to weigh for Gibraltar. There you will face examination, and I have no doubt be found wanting. So severely short of what an officer needs to be, I doubt you will survive in the service.'

'Should you succeed in this farrago, I will use all the means at my disposal to destroy you.'

'Oh, no doubt you refer to the Spanish silver you took in another questionable operation? If I have my way, you won't see a single dollar. Now, I believe I just gave you an order.'

'One it gives me,' Pearce spat over his shoulder, 'a real pleasure to obey.'

Back aboard HMS *Hazard* it took time for his temper to cool, for his mind to turn to ways in which he could confound Jervis and see Toby Burns stand accused of the cowardice of which he was guilty. He had survived the machinations of Lord Hood to earn his respect and had outwitted Hotham when he and his slimy clerk Toomey sought to send both him and Henry Digby to perdition.

Jervis might see himself as superior to the aforementioned pair of admirals. But he was no better, so the John Pearce mind began to turn towards a defence of his actions and one not even a wholly prejudiced court could find fault with. He was leaving a theatre in which he had seen so much action, one in which he had a high degree of professional success. If this brought on regrets, he was going home to the woman he loved and a son who could be walking by now, something he longed to see.

'To hell with Jervis, though I doubt Old Nick would have him.'

By David Donachie

THE JOHN PEARCE ADVENTURES
By the Mast Divided • A Shot Rolling Ship
An Awkward Commission • A Flag of Truce
The Admirals' Game • An Ill Wind
Blown Off Course • Enemies at Every Turn
A Sea of Troubles • A Divided Command
The Devil to Pay • The Perils of Command
A Treacherous Coast • On a Particular Service
A Close Run Thing • HMS *Hazard* • A Troubled Course

THE CONTRABAND SHORE SERIES
The Contraband Shore • A Lawless Place • Blood Will Out

THE NELSON AND EMMA SERIES
On a Making Tide • Tested by Fate • Breaking the Line

THE PRIVATEERSMEN SERIES
The Devils Own Luck • The Dying Trade • A Hanging Matter
An Element of Chance • The Scent of Betrayal • A Game of Bones

HISTORICAL THRILLERS
Every Second Counts
Originally written as Jack Ludlow

THE LAST ROMAN SERIES
Vengeance • Honor • Triumph

THE REPUBLIC SERIES
The Pillars of Rome • The Sword of Revenge • The Gods of War

THE CONQUEST SERIES
Mercenaries • Warriors • Conquest

THE ROADS TO WAR SERIES
The Burning Sky • A Broken Land • A Bitter Field

THE CRUSADES SERIES
Son of Blood • Soldier of Crusade • Prince of Legend
* * *

Hawkwood